The Island Murders

A DI Bruno Peach Mystery

ACORN BOOKS
www.acornbooks.co.uk

James London

The Island Murders
First edition published in 2018 by
Acorn Books
www.acornbooks.co.uk

Production and layout by
Andrews UK Limited
www.andrewsuk.com

For Annabel Wright
whose love of crime stories and the Isle of Wight
helped Bruno Peach a little on his journey.

The Island Murders

Chapter 1

Sunday 20th July

Detective Inspector Bruno Peach had taken off across the ancient humpback bridge in Beacon Alley a thousand times whilst on his way to meet Anita Burton in her flat above the post office in Niton, an unremarkable village on the southern tip of the Island. The Norman church nearby, with its table top tombs, had been used by smugglers to hide fugitives and contraband. As Bruno turned into the Alley, just for a few seconds memories of those tender, passionate nights returned.

Beacon Alley was a cross-country shortcut that led to the main Newport-to-Niton road. At its widest it was four metres; at its narrowest just two, with passing places every two to three hundred metres or so. In daylight it frightened Bruno. When the passing bay was on *your* side, you pulled in and – following a hand salute from the passing speedster – drove on. In darkness however, you could drive fast, because the headlights of approaching cars would light up the road for some distance.

Bruno had first used the shortcut one hot summer night twenty-five years previously, when Anita, the village postmistress, had phoned Godshill Police Station at 1:00 am, reporting hooded burglars trying to break into her post office through an iron-barred ground-floor window in her back yard. The robbers had failed to wrench out the window bars when a chain fixed to the rear of a fifteen-year-old stolen truck had snapped, creating a great deal of noise. They had given up, leaving behind finger prints... and a useless set of bar cutters.

The prints were never matched to known Island criminals, and there were no leads or suspects, so Bruno's report of the attempted robbery remained in the unsolved crime files in Godshill Police Station. At the time of the incident, he had been on night duty at the station, a small cottage office in the High Street manned by a single officer. When called out, he would have to divert the phone line to the Island's main police station at Newport.

Anita Burton, then thirty-seven and a divorcee, lived alone above her post office. She'd been relieved as she greeted the arrival of the police car at 1:50 am, wearing night clothing – a pink bed jacket that covered her back and shoulders and a similarly-coloured low-cut ankle-length silk nightgown. On that warm summer night, her firm body beneath the negligee had been enticing, as had Bruno Peach's youthful twenty-seven-year-old body, wearing a police uniform and a crisp white shirt, a hidden reminder of Anita's life as a sailor's wife. She was pretty and still youthful, with a penetrating eye. Professionally, she was helpful and kind to the elderly and was much admired as the postmistress of the village of Niton. She enjoyed being admired, and being the centre of attention. Stories linking her romantically with various men from the village had circulated; some were married or divorced, the rest with neither the money nor status to match hers. Whether true or false, nobody knew if anything had ever come of them.

After examining the crime scene, bagging up the useless bar cutters and reporting to his sergeant at Newport Police HQ, Bruno had been writing up Anita's statement of the attempt to rob the post office when he'd accepted her offer of a cold beer. His pleasant manner when asking the necessary questions to draw up the statement had prompted Anita to ask *him* personal questions in return. She'd discovered he was single, lived alone in a flat in Newport, and did not have a girlfriend. He cycled to keep fit and looked after his recently widowed mother, who lived in Shanklin.

Bruno had been relaxed in her company and did not shrink at her advances, soon being drawn into her bed to begin an affair that had gone on to last for ten years. In that time they had occasionally spoken of marriage, but she liked her role at the centre of village life too much to become 'just' a policeman's wife. Eventually, their relationship faded, and approaching fifty, she married the solicitor who acted for her in the sale of the post office, exchanging her village celebrity status for the respect accorded to a senior Island solicitor's wife.

Anita's new husband changed her life completely, enabling her to avoid the loneliness that had crept in and resulted in her decision to sell Niton Post Office. He had dismissed her concerns, relieved her of all responsibility, and she was thus happy and cared for.

***

Godshill was the most photogenic village on the Island and its fifteenth century church and world famous tea gardens attracted tourists from all over the globe. While Bruno had worked there, those journeys along Beacon Alley to Niton had been exciting. He'd always driven fast along the narrow winding road, impatient to enjoy the imminent intimacy.

On *this* early Sunday morning though, despite his mind evoking thoughts of Anita – who had been married to husband number two for ten years now – the rear chassis of Bruno's car did not bounce off the road surface from driving too fast over the bridge as it often had done. This time he drove cautiously and parked three hundred metres in from the Godshill road, in a space belonging to a dark house set some way back from the alley and in full view of the bridge.

Despite a calm exterior, Bruno was gripped with fear at beginning an investigation into only the third murder in his thirty-odd years as a policeman.

At 6:00 am that morning, a forty-four year old man had been found by a dog walker battered to death on the riverbank beneath the bridge. The walker had stopped to relieve himself in the undergrowth near to the bridge when he'd heard his dog barking at something it had found underneath it. After getting *just* close enough to see what had interested his ever-faithful companion, the man had immediately reported to Godshill Police Station via his mobile what looked like a body under the bridge. He saw no one other than the dead man until the police arrived.

As the Island detective responsible for investigating serious crime, Bruno was driving that familiar route so to arrive as early as possible, in the hope of searching for clues before anyone else turned up and disturbed the scene.

The corpse of the murdered man lay along the river bank, under the two hundred-year-old stone bridge which spanned the East Yar river, hidden by low-hanging trees and fully-grown shrubs and bushes.

Waiting for him at the crime scene was his old friend Andy Welsh, the current resident Godshill police officer, who had thankfully arrived first to prevent any encroachment over the ground surrounding the body, allowing Bruno to be the first to examine it. Andy was twenty-eight years old, already with six years' service. He was married and lived in the flat above the police station in Godshill. His wife, Carol – a lively and efficient woman four years younger – was the manager of *The Smokey*, the restaurant a stone's throw from their home.

"It's a grim sight, sir. Plus it's wet and muddy, so be careful you don't slip. I didn't get closer than a few feet. I'd leave him to the medics if I were you."

But for Bruno, it was at the close proximity to the body where important clues might be found. "I need a close look," he explained, donning his crime scene suit and a pair of plastic gloves as he talked, kit he always carried in his car but hoped rarely to use.

"I'll go first then," said Andy. "It's dark under the bridge and I've got a torch"

It was a clamber down the slippery riverbank and then a few metres crawl along to the body. The ground under the bridge was damp, flattened and narrow. It would have been difficult to pull a body along the bank under the bridge far enough to completely conceal it. To return from the bank, the murderer would have had to have exited backwards, climbing over the dead man or dropping into the river, which was a good few metres deep under the bridge. At a guess, the dead man looked around six feet tall and twelve stone in weight. It was cramped and tight beneath the low arch, necessitating the murderer's close contact with the corpse. *This might yield clues,* thought Bruno.

The dead man wore shorts with pockets front and side, out of which Bruno eased a wallet, credit cards and a driving licence. These gave his name as Samuel Peters and his address as one of the upmarket apartments in Cumberland House, situated on Festing Grove in Southsea. The driving licence revealed that he was born on the twenty-eighth of April, 1971. The wallet still contained £80 in notes and a small zipped compartment with change, immediately suggesting that robbery was not a motive for this man's murder.

Bruno had seen many corpses in his years as a police officer. Mostly they were from motor accidents, found lying amongst the mangled wreckage of cars before being cut free by the fire brigade and taken away by paramedics for identification. Drownings were equally gut-wrenching – both visually and nasally disgusting. A deliberate killing, however, was worse than any of these *and* required a detective's thorough, careful examination before anyone could move the corpse. It was a horrifying task for the two policemen who had to examine this one.

"Andy, I can do this," said Bruno to his equally petrified assistant.

"I'm okay, sir, and you need the light from my torch."

Completely covering the corpse's head was a plastic bag from Tesco, held in place by a second bag tied around the neck. The latter had not been successful in stopping blood from a head wound from seeping down past the neck and forming a thick, black congealed mess around the shoulders. Bruno took fifty or so photos of the scene on his mobile in a quick blast.

Whilst Andy directed the spotlight, Bruno untied the plastic bag from around the victim's neck, enabling him to peel back the second bag that covered his head. This allowed the two professionals to confirm beyond all doubt that the victim *was* actually dead. Blood had congealed across the poor man's face and into his eye sockets. The bag seemed almost glued to his blood-impregnated hair, forehead and crown. Bruno did not attempt to further remove the plastic bag, leaving it for the forensic clean-up technician and the scene of crime officer – SOCO in police parlance. Nevertheless, he was able to see that the man had surely been killed by a blow to the back of the head, most likely with a hammer or blunt metal instrument, crushing his skull and no doubt killing him instantly. The plastic bags suggested that he had *not* been felled there, under the bridge. Blood had now saturated the victim's jacket collar and shirt.

Beneath Andy's well directed spotlight, the DI searched for clues amongst the gory mess and the ground surrounding the body, before stepping back and allowing the doctor and SOCO to conduct their inspections. As he did so, he noted that the grassy bank was wide enough to prevent the body slipping into the river.

In due course, the body would be released to the paramedics who would relocate it to St Mary's Hospital mortuary in Newport for a post-mortem and further forensic checks – and for some unfortunate soul to identify the body. As for now, the doctor informed Peach that the victim had been dead since around dusk the previous evening.

Coming from Southsea and having been discovered on his Island patch, the victim was Bruno Peach's responsibility to investigate. Once they had removed the body, he and Andy Welsh re-examined the verges either side of the bridge, which had now been sealed off to the public by another officer who had arrived from Newport.

"We often walk down here for a picnic on fine evenings," said Andy, as the two men crawled around on hands and knees, looking for anything that might prove to be a clue. The walkers' trail had plenty of footprints, far too many to identify which were the killer's.

"Why do you think he was placed under the bridge?" asked Bruno.

"I don't know," said Andy. "His body was dripping wet from the dew and the morning mist from the river."

"It isn't secluded enough to have remained undiscovered for very long. Perhaps the bridge is significant. If the murder had taken place *near* to the bridge, would it have been necessary to drag the body *underneath* it? The killer could have just left it in the surrounding bushes and undergrowth."

"Perhaps he was killed under the bridge after he and the murderer climbed down *together*?" Andy proposed.

Bruno nodded thoughtfully. The underside of the bridge had marks that might have stained clothing and the pitted brickwork could well have caused unwanted scratches to the murderer. Judging from the difficulty a person would have had in moving a dead twelve-stone man, for now he went along with Andy's conclusion that the victim must have been killed close to where he lay.

The lack of a holdall or back pack containing items such as a compass, map, protective clothing, some kind refreshment or even a first aid kit indicated that the dead man was not on a walk. Although he was from the mainland, as he was murdered on the Island there was every reason to believe his murderer was an Islander.

Without a trail to follow locally, Bruno decided to start with what he *did* know and visit the victim's home in Southsea immediately, in order to find out what he could and to report the circumstances of the death to any next of kin. He left Andy to return to Newport HQ to set up the incident room with instructions to protect the crime scene from passers-by... and to keep a lid on the news of the death for as long as possible before it began to be covered by the local – or, Heaven forbid, national – newspapers.

***

The Island police worked closely with the mainland Hampshire force and the Desk Sergeant at the Newport station arranged not only for the Portsmouth constabulary to issue a search warrant but also for an officer to accompany Bruno to visit Sam Peters' home that afternoon. During the scheduled early Sunday afternoon fifteen-minute hovercraft journey to Southsea across a calm Solent, Bruno rehearsed his start: to find out exactly *who* Sam Peters was, and to garner details of his visit to the Island. With a little luck, the contents of his home should help reveal the former.

Bruno was met at the Clarence Pier Hovercraft passenger terminal by Detective Constable Tom Craven, a young man of twenty-six who was particularly keen to take this opportunity to learn from an experienced detective, having been assigned by his superior to assist DI Peach. He walked the Island detective to a car and they set off for Cumberland House.

The drive afforded Craven the opportunity to grill Peach about the murder in a manner which he thought would impress his senior; in appreciation of the genuine keenness shown, Peach responded helpfully with everything he was prepared to reveal at this stage. It was still under twenty-four hours since the killing – and much less since the DI had witnessed the horrific scene that morning of a man battered to death, his bloody corpse lying helplessly beneath the bridge. Yet Craven's enthusiasm was contagious and somehow banished a multitude of dark thoughts that had overcome his older colleague during the trip over from the Island. He now accepted that he was hunting a vicious killer, one that would likely demand every facet of his experienced detective skills to apprehend.

"Did the crime scene reveal anything, sir?"

"He wasn't killed *exactly* where the body lay," said the DI. "We're still waiting for the post-mortem and forensics reports." He paused for a moment, a snapshot of the scene flashing through his mind's eye. "The victim was savagely beaten up and struck by a heavy blow to the head. It's a local nature walk where the body lay, a river bank... which has told us nothing about the killer. The possessions found in the pockets of the deceased's clothing revealed little more than his name and address."

The ten-minute car journey saw them soon arrive at the apartment in Cumberland House. The building looked out across a man-made lake with paddle boats, and further beyond to the Solent, the Napoleonic sea forts today still visible in the distance. On a sultry, warm, mid-summer afternoon such as this, the swan-shaped paddle boats were always in full use, a queue of families waiting in line for the turnaround.

"So this is where we start," Peach said to his young assistant as they climbed out of the car, "his home should tell us about him and hopefully reveal some clues that will lead us to the killer," said Bruno, perhaps a tad too optimistically.

Wearing protective gloves that crept up his arms like a wicket keeper's, the police locksmith gave the two detectives access to Sam's apartment. Once he had departed, Tom Craven took photographs of the layout of the apartment as it stood before any interference, whilst Bruno planned the precise order of their search of the apartment. Bruno's discomfort at their uninvited intrusion into the dead man's life was mitigated by his belief that a thorough search of where the victim lived *must* provide a clue that would give them a positive lead if nothing else.

Sam Peters' residence was a well-appointed, large, ground floor apartment: three bedrooms, two bathrooms, a spacious entrance that led to a kitchen through the lounge. The bedroom which faced the sea across the canoe lake was arranged as an office, with a broadband router, a desktop PC, printer, cables in many different places, two desks, plenty of papers, a bookcase and some files. Finding a clue amongst these possessions might take some time, even with DC Craven's help. The younger man noticed on the hall table an invitation to a tenth wedding anniversary party two weeks hence, 'From your sister Wendy and Jack'.

"Go through the address book – it's on one of the desks – and see if you can find out her address," said Bruno.

Tom found the page quickly. "If her surname is Paterson, it's in Southsea, sir, only ten minutes from here in the car," he replied.

Telling Wendy Paterson that her brother had been murdered was an unenviable task, but one of the utmost importance.

"We'll see her before we start here," said Bruno. "Leave the talking to me, and you write down everything that is said – both by me and whoever we see."

During another short car journey, this one to Wendy Paterson's home in Haslemere Road, Tom remained silent whilst Bruno assembled the correct words in the right sequence and anticipated the shock their news would solicit. There was *never* a script for a visit such as this.

The two sat outside a few doors down in silence for almost fifteen minutes after arriving. Bruno knew he had to be confident, clear, sympathetic and somewhat unemotional, stating only facts... and this without knowledge as to whom the killer might be. Above all though, he must be kind and show empathy towards a bereaved relative at the shock news he was about the give her.

When he had composed himself, he confirmed Tom's actions to him: particularly requesting careful noting of references to times, places and other individuals – even just a name could lead somewhere. Conscious that this could often be an emotional moment for a young policeman, Bruno placed his hand on Tom's shoulder. "You'll be OK," he said, an almost fatherly kindness is his voice.

***

It was a large mid-terrace house with the name *PANTASAPH* embedded in a stained glass rectangular panel above the door. The detectives' silent prayer that someone be home was granted and the door was opened by a trim, well-dressed lady, seemingly in her late thirties.

"Wendy Paterson?" chanced Bruno.

"That's me," she answered, smiling nervously.

Bruno introduced himself as a DI coming from Newport Police, with his colleague DC Craven of Portsmouth CID. Mindful of her nervousness at being faced by two strangers on the doorstep, they both presented their photo identity.

"May we come in Mrs Paterson?"

"Yes," she said hesitatingly, as if not really meaning it. Still, she turned and led them through a tidily kept house to an open-plan kitchen with a centrepiece pine table surrounded by chairs and the noise of a washing machine gurgling in the background.

"Are you alone in the house?"

"Yes, my husband is out."

"I think it's best if we sit down," said Bruno, and waited for the increasingly nervous woman and his younger colleague to sit down before himself pulling out a chair. "We've come about your brother, Sam. I'm afraid that we found a man dead on the Isle of Wight in the early hours of this morning, and have reason to believe it's him."

"Oh goodness, are you *sure* it's my brother Sam?" Wendy said after a slight pause.

"Well, we found Sam's wallet in the man's pocket, and unfortunately a comparison between the photo on the driving license and the victim's face leaves us in little doubt, I'm sorry to say."

With her body language seeming to suggest acceptance yet having some strength behind it, Bruno explained about the identification process and the need for such action.

Part way through a sentence, she stopped him.

"What was he doing on the Isle of Wight?" She asked.

"We thought *you* might be able to help us with that question," Bruno replied, an inquisitive note introduced to his voice.

Wendy stared at them and locked her lower lip into her mouth, like a punctured tyre, before she turned away and began to weep quietly for what seemed longer than the minute it was. Hesitatingly she confirmed that their parents were dead and she was his only living relative.

"Oh dear," she sighed. "Poor, poor Sam. How did he die?"

"Mrs Paterson, this will be difficult, but can we talk about him? It would help us tremendously if we could?" said Bruno, keen to make the most of this time with her.

"Of course, but may I call my husband first?" she said. "He's playing football. He does that on Sunday afternoons."

"Go ahead, and please, take your time."

She left the kitchen and, out of earshot, called her husband. After a few minutes she came back and sat down and said "He'll be home in twenty minutes."

It was a relief to the two detectives that some support from someone close would soon arrive.

"Actually I know very little about Sam – I've never met his friends. Jack and I didn't intrude into his life," she ventured.

Tom set about making coffee, while Wendy, clearly distressed, sat in silence, watched by Bruno – who hoped she would reveal everything she knew about her brother.

"When he came to see the children, they loved him. We have three girls, they're at the local primary school. Every week he brought sweets, colouring books, that sort of thing... but always before Jack came home. He said he didn't want to intrude on 'family time'.

With a slight panic, Bruno glanced upwards, as if he might be able to see whether the girls were here, perhaps listening in on what he'd just been discussing....

"Don't worry," Wendy said, clearly seeing the DI's concern, "They're over at my mother-in-law's place this afternoon."

"Did your husband get on with Sam?" Bruno asked, keen to keep the information flowing.

"Well... they got on, but definitely weren't 'mates'. To be honest, Jack thought Sam was strange."

"Why was that?" said Bruno.

"Jack's a team player, has lots of close friends... but Sam was always a loner. To Jack he seemed odd; obsessed with his work and he wasn't married. My girlfriends thought he was wonderful. *They* said he was an eligible bachelor."

"So he met your friends when he called?" enquired Bruno.

"Yes, those that live nearby, they are often in and out, all day long... but admittedly he usually made himself scarce when they arrived."

"Did he get to know any of them?"

"No, but he had girlfriends, I'm sure... just... none that *I* ever met."

"Have you been to his flat?"

"Yes, it's facing the sea in Southsea. A lovely flat."

Tom eased the tension with coffee, and in a few minutes Jack arrived. The couple retired to their front room privately, to confront the reality of this family disaster. He seemed an uncomplicated, dependable husband, who understood the seriousness of the situation.

"Inspector, how can I be of help?" Jack asked, returning after a relatively short time with Wendy.

"Please, tell me everything you know about your brother-in-law," said Bruno.

"I know very little, mostly only from Wendy," he said. "Sam lived in Southsea, but we rarely saw him. We think he used to go away a lot."

The unexpected, unexplained murder of their nearest family member was difficult for Jack and Wendy to understand, the crime of murder being far removed from their day-to-day life.

Bruno understood their shock and silence, but needed more from them before he could leave them alone with their grief.

"When did you last see him?"

Jack could not recall, but Wendy had seen him ten days previously, at about 3:00 pm with the girls.

"I don't think Sam ever made enemies," said Jack.

"How do you know that?" said Bruno.

"Well, he avoided confrontation on anything."

"If you never saw him how do you know that?"

Jack shrugged his shoulders and said. "It was the impression I got from the little contact I had with him over the ten-plus years I knew him. He had plenty of money."

"And *how* do you know that?" said Bruno, a phrase he had clearly found particularly useful over the years.

"He was a surveyor. He had property dealings and although he didn't tell us any of the details, we gathered he was always buying and selling things. He never told us when he made a profit, but he knew what he was talking about."

"He helped us, you know; he did the survey when we bought *this* house. That saved us money, and he paid for a new kitchen and bathroom. Wendy was always concerned about him. She talked him up to her female friends, but he kept away. He lived only a little more than walking distance, two miles away from the only family he had, us, but it could have been that he lived in a different country."

"What did he do with his time?" said Bruno.

Both interviewees realised that neither could shine a light on the details of the bachelor's existence.

"I'm afraid we'll need one of you to help identify Sam as soon as possible," said Bruno.

"We will do it together," said Jack. Bruno duly provided details of time and place to him and warned that the identification of Sam, due to his injuries, would be unpleasant. They agreed to attend that evening.

"One final question, so we can tick all the boxes." said Bruno. "Can you tell me where you both were yesterday?"

"We were here," said Jack. "Wendy and I had a 'breaking up for the school holiday's party' for the girls."

"Was that all day?"

"Yes, all day," confirmed Jack.

"Thank you," said Bruno.

"If anything comes to mind will you call us straight away?" said Bruno as he and Tom presented cards with contact details.

***

In the car on the return journey to Sam Peters' flat, they agreed they had learned almost nothing about their victim.

"What did *you* make of the Patersons?" asked Tom, a little gingerly.

"When relatives don't get on it's usually six of one and half-a-dozen of the other," said Bruno. "Wendy had no problem with Sam, but Jack didn't like him – which is probably why he kept away. I'll meet them at St Mary's mortuary this evening, and see how they react to seeing the body. Meanwhile, let's try to discover what kind of man Sam Peters was from the contents of his flat – after a recap of what we *do* already know."

"Well... he worked alone, lived alone and was, by ordinary standards, rich. So, it's not impossible for him to have had enemies or even be known to thieves," Tom summarised. "Some people he came into contact with would surely envy him. Very few people isolate themselves from everyone without reason; maybe this helps by narrowing it down to a few suspects."

By this point in the conversation, the two were back at the apartment with its spacious ceilings and sea views. Bruno awarded Tom with a brief smile of appreciation for his respectable summary and the two got to work.

A black leather shoulder bag lay on what seemed to be Sam's main desk. In one compartment were business cards: *Samuel Peters FRICS,*

Chartered Surveyor, a contacts book, recent business correspondence and a few invoices. Unzipping the second compartment revealed a laptop computer along with the expected leads and peripherals.

Various mundane office objects such as a flat decorative glass tray filled with pencils and erasers lay on another desk, this one set before a feature window with a picturesque view across the boating lake to the sea. Everything was neatly stacked and identifiable.

"I think we'll need to read everything in those," said Bruno, pointing at several A4-size handwritten notebooks stacked in a bookcase, all categorised under subject headings such as *Geological Strata of South West Wight, Rock formation: Isle of Wight*, and *Field Exploratory Results & Charts of Areas Searched.*

"Geological study books and surveys," said Tom, "at least *that* explains what he was doing on the Island."

The two continued their search in silence for a while; the discovery of each new folder or drawer necessitating a sifting, brief read and cataloguing. Stacked up in one corner were plenty of books – once inspected, confirmed as having been borrowed from Southsea Public Library – on geological subjects and regarding precious metal extraction, including a prospectors' manual, a history of gold mining, and a set of Ordnance Survey explorer maps of the Island.

A page-a-day desk diary had just been unearthed, with recent entries promising enticing information, but the time had now reached 6:00 pm and Bruno was beginning to tire. It had been a long time since his early morning call to visit Beacon Alley, and if he was still to meet the Patersons at the St Mary's mortuary at 7:30 pm, he needed to leave. "I'm whacked, let's get out of here," he said. "Are you OK for tomorrow, Tom?"

With an eagerness that had long-since vanished from Bruno's own police work, Tom replied, "I can't wait, sir! You say what time and I'll collect you from the ferry terminal. Don't worry, we'll find who killed Sam Peters from this lot."

As was standard procedure, the family was denied access to the Southsea apartment until CID decided to release it back to them. Back at HQ the IT specialist made hard copies of the documents found on the laptop. Putting these together with the diary, Bruno hoped not only to find a motive, but also a potential suspect or two. A good start, he thought, would be determining whether the killer was from the Island or the mainland.

Chapter 2

Although Bruno was tired, his thoughts were starting to come together. Everything suggested it was an Island killer and he was confident that their identity would be discovered from the documents in Peters' flat. Despite what you see in the movies, people are rarely murdered by strangers, and almost never without motive.

He was relieved to have already broken the news to the victim's sister and brother-in-law – the longer after the murder the harder it became somehow – and promptly at 7:30 pm he had witnessed their positive identification of the body. DC Tom Craven had been an enormous help in dealing with Wendy and Jack, both of whom had remained calm upon receiving the awful news. At the morgue they had positively identified the body without fuss, but could offer no further information about the deceased upon DI Peach's outwardly casual yet probing questions.

On some evenings, Bruno dined at Bentley's Fish Restaurant in Newport High Street with a friend, Janet Gibson; he found her company refreshing, revitalising and rather comforting. Without doubt he needed such psychological assistance tonight – and he also knew she'd genuinely want him to describe every detail of his eventful Sunday.

Having arrived earlier than his companion could – perhaps deliberately – the exhausted detective sipped cold beer from a tall logo-emblazoned glass and wrote up the main events of the day in his own well-worn police notebook.

Janet Gibson was headmistress of one of Newport's five primary schools and had moved to the Island from Yorkshire after her parents retired there. Her six-year marriage had ended when her husband, on completion of his PhD studies, had traded her in for a younger model, one Celina Bolt, unsurprisingly a fellow PhD student.

Janet's time on the Island had seen her eventually recover from the disappointment of that failed marriage and the collapse of the plans that she and her former husband had made together. She had put *everything* into the marriage, both materially and emotionally, until that afternoon when the bottom fell out of her world. Not even two hours after receiving the PhD for the work that she thought she'd supported him through, he had stood on the university steps and declared his love for a plain-looking young girl simpering next to him, heartlessly informing his shocked wife that his chosen solicitor had already been instructed to commence divorce proceedings.

Janet had known Bruno for three years. Initially she was reluctant to see him socially, believing that a dull, institutionalised policeman could not give her the psychological lift she needed. She eventually overcame the gender hostility that her marriage had provoked, which had been difficult in a profession dominated by women. She wanted a relationship with a man who was interesting and fun, who would open some of life's closed doors and ultimately help her to forget the more painful memories of the past.

Although Bruno Peach did not initially seem particularly full of fun, a contact at the local police *was* useful for a school head. So after a routine visit to the school, talking about road traffic to eight-year-olds, she accepted his dinner invitation to Hambledons in Ventnor, a restaurant run by a Cordon-Bleu chef, no less. From then onwards she had begun to see that he was not the dull, unimaginative person that many of his profession came across as, and that his particular role in fact required initiative, flair and dedication for him to be as successful as he was.

Janet had since become one of the select few to whom Peach spoke about cases; as a perfect counter to his own traditional policeman's nose, she understood that you could never *entirely* trust your gut instincts. The teaching skills she had perfected meant it was natural for her to hold a 'road map' of an investigation in her head, and with an uncluttered, organised mind she helped Bruno exclude the irrelevant and focus on the facts which could be proven.

***

Bruno and Janet's fish-and-chip shop venue had a licensed sit-down section serving locally-caught fish fried in thick batter with golden chips, a side of peas (mushy ones for the traditional), pickled gherkins and an excellent homemade tartare sauce. Beer from the famous Burts of Ventnor was available, as was a pleasant and not overly-crisp dry white wine from the Island's Adgestone vineyard. Such a meal was always made to the same consistent high quality it had been for years, and this Sunday evening proved the perfect opportunity for Bruno to relax after his long, exhausting day.

Janet sensed a need for him to unscramble his mind. Knowing that everything he told her was always kept in the strictest of confidence, she had been the only person outside of the force he had already informed of the early-morning discovery under the bridge in Beacon Alley.

"We know his name, he lived in Southsea, he's been identified by his sister... but otherwise there's not a huge amount that we know about him," said Peach. "He was a property surveyor of sorts, and had a rather interesting hobby – it appears that he came over to the Island at weekends to prospect for gold and other precious metals. Our victim was some kind of treasure-hunter."

"That's more than 'not a lot,'" said Janet, "that alone *could* help lead you to the killer."

One of Janet's endearing qualities was the 'schoolmarm' way in which she treated her friend, manifesting itself not only in the manner in which she often spoke to him, but also whenever they met, on parting she would hand over a see-through plastic wallet containing printouts of three or four articles from the internet, mostly from the member's section of the Guardian – that left-leaning paper ever popular with a similarly socialist-inclined teaching fraternity. With Peach regularly guilty of focusing on his locality to the exclusion of everything else, Janet's articles were an attempt to keep him updated with what was going on in the rest of the world.

This package he always looked forward to, even treasured. He knew that today it would certainly dull – if not erase – the image of the victim's battered skull wrapped in that thin, plastic Tesco-branded shopping bag. With a little luck he would sleep soundly enough, waking refreshed to meet Tom Craven in the morning.

Chapter 3

The following morning at 8:30 am prompt, DC Tom Craven arrived at the Southsea Hovertravel Terminal to collect Bruno and take him to Sam Peters' apartment.

The password to the dead man's computer records had been deciphered (using 'rainbow tables' according to the smiling police IT expert) and the data replicated and printed, enabling the two detectives to read around one-hundred pages of correspondence with various third parties, as well as reports of building surveys undertaken by him in the counties of Hampshire, Dorset and Sussex going back one year.

"I had him work on it overnight," said Tom. "I made it clear that it was vital to a murder case, so turnaround time for accessing the data was of the highest priority. But even if I hadn't I get the feeling we'd still have the documents in our hands – the guy lives for solving puzzles, and this is exactly his kind of thing."

"He'll get rewarded for that," said Bruno. "Did he mention anything about the contents?

"Not much, no. Once he's 'in', that's his job done and he's already moved onto the next puzzle. He just said it looked like normal business docs."

Bruno split the file into two and gave one of the equal halves to Tom. "Hot off the press, then. Let's deal with it first."

Tom nodded and his senior set out their task.

"We're looking for any sign of dissention between our victim and one of his clients, OK?"

As Tom's mouth began to form a 'd', Bruno helped him out.

"Dissention. Conflict. Lack of agreement or harmony..."

***

At this early stage of the investigation, it only took the men an hour to make it through every page of text, and neither found anything obviously contentious in Peters' correspondence with his clients.

It felt to Peach like turning over an interesting stone only to find nothing at all crawling about beneath. The dead man's business appeared to have been conducted on an above-board basis, and was not riddled with dissenting clients who might have decided to act in a violent way towards him. Despite the lack of a smoking gun, reading the documents had not been overly arduous, and the time spent had helped them get a handle on the victim's personality.

"OK then, now for the personal stuff," Bruno said, picking up Sam's current year diary. The first entry was a Wednesday:

> WEDNESDAY JANUARY 15th
> *Back from skiing in Davos, very fit, must keep it up.*

Then a blank before the next page of writing:

> FRIDAY JANUARY 17th
> *Visit to Island. Survey for Watt & Co in London. Travelled by car via Portsmouth car ferry terminal to Fishbourne. Inspected and compiled a report on the derelict Havelock Hotel, situated on the eastern shore of the Island, three miles southeast of Ryde. Valued as a development site – Discussed my valuation with Philip Coulter, before inserting figure into report. Wrote report in Bembridge Village tea house Friday pm – Emailed to Philip at Watt & Co Insurance assessors, One Liverpool Street, London, E1 6QY.*

Tom took one step towards the filing cabinet and quickly found a file for Watt & Co, extracting a report. After some preamble it read:

> *The Havelock was opened as a hotel in January 1901 in the month that Queen Victoria had died at Osborne House in the west of the Island. Until the nineteen-twenties it had been the best hotel this side of the Solent, hosting Royal dignitaries and members of the gentry during the sailing regattas of Cowes week. Situated twelve miles east of Cowes, it had been a bolt-hole for those wishing to avoid the snobs and social-climbing bores of the Royal Cowes Yacht Club before, during and after racing as well as during bad weather. During World War Two, in the build-up*

to the D-Day invasion, the hotel was regularly the venue of high-level war cabinet meetings attended by Churchill, Eisenhower and Montgomery. The Havelock remained the Island's premier hotel until the summer holiday exodus to Southern Europe's beaches on cheap package tours began in the nineteen-sixties.

Bruno knew the Havelock Hotel and could remember seeing its final years housing guests as a boy in the nineteen-seventies. Growing up on the Island, during long-distant summer holidays he had cycled to the remotest parts he could reach, picnicking in the deserted fortifications on top of Culver Cliff, looking down on the eastern coast and the old forts in the Solent and the Havelock. The hotel had by then become a 'social housing provider,' open all year to cover the overheads by taking in permanent guests, or 'cheapies' as the staff called them, booked in by Ryde Social Services who could offer no more social housing elsewhere.

In winter, the cheapies earned enough to cover the rates, gas and electric and no more than essential maintenance. On dark windy nights, the lounge, saloon and public bars would fill up with locals until well after the legal closing time. Many, though barely able to stand, would speed off in their little saloon cars along pitch black, high-hedged narrow lanes to isolated cottages in the sparsely-populated farming areas near the centre of the Island. It was a rare occasion one would be stopped by the police, but even when so, the friendly, local PC would smile, share a joke and allow passage after being told of any newly-brewing scandals overheard in the rooms of the Havelock earlier that night.

Policemen on the Island had kept the peace. They did not pursue petty criminals or vandals for minor offences. It was an anathema to them to fill in forms and spend their days in Magistrates' courts presided over by unelected nobodies whose half-day-a-fortnight court sittings dishing out sentences to alcoholics, shoplifters and wife-beaters satisfied their inflated egos.

After his long service as an Island copper, Bruno understood how its culture differed from the mainland; he was acutely aware that in many places here, policing remained the same as it had been in the seventies. Most of the born-and-bred working-class Islanders – 'Caulkheads' as they were known – were still employed in low-paid seasonal roles, were poorly educated, in-bred, and plenty had never left the Island in their lives. Island police were not officious crime-solvers banging up petty criminals. To keep families together, they tended to act as judge and jury over petty criminals, whose reactions to being caught and being let off were humble and conciliatory. In most cases they became reformed characters and law abiding citizens, a fact that would shock and surprise your average generation-X city copper.

When the Havelock had visibly had its day and fallen into an ever-worsening state of disrepair, the owners wouldn't accept that a property was only worth what somebody would pay for it, their own valuation falsely based on its once pre-eminent status. Rejecting sensible (but in their eyes paltry) offers, time after time they held out for more... until 1999 when the property became literally worthless.

Facing the east winds of the Solent, the exposed fabric of the building had deteriorated in no time at all. The wind-driven sea salt had eaten deeply into the brickwork, loosening the mortar and resulting in both crumbling walls and collapsed ceilings. Carved masonry of any worth had, unsurprisingly, been stolen; every single one of the window panes had been smashed by vandals. Joined by squatters and transients, they had also burned doors, floorboards, stair banisters and even the wooden window frames, creating warmth during the colder nights and a pleasing flame-based backdrop for beach parties on fine summer evenings. The heavy, much-sought-after welsh roof slates had disappeared, no doubt quickly turning up for sale at the yard of a less-than-scrupulous architectural salvage company who happened to have mislaid the receipt for the purchase thereof. This had left the roof rafters exposed to the elements, most now resting precariously on crumbling stone walls, propped up by local authority-funded scaffolding. To complement this vision of ruin, a Mex Hire fence enveloped the site at a distance of twenty metres all round, displaying fixed metal 'Keep Out: Danger' notices, themselves now visibly weathered.

The shoreline, one hundred metres from the hotel, sloped sharply down to a shingle beach. To the south lay Culver Cliff and the small towns of Sandown, Shanklin and Ventnor. Here, cliffs were well known to slip into the sea on a worryingly regular basis, edging now uninsurable cliff-top buildings ever closer to their inevitable destruction.

***

In his report, Sam had recommended that the Havelock Hotel location offered excellent opportunities to be developed as a holiday camp or caravan park, but never to host the kind of building it once did; the market for a super-luxury hotel on the Island simply no longer existed.

Like his general business document, apart from confirming that Sam was in fact working on the Island on that day, there was nothing in the report or the diary that could be linked directly with his demise. Tom added the name Philip Coulter – the man for whom the report had been undertaken – to a list of names he'd like to contact at some point in the investigation.

The diary entry for Friday the seventeenth continued:

EVENING
Decided to remain on IW for the weekend to explore local geological formations. Stayed Friday and Saturday at The Haven B&B in Bembridge. Was warm and comfortable. The only guest! Weather cold and wet with an east wind off the sea. Pub supper at the Crown, also in Bembridge. Returned to read Jasper Jenkins, Island Historian: Geological Formations of the Island. Tells of how the rocks, laid down layer upon layer 140 million years ago, contain visible remains of many plants and petrified fossils. Evidence that the Island had once been covered with sea water can be seen in the marine gravel found on top of Chillerton Down, 600 ft above today's sea level.

SATURDAY JANUARY 18th
Out at 8:30 am. East wind too cold to explore the exposed Chillerton Down. Drove to Sandown, and walked west along the cliff top towards Shanklin surveying the rock and clay outcrops.

As a local, Bruno found Sam's diary entries of his Island tour interesting, particularly the next note which initially intrigued him. On the diary page Sam had written a reference to a certain page of the Jasper Jenkins book he'd listed, a well-read copy of which sat in his bookcase.

"Read page sixty-two of that Jenkins book to me, Tom. It might lead us to something," asked Peach. Tom began:

"Placer, or alluvial, deposits of gold result from the erosion and washing-away of gold contained in rocks by the action of wind or flowing water. The earliest known method of humans extracting gold came from the washing of river gravel. Gold forms *after* the major mountain-building tectonic activity has ceased, when erosion of the uplifted areas is linked to widespread deposition in river systems. Placer deposits form in flowing water downstream from the source region in active river channels. These deposits can travel long distances downstream, although most form within ten miles of the bedrock source. Bars and islands of braided streams where the deposits of gravel usually accumulate are relatively common places for gold to become concentrated. Prior research of the Palaeogene Hampshire Basin has hinted at possibilities of gold deposits in the outcrops around high points on the south of the Isle of Wight."

When his young assistant had finished the paragraph, Bruno re-read the note which now made more sense:

> *Investigate if anyone has followed up on Jenkins' Palaeogene theory, particularly in stream beds of E & W Yar rivers.*

"So our murdered man thinks there might be gold in the Island's rivers, does he?" Bruno mused.

When he saw his superior had stopped reading, Tom spoke up. "Do you think that anyone has *really* searched for gold in those rivers?" he asked.

"Who knows? My hunch is that few would have considered doing so as being a time-worthy exercise... but it certainly would explain Peters' reasons for spending so much time on the Island."

"Perhaps he *did* find some gold there. You never know," said Tom, barely containing a laugh.

"Possibly," Bruno replied, rather less dismissively. *And it would give us a decent motive for his corpse being found under the bridge across the East Yar river at Beacon Alley* a voice in his mind said. Although not willing to draw that conclusion *too* quickly, years of experience had taught him that early hunches were often well worth looking into. "Back to the diary for now though," he stated with a down-to-earth tone, perhaps designed to ground the younger policeman's mind from wandering off into wild riches obtained from riverbeds.

> SUNDAY JANUARY 19th
> *Walked the coastal path from Shanklin through Luccombe to Ventnor descending to the shore. Continued out along the beach beyond – three hours; returned through the landslip – four hours. Late afternoon returned to the mainland on the ferry from Fishbourne to Portsmouth.*

Then a blank page. And another. Bruno licked his finger and thumbed through more until writing was found.

"A two week gap then," said Tom, keen to show his focus was very much on the here and now.

"Yes... almost," agreed Bruno.

SATURDAY FEBRUARY 1st

Returned to the Island on the 8:00 am Portsmouth-to-Fishbourne ferry. 9:30 am: heavy rain grew into a giant storm. Parked in the Military road car park high on the cliff tops between Ventnor and Freshwater and waited for the rain to stop. Found it was an ideal lookout to observe the cliffs – should see a mile each way on a clear day. Exciting to watch the wind-driven, sand-filled rain pound the face of the cliff. Foam-filled waves lashed the shore, hurling pebbles and rock at the vertical stone with the force of a sledgehammer, driving saltwater into the cracks and crevices. Every now and then, segments of this age-old barrier would fall away in the relentless punishment, finding a new home at the bottom of the English Channel. Sketched the newly exposed cliff surfaces, took photographs and drew a map from which to read the cliff surface and different layers on a return visit. I was completely alone."

"Seems to be more than a diary," said Tom.

"Yes, we're even treated to some poetry," Bruno agreed, his helper not knowing him quite well enough yet to tell what might be a joke and what definitely wasn't.

Around noon, the tide changed; wind and rain eased. Climbed down to the rock-strewn beach and examined the layers that had fallen from the cliffs. They were a different colour from the sand around them, almost black. Collected three fist-sized samples. Left at 3:45 pm after looking at the beach's other rock formations. Drove eight miles inland, north, through deserted tourist areas, searching for a B&B. Eventually, after dark, saw a 'Vacancies' sign swinging from a pole on the outskirts of Godshill. An uninviting bungalow, the noisy gravel drive would have alerted its occupants to my arrival. It was unlit, although a faint glow shone into the hallway from inside. On the steps of the front entrance, I pushed a rasping Victorian wind-up doorbell that made a screeching noise. It set off voices which I strained to hear.

***

"Dick," a woman's voice called, "there's someone at the front door, but I'm going to ignore it."

"No," a faint male voice called from a distance.

"You bastard, Dick. I told you to change that sign days ago."

"We need money, sweetheart," he shouted from the lavatory. "Go and see who's there."

"Fuck you, Dick. If you leave the board stuck up, you should turn the heating on in the guestroom," she said, as she inched the hall curtain aside to see the visitor. After a long stare and a grimace, she switched on a doorstep light.

Sonia Potter dreaded the day each year when they put the 'Vacancies' sign back up and began taking in guests for bed & breakfast; it had never been her idea to do this and she tried to do as little as possible every season. On the first sunny day each year, and always when she was out, the first punter would have checked in before she returned. Usually with couples, only one would come to the door. If she was the one to respond, they would usually go back to the car to 'consult with the wife' and then quickly drive off.

She could see the caller was alone at the door on this miserable winter evening. Sonia wondered if (or more accurately hoped he would be) a 'consulter'. She opened the front door, stared at Sam, and spoke, putting only the smallest effort into her politeness.

"Can I help you?"

Sam stared back. The woman in front of him was thin, skin hanging loosely off her frame. She really was just a bag of bones, covered from chin to thigh in a roll neck sweater, a tweed skirt, woollen stockings and slippers. This vision that wouldn't have been out of place in a nightmare was as unappealing as the bungalow, but at Heaven knows how late on a dark and wet winter's night, and after such a tiring day in the battering wind and freezing cold, Sam was simply too tired to look elsewhere.

"Hello, I'm looking for a room for the night."

"Just you?"

"Yes."

"How long for?"

"Just tonight."

She looked him up and down and sniffed noisily, she was used to unwelcome guests.

"Wait a minute, I'll ask my husband, we're not *actually* open," she said, and receded back into the hall.

"It's a man for one night" she called out.

"On his own?"

"Yes."

Dick did not like singles, but on a day like this, no one else was going to turn up. Maybe it was a case of *a bird in the hand...*

"What's he like?" he asked.

"Driving a Volkswagen."

"New?"

"Hmm, looks old."

"What's he doing in Godshill at this time of year?"

"How should I know, why don't you get out of the shithouse and come and ask him?"

"It's thirty-five quid a night," he called out.

Sonia returned to the doorstep and said, 'It's thirty-five pounds per night, including breakfast. We don't take credit cards, so it'll have to be cash. In advance.'

As Sam nodded his acceptance of these terms, she stood aside to enable him to enter, closed the front door behind them both and gestured at him to follow.

The room she took him to was – somewhat surprising to Sam, at least – clean and comfortable with a double bed and a walk-in shower. It was an improvement on the bungalow itself, being an extension tacked onto the back. It looked appealing enough, but as Sam entered, he shivered; it was freezing cold.

"What time do you want breakfast?" his landlady for the night asked whilst turning on the large radiator and drawing the curtains across a window that looked out towards a garden.

"How about eight?" Sam proffered.

At that moment Dick appeared; a bald headed, short-ish man, in his fifties and with an instantly detectable friendlier air than that of his wife.

"I'm Dick, Dick Potter," he said and offered his hand. "Have you come far to visit the Island?"

"No, I am visiting, touring," replied Sam, clearly unwilling to go into too much detail. "Let me get my bag."

On his return he handed over the £35 in cash, took a key, and on Dick Potter's recommendation drove back to Godshill to the George Inn just in time for a pub dinner. When he returned, the room had thankfully warmed up, with the addition of a portable electric radiator – no doubt from Dick rather than his wife.

***

SUNDAY FEBRUARY 2nd

8:00 am breakfast, cooked by Dick Potter and served by Sonia, trying her best to be pleasant. Returned to the Military Road car park to re-examine the cliffs after yesterday's storm. After Saturday's high tide the rock fall at the base of the cliff has remained where it fell. On the beach examined the different coloured layers and geological strata now clearly discernible. Photographed the collection of broken cliff and measured its distance from the cliff top. The rock strewn amongst the sand at the base of the cliff was dense quartz rock.

This quartz seam would be impossible to approach from the summit of the cliff, at 250 ft high. It would be laying at an angle, around 50 ft deep from the surface, which, if tilted upwards at an angle of rise estimated at one degree, would surface half a mile or so inland from the cliff top. The seam was approx. 6 ft in depth and, assuming gold is always present in quartz, this could be a highly valuable discovery.

Gathered a bag of the broken quartz rock to add to yesterday's samples.

Weather forecast for the Solent for the weekend is very bad. Returned via Godshill and Newport mid-afternoon to Fishbourne car ferry and went home.

"Now we know what he was up to," said Tom. "Do you think that's true about gold and quartz?"

"I don't know, but our dead expert seems interested enough."

"And a motive?"

"It's a beginning, certainly. Worth looking into, it could lead us somewhere."

"What about the Potters?", Tom asked keenly. "They're the first people on the Island he seems to have spoken to – if we believe the diary."

"No reason not to. We should see if he told them what he was doing."

"If he was only there for one night, they probably won't even remember him", said Tom, dejectedly.

"We'll find out," replied Bruno, "*after* another page of that diary..."

MONDAY FEBRUARY 3rd
Crushed a handful of the shale and quartz rock with a sledge hammer behind the garage block at home. Produced a mixture of miniscule particles, dust and metallic splinters and grains.
Used a 15" circular plastic bowl and water from garden hose to make a dust soup. Washed away the dust then repeated again and again. Eventually, all that remained in the bottom of the bowl were insoluble gritty metallic particles.
Working like an ancient gold prospector would have done was rather exciting, but tiring. Ten kilos of rock produced three hundred grams of insoluble metallic particles.

Bruno knew that in the mid-nineteenth century, gold prospectors had laboriously used a pan to process streambed material, until they developed methods to simplify panning that required different skills and equipment. Sam was copying their early method, and his enjoyment of this – plus, surely, the potential rewards – was clearly what was drawing him to the Island.

Chapter 4

Monday 21st July

Bruno felt surprisingly comfortable, given that he was in a dead man's apartment with a fellow policeman he had never worked with before, sorting through the former's personal effects. *Not many other professions put on in such extraordinary environments*, mused the detective as he continued reading the diary, his keen underling eyeing the same text from a close but thankfully comfortable distance.

> TUESDAY FEBRUARY 4th
> *Called Southampton University, spoke to a Professor Bartlett (Noel), head of the department of Geology. Explained briefly what my survey had produced. He invited me over. Friendly and helpful. Gave him the three-hundred grams of particles, which he agreed to analyse in his laboratory and call me with his results.*

> FRIDAY FEBRUARY 7th
> *Bartlett phoned at 4:00 pm and invited me back to his lab.*

***

Professor Bartlett was visibly excited. "Your samples contain an amazingly high concentration of gold," he explained as he walked Sam through to his laboratory full of scientific devices. "Let me show you the results."

On a bench were displayed several plastic cups on which he had stuck paper labels.

"I have numbered these cups one to seven," he said, pointing to the workbench. Your three-hundred grams of quartz rock crystals contains in cup one, dust and earth; cup two, silicon crystals of a type usually found in quartz; cup three, quartz itself; cup four, one gram of lead; cup five copper, two grams; cup six, three grams of silver; and finally, in cup seven there are *thirteen* grams of gold! As this was produced from ten kilos of quartz rock, it represents nineteen grams from *ten thousand* of precious metals – the lead, copper, silver and gold. Compare that to, say, a gold mine in Kalgoorlie in Western Australia which would only have to yield one particle of gold in *one hundred thousand* to be profitable... a mine working on the statistics of your sample could be more than a hundred times as profitable as the industry standard. Of course, this *may* be all there is – one quartz rock broken off thousands of years ago, found lying in the sand on the beach. But if it's part of an *existing* quartz seam, there is huge potential in its value. We need to go and take a look."

Bartlett made coffee and conjectured about the possibilities. He was keen to know specifically *where* Sam had got the rock from... and *when*, certainly more keen than Sam was to *tell* him at this, their first meeting.

"At twelve hundred US dollars an ounce, your thirteen grams of gold are worth almost six hundred dollars. How do you feel about that?" Bartlett asked.

"Perhaps I got lucky with a single rock?" Sam proposed.

"It is worth my investigating the rock formation with you... you may have found an outcrop that's many thousands of years old. If it were as big as, say, a house... well, surely I don't need to tell you what it could be worth," said Bartlett.

"I would be very grateful for your help, of course," said Sam, "but I can't spare the time just now to go with you."

The questions continued. "Who owns the land you found your samples on?"

"The land's public, I think – I found them on a beach," Sam answered.

"In Portsmouth?"

"No, not in Portsmouth."

Bartlett waited for Sam to expand.

He didn't.

"We should go back to the spot; it might be just a rock or boulder rolled in by the tide, but perhaps if it broke off a cliff..?"

Bartlett was getting too close for comfort, and Sam was glad he had thus far stayed silent on that front. He gave Sam the cups containing the separated samples. Despite his eager questioning, he refused to accept payment for the analysis; Sam therefore felt comfortable enough in promising to call him one week later to arrange taking the academic to the all-important spot. In return for the goodwill Bartlett had shown, he conscientiously dropped £50 into the student union welfare box.

Sam considered Bartlett's estimate of the potential profitability of the seam a somewhat unwelcome surprise. If it were six feet thick, it could run inland for some distance. At the depth he felt it was most likely located, it would certainly be mineable by a commercial company. In British law, mineral rights belonged to the owner of the land; Sam considered the possible route such a quartz seam might take and decided it would likely be somewhere on the Downs – which he guessed would be owned by the local government. He needed to put some thought into how he might gain from the situation, so until Sam could remove this obstacle, he decided to put Bartlett off.

***

SATURDAY FEBRUARY 8th
Re-visited the Island alone. Using ordnance survey maps, traced the fall of the Downs from the cliff top high point at the Military Road car park, and determined that the rainfall on the Downs eventually dropped into and formed the source of two Island rivers, the East Yar and the Medina.

Bruno looked up at Tom.

"So we have a man, murdered by a blow to the head," he said. "We have identified one reason for his presence on the Island, in fact, a potentially lucrative and thus *life-changing* reason. Apart from our dead gold prospector, at *this* point it seems only one other person knew of what he'd found – this Professor Bartlett. And although we don't know yet whether he was ever told the location; wouldn't you agree our victim makes it clear in that last entry that he was very keen to find out where it was? I'd therefore say he's definitely a person of interest to us."

"I'd certainly agree," said Tom.

"He stayed for one night at that B&B, but going by our victim's notes, the owners wouldn't know him from Adam," continued Bruno, Tom ever attentive to his words, "and would have no idea what he was doing. So, focusing on the professor, to gain such a position one has to be clever at their chosen subject, but the pay is far from generous. What if he realised quickly that *this* could be his golden ticket?"

"There's definitely plenty of questions we could ask him, even if he doesn't have blood on his hands," Tom suggested.

"Agreed, but first we should speak to the manager of this apartment block. Let's see what response we get when we tell the landlord their tenant has met their demise. Plus there's plenty more of this diary to get through."

***

Sam's address book provided the phone number for the management company's secretary, who in fact lived across the hall in the adjacent ground floor apartment. Her name was Sarah Bates and she lived alone. When Bruno explained that Sam's murder was the reason for being in his apartment, she was visibly upset; she'd lived in the building for nine years and knew most of her neighbours very well.

The conversation had been routine up until the point Bruno had asked Bates when she'd last seen Sam Peters.

"Sunday just gone, quite early in the morning. Around seven am," she had stated.

With the time of death clearly established as the day *before*, this assertion was of great interest to the two detectives, although both were well-practised enough not to show it.

"Can you describe what you saw that morning?" Bruno asked.

"I was in bed and had been awake for a few minutes when I heard his front door close. I hadn't seen Sam for a few days and so I jumped out of bed to look out of my window. It was bright and sunny, but I guess it was supposed to rain, as he was wearing his raincoat."

"And you're sure it was him?" Tom asked, subtly enough.

"Oh yes, his raincoat is very distinctive. It hangs almost down to his ankles rather than just to his knees. He also had a baseball cap on."

"You say you 'jumped up' to see him...?" led Bruno.

Bates sighed. "I was being nosey," she admitted. "He's had a lady stay with him recently. I was... interested..." she tailed off.

"What do you know about this woman?"

"She was well-dressed and looked quite well off to me. Taller than most, and I'd guess in her late forties. I couldn't describe her looks though, I never really caught any more than a sideways glance at her face."

"Would you mind showing us where you were standing when you saw Sam walk away from his flat?" Bruno asked.

Sarah agreed, and led the two policemen across the hallway in her apartment and then through into her bedroom. There were net curtains across the window.

"Ms Bates, if my colleague Tom acts as your friend Sam, would you mind showing me exactly what you did when you heard the flat door close?" asked Bruno.

And so, after Tom had walked back to Sam's flat and readied himself, their ad-hoc reconstruction began. Sarah Bates laid down on her sleep side and the second she heard Tom close the flat front door, she repeated her actions the previous Sunday morning. She got out of bed and walked around in front of it, stopping at the corner of the window nearest her door and peering through the net curtains. By this time Tom had almost reached the front garden entrance and was about to turn right onto the pavement and off down the road.

"Did you pull the net *back*?" asked Bruno.

"I *never* do that, Inspector. If someone turned round, they'd see me... and I'd get a reputation as a curtain twitcher!"

Bruno thanked her for her help and left, meeting Tom back outside. No sooner had he shut the door behind him, than Tom fired off his burning question.

"What do you think? *Could* she have seen him?" he asked.

"Of course not. Unless the rules of physics have changed, she couldn't have seen Sam at seven am on *Sunday*, when he had most *likely* died the evening before, and his body had most *certainly* been found an hour earlier the same morning. To be frank, I could hardly see you through her net curtains, *and* you'd nearly reached the gate by the time she had a view from her window. Obviously a case of mistaken identity. But if it wasn't Sam, who *was* it?"

"Do you think she's even right about the clothing, then?" said Tom.

"The raincoat, yes, probably," Bruno replied "Let's remember that, because whoever was wearing it might still have it."

Chapter 5

Took 8:00 am car ferry to Fishbourne, booked one night at the Potters' B&B. Returned to Military Road car park to search for the quartz inland from the cliff at Reeth Bay to the east of St Catherine's point. Estimated that if the quartz seam's upward incline continued at the rate of 1 ft rise in 200 (and the ground remained level) it would surface in the area of Chale, a mile inland to the north.

Walked from cliff edge by compass straight lines due North for 1½ miles. Nothing visible in the long, tufted grass covering the wet, uneven moor. Returned to starting point along a parallel line 200 metres west. Planted small flags in the turf as a guide along a straight line.

Covered three miles over rocks and up & down inclines, felt like much further. Repeated the exercise a second time 200 metres east of centre for 1½ miles, found nothing. Completed a third search 200 west of centre – Nothing. Total distance searched on foot nine miles across boggy uneven ground.

Gave up, exhausted!

Not wishing to arrive at Potters before bedtime, dined at the Village Inn in old Shanklin, close to Shanklin Chine. Interesting place; in the days of sailing ships (before it was opened as an early tourist attraction by William Colnutt in 1817) the Chine had been a refuge for smugglers! Landing their contraband at the inlet, they vanished into the thick undergrowth, leaving their spoils well hidden, to be collected after dining in style at one of the hostelries in the Old Village once the customs officers had gone home.

After two pints of Burts' ale at the Crab Inn and a local breed beef steak pie, drove back to the Potters'. Slept well after a long day. Will go again in the morning. Optimistic of finding a quartz outcrop tomorrow.

*SUNDAY FEBRUARY 23*rd
Departed Potters on a friendly note after a decent fry-up.
Continued trekking St Catherine's Downs. Extended search either
side of previous markers. Examined rocky outcrops.

***

Monday 21st July

By mid-afternoon Sam Peters was soaked up to his knees, had found nothing and now believed that he may have erred to have assumed the quartz would surface here on the Downs. It had been a pretty wild guess to assume it would and he now somewhat regretted not bringing Bartlett, whose experience would have helped. Rather than the guesswork Sam was relying on, the professor's contribution to such a search would have been based on his knowledge and experience of fault lines.

He decided to give up as the weather was deteriorating, but it was a long way back to the Military Road car park – at least a mile and a half. Looking up, he spotted a person approaching from the west, a lady with her dog; it looked like an Alsatian. It must have been an older dog, or surely it would have been running about instead of plodding along, trying to keep up alongside its mistress.

"Good afternoon! Awfully drab isn't it? But it's almost March and spring will soon be here," the lady said, in a friendly, educated, upper-class tone. She was well dressed, with green wellingtons, brown waterproof slacks and a Barbour wax jacket, scarf and hat. She was rather a handsome woman, he guessed aged somewhere between forty and fifty. "Where are *you* going?" she enquired, with a pointed emphasis on the word 'you', implying that whatever it was, he was obviously stupid to be doing it.

"Just walking back to my car on the Military Road." he replied, a little less sheepishly that he felt internally.

"That's *miles* from here, and torrential rain can only be one minute away – look over there," she said, pointing to the large black clouds approaching from the sea. "On these Downs you'd surely get lost in the mist, it's far too dangerous. My house is only a few hundred metres from here, behind the copse," she pointed ahead. "Come with me for now, I'm headed home. If we hurry, we'll avoid the rain," she added, striding out.

Grateful for the offer – although it had almost felt more like a command – Sam followed, only now realising the serious danger the ominous clouds could potentially bring.

Within two minutes, when the first spots of rain fell, Sam's female companion was proven right.

She had led him to a two hundred-year-old farmhouse hidden behind a copse of equal vintage which lay in a natural dip, sheltered from the winds that drove in from the sea across the Downs. Arriving *just* before the heavy rain had begun, they had both avoided a severe drenching.

They entered through a rear door into a traditional low-ceilinged farmhouse kitchen, complete with wheel-back chairs. A wooden picture rail encircled the walls at head height from which, on triangular brass picture hooks, hung framed prints of the Island from bygone years. The pictures had clearly sat there for many years. The room was pleasingly warm, but its appearance tired and dated – as, Sam would later learn, was the rest of the farmhouse. The ambience of the kitchen was in complete contrast to the lady who had just rescued him from the gale force wind that he now felt blowing cold air through the creaky ill-fitting doors, and the rain that beat noisily against the window panes.

As Sam's gaze fell on the source of the kitchen's warmth – a black, coal-fired cast iron stove that roared away against a kitchen wall – his companion spoke.

"My name is Phyllida Glassman, pleased to meet you," she said. "Welcome to my home, Roud Farm... which, I must admit, has seen better days."

Sam introduced himself saying he was visiting the Island for the weekend and staying in a B&B back at Godshill.

With the history of the farmhouse a pleasantly neutral subject about which conversation could commence, Phyllida explained that the seventeenth century stone fireplace in the adjoining lounge was built using stone from the original Appledurcombe House, which had burned down in the mid-seventeen-hundreds. The house had been the ancestral home of the Worsley family; James Worsley – a companion of Henry VIII – had been knighted and made captain of the Isle of Wight in 1509.

She continued to describe the farmhouse's features while placing a metal kettle over the open lid of the black stove.

"In fact, much of the Appledurcombe stone was used to build the walls of this house," she continued as the water boiled, soon pouring it into a silver teapot to brew.

At Phyllida's invitation, Sam followed her into the adjacent living room and sat on one of the chairs in front of the roaring fireplace, its age and provenance easily apparent to anyone who had worked in his industry for a decent length of time. She served up the Earl Grey tea with a slice of lemon, and offered from the tray she had brought in a small spread of chocolate biscuits. Sam picked one up, nibbling on it as politely as he could.

"So, tell me, what were you doing walking the Downs on a freezing wet winter's day such as this?" she asked.

"Searching for treasure," he explained, noting a slight raising of her eyebrows. "As a former Roman province, the Island is rich in as-yet-undiscovered Roman artefacts." For some reason he felt comfortable enough to tack on additional information for her. "I'm also keeping an eye out for outcrops of quartz seams, which can contain precious metal deposits and old fossils, which are widely collected."

"And what have you found today?" she asked, expectantly.

"Nothing" replied Sam, with the tiniest glimmer of embarrassment.

"And is this your first foray, or did you come yesterday as well?"

"I did come yesterday... but to be honest I found nothing then, either."

"Oh. When did you last find anything interesting?"

Sam thought back to the quartz samples he had taken to the university, but did his best to outwardly put on a sheepish smile that hinted at a general lack of success.

"Oh. Well, I wouldn't have thought it's worth doing then," she replied, "Certainly not in *this* awful weather."

"But it *can* be very rewarding... and it's a healthy outdoor hobby," he said, trying in his bedraggled state to sound enthusiastic and to give credibility to his activities. "Although... perhaps not so much on a day like this."

This was now becoming a conversation Sam didn't particularly want to have with a local landowner. Treasure hunting was naturally a rather secret activity, and usually so was what you found. Besides, he had no idea who her connections might be. He did his best to steer the conversation back to the house and its history.

In fact, Phyllida spoke not of the house, but of its occupant, herself. She was relaxed and clearly pleased with the opportunity to talk about her own history. Perhaps, Sam thought, companionship and the opportunity to talk about old memories were the real reason she had invited him into her home. Yet as long as the conversation stayed away from his own particular interest in the Island, he was more than happy with it – her style and warmth was the very antithesis of the isolated farmhouse which was her home.

The heavy rain continued for more than an hour, while darkness closed in. During this time Sam learned that Phyllida had been a widow for six months, having lost her husband towards the end of the previous year, after many spent nursing him through his Parkinson's disease.

"Twenty years ago farming had been his idea," Phyllida said. But although her husband had been born into it, she explained, they had struggled. To make matters worse, ten years ago he had fallen ill, necessitating the leasing out of parcels of land for grazing and outbuildings for livery, milking and sheep shearing. The income from these leases just about covered their expenses and provided them a frugal existence that she portrayed with a kind of upper-middle-class respectability.

"This is a rather quiet place for a lady to live alone isn't it? A mile from the nearest neighbour,?" enquired Sam.

"There is one farm labourer's cottage a quarter of a mile from here. If I need any muscle I hire him for half a day or so. But... I'm not going to stay here. It's taking rather a long time to sort out probate on my husband's estate, but once that's done I shall be off. I'm hoping it won't be long. The farm is all I have, and so until it is sold I'm living off the bank. We never made anything to put into savings from the farm."

By now the rain had ceased. Briefly pulling the curtains back, outside appeared pitch black, the moon nowhere to be seen.

"You said your car was in the Military Road car park?"

"Yes," said Sam.

"Well I'll take you back there, then." she said firmly.

He was concerned for her safety, her being out on a wild night, but his company was pleasant and he accepted her kindness.

It had begun to rain again by the time they got to his car.

"Thank you for rescuing me," he said, before opening the door.

"It was a pleasure – my good deed for the day," she said. "If you want a local guide the next time you come over to the Island, give me a call, my number's in the book: Phyllida Glassman, Roud Hill Farm," she called out, as Sam ran to his car through the cold, black, wet winter night.

***

Sam arrived in time to catch the 8:00 pm Fishbourne car ferry to Portsmouth. He had enjoyed his chance encounter with Phyllida Glassman; it had enlivened his tiresome search for the quartz seam and given him some much-needed respite. He realised now that she had rescued him from a genuinely dangerous situation, one he had carelessly ignored and thus he was beholden to her for helping.

Almost as soon as he returned home, he looked her up in the phone directory and made a note of her number. Although he lived surrounded by people, he thought, his lonesome life was not unlike hers day-to-day.

***

SATURDAY MARCH 1st
Returned to the Island and stayed at the Potters' for one night.

***

By 4:00 pm on the Saturday, the confidence that Sam had built up during the journey across on the ferry had now withered away; it had now just been an unsettling and disappointing day roaming the Downs. With every step he took, Sam wondered why he had not brought Professor Bartlett along to help.

Over breakfast on the Sunday morning he watched the Potters in the kitchen, sitting at a round table and listening to Radio Solent.

Sonia, as expected, had a disagreeable look. Almost the very second Sam finished, she pounced on the metal toast rack, returning the uneaten half-slices to Dick, who scooped out the remains from Sam's butter dish and spread it over two of them.

"What's he up to, all those pans on his back seat?"

"He's divining."

"What's that?" Sonia asked.

"It's what gold prospectors do. They gather mud from the bottom of rivers into pans and wash out the mud to see if there are any gold crystals left in the pan."

"Like those men with metal detectors who wander about on other people's land looking for gold coins? Hah, bloody stupid. He'll never find anything on this island," she said.

"I dunno' about that," Dick mused, "The Romans were here in sixty AD, and they would have left things. There were no banks back then, so they buried their treasure. I bet some of it's still there."

***

Sunday 2nd March (am)
Bored with trekking the Downs in these winter conditions. Abandoned search for the quartz seam.
Time to bring Bartlett in???
Parked in Niton High street. The source of the East Yar river lays near to the centre of the village of Niton at the roadside and is marked with a carved stone half-circle. Sculpted into this is the text 'River Yar Source: Sea 19 miles.' Turns out finding a river's source is easier than a quartz outcrop!
The East Yar is the most likely to yield up sediment of interest, being the longer of the two rivers. These kind of streams transport sedimentary grains from steep inclines along their riverbeds until they settle into basins created where the gradient is a degree or two steeper. Draining down from hills above Niton football ground, through fields and under a concrete paving slab-covered roadside ditch, just at a trickle, the spring source of the East Yar river!

***

It was a warm early March day which signalled spring was coming. From the source in Niton, Sam followed the trickle on foot into a stream for a spot to take a sample from the bed of the river. After recent rain the trickle was flowing quickly, not impeded too much by rotting leaves and twigs from late Autumn. The stream passed the parish church of St John the Baptist within a few feet of the gravestone of one Grace Mary Baguley 1899–1982, on which was carved the inscription:

I Must Go Down To The Sea Again

She lay at peace amongst several dozen headstones of former Niton village residents of a similar age, some no doubt her friends in life. To Sam, the headstones confirmed the wisdom of burial in the ground.

The church of St John the Baptist in Niton dated from 1228. The name of its first rector, The Reverend Johannes Gaignard, 1228–1244, was written in gold leaf on an oak board which contained two columns of names in chronological order, all the way through to 1996 and the present incumbent, Sandra E Lloyd. Sam signed the visitor's book below a Freda Cox from Stafford who had visited the previous day. Her note said that she'd been stationed on the Island as part of the Land Army from 1944 to 1946.

One hundred metres beyond the church gate, the concrete paving-covered East Yar was joined by a small tributary descending from higher ground, carrying the rainfall from the hill at the top of Pan Lane. The additional flow looked to Sam as being a similar rate to a bathroom tap when fully opened. After crossing Niton's High Street underground, the river continued to Whitwell where a substantial tributary, itself called the Yar, flowed into it. The conjoined waters then meandered across fields, some grazed by animals, others planted with corn, wheat and oats.

Sam drove the road towards Godshill, passing several small streams that emptied into the East Yar, although none wider than eighteen inches or so. The farmland through which the river ran dropped away from Niton towards Whitwell, with the direction of flow always steadily north, without bend or fall – meaning no natural gullies or basins to collect miniscule particles.

Eventually Sam parked up and followed the river on foot as far as he could. On the outskirts of Godshill though, he was unable to maintain contact with it as it traversed private farmland towards the farm.

A lady in the kiosk of a model village nearby directed Sam back to Beacon Alley off West Street. Three hundred metres along a narrow country road he came to a humpback stone bridge which crossed the East Yar. Signposts on the banks of the river indicated it was a designated walkers' footpath – reference GL18 – and showed a distance back to Roud of three quarters of a mile.

***

SUNDAY 2nd MARCH (PM)

Sunday pm. From its source in Niton to the Beacon Alley bridge, the East Yar has grown into a proper river. The riverbanks in the vicinity of the bridge near Beacon Alley appear to be a good place to pan for gold. Either side of the bridge are deep pools, gullies and basins in which there could be deposits of particles accumulated over centuries.

Examined river flow either side from the bridge for two hundred metres. To the west are large rocks, narrowing the width of the river and causing the flow of the water to increase; it twists and turns, creating both gullies and pools. Beneath the bridge at its centre, the water is ten feet deep, fast flowing and clear, revealing a red muddy bottom, consistent with the red earth seen along the banks on either side up to the grass verge which borders the walker's track.

Explored the banks either side of the bridge. Within view from the bridge, set back 150 metres from the north bank is an old house with views of the East Yar from its two floors. Built on a mound a couple of metres higher than the passing road, it would survive any river flooding and the high ground gives it a good commanding position. Thick shrubs, a closed farm gate and a wire fence prevent access, although it is untidy, tired, and looks uninhabited. From most windows, walkers on the towpath would be clearly visible.

***

So as not to be seen from the house, a passing car, or by a walker, Sam slid down the river bank and crouched beside the fast-flowing water, and from as far below the water line as he could reach, dug out a half-kilo of sediment, placing it in a plastic box marked with the number '1'. He then moved thirty metres towards the bridge and repeated the task, putting another half-kilo into a box marked '2'. At the bridge, the river narrowed and reached a depth of ten feet at its centre. From under the bridge, he took a third sample from below the bank, placing it in box '3'. He then repeated the exercise both thirty and sixty metres downstream from the bridge, filling boxes four and five with more sediment, providing sufficient volume for analysis.

At 2:30 pm rather than return to search for quartz on the Downs, Sam went to visit Phyllida Glassman, armed with scones, jam and cream bought from the local farm shop.

She was home, and very pleased he had called by. "Are you treasure hunting, or did you just come to see me?" she asked him.

Sam gave her the answer she wanted to hear, and after tea he accompanied her whilst she took her dog for a walk, during which they talked about the weather, the Island, and what she would do once she had sold up. Phyllida took the opportunity to show him some of the marshy tributaries that trickled across the Downs and descended to the source of the East Yar at Niton.

"I'm really very glad you came back to see me," she said as they walked the Downs' trails. She spoke intimately, as if she already knew him well.

"If I had not led you to safety that day, the storm might well have killed you," she said, taking his hand.

Sam wondered if she might need help from him.

Having returned back to the farmhouse, and after more tea, as darkness closed in he said goodbye, promised to keep in touch, and returned to the mainland mid-evening.

Sam was lifted in spirit. He'd met a friendly, capable woman who seemed to be a few years older than he was, a widow who'd shown an interest in him... he wondered whether she had any faults at all, and yet could only think that she had scorned his treasure hunting as a complete waste of time.

Then again, no one was perfect.

Chapter 6

Monday 21st July

After two hours discussing Sam's diary entries, Bruno suggested lunch.

"It's time for some air. Let's go to that café by the canoe lake," he suggested. They could both see it from the front window of the flat.

***

"This place opens at 7:00 am," said Tom as their food was served. "You can sit and watch Sam's apartment from here."

"Is that important?" said Bruno, tucking into his tuna salad.

"It could be," replied Tom. "He could be spied on – *if* somebody wanted to do that," he added.

The two policemen discussed what they'd learned so far about Peters from his diary. Bruno concluded he was tired of working alone and had met Phyllida just in time to maintain his interest in finding the quartz. But personally, save for his newly acquired obsession with the Island and the possibility of finding a valuable gold seam thereon, there was no mention of club memberships, friends or any other kind of human connection; a kind of invisible man, they agreed.

"Do you think it's odd there's no *last* year's diary?" asked Tom.

A valid observation from the rookie, thought Bruno. He imagined most people who kept diaries had one for every year, but after a brief discussion they concluded it was likely just a 'this year' thing, spurred on by his interest in the Island.

***

Having eaten, they took a walk along the shingle beach – always with the apartment in view, and from where they could see across the Solent. To Islanders, Bruno considered, Sam was an intruder, a thief, plundering their birth right – something that could easily inspire hatred and a vicious response. It was a danger he could have overlooked. Treasure hunters normally belonged to clubs, feeding off other member's motivation. To become the 'star finder' was often the accolade they sought; it was often more important to them to be *named* the finder than to receive any financial reward, which under British law had to be shared fifty-fifty with the landowner. Yet the contribution of metal detecting to the understanding of the country's past is immense. Thousands of these dedicated searchers have made discoveries of such importance that they have on occasion re-written known history.

"What was his *reason* for the hobby?" mused Tom, clearly thinking along the same lines as his senior colleague.

"It's intrusive, obsessive and at times aggressive plodding around, alone, all over other people's property. Fits his personality to a T," said Bruno. "That's how I see it."

As Sam was a self-employed building surveyor, he worked from home, making contact by e-mail and telephone. With direct access to most of his employer's networks, he would have been able to send in reports to the correct person without any face-to-face contact. To his employers then, he was invisible. Payments for work undertaken by him were made against his invoices by bank transfer. Transactions by credit card showed nothing unusual, neither did those on his current account – although he had an unusually high cash balance at Lloyds Bank of £436,000, in an account which received regularly credits of several thousand pounds. Sam was notably careful with his money, a sheet of his ledger balances indicating that he knew to the penny every sum that was owed to him. And as the owner of an un-mortgaged and valuable apartment, he was clearly a man of some wealth... but surely money couldn't be the reason he'd been the target of a murder?

***

Back at Sam's flat, Tom found for Bruno a summary of cash due to Sam as of the thirty-first of December, the previous year end, taken from his invoice sales ledger:

Personal Accounts to December 31st

32 Client Ledger Accounts		10 with outstanding balances
December 31st	5 accounts not paid:	£28,000
November 30th	3 accounts not paid:	£7,000
October 31st	2 accounts not paid:	£4,000
Total monies owed:		£39,000

"So he was owed £39,000," noted Bruno. "You think that's a lot?"

"I would say so, yes, for most people" replied Tom.

"Then let's keep in mind the fact that someone *might* have done the unthinkable rather than actually pay up. It's not uncommon, sadly."

"Agreed," Tom admitted.

"Well, let's continue with this diary and see if we can put some flesh on the bones of Sam's Island crusade."

*FRIDAY MARCH 7*th
*Accepted Bartlett's invitation to lunch on the 9*th
Will take new samples.

*SATURDAY MARCH 8*th
A very enthusiastic, friendly welcome from Bartlett.
He told me that it's about turning over stones, and that I've definitely been turning over the right ones!
When I presented the latest results, he cut to the chase, saying he appreciated I don't know him particularly well, so he gave me his CV to reassure me of his credentials.

This prompted Tom to rummage around in the filing cabinet, soon pulling out a file marked *Bartlett*. It contained the following details:

Gained a first in physical geology at Southampton University.

After university joined GOG (Geological Oil and Gas) a Texan company working on deep sea vessels exploring the sea bed, drilling deep into the ocean floor. Their purpose was to search for oil and explore the sediments and sea bed crust. At sea for months at a time, it was a very well paid but unsocial existence. Worked with GOG for six years.

1996: Accepted a teaching post at the University in Southampton.

1999: Obtained a PHD in physical geology.

2000: Married Jane, two daughters, Jessica and Miriam.

2008: Senior professor in geology at Southampton University.

Hobbies: Exploring the Dorset Jurassic coastline, discovering fossils, history of which regularly published in the Dorchester county geological magazine. Regular talks given about the coastline and new discoveries to schools, clubs and local television. Several listed publications.

Bruno and Tom concluded that for Bartlett to make a major gold discovery on the Island after twenty years of teaching would exceed his wildest dream and become a legacy that defined his career. His was not a pure research lab, it was for teaching university students first degree Geology. He may have appeared to be a high-flying scientist but, in all honestly, he did not stand out in his profession. In his early career he had avoided the treadmill of teaching, but after gaining a PhD, he'd sunk into it.

Sam's diary continued with what Bartlett had explained to him during lunch:

> Bartlett produced the latest results of the riverbed samples, and explained what his role might be in assisting me to develop and document what I had found. The following is a summary of his comments.
>
> - A high concentration of minerals in first batch.
>
> - These are certainly alluvial deposits from the bed of an ancient river.
>
> - Important to understand the geological strata through which it flows.
>
> - Gold always occurs where there is quartz, often in the sediment of river beds where streams have washed the gold crystals from a quartz seam or outcrop downstream to gather in sediment at the bottom of inlets and pools.
>
> - There are hundreds of hydrothermal veins in the south of England associated with quartz that create placer or alluvial deposits in the lower cretaceous geological location which covers the Wessex basin and the Weald of Kent & Sussex.
>
> - He said that the samples are from one of these areas, referring to the second batch of particles. The Weald beds deliver deposits across the southwest of the country. Ammoclinal fold occurs at Alum Bay on the Isle of Wight where the strata changes from horizontal to the vertical in a few hundred metres and reveals the most colourful array. Alternatively inland, a mass of different rock formations near to the surface might contain a quartz seam.

- *This was the first time he had mentioned the Island, and with his knowledge of the Jurassic coast, he'd got to near to where I had discovered the quartz.*

- *He went on to explain that in the UK, gold has been mined in Scotland and Wales in small amounts; he felt the deposits I had found would create quite a stir.*

- *Bartlett asked if the samples were from the same bed; I replied they were from different rock pools. He produced a little black book, and read out what these latest samples contained:*

- *Cups 1,2,4 and 5 contained identical amounts of flaky gold particles, none greater than ½ mm thick, in all a total of 20 grams. Pot 3 contained almost 10 grams. From 2½ kilos of sediment I had collected over a full ounce of gold flakes.*

- *The professor suggested that should this information be published in any geological paper, hundreds of amateur gold searchers clubs would converge on the site, each with a legitimate right to be there. He asked whether or not I had lodged a claim or registered your finds; I replied in the negative. He advised I wait until I had mapped and documented the area, and had obtained permission from the landowners.*

- *Having registered his analysis in the university register, Bartlett took me to the car park and returned to me the plastic cups with their content, along with a pouch containing 27 grams of gold. Again, he refused payment for his work on the condition I take him with me next time. I agreed.*

- *This project needs thought. I'd rather my casual walks in the countryside turning over stones does not become an overbearing pastime. I need help contacting the landowners, but do I really need the academic?*

From Bartlett's file Tom read out an e-mail dated Saturday March 8th.

Sam,

Tell no one what you have found, where you live, how you earn a living... nothing personal. If your discovery became public knowledge, prospectors from the poorest countries in Europe would descend on the Island in their droves. Imagine that – it would be like every other gold rush since the California strikes in the mid-nineteenth century, when miners were trampled to death in the stampede to lodge the best claims, and many froze to death on the long marches to the gold fields.

Many had set off by wagon train to cross America from the Eastern States, meeting those who had set off from those same Eastern states by sailing ship, and had survived the perilous journey south, around Cape Horn, then turning north along the windy uninviting coastline of Chile – the conventional route before the Panama canal was opened. Many were lost at sea in violent storms around the Horn, or died from cholera, which on arrival at a mine would spread like a bush fire.

These were men desperate to try their luck and who came with nothing. Everything had gone towards paying the fare for whichever hardship journey they had chosen. They had abandoned their wives and children to fend for themselves in the hope of making a fortune in California. Joining them were soldiers of fortune who had fought in and deserted from the Mexican War of 1848, trekking north to the gold fields in San Fernando and the Sacramento Valley around the fast flowing Sacramento and San Joaquim rivers.

None of these men knew the first thing about mining, but the bright and malleable metal was their shining star, and they could begin with just a pick, a shovel, and a tin pan.

With their bare hands they picked gold out of rock crevices – nuggets weighing one to six ounces were commonplace. The 49ers were hungry and desperate, gambling their lives on striking it rich in a place they'd never been, three thousand miles away from their homes, their wives and their children.

I know you cannot compare the social conditions of 150 years ago with today, but what lies *in the heart of man* has not changed, believe me.

So, to your immediate actions. The rights to mine and ownership of the gold *have* to be sown up. That's where I can help. I will locate the quartz vein and estimate the potential value of the gold and silver deposits from its height, width and length.

Attached to the e-mail was a scanned pamphlet on gold mining by Noel Bartlett, dated 2004. He had highlighted the introductory paragraph, which read:

Noel Bartlett, professor of geology at Southampton University, potters around Dorset in an old VW Camper Van on holidays and at weekends, sometimes with his wife and two daughters, other times alone. He has even been known to take students and impress them with his knowledge of the geography of Southern England.

"Bartlett brings Sam Peters' work to life doesn't he?" said Bruno.

"Yes," agreed Tom. "So surely it would have been a no-brainer for Sam to let him lead the project. What was holding him back?"

"Simply that he didn't trust anyone; he was not a team player. I'd guess something happened to him when he was young that made him frightened or at least wary of people. But without Bartlett he was going nowhere; he was smart enough to realise that and in the end involved him. Yet that dithering may well have led to his death. Not at Bartlett's hand, necessarily, but maybe his activities on the Island were being noticed by others?"

Chapter 7

Monday 21ˢᵗ July

> *MONDAY MARCH 10ᵗʰ*
> *Received a call from Bartlett, left a message saying he's free next weekend. Did not reply.*

On the same page Sam had noted the following extract from The Treasure Act of 1996:

> *16.3.1 The Crown Estate owns the rights to all gold in the UK. Before panning, ensure one has permission from the owner of the riverbank (in writing). It is the owner of the riverbank rather than the surrounding arable or pasture land whose permission is needed, although to avoid trespass the latter may also be required.*

The diary then continued:

> *SATURDAY MARCH 15ᵗʰ*
> *Planned to stay at Roud Farm tonight. No space on the car ferry. Decided to travel from Portsmouth Harbour by Hovercraft and arranged for Phyllida to pick me up at the terminal in Ryde.*

***

Sam left his flat at 7:30 am to walk to the bus stop to catch the bus to Portsmouth harbour. Parked outside his apartment was a red Ford Fiesta hatchback. It was Bartlett's car, the one he had driven to the car park to return Sam's samples. He confirmed it was Bartlett's *actual* car by the University of Southampton car park sticker on the inside of the front window. Placing his hand on the warm surface of the bonnet proved it had not been parked too long – perhaps twenty minutes. But where was Bartlett and what was his intention, arriving so early?

Having Bartlett under a cloud of suspicion in Sam's mind troubled him. He forgot about his mission to the Island and began searching for the professor – first the rear apartment gardens, then the two entrances to the building. With rising panic, Sam reached the edge of the grounds of the canoe lake. On the far side was the café, which had opened thirty minutes before. As he looked up, Sam saw a man appear in the doorway of the eatery and call to him – it was Bartlett.

"Sam! Sam! I didn't want to wake you so I thought I'd have breakfast and come by later, at about 8:00 am. Not off to the Island today?"

"Too busy, and there are no car ferries today," Sam replied.

"I'm on my way to see Harry Felt, the smelter in Emsworth, so I thought I'd drop by and see how you were getting on with the permit," Bartlett said, seemingly sincerely.

"I am dealing with it on Monday."

"Good, good," came the reply.

Bartlett's appearance so early made Sam no less suspicious, but he accepted the academic's offer to join him for a full English breakfast.

"Sam, I want to talk about the way forward and how you can maximise the potential of what you have discovered before the whole world finds out what you are up to," Bartlett said as the two men waited for their food. "I do appreciate you want to protect what you have and keep the rewards... and I don't want to take anything away from you. However, what you have delivered to me for analysis so far, are just the surface scrapings of a substantial gold deposit somewhere in the area that emanates from a lucrative, mineable quartz deposit. From my experience, the intensity of precious metal in your rock and mud scrapings would have been washed out over thousands of years from a large quartz vein, most likely from high ground. The land that the quartz vein runs through will no doubt be owned by someone who will be unaware of its value, and the *only* way you will benefit is if you bring the owner a complete proposition." A small pause and he then continued, "This is what you'll need: certified proof of the value of the deposit, a detailed plan to exploit the value of your find, and what's in it for the owner. To achieve that you really will need assistance from a reputable international mining company with the resources to undertake the entire job. There'll be planning, surveying, engineering, processing and marketing of the precious metal, and you'll need someone with the expertise to sell the scheme not only to the owner, but likely also the local authority in whose territory the land lies."

Sam could not disagree with anything Bartlett had said – in fact, he knew he was lucky it was him to whom he had taken his samples in the beginning, or he might never have known the value of what he had discovered. After a slight pause, he said "If I am to succeed, we'll need an agreement to be partners."

"Well then, "Bartlett said, smiling, "I've brought you this to look at," and handed Sam two pages of A4 paper, on which were typed a financial proposition that agreed that the two would share anything they found. In addition, the document proposed that joint names would appear on all published material, and any statements made about their activity would be agreed jointly before being issued. Such an agreement gave academic credibility to Sam's treasure hunting and enabled him to ride on the qualifications of a professor of geology – in return, giving Bartlett what *he* wanted – fortune. The division of money and labour that Bartlett suggested was:

- *The gold extracted from the river panning would be used by Sam to pay all expenses, including for accommodation. Nothing to Bartlett.*

- *Bartlett and Sam would map the location of the quartz rock.*

- *Bartlett would initiate the approach to a mining institution and together they would negotiate a deal as finders. Such a deal could be substantial, either as a percentage or as a retainer. Bartlett and Sam to share equally what could be negotiated.*

- *A parallel deal to be negotiated with the landowner, with Bartlett and Sam as finders and ongoing contact agents between them and the mining company.*

An important clause also stated that they would keep each other informed of any related actions either might take in furthering the project.

"Keep it for now, and let me know what you think," Bartlett said, clearly but tentatively.

Sam knew that without Bartlett's help he could not capitalise on his discoveries. If he was to progress his discovery, he knew this was his best chance or it would drain away. The contract was both clear and fair, and so he decided the two should sign it there and then. Bartlett took a second copy from his bags, and each man signed both contracts, taking one copy for himself. The agreement had been completed before the two fry-ups had even arrived.

Although Sam had no reason to continue to harbour feelings of distrust towards Bartlett, they did not completely disappear with the signing of the contract. But he was happy, because he now had a partner

– someone to hide behind – and a contract that clearly and fairly stated the basis on which they would work together.

During breakfast, and for some time after, Sam brought Bartlett up to date with the work he had done so far and they agreed a firm time to visit the Island: early the following Saturday. Bartlett departed, although Sam was pretty sure it was *not* to visit Harry the smelter in Emsworth.

Back at his flat, Sam made plans for the ensuing week, beginning with a delayed visit to Phyllida Glassman at Roud Farm later that afternoon using the car ferry, where bookings were now available.

***

SUNDAY MARCH 16th
Spent *night at PG's. who left early Monday morning to visit sister.*

MONDAY MARCH 17th (AM)
Visited Newport Council office. Spoke to Arnold Harris, Chief Environmental Officer, who handled mineral rights enquiries. He explained that although the local authority knew who owned the land through which the Island rivers flowed, it did not mean that the riparian right to the river banks were owned by the landowners. Fishing rights were often sold on. Harris advised me to get a lawyer to find this out and apply to the several landowners, thus any agreement would be properly executed. He recommended Peter Noway of Noway & Co Solicitors in Ryde. According to him they are the best land solicitors on the Island. Harris also informed me that if I was prospecting for Gas, Coal or Oil I would need to apply to his Department for a permit, and if I wanted access to any river bank I'd either need the permission of the owner of said bank, or, if on public land, permission from the Newport Council. This would mean completing an application form, which he gave me.

The document Harris handed Sam asked for plenty of personal information; name, age, address, how long he'd been there, and a request for a copy of his passport or driving licence were all required, as was a section where he should describe his intentions before giving an estimate of the time he expected it would take to complete his objectives. Harris had in fact already asked these questions during their meeting, where he had shown a professional interest combined with an obvious negativity in his responses. Arnold Harris did not like treasure hunters.

Monday March 17th (pm)
Visited Newport Public Library archives. Read up on Island mining history.
Stayed again at Dick Potter's gloomy B&B.

Tuesday March 18th
Wanted to finish taking alluvium samples from the East Yar beyond Beacon Alley. Sonia Potter asked what I was doing. They are a nosey couple. After breakfast, Dick was readying himself to walk into Godshill at the time I was leaving. He asked me if I were going to the river as I paid for the one-night stay. I replied that I was continuing my East Yar river walk, and he offered to accompany me to the village. Unable to think of a reason to decline him, we walked together. Left car on the drive as my route would bring me back round to the B&B.
On the way down, Potter fished for more information, asking if I always took the same route. I replied that I would be starting where I left off last time. He pushed further, saying, "and after that?" I told him I considered the Island a walker's paradise, and that there were many places to see. Thankfully by this point it was time to part ways, but not before he asked me if he would see me again. I smiled and continued on my way.

Hopefully not, thought Sam; the Potters were a miserable couple.

It had rained before daylight, adding freshness to the morning. With a backpack tight against his shoulders, Sam clambered over the fence at the bridge and slid down the wet dew-covered bank to the water's edge. After the early-morning rain the river was deeper and flowing faster, the reeds which grew on the bottom lay flat and the bed was clearly visible. He walked the trail besides the bank for a mile marking positions, taking samples from the pools that had formed beside the fast-flowing water, and recording each position both in his notebook and on the side of each plastic container. Now he was enjoying the smell of the rain-soaked green fields each side of the river, all the while searching for the shallow ridges from which to scoop out sediment. He was intent on completing his survey of the three-mile stretch as far as the farmer's fences that made the river banks inaccessible before having to return home to Southsea. He knew he was near to the limit of how far the particles washed from the quartz vein would travel towards the mouth of the river. Even after thousands of years, around fifteen miles was the maximum distance according to the text books he had been reading carefully. He saw few other people on the trail – only two couples at some distance apart passed him during his somewhat muddy work.

Then, after an hour, through a gap in the bushes, he noticed a man who seemed to be following him from some six or seven hundred metres distance. The features he could not recognise, but Sam quickly realised the man walked with an unmistakable gait – It was Dick Potter! Sam chose to remain visible through the gap, and watched until he was sure Potter realised he'd been spotted, then vanished behind some bushes.

Sam immediately felt like he had about Bartlett; an internal, nagging suspicion that he had revealed too much of his activities to the Potters. So, well-hidden in dense laurel, he sat down, drank from his water bottle and contemplated what he should do. His gut feeling was to vanish from his sight, return to the uninviting little B&B, collect his car, and if he never stayed another night there, he wouldn't have to see the man again.

Instead, he continued walking for half a mile – without collecting samples – until he reached the fence barrier which acted as a diversion away from the river. Here, he stood amongst the bushes until Potter caught up.

"Good morning again," Potter said as Sam stepped deliberately and firmly into his view.

Neither man was startled.

"Hi," Potter continued. "You talked about the East Yar trail, so I thought I'd try it. You saw me in the distance, didn't you?"

"I did, but I kept going to finish this stretch," Sam replied, the lie flowing easily from his mouth. However, to his surprise, now Potter was there Sam was displeased with neither the company nor the chance of conversation.

"Getting away from 'er indoors," Dick said. "Let her clean up, change the sheets. It's a lovely walk as you said; I can't believe I've never come here before, still, you never know what's on your own doorstep do you?" he continued quite pleasantly. "I saw you bending down at the water's edge, what have you found?"

"I'm testing the sediment," said Sam. "Geology is my hobby. I find different things every time."

"And what do you find in this sediment?"

"It depends on the surrounding rock formations and what's upstream, but sometimes minute quantities of gold."

The mention of gold noticeably aroused Potter's interest. He was a 'quick buck' kind of guy, with a prospector's mentality – he'd lift a bin lid or turn over a stone, looking for something valuable... so perhaps he had the patience to pan for gold shards. His thoughtful response suggested that he may yet be of some use to Sam.

The two continued walking together around the detour to reconnect with the river, while Sam casually enquired what Dick did during the days. It transpired that he scratched a living from the B&B in the spring and summer and claimed jobseeker's allowance in winter – exactly as Sam has suspected. His questions about the river were persistent and logical, and he understood Sam's explanations about the uniqueness of the Island and its importance in the science of geology in the United Kingdom.

By the time they had walked for another hour back to the bridge, Sam had seen an entirely different side to Potter's personality than that which he had experienced until now. With the negativity and cynicism of his attitude in the B&B no longer present, Sam believed that he could possibly be of some help.

Sam's panning of the riverbed's alluvium deposits had shown that it could deliver a worthwhile yield in itself, however for him, it was the quartz vein that would lead to greater riches and therefore it was this he must concentrate on first and foremost. But having mapped the river basin, he knew that one could pan for gold and get a decent return in several places up or downstream from Beacon Alley. However, to maximise the take from the river's alluvial deposit he needed help from somebody with a bit of muscle, a follower rather than a leader, who could be incentivised with a share of the spoils. Although it would be a bad idea to convert the streambed material into saleable metal on the Island, that could be done elsewhere. It was the hard graft of the panning that would perfectly suit someone like Potter.

It was an interesting proposition, but one that Sam was not ready to make just yet, not least because having signed their contract, he could not speak of any of this to Potter without Professor Bartlett's agreement.

TUESDAY MARCH 18th (PM)
Returned home late. Called Bartlett at 8:30 pm and invited him to the Island at 10:30 am on Friday 21st March.

***

When they met at the car ferry terminal, Bartlett was as excited and enthusiastic as a child setting off on holiday, now finally being taken to the Island by Sam.

On the car ferry over to Fishbourne, Sam gave Bartlett the form from Newport Council to complete.

Bartlett was quite delighted to be elevated above the ordinariness of his everyday job to pursue this geological exploration with Sam as his partner, and – for once – to be a decision-maker. Although he was not overly enthusiastic at including a third person so early in the relationship, he did not veto the idea, and so Sam had arranged for the two to meet Potter in Godshill for lunch.

Before the meeting, to the professor's delight, Sam took Bartlett to the East Yar at Beacon Alley, and showed him the pools that produced the gold-enriched alluvium sediment.

***

At noon, a cleaned-up Potter arrived at The Smithy Restaurant to meet the two partners, Sam not only having convinced Bartlett that morning of the man's potential usefulness, but also persuading him that *he* should make the pitch.

The plan they hatched was that Potter would pan for gold riverside, as well as collect, weigh and record the metallic granules. Sam and the professor would analyse, grade and organise the smelting. Potter would be paid for doing the hard graft. How much he'd make, how many hours were involved and whether they had permission to pan for gold on the river were Potter's only questions. In response to the first two questions, Sam and Bartlett agreed that Potter would be paid £10 an hour as a minimum guarantee against earnings from the selling of the gold, until such a time as the money began to flow in from the smelter; for now he'd be required to complete a timesheet which detailed both activity and location. In answer to the third, Bartlett explained that permissions were being obtained to treasure-hunt on private property. They had agreed that – certainly at this stage – no mention of the hunt for the quartz would be made to Potter.

Potter was, as Sam had suspected he would be, very keen, accepting the deal right there. He agreed to spend as much time as possible panning on the river banks, at fourteen locations Sam had designated as suitable. The agreement was to pay him twenty per cent of the value of his panned gold as certified by a licensed smelter. Sam supplied Potter with a number of YouTube links on how to pan for gold and left him with a complete panning kit.

The locations Sam had selected for Potter to pan at the riverside were all more or less in total privacy. However, to obstruct the view of passers-by who might become interested, Sam provided him with a tent as used by fishermen, along with fishing gear, a rod, line, net and handbook on coarse fishing. Dark green clothing would act as camouflage, making it difficult to see him from any of the river's access points. This was an extension of the kit that Sam had used himself. Having come round to the idea of Potter doing the graft, Bartlett expressed his confidence that Potter would actually do quite well.

***

FRIDAY MARCH 21st (PM)
Dropped Bartlett at Fishbourne late afternoon; stayed the night at PG's who has now returned. Will look to start Potter tomorrow.

SATURDAY MARCH 22nd
Started Potter at position one where I previously panned successfully unseen for several hours. Good news – he took to the laborious and time-consuming task like a duck to water, allowing the fast flowing stream to wash away the sediment leaving clear shining grits in the bottom of the basin.
Spent the morning explaining to him the various locations, taking it in turns to pan in position.

SATURDAY MARCH 29th (AM)
Headed over to the Island with Bartlett. Drove to the cliff-fall on the Military Road, where, from the beach, he confirmed that the exposed edge fifty feet from the top of the cliff was a thick quartz vein!

***

Sam was relieved at Bartlett's observation; it was *real* confirmation from a geology expert of what *could* have been just 'pie in the sky'.

Bartlett continued to prove himself as being the knowledgeable field geologist he was, his enthusiasm allowing an entirely different character to shine through compared to the somewhat downtrodden university lecturer who had analysed his early samples. He explained about erosion, the effects of landslip and something called slumping, where after heavy rain clay flows like a river of mud. These, he detailed, combined with 'soil creep' caused by exceptional rainfall and drainage towards the ocean, would in fact expose the quartz *nearer* to the cliff edge than Sam had anticipated.

Peters and Bartlett retraced the former's earlier steps, keeping to the still-visible markers for a mile inland, where the ground rose gently across St Catherine's Down to the chalk basin near Niton, the village where the sources of the rivers Medina and East Yar could be found. There, the ground began to fall, reversing the drainage channels towards these two rivers flowing north. It was in the area of the two drainage basins that Bartlett confidently predicted the quartz vein would surface.

He explained to Sam, "In the last Ice Age, the rivers had been larger, carrying huge volumes of melting ice, causing the sea level to rise, eventually isolating and confining the rivers to the Island. Whilst the northern part of the Island was irregular lowland, on the southern side the central down – surrounded by a thick belt of Gault clay or blue slipper – would have created a bowel broken by ridges and minor hills."

About a mile in from the sea and after two hours of searching across Downland trails and rough pasture along a route Sam had not walked before, they came to a South-facing landslide, four hundred metres across and due north from the cliff outcrop.

According to Bartlett it was "the perfect opportunity to check the direction we are walking in is correct."

The slide had been created where the sand and chalk had shifted towards the sea a mile south. The embankment was covered in soil and grass, but the professor predicted that by digging a vertical slice with decent shovels, quartz may well be discovered.

With the weather worsening and with the evening closing in, the two men agreed to return the following morning with suitable picks and shovels.

Earlier that afternoon, Sam had called Phyllida who'd suggested he bring Bartlett back for dinner and offering to provide him with a bed for the night. She even said she could provide the digging equipment Sam had mentioned that he needed from the sheds around her farm.

Sam did not explain Phyllida to Bartlett, who was simply pleased to rest for the night nearby and aim to begin a serious search for the quartz the following morning. Nor did he allow *her* to think the academic was another treasure hunter, explaining that he was a geology professor from

Southampton University who was conducting a geological survey over the Downs and with whom he had become friendly.

"How interesting," she said. "I hope you find something valuable that we can all share in."

***

Over supper, Bartlett talked about fossils and how successful he'd been in Dorset, where he had found remains of many species that had been extinct for five to ten thousand years. Phyllida pretended to show vague enthusiasm without disguising her total lack of interest. To Bartlett, she came across as a farmer's wife who had been fully prepared to live a dull and unsuccessful life, not as the sophisticated woman of the world Sam saw in her.

The widow Glassman had roasted a chicken, which she served with roast potatoes, carrots, cabbage and a bread sauce, accompanied by a bottle of red wine. This was followed by apple crumble and custard, the meal demonstrating her mastery of the culinary arts (to Sam, at least). Refusing any offers of assistance, she ushered the men into the lounge to watch Saturday night TV whilst she cleared up in the kitchen alone.

Out of earshot, Bartlett commented to Sam, "She seems too good to be true, you should hang onto her!"

This comment was encouraging for Sam, as he was still in the early stages of trying to fully work her out. He already knew she went away a lot – always to visit her sister – but she'd never said where that was, or for how long she'd be away. Furthermore, strangely, whenever he stayed over, the house always felt as if she had returned no more than half an hour before him. There was no evidence of what she occupied herself with living alone in the farmhouse, even how she had passed her time when her husband had been alive. He knew that it was the nature of a farmer's life to live a solitary existence but as the Glassmans had not worked the farm itself, how the two had passed their time – and how she passed it now – was very much a mystery to Sam, who liked to know where he stood.

Chapter 8

The following morning the weather had improved. It was a warm day and Phyllida provided a packed lunch so Sam and Bartlett could put in a long day. They dug bore holes at ten-metre distances back from the south-facing landslide. On the third hole, thirty metres back between the two-hundred metre markers Sam had set weeks before, they found the quartz seam just one metre below the surface. Like grave diggers, they enlarged their hole to a metre diameter, and then to two metres. The solid rock plane Bartlett had predicted was definitely there, one metre below the surface.

It had taken nine hours of back-breaking digging to find the quartz vein. When walkers had passed, thankfully none closer than four hundred metres, they stopped digging until they were out of sight, so as not to attract curious enquiries.

Once they had chipped off samples and Bartlett had estimated the width and girth of the quartz, they filled in the hole and spread grass sods over the area so it no longer looked disturbed. Over the exact spot they rolled a fifty-kilo stone and recorded the position with recognisable co-ordinates, marking it clearly on their ordnance survey map. By late afternoon they had plotted the course of the quartz seam for two hundred metres along the line back to the cliff.

From outcrop to a hundred metres back, the depth varied between one-hundred and one-hundred-and-twenty centimetres, but remained constant after that. They took more samples and drew a map of the pathway back to the cliff, where they discovered another outcrop equidistant with small deposits in undulations – both were recorded on drawings headed Q1 to Q4.

After an exhausting day of digging, they celebrated their successful weekend at the Chale Inn. With a major triumph in finding, tracking and mapping the quartz and a thumbs up for Potter, Bartlett was confident of the mining project... but he reminded Sam that everything depended on approvals being granted.

Having completed the formal application on University paper, Bartlett left it with Sam to present to the Newport council office the following morning.

After dropping Bartlett at the Fishbourne ferry, Sam returned for Sunday night at Phyllida Glassman's, where he prepared for his second meeting with Arnold Harris early on Monday, hoping to progress their application for access.

MONDAY MARCH 31st (AM)
Checked on Dick's progress – excellent – he had panned the second base I had designated which produced ten kilos of good quality metal particles for processing. Loaded up my car.

Must give cash to Potter on my next visit to maintain his commitment. Need to convert the raw gold into cash. Find a bullion dealer who will buy from me.

MONDAY MARCH 31st (PM)
Arnold Harris was thirty minutes late. Unhelpful. Insisted on discussing the application for a licence standing across a public counter with comers and goers listening to our conversation.

"Tell me about yourself," Harris began, as if I was applying for a local authority job. "What do you hope to find on the Island?" he asked, reading from clip board notes. "Building surveying will not persuade the committee to issue you a permit to dig local authority land."

I told him the investigation is being led by the head of geology faculty at Southampton University and that I'm simply Professor Bartlett's assistant.

"What's his name?" Harris asked me, ignoring the correspondence attached to the application I had just given to him.

I told him it was Professor Noel Bartlett, pointing out that Harris had his CV there with the application. Harris wrote my response down without referring to the application and then told me Bartlett would have to "apply separately!"

"That is his application, I am the courier," I explained again. Harris, ever the bureaucrat, asked me what Bartlett wanted to do, to which I responded that he had written it down and that it was attached to the completed form. Despite everything required

being there, he did not seem interested to read the documents I presented to him.

I explained that we want to study the soil composition on the Island and search for minerals. The response? "There are no minerals on the Island, only coloured sand at Alum Bay and you don't need a permit to study that."

"What about the quarries?"

"They're dangerous, privately owned, and no access is permitted."

"We want to examine the landslides and slippage close to the cliff face."

"It's been done," he told me. "All of the surveys are in Newport library. Ask them to look up what you want from their archives – it's all there. Save you wasting your time coming over here. Yes, the committee might issue a permit to a University Geologist, but to you, it's no, probably a no."

I reminded him once again that the application <u>was</u> made by the professor, in his name, and linked to a university research project. I was as clear and emphatic as I could be.

Then he left me standing at the counter, without a goodbye or good day.

Bartlett agreed that Harris was an unhelpful bastard and neither of us could work out why.

Bartlett confirmed everything I had said to Harris directly by e-mail, and requested an acknowledgement that he was requesting permission to undertake geological explorations on the Island. Harris acknowledged receipt of 'an application' but nothing more.

***

"Why is there so little mention of Phyllida Glassman in his diary?" said Tom to Bruno. "They're obviously getting on well by this point."

"You mean what they were getting up to together?"

"Yes," said Tom.

"It's personal I suppose. You wouldn't detail your love life in a business diary, would you Tom? This is more like an office diary than a traditional one. To Sam Peters, 'personal' means private."

Having read and discussed Peters' diary entries page-by-page, they still didn't feel they knew enough about him to begin to understand why anyone would want to murder him.

"Why was he so keen to pay Potter?" asked Tom.

"Because Potter's a working man. People like that don't live in promise-land, they need cash in their hands," said Bruno.

"To me the diary comes across as boring and overly reflective; it tells us nothing important," stated Tom. "In fact, I think it tells us that *he* was boring," added the younger man.

"I'm not so sure about that," said Bruno, "But I do know that until we have a more complete picture of him, we shan't know why someone would kill him."

"What about *last* year's diary, and the year *before*, were they thrown away on the final day of the year? I just don't think people who keep diaries do that," said Tom.

"If he *has* sanitised himself, we need to find out why... unless life before this year's diary has been sanitised *by someone else*. I think it's time to look at his business contacts. I'm sure we'll find something to help us build the whole picture we need. We know enough about him from this diary to know that his big secret is the gold – and surely that *must* be connected to his murder. Let's look at the people involved in his day-to-day business."

"That Arnold Harris appears to have spoken as if he knew everything about the Island," said Tom.

"And, as the man in the area who processes all kinds of forms, everybody who lives there, I'd bet," said Bruno. "He didn't want to rubber stamp Peters' submission, he was clearly being deliberately obstructive, and as a local government officer surely it's his job to process applications? Perhaps he has a hatred for mineral searchers wanting to take anything away from the Island? And maybe that's his normal manner in response to any stranger returning with completed versions of *those* documents?"

Bruno thought for a moment and then continued, "But it seems too *powerful* a rebuttal for an uninterested person. There's intense competition between treasure hunters, and Harris would know – or have a list of – everyone who'd applied to the council for permission to search over public land."

"Then let's talk to him about the attitude Islanders have to treasure hunters. Personally, I'm surprised it isn't the Islanders who do most of the treasure hunting," said Tom.

Bruno wasn't surprised, though. He knew it just wasn't in their nature. Most were simply happy with their existing life on the Island.

Chapter 9

The name 'Dick Potter' in Sam's diary had not immediately rung a bell with Bruno. He hadn't made the connection with a *Richard* Potter, a Shanklin resident who had been a suspect in the Godshill Butcher's murder case, six years previously.

That had been Bruno's second Island murder case, and remained unsolved. He considered the case a personal failure, feeling he had not recognised clues which might have trapped the suspects into mistakes and lies. In his eyes, he had failed to correlate all the times, places, suspects and connected person's statements, of whom Richard Potter – or Dick, if they were the same person – had been one.

The feelings of failure troubled him still, and when he had re-examined the murder file years afterwards, putting the statements, times and places together with a more experience eye, he could now see a number of suspicious elements – but could just not persuade the station Super to let him actively investigate them.

"It will draw attention to our previous inefficiencies," was his boss's opinion. "And we've enough to do without trawling back through old crimes, especially those which we ourselves failed to solve."

Although Bruno's new list of contradictory statements added up, he had to agree that no Island judge would give the Police a second bite of a cherry they hadn't nailed the first time.

Whenever a crime that reminded him of the Godshill butcher murder became his case, he secretly believed that a superior being was giving him a chance of redemption. The positivity exuding from DC Tom Craven was making him feel as comfortable and in-charge as one could with a brutal murder.

Normally a man who kept his cards close to his chest, on this occasion Bruno decided to share his thoughts about the 'two Potters' to Tom.

"We should speak to him right away," the younger man said, the eagerness clear in his voice.

Bruno, ever able to keep one foot grounded in the world outside of the force, reminded his new colleague that there wasn't a shred of evidence to link Potter with Sam Peters' murder, just as there had not been to the Godshill case. But he had to admit that it was certainly a fact that Sam was working with Dick Potter at the time of his death.

Newport police records confirmed that the Richard Potter of the Godshill murder case *was* Dick Potter, linking his movements from his address all those years ago to his current residence the bed and breakfast bungalow he ran with his wife on the outskirts of Godshill.

***

Stanley Musgrove, the local butcher in Godshill, had been Sonia Potter's brother-in-law, married to her sister Stephanie, or Steph as she was well-known in various parts of the Island. She was Stanley's second wife; Carol, his first of just over three decades having died the previous year of natural causes.

Musgrove had been killed in his butcher's shop on Godshill High Street, late on a Saturday afternoon just before Christmas, sometime after shutting up for the weekend. Several witnesses saw him screwing up the shutters at about 4:00 pm as dusk enveloped the high street. But he did not leave the shop. The murderer had struck after Stanley had finished locking up, with the shutters in place preventing any passer-by seeing through the shop front window. The murderer had extinguished the shop lights, pulled the door shut until the Yale lock clicked shut, then left on foot apparently unseen along a dark, deserted High street.

The butcher's life was extinguished by a heavy blow to the back of his head from the blunt edge of a meat chopper taken from inside the shop. He was found face down on the shop floor, his head in a pool of blood, the cash takings still counted and bagged up on the counter beside the till. It had been obvious what they were, placed by Musgrove not long before in a brown lockable leather purse issued by Lloyds Bank – with their logo clearly visible – ready for him to deposit in the pavement safe he'd regularly pass on his way home. It lay beside a carrier bag containing two pork chops, a string of sausages and two kidneys, all separately wrapped. It appeared nothing had been taken from the shop or from Stanley's person, so robbery as the motive was ruled out.

In her statement to the Police, Stephanie said that when her husband did not come home, eventually she went to the shop and found him lying on the shop floor in a pool of blood. She called 999 but the ambulance paramedics who arrived certified him dead, a state which it turned out he had been in for around two hours.

The police, one of whom was a younger Bruno Peach, arrived at the same time. It was he who took Mrs Musgrove's statement, and he found himself rather disturbed by her unemotional and calm demeanour in the face of such a tragedy. Although she appeared frightened and upset to a degree, she answered his questions with extreme caution.

Stephanie had said that on Fridays, Stanley would call into the Castle Inn for a pint before arriving home at around 6:30 pm. Coming out on a cold winter evening was not something she did on a whim, however when he hadn't shown by seven, she drove to the shop to see if he was still there.

However, when interviewed at a slightly later date, there was a minor addition to her story; she said that she had stopped at the Castle Inn en-route to see if he was there before travelling on to the shop. The words she used was that she had 'just looked in', but although most of the Inn's regulars knew her, not a single one remembered seeing her that night. Peach accepted it was *possible* that no one saw her if her stop had been extremely brief, but personally had felt that she was lying.

A murder is a rare occurrence, especially on the Island. In the majority of cases, the culprit is usually someone very close to the victim – a husband, wife or lover. Police are trained to carefully observe these relations, looking closely for any sign of anxiety or guilt, following up anything detected with close scrutiny.

So Stephanie Musgrove had become a 'person of interest', with no verifiable proof of her whereabouts until she arrived at the butcher's shop and called 999 a little after seven o'clock that evening.

A similar unusually emotionless response to the murder was noted from Steph's sister, Sonia Potter, who arrived with her husband Richard, to offer her comfort and support. The two sisters were definitely peas from the same pod. Steph had called Sonia while forensics and the medics were still in attendance, recording the facts relating to the body. Sonia and Richard had then apparently driven from Shanklin – where they lived at that time – to support her.

Although Steph was on the heavier side compared to Sonia's slight figure, they had distinct facial similarities. As teenagers the sisters never had boyfriends; single lads had been put off by their domineering personalities and need to have their own way in every part of a relationship. They were neither tender, loving, interesting, generous nor funny and had a clear and somewhat unhealthy obsession with money. They were known by other locals to offer sexual favours to men who would reward them with money, and not always their own.

As they grew older, they were often the 'perks of the job', or 'bits on the side' for married men who revealed the slightest hint of unhappiness in their home lives. The sisters would show not the slightest concern for the wives and children whose lives they helped to wreck with their enticing behaviour, ensnaring near-happily married men with families into sexually-charged relationships. They would show the same disdain for the men themselves once any attraction had faded – or, more likely, money was no longer forthcoming. They sunk their teeth into their victims, destroying marriages without care yet with absolutely no lasting benefit to themselves.

Even with the combined opposition from Stanley Musgrove's two daughters, he had been unable to escape Stephanie's clutches. Only three months into his life as a widower, grieving and vulnerable, she had struck whilst the iron was hot.

During their three-year marriage there was continual hostility from Stanley's daughters towards Steph. She was unlike their mother, who would turn up to run the cash till on busy days, and scrub the shop clean after closing. All their young lives the shop had been a family business, and together with their mother, each girl had worked in some capacity in the shop.

Steph had been interviewed at length as she had at least one potential motive for killing her husband. Her demeanour was off hand and she was clearly irritated by the length of her interview with the police. She displayed a lack of interest in finding her husband's killer, which suggested that she knew more than she would ever tell. Simply discovering her dead husband's body did not implicate her in his death and there was no hard evidence against her. Despite the suspicion and her unverified stop at the Inn, her story that she arrived at the shop a little after seven pm stood up to questioning.

Stanley, with no known enemies, was a good honest businessman. He paid his debts on time and was a well-respected member of the Godshill community, and his daughters were recognised for their local charitable activities. Like all successful butchers, he had a 'way' with ladies – a pleasant rapport. He listened to them across the counter, and was genuinely interested in the problems of their lives, offering advice and consolation where there was an obvious need.

The true motive for his murder never came to light, but his death clearly fuelled Steph's greed. When probate had been obtained after several months – and during a period of intense family animosity towards her – it was time for her to move on... and as far away from the Godshill gossips as her courage would allow. She sold the butcher's business in its prime High Street location, along with their spacious four bedroom detached property, moving away to live in Bournemouth. There, she was able to avoid the gossip, constant resentment and animosity from her step children, from whom she chose to detach herself completely, immediately after Stanley's funeral.

In an Island community one's private life is never private. Past deeds, misdemeanours and lies are constantly regurgitated and Stephanie's was no exception. The details of her entire personal life were exposed in full, with the Godshill gossips discovering and questioning witnesses to past relationships. Much was made of her previous marriage – in fact her second – to Andrew Pumpkin, a Cowes Solicitor, who had also met an early and *supposedly* accidental death. Various rumours circulated, including the antics she got up to during her *first* marriage, that to Rod Fletcher, a Shanklin longshoreman. The most serious gossip mongers even spoke to the police about their suspicions that two dead wealthy husbands – Pumpkin and now Stanley Musgrove – could not be a coincidence and needed investigation. But, as every policeman knows, coincidence is very different from evidence. All of these rumours were recorded in police files – as one never knows where the vital piece of evidence will come from – but had detracted the police greatly from the core investigation into Stanley's murder, resulting in time being wasted looking down blind alleys. On reflection, Bruno felt that the cloud of suspicion around Stephanie Musgrove and her murky past overly influenced his and his colleagues' thinking so much that their focus on the murder of Stanley Musgrove was somewhat diluted.

And Stephanie's behaviour, so scorned by the gossips, was also reflected in Sonia's sordid relationships. To anyone who looked closely enough, there was a clear pattern common to both sisters.

Chapter 10

Bruno recalled that Steph and Sonia's mother, Vivienne, had died of a heart attack aged sixty, whilst playing the one-armed-bandit in her husband Gerry's Odd Fellows club. Her last spin of the reels won the five hundred pound jackpot, causing an endless stream of ten pence coins to spill out over the top of the tiny silver winnings cup. As Vivienne bent forward to stop them from escaping and rolling all over the floor of the club for anyone to grab, she kept going, collapsing face down onto the beer-soaked carpet, dead of a heart attack. The machine, unaware of the scene as inanimate objects generally are, continued to play its joyful music and spewed more and more coins out, each one bouncing off Vivienne's immobile body. Eventually it spat out one last ten pence piece, played a final 'ta-dah' and then fell silent, the poor woman buried under a mound of coins.

Gerry, who had been getting a round of drinks whilst she made her winning pull, wailed and fell down onto both his knees. Holding his wife's heavily made-up and now swollen face in his two hands, he performed the appropriate functions on her chest as best he could from seeing it done on TV programs, and blew air into her lungs, all to no avail. With tears now dripping from his chin, he gently eased down her eyelids, and after picking off the coins that had stuck to her jackpot-winning, smiling face, with the help of some other kind members carried her to the secretary's office. There they lay her body across a three-seater settee to await the ambulance paramedics, who sadly confirmed she was dead.

Almost immediately, Sonia, moved back temporarily into her parents' house, although she hated living with an old man, doing his washing and scrubbing the lavatory. She believed she was never cut out for a life of work. Not for her a penniless Island workman with nothing; she targeted the established professional or manager and began working in their office or home as a simple clerk or a cleaner, until she enticed them to get their leg over.

Her previous conquest using this method had been the manager of a greetings card factory in Newport. She'd worked there as a temp until he gifted her a permanent job in return for regular sex on his five-seater office couch after the offices had closed, followed by a pint of local ale and chicken-in-a-basket at the Wharfside Inn. *Dennis* was happy with this arrangement and – as plenty of established married men do – enjoyed the best of both worlds, something he felt perfectly entitled to.

Sonia had not been Dennis's first office romance, and in the past he'd successfully flicked on these casual relationships when they were in danger of becoming too intense. But Sonia was different. Greedy and envious of his wife, she would not be disposed of like the others. When this hardworking thirty-five year old man, with a wife, two children and a job for life with prospects was promoted and transferred to a mainland office, he tried his hardest to end their fling, but *she* was having none of it. Sonia left home and moved into a room above a shop opposite his new office, so she could spy on his comings-and-goings. She told him she'd never let him go, so – having asked her what would convince her to leave him alone – he paid her off with £7,000 taken from the till. Sonia gleefully pocketed the money, but it didn't buy her off as she had suggested it would.

Three weeks later, the night before a surprise branch audit, he asked her for it back lest his theft were found out before he could replace the money in full, which he intended to do. Although every penny was still sitting untouched in her bank account, she refused. Dennis was found out and was jailed for two years.

At the end of his trial, she turned up in disguise – although easily recognisable to him – and sat in the public gallery with a sadistic smirk on her face, watching him be convicted. She never contacted him again, although she *was* tempted to contact his wife and tell her *why* he had stolen the £7,000. Surprisingly, *that* evil act she resisted.

Once that money was spent, to get away from her father, she worked half-days as a waitress in Fatboy's Café. This provided her with enough pocket money to spend the afternoons applying for something better. It was at the café that she met Dick Potter, a ladies' man who soon arranged afternoon dates with her at his home... until his wife, a legal secretary, caught them together in the marital bed on an unscheduled early end to her working day. She kicked him out that very afternoon, so Sonia, buttering her father up with a promise of rent money, persuaded him to take Dick into his house as a lodger.

Dick Potter convinced Sonia that he could give her everything she wanted. By the time she had learned what he was *really* like – a penniless Island workman with nothing – she had married him, not for love, but in the hope of escaping from domestic drudgery looking after Gerry. Daily examination of her now skinny, drawn features prompted her to settle for what she now had.

Dick had pretended to be an antique dealer, but in reality sold second hand furniture that he collected from house clearances. He was as close as you can come to a modern-day rag-and-bone man.

When Gerry was run over and killed by a drunken lorry driver in Shanklin High Street, Sonia got her doctor to certify her as unfit to work as a result of depression resulting from her father's death. This doubled the life insurance company's payout, as it made her a 'dependent next of kin'. Together with the money Dick had obtained from his share from the recent sale of his previous marital home, the couple had just enough to buy the modest bed-and-breakfast bungalow in Godshill.

Sonia and Dick began attending St Paul's Church in Cowes as Samaritans, although not because they had 'found God'. The congregation at the church contained the highest proportion of elderly residents on the Island and had been specially chosen by the couple for a particular and rather ungodly purpose. They stole antiques from homes of the oldest people in the congregation they regularly visited and 'looked after', sneaking them out from the homes of the bedridden and forgetful by the back door. They lived in expectation of an inheritance from various members of the congregation who they befriended; they regularly attended services on Sundays, looking out for any elderly, vulnerable men or women who looked as though they might die soon so they could be targeted for this purpose. They took the churchgoers on outings, collected their pensions from post offices and went out to get their shopping – all the while short-changing as much as they dared – and drove them to church flamboyantly, so as to publicise their connection.

One day, £2,000 in cash went missing from a biscuit tin in one of the old dear's houses whose only visitors were Dick and Sonia and the police were called. With the victim suffering from Alzheimer's (although not as badly as the couple told everyone) and no proof that the £2,000 existed in the first place, the police concluded the cash was a fantasy and did not even officially interview the Potters. However, the Vicar and his wardens knew the member of their congregation well enough to believe her and took a rather different stance. They banned the two thieves from both their 'benevolent' church-related social activities and also from the church itself.

Having perfected the art though, it was too lucrative a pastime to give up, so they simply moved to another church away from the area. Although just a short walk away, they seldom went to Godshill, preferring instead the anonymity of bigger congregations in Ryde and Cowes.

***

Bruno understood how Sam Peters' death could benefit Dick Potter, but he was too astute to think Dick Potter would carry on alone, and he did not think Potter was a murderer. The similarities between the two killings – the Godshill butcher and Sam – had to be no more than a coincidence, surely?

The two victims were both struck violently from behind. The Godshill murder weapon was the blunt end of a meat-chopper; whatever instrument was used to kill Peters was presumably still in the possession of the killer. The seemingly sudden nature of the attacks was, admittedly a further similarity. Neither Stanley or Sam appeared to have struggled or fought back; this meant the fatal blow could have been delivered by an attacker of either gender, and furthermore, in each case was most likely by someone known to the victim.

The detective was thinking about how Sam, having discovered the quartz seam, was surrounding himself with the people he needed to progress his project further. The activities going forward required professional or manual skills that Sam did not have, knew not much about, or would rather not spend his time on – hence bringing Bartlett and Potter on board.

"Apart from our central characters, who do we have on the periphery," Bruno asked Tom.

"The Assay Office, local authority personnel... but they're not suspects, are they?" said Tom, a little surprised.

"Don't let's write them off yet," replied Bruno. "A lot of scheming people work in dull public service jobs where nothing happens. Something exciting or life-changing like finding gold in a river they live near to could easily give someone nefarious ideas."

Bruno was aware of the short window in which to search Sam's possessions and study his treasure-hunting activities, so they returned to the remaining diary entries and the contents of his flat, determined to complete the task that afternoon.

Mindful of the need to speak to every person who might be a connected to Sam's personal and business activities, Bruno concentrated on the detail from his client files. He wanted to start interviewing connected persons with knowledge of at least *some* aspect of Sam Peters' life. He was anxious not give the murderer time to cover his tracks, or allow clues that would only be visible a short time after the killing to disappear. Plus, if he was very lucky, a guilty interviewee might panic and reveal themselves if he could get to them so soon after having committed the crime.

Turning to his notebook, Bruno reviewed his list of current suspects:

Noel Bartlett	Southampton University
Dick Potter	Potter's B&B
Peter Noway	Property Solicitor, Noway & Co
Arnold Harris	Chief Environmental Officer
Phyllida Glassman	Personal relationship
Harry Felt	Smelter, Emsworth

"One of these could easily be the killer, provide us with a clue, or perhaps lead us to someone of importance," said Bruno, tapping the page.

"What about the brother-in-law, Paterson?" said Tom.

"Carry on," said Bruno.

"Well, *he* knew about Peters' money, he knew he was well off... and *you* know the stats on family murders," said Tom.

"Hmm. Park Paterson, he's confirmed as being at the girls' party on Saturday evening." Bruno replied, but with no negativity. He paused for just a moment, then, smiling, said, "And Tom... I'd like it if your boss would let you continue working this case with me. I think we can solve it together."

"I hope so," replied Tom, "he *has* to let me carry on!"

Bruno had no problem making it clear that he liked working with this young detective, and as well as finding him useful, hoped he would be able to teach him something.

***

That evening Bruno received an e-mail from Portsmouth police HQ, asking for a progress report on the Peters investigation; it gave him only twenty-four hours to release the apartment and its contents to the victim's next of kin.

After the last entry the detectives had read, Sam's diary entries became more of a journal, written up but not dated. Perhaps this was due to the pressure of the project, or maybe he felt it inappropriate to write in an organised way about his private and personal visits to the Island? Personally, Bruno believed it was because of the complexity of the need to interface with a number of individuals, and that had taken the edge off his initial excitement about the treasure-hunt.

Interestingly, visits to see Phyllida Glassman were no longer recorded in the diary. Sam Peters was not an obvious ladies' man, so one would have thought that a new relationship such as this would have had a major impact on his ordered life. With Potter panning the river pools, although there was plenty of work to do, surely it wouldn't have been too difficult for Peters to slot his building clients into a decent timetable, organising his life so he could meet the demands of a new romance, even with his complicated business situation.

Frustratingly, Peters was a man without friends; this, of course, made it difficult for Bruno to identify his *enemies*, in particular the one who was prepared to kill him for a reason so far unknown.

Bartlett, the Potters, and Harris all knew what he was up to in one way or another, but did any of them have motive enough to kill?

Then there was Noway the solicitor, only briefly mentioned, the Smelter about whom little was known at this point and the ever-elusive Phyllida Glassman.

Potter had panned the East Yar pools with Peters paying him £400 as an advance; this meant that he had more to come. Given the size of the Potters' activities in Godshill in their small B&B, to them the money was a gift from heaven. That he could have high expectations was a factor, but his anticipated reward would not be *unrealistically* high. From his perspective, he was panning in a backwater of England without any real knowledge of gold mining. He was totally unaware that anywhere else in the world, yields of the proportions he was passing on to Peters & Bartlett would have created a classic nineteenth century gold rush! In Western Australia, the amount of bullion so far achieved would have already resulted in a stock market flotation – this was how companies and individuals there made money from the merest sniff of a gold deposit. However, for it to be a successful flotation, a prospector would have to show *legal ownership* of the *source* of the gold.

A point both Bruno and Tom felt was of immediate importance was that lack of permission to pan for gold in the East Yar was putting *Potter's* activity in danger, particularly with Peters' demise.

***

From Sam's filing cabinet, Tom pulled out a folder that caught his eye marked *Hamdens*. It contained drawings and enlargements of ordnance survey maps of the Southern coast of the Island, sections towards Freshwater in the far West of the Island, and an enlarged land drawing of the area north of the car park from the point of the cliff fall. The drawing showed a marked point 1.9 kilometres inland from the Military Road where Sam and the professor had found the quartz outcrop had surfaced. At the bottom of the page were the words *Bartlett/Peters Associates*.

The folder also contained correspondence between Nick Hayes, the Managing Director of Hamdens Mining and Engineering, and Noel Bartlett. Each letter to and from Nick Hayes, was copied to Sam Peters at his Southsea apartment, and on the Hamdens file.

So, Tom thought, *who are Hamdens and what's their connection with Peters' explorations?*

Tom pointed out to Bruno one particular piece of correspondence that confirmed a date and time for a morning meeting at the company's head offices in Finsbury Square. As if deliberately answering the question Tom had asked himself, the letter provided a summary of Hamdens, explaining that they were a mining and exploration company, with a client list that included pretty much all of the main gold mining and oil companies worldwide.

It didn't take long to find a report of the meeting.

Hamdens
Finsbury Square

June 1ˢᵗ, 10:30 am

Present –   Noel Bartlett
Sam Peters
Nick Hayes

Participants discussed setting up a gold mining plant in a South of England location. NB indicated the depth and location of the quartz seam as being one to two meters beneath the surface across a more-or-less level grass-covered cliff top. NH of Hamdens displayed great interest, and accepted NB's refusal to reveal the exact quartz location at this time.

NB & SP confirmed that no signed agreement to go ahead with mining yet existed.

NH reported on the sample of quartz Peters had sent him for analysis by them. His response was very positive. He confirmed sample contained a significant level of gold, higher than many profitable mines in various parts of the world. Stated that concentrated in a small area, it could be extremely profitable.

NH stated that before the discussions could be taken further, the legal rights had to be watertight.

NH   agreed to draw up a contract covering NB and SP's involvement, after which Hamdens would negotiate with the landowners.

A note from Professor Bartlett concluded it was a satisfactory meeting from his and Sam's point of view. A number of points to action were listed.

Bruno and Tom's first visit was to see Bartlett, which they arranged to do first thing next morning.

Chapter 11

Bruno and Tom met Bartlett at the University in Southampton in his head-of-faculty office surrounded by books, papers, samples and various relics from field explorations. He was horrified and very disturbed at the news of Sam's murder, which clearly came as a complete shock to him. Was his murder connected with their discovery of quartz, illegally mining for gold on the riverbank or something else? These were Bartlett's immediate questions.

"We don't know at this point," stated Bruno, truthfully.

From his demeanour, Bartlett seemed very sad at the unexplained murder of his business partner and by now, the DI suspected, his friend. He was pleasant to the police, and stated he was willing to help in any way to find Sam's killer.

"I can't see his murder being connected with our gold mining project, in my opinion," Bartlett said. "No one knew enough about it to have a reason for removing Sam from the picture. Sam's objectives were difficult to pin down at first; was he a serious prospector or was he just a lucky treasure hunter relaxing from a strenuous job? When he came to me with his samples I was amazed at their quality and consistency, and I offered to help to go to the Island and plan the exploration of his fantastic discovery... but I assure you, my preamble contained the caveat *signed agreements from the landowners first*. But Sam and Noway waffled along, not appreciating that time was always of the essence."

"*Noway*," said Bruno. "He's a solicitor, yes? So he's handling the riverbank permissions I take it?"

"Yes," replied Bartlett. "My interest was in the much more serious business of the quartz deposit as a geological find. That's why I drew up a contract between us, and introduced Hamdens to him."

Taking Bartlett's demeanour into account, and looking around the office, Bruno did not see Bartlett as a tired uninspiring University lecturer trudging through the backwaters of academia as Sam's diary had suggested, but as a dedicated professional with commendations going back two decades for the efforts he put into his teaching. His exam success rate surpassed most other faculty heads at the University; a desktop silver photo frame displayed a loving picture of his wife and two children. All of this totally went against the view that he might be a lonely dysfunctional person in a dead end job.

Bartlett was supported during field trips with students by his wife, who came along with responsibility for organising, preparing food, and where required, finding lodgings. He inspired his students with an incredible depth of knowledge of his subject, and an unwavering and long-lasting commitment to them. He gave guest lectures at Oxford and Cambridge Universities on field geology, and his books were set books in many degree courses throughout the country. Geological exploration and the imparting of his knowledge to his students was his life.

Bruno snapped back into the here-and-now as Bartlett spoke again. "Sam made a truly remarkable discovery," he said. "From the time he brought his first batch of samples to me to analyse, I knew he really *had* struck gold."

"Unlike winning the lottery, where you have a prize which no one can take away from you, he had his hands on a prize, but it wasn't strictly his. Handled properly, he could have done well and probably become very rich as a result. That was why I was willing to help him by analysing the panned metallic substances and help him locate the quartz seam from which the gold in the river bed was derived."

"I was excited by what he brought me because it *must* have come from a source that had commercial potential, which is very unusual. It took weeks for him to take me to the Island, but when we finally located the quartz it was *spectacular*. It has enormous value and can easily be mined commercially. The gold panned by Sam and his associate Potter has been washed from the quartz seam by rain water into the bed of the East Yar over several thousand years, and is relatively small beer. Although as a hoard for treasure, the returns were substantial."

"I advised him to secure the rights to mine the seam *immediately* before doing anything else. That was a while ago. Afterwards we had a few short conversations about getting the mineral rights from the owners, but it was always the same answer: "Noway is doing it." I suspected he'd come up against problems, but he didn't confide them to me. He was secretive, but there was an immediacy that he just didn't grasp – he was effectively stealing until the permissions were signed and sealed. Yes, I agreed for him to use my name and the University's... but it was to speed up the chances of getting the proper licences. To tell the truth, I *wanted* him to use my name. I'm an academic, so recognition for the geological aspects of the find are my primary concern. Put simply, I want to have my name on the book. Obviously, financial reward is also nice and I wouldn't have – nor will I – turn that down."

This was the perfect opportunity for Bruno to ask the all-important question, "So how does his death affect you?" he enquired.

"Personally? Well, as you may be able to tell, I'm devastated that our journey together in this life has come to an end. It is also sad that we cannot share in this venture together. I shall continue forth with a heavy heart. Hopefully it will prove rewarding financially, but to be honest, with the news you have brought to me, I do not feel particularly enthusiastic about continuing, though no doubt I shall. I will assume ownership of whatever Sam negotiated with the relevant owners of the mineral rights with a very heavy heart... someone has to. I will also, of course, accept any legitimate claim from his estate."

"Do you know his next of kin?" enquired Bruno, wondering if Bartlett's 'agreement' to take the whole project on board would be as simple as he made it sound.

"No, I don't believe I do, Inspector."

"And what will you do now?"

"Well, everything really does depend on the permissions from the landowners."

"And do you know who they are? Will they give their permissions?"

"The riverbank owners, yes, I believe they shall."

"I sense a 'but' coming," noted the ever-astute Tom.

"The owner of the land where the quartz seam can be found is a completely different kind of person. He is not an Island farmer, in fact his reason for owning farmland on the Island is unclear. But he will not mine the gold for financial gain", Bartlett explained almost with a simultaneous sigh.

"Why not?" Bruno asked.

"He is a rich man, and the Island farm on which the deposits lie is being developed as a winery apparently. It's his escape. He arrives by helicopter and leaves the same way."

"Would he have dealt with Sam?"

"I doubt it. What Sam had to propose was a big project which could only be successfully and profitably undertaken by an organised business of considerable size. To exploit the quartz, the landowner would have had no need for Sam, to be perfectly honest. Someone of existing wealth could easily just go direct to Hamdens or anybody else for that matter. Gold mining, like the diamond or oil industries is a closed business. In mining, you don't *make* anything, you *find* things in the ground or under the ocean. The big money drives the exploration; what you are doing and where is therefore highly secret and is information that must not fall into the hands of competitors. You really cannot do a deal in mining as an outsider... or in Sam's case as a treasure hunter. That is why we went to Hamdens."

Bartlett looked at the policemen; Bruno's almost imperceptible nod encouraged the professor to continue.

"Since we discovered the quartz, Dick Potter has carried on panning the river bed and delivering the metallic findings to Sam. This seemed like a good idea at the time, but it opened the knowledge of potential riches of one form or another to someone whose background we know nothing about, who could even be the Island gossip. If that were the case, a lot of what we thought was confidential could have easily become common knowledge by now."

"Even though I quickly considered him a friend," said Bartlett, "he played his cards close to his chest."

Without argument the academic handed all of his paperwork related to Sam and their mining project over to the two detectives at their request.

***

As they walked back towards their car, Bruno and Tom agreed that the picture of Sam Peters painted by Bartlett was consistent with that which was evident from his files, his apartment and, of course, his diary. Both agreed that it seemed that Bartlett would help them if needed, and although he must remain a suspect for now – as someone with a significant amount to gain from Sam's death – their policemen's guts were telling them that he actually had more to lose from it.

Chapter 12

Amongst Sam's paperwork had been a file named 'Tax Returns', the contents of which included paperwork going back a number of years, all of which was rubber stamped by *L Prendergast*. A business card tucked inside the file had revealed a Portsmouth-based address for Prendergast's one-man accountancy firm, and today felt to Bruno like a good day to get some information about Sam's finances.

On their journey, Bruno and Tom reflected on their earlier meeting with Bartlett. Bruno needed time to think through Bartlett's responses. He felt there had to be something in them that shone a light into a dark corner. Was Bartlett *only* interested in the academic aspect of the gold strike, or was that just an impression given for their benefit? He *had* certainly been quick enough to say he would carry on without Sam.

Many academics have blown-up egos when it comes to their subject; they can be controlling people and unable to delegate... so why did Bartlett leave the legals to Sam?

Bruno asked this last question out loud.

"Because Sam was a businessman and familiar with legal contracts," Tom replied.

"True, but it wasn't his gold," said Bruno. "*Peters* discovered the gold, but I'm not sure that Professors play second fiddle. Let's check on his CV and watch what he does now that his business partner is dead."

***

Larry Prendergast's office was in Landport Terrace in the Southsea business district. After making a surprisingly good coffee for his visitors, the accountant told them that he'd been Sam's accountant for twenty years and had always completed and filed Sam's annual tax return on his behalf, most recently the previous January. He stated that Peters was relatively cash and property rich, confirming the half-million pound sum in Lloyds Bank had been accumulated mostly from profits on property purchases and sales over the past twenty years. Several profitable sales had, after tax, added up to that sum and all was correctly recorded and reported to the revenue by Prendergast himself.

"Property was his hobby," said the accountant. "It's not *that* large an amount over a twenty-year period. I prepared his accounts and had one meeting annually to advise him on tax; I always tried to persuade him to invest some of his cash into equities or high interest-bearing certificates, but he was always on the edge of a property deal, he claimed, so he wanted to have liquid funds available instantly."

"I didn't know him well personally. I asked him the same questions every year, used his answers to complete his tax return, he'd write a cheque for tax due and then relied on me to file his tax return and pay HMRC on his behalf."

"He could have done it himself," Prendergast added, "but he wanted to be sure it was filed correctly and that the tax was right. Then if he ever became the subject of a tax investigation, which sole traders often are, I'd have all the working papers and he could just leave it to me to handle."

"Do *you* know why anyone would want to kill him?" asked Bruno.

"For his money?" was the accountant's obvious answer.

It was an interesting point that Sam was keen to keep a substantial cash reserve, on which he could draw anytime.

***

"I'd say that we can forget about Prendergast as far as being a suspect," said Bruno to Tom as they opened the door of the car. "He's simply the necessary professional advisor you would expect a man of substance – as Sam Peters clearly was – to have used when needed."

Bruno handed to Tom the copy of Sam Peters' previous year-end tax return that Prendergast had given him. It showed that he'd earned just over £143,000 before tax, which – for a man with modest tastes and no mortgage – left a significant surplus, even after the amount owed to HMRC was paid in full.

"Next up?" Bruno asked.

"Next up is Peter Noway," Tom replied. "At first he 'politely' informed me that he couldn't discuss a client's business with anyone without prior written permission from the client themselves."

"A common solicitor's response."

"Yes, so I gave him the common policeman's reply: if he wished to avoid the processes available at my disposal to *compel* a meeting, then perhaps he should re-think his answer!"

***

Noway was a short man – around five foot six, aged mid-forties, and with dark black hair matching his three-piece dark undertaker's suit. He was an old-fashioned dresser who actually turned out to be a pleasant, if fussy solicitor with a good reputation; his sixty-year-old secretary, Madeline, was efficient and friendly. Noway's firm had some longevity, having been started by his father in the nineteen-seventies as a sole practitioner until a stroke in 2004 forced his retirement and had persuaded his son to abandon London and return to the Island to take over the practice.

Noway junior had qualified in Birmingham, his father's home town, and worked in London as a company property lawyer for British Securities, a company who developed commercial offices and shopping centres. He was smart and brought to the Island land-buying and selling skills as well as his mainland contacts. His methods of purchasing land and buildings using London banking connections made previously *im*possible deals possible. He introduced his Island clients to bankers and financiers, who helped gear up their assets and stretch themselves in the process. One or two, in attempting to achieve the unreachable had gone bust, usually from ignoring his advice, but generally he invigorated the Island property scene.

In particular, Noway awakened the potential of the Island farmland market to two of his London friends. Both had bought parcels of considerable size and value, one a farm of 1100 acres called The Chesneys, the other 850 acre Balham Farm. At eight or nine thousand pounds per acre, these two purchases alone brought substantial capital to the Island. The Chesneys had a two mile boundary along the East Yar beyond the bridge at Beacon alley, and was one of the landowners relevant to Sam Peters' panning activity.

When Bruno explained his reason for visiting, Noway called his close friend Oliver Medwin QC in Winchester, who confirmed that with regards to client confidentiality, if the client had been murdered it might be seen as obstructive not to let the police have sight of anything that could help them find the killer.

Noway told the two detectives that he'd been instructed by Sam Peters to write to a group of Island landowners to request permission for him to enter onto their property and undertake a geological survey of the river and riverbanks, taking samples of sediment and alluvium from the bed of the river. His letter promised that all discoveries of note would be reported to them through him in writing within forty-eight hours, and as per the prevailing convention, any profits accruing, would be shared fifty-fifty between the landowner and himself.

"It was a fairly standard request from a hobby treasure hunter and not one that was usually refused by most farmers or landowners," said Noway. "My letter also confirmed that Peters had been referred by the Island's Environment Officer, Arnold Harris from Newport Council."

At Bruno's request, Noway indicated on an ordnance survey map the positions on the riverbank where Peters requested permission, and gave him a list of the landowners with riparian rights relating to these particular locations.

"I had received replies from all seven landowners giving permission without the usual clutch of irrelevant questions," said Noway, "so last Friday – the eighteenth – I invited Mr Peters to come and collect the details... to which there was, of course, no reply."

Despite his early reticence, Noway had been helpful and friendly, with Bruno and his assistant departing after polite handshakes. He had a feeling that Noway had provided them with something that needed a little more looking into.

***

"So Potter is now legally entitled to crawl over the land and take what he wants?" asked Tom, the two of them now en-route to the hovercraft terminal at Ryde.

"Yes... except that Potter wouldn't know that yet, and neither would Bartlett," Bruno replied.

"And legally they are *obliged* to share the gold with these landowners. Is that something we should investigate?"

"Yes," Bruno affirmed. "I don't believe any of the landowners would be connected with the murder because as yet they know nothing about what Sam has been up to."

Bruno later sent the list of landowners to the Newport Police desk for them to run a check for anything that stood out.

"On reflection, something about Noway's manner made me a little uncomfortable." Bruno said to Tom. "*I* reckon there's more to his connection with Peters' gold mining activities than simply taking instructions to write a few basic letters about treasure hunting. He said that he had acted for three of the landowners on boundary matters, and that it was his business to know every farmer or landowner throughout the Island."

Bruno, thinking hard, paused a moment and then continued.

"Say Peters, for whatever reason, revealed to him the value of what he had found, that he has discovered significant gold deposits in the East Yar, and that a quartz vein not only exists, but a gold mine is a proven commercially viable prospect. How would that change Noway's position? As the main property lawyer on the Island, surely he keeps himself aware of almost all the goings-on in such dealings? But he'd also need to maintain a professional confidentiality between each client."

A light suddenly flashed in Tom's mind. "What if Peters wasn't the first to discover the quartz?" he proposed.

"Interesting..."

"Isn't is possible that a previous or current landowner would know about it, and if they do it's a sure bet that Noway does as well, yes?"

"Right. But his 'professional interest' would mean that information would be kept confidential from other parties such as Sam Peters."

The two men thought in silence for a moment before Bruno continued airing his suspicions.

"He mentioned that at one point Sam had become interested in buying land on the Island, but he had dissuaded him, saying unless he was lucky or paid through the nose Peters wouldn't get a chance to buy any freehold land. Isn't that strange when he implied he always kept his ears open for any Island deal?"

Tom nodded in agreement. "I don't think he's given us the full picture, has he?"

"No, because *we* didn't ask him the right questions," Bruno concluded. "Tomorrow morning is our last chance to search the apartment, so let's begin early, Tom, and then we will see the others."

"Harry Felt the smelter, Phyllida Glassman and Arnold Harris?" Tom replied, looking at his notes.

"Correct. And if others crop up, we'll see them too," said Bruno as he dropped Tom at Ryde hovercraft terminal for his end-of-day crossing back to Portsmouth.

Chapter 13

At breakfast in the canoe lake café the following morning, Tom had no sooner sat down than he handed his mentor a copy of the local paper, the *Portsmouth News*. Glancing at the front page Bruno let out a sigh.

LOCAL MAN FOUND MURDERED

Portsmouth resident Sam Peters, a property surveyor, was found dead by a dog walker last week. On the morning of the 19th July a body, later identified as Peters, was found lying under a bridge on the Isle of Wight having suffered a fatal wound to the head, believed to have been inflicted with a knife. No further details have yet been released by the Island's constabulary, other than that the investigation is being led by Detective Inspector Bruno Peach, best known to the public for his work on the infamous *Godshill Butcher's Murder* which remains unsolved to this day.

"Oh they just *had* to remind everyone of that, didn't they." Bruno said, clearly dejected. "Plenty of people will know about this now, although we've got another few days until the local Island paper goes out; that might help us a little."

"At least it was in the bottom left, and not the headline story," ventured Tom.

"Thank God for small mercies," Bruno replied, sarcasm oozing from his voice.

Breakfast was eaten mostly in silence after that, each man examining their notes of the meetings with Bartlett, Prendergast and Noway. When they'd both finished eating, Bruno realised it was upon him to lighten the mood.

"Speaking of small mercies," he said, "at least we've crossed one suspect off the list. Come on Tom, let's go see what we can achieve today."

***

Back at Cumberland House, they continued with a thorough and final examination of Bruno's apartment, its contents and his filing cabinet records. Amongst the various business files, Bruno discovered a remarkably important three-page letter from Peter Noway. It was a draft of a will... that of Sam Peters, dated the fourteenth of May, that same year.

The bequests were few. There was a relatively small sum of £10,000 each in cash to his sister Wendy and her three daughters, making a total of £40,000. The remaining assets, including the apartment in which the two men were currently standing, his personal belongings, his car and all monies in his bank accounts save for the aforementioned monies were left to a certain Phyllida Glassman.

Bruno noted that it *was* only draft will and contained a number of legal caveats; there was a no evidence that it had ultimately been finalised and signed.

"You *were* right about Noway not telling us everything," said Tom.

"*And* this throws new light onto the relationship between Noway, Sam and Mrs Glassman," said Bruno, after Tom had digested the contents of the letter. "How long had he known her?"

"Two months, thereabouts," Tom answered.

"Would he really have contemplated leaving everything he had worked for for over twenty years to someone he'd known for just *two months*?" Bruno asked, not necessarily expecting a reply.

"He'd fallen in love with her, you know how that affects some people," said Tom.

In fact, Bruno did not. "We need to see her as soon as possible and try to understand their relationship. Let's see if she knew about his intentions to leave her his fortune," he said.

Their request to retain the contents of the business files for further examination was agreed by Portsmouth CID, who removed them to an office at Portsmouth, allowing Bruno further time to examine them if necessary, in view of new discoveries.

"The value of the gold and silver so far accumulated by Peters and Potter, and the potential value of the contents of the quartz seam convinced them to treat those associated with these activities seriously. Even for Peters it seems that it had ceased to be just a hobby," mused Tom. "We need to find out what he was doing with the rest of his time on the Island, once he'd mapped the quartz and set Potter to work."

***

Peters' diary recorded that following their discovery of the first quartz outcrop they had concealed it by covering it with a massive stone that needed two men to move. It had taken Bartlett and Peters several visits during April to St Catherine's Down to map the area of the quartz seam. These were recorded as follows:

TUESDAY APRIL 15th
Mid-day discovered more quartz outcrops on a ridge 1.9 kilometres and parallel to the cliff. Already planned to stop at 2 kilometres; Noel concluded that it would have become exhausted or turned down at that point. This extent of the quartz lifted our spirits to exceptional heights. He had calculated from the metal content of my alluvium deposits that the seam was a rectangle over several hundred metres, possibly two kilometres. Its breadth and depth confirmed the precious metal content could be enormous, outstripping anything ever found in the UK or Europe. Marked the spot on OS maps with angles & lines to other prominent undulations. Took readings on an instrument that predicted the size of the quartz.

Peters' sketch of the location showed where they began their search and consisted of measurements with compass marks from the cliff-face inland. At each one hundred metres there was a description of the terrain and soil until at nineteen hundred metres they had located quartz rock visible through the moss and broken earth.

Mapped the size and depth of the quartz beneath the earth, by digging small holes, the deepest 140 cm over a large area.

The entries in the diary revealed a consistent level of activity by Peters, Bartlett and Potter to establish the operation as a viable concern, which brought into play Harry Felt and a London connection, who would buy the gold ingots.

FRIDAY APRIL 18th
Collected a second gold ingot from Harry plus an one-eighth kilo silver ingot. Took a third 15 kilo load of metallic particles for processing.

WEDNESDAY APRIL 23rd
Deposited two gold ingots and one silver ingot into Lloyds bank deposit box Southsea Branch, and caught the 1:20 pm from Portsmouth City to Waterloo. Visited L. Stein Ltd, gold dealers, at Hatton Garden. Met David Samuel about buying the gold ingots. Charming man, explained they'd been dealers in Hatton Garden for nearly 200 years and only bought from licensed dealers. However, subject to references he agreed to propose us to the licensing committee – and that Noel Bartlett, possibly on behalf of Southampton University and as Professor of Geology, should be the principle applicant. This would carry weight. Provided Bartlett's CV as in the Newport Council application. Paid him £200, the license application fee. Promised to return with the gold when properly licensed. Illustrated the importance of obtaining the proper authority to mine the precious metal.

THURSDAY MAY 1st
Spoke to Harris at Newport Council. Reminded me that the Council would not entertain an application from me to treasure hunt over council land, until I had the permission of the landowners of the river banks along the East Yar. Suggested I visit Noway & Co – property solicitors in Ryde who specialised in land transactions on the Island. Said he could approach the landowners on behalf of Bartlett and I.

FRIDAY MAY 2nd
10:30 am Met Peter Noway, Solicitor in Ryde. Knows Arnold Harris well. Understandable given that Noway is a property lawyer and Harris's job is dealing with planning applications and property matters. Noway accepted my instructions to approach a list of landowners with riparian rights to the river banks, explaining to them that I wanted to search for treasure and pan for precious metals on their land and along the river banks. He saw no problems in obtaining the permissions. Outlined to me the rules governing any treasures I might find. "Sign up to these

and everything will be legal," he told me. Said he'd give them three weeks to reply. I gave him £500 on account. Then visited Godshill, paid Potter £400 cash and collected another sackful of metallic substances. He was happy, the cash cemented our deal.

Chapter 14

Harry Felt was the next person on Bruno's to visit list.

When Tom and Bruno arrived at his smelting plant, he was hard at work and dirty but not so as to be unable to break off and leave his task to the two foundry men working alongside him. He scrubbed up, took off a white overall and walked the two detectives to a workman's café called Apollonia, two hundred metres from his foundry. The eatery was run by a polite young woman with a mid-European accent. Over scrambled eggs on toast and tea for Bruno and Tom, and a jacket potato, baked beans, tea with milk and two sugars for Harry, they discussed Sam's murder.

On being told the news, Harry quickly became upset, but as a working man tried not to show it too much. "I assumed you came to discuss some irregularities in Sam's gold mining activity, not his death," he said.

"Can you tell us all about your involvement with him," said Bruno.

"Sure, but first let me explain something about myself," he insisted. "I've worked in foundries since I began as an apprentice. I started this business thirty five years ago to work in bronze for artists, iron and steel for architects creating objects to decorate the interiors and exteriors of buildings, and base metals for hammering into sculpted edifices."

"I agreed to work for Noel Bartlett because I've worked for the University in the past and I have the quarter and one-eighth kilo moulds into which to pour the molten precious metals – this produces regulation-sized ingots. Making ingots in gold and silver is the same as bronze statues from plaster casts for artists and I can handle the quantity of material that Peters brings to me. I have a clean, modern building – as you could see – and the furnace equipment is state-of-the-art. Peters delivered a high quality mix of gold, silver, copper, lead and others, but the precious stuff predominated. Of course I could not indicate the carat. That could only be done by an Assay Office; my end product *might* contain impurities."

"It was a time-consuming job, lots of impurities to burn off, then separation. I didn't know how long it would take or what its worth until I'd done it. When I asked him where it came from, he said 'a riverbed'. He told me he could deliver tons if he were to pan the riverbed. When he asked what I would charge him, I was cautious. I had no idea how long it would take, so we struck a deal."

"When he mentioned an Assay Office, I said to him not to take the bullion there unless you are prepared to tell them *how* and *where* you mined it... and if your explanation isn't satisfactory they *will* investigate you. Of course, if you own the river it came from it would be fine. But I didn't get the impression he did. That was it, off he went and came back when I had done the job."

Harry was a clear talker and Bruno and Tom let him carry on.

"When I had done it, he returned. I told him it took three times longer than I'd estimated, and here's why. The analysis was complicated, I had to divide and sub-divide in my crystal separator until I was *certain* I was smelting gold. There was silver, copper, iron and some tin in the fifteen kilos he gave me, but *most* of the impurities burnt off during the process."

"The precious stuff was less than half a kilo, of which about five ounces was pure gold. That's more than six thousand Dollars at today's prices. The rest was worth about five hundred pounds, mostly in silver.

"But, I told him, he wouldn't get that from the buyers *he'd* have to deal with. I told him that I could get the Assay stamp but it's extra work and we cut it differently. So I proposed we split three ways. Somebody mines it, that's hard graft. I refine it and deal with the Assay Office, there's plenty of hard graft there as well, then at the end Peters collects, delivers and does the business. I was being realistic – it was worth doing, but it *was* dodgy, and I needed more than wages. Sam had two thirds of the value realised to sort out with his associates Potter and Bartlett".

Bruno realised that it was from *that* moment that Sam's hobby and passion became a business. The rewards were potentially enormous, however they were coming from activities where he had no permission from the landowners and riverbank rights holders to take the gold. It was effectively stolen property – and therefore illegal. Harry Felt knew this, and realised it might leave Sam vulnerable to criminals.

"What's your opinion of the whole set up?" said Bruno to Harry, trying to stand back for the details which were important but complicated.

"Peters was a nice man," the smelter replied. "Worked in construction, I think. Told me that gold panning was his hobby. Bartlett, a geology professor at the University was in it too, that's who gave him my name, but he had *big* ideas. I get hobbyists come to me all the time; sculptors who want me to cast into bronze, and not all artists who work in iron like doing their own welding. For them I work to drawings; for Peters I processed metal particles producing gold, silver and lead, and worthless shards of materials from a river he'd been panning. He produced a very high concentrate of precious metal... for a hobbyist truly extraordinary. The precious metal content from that panned alluvium he brought to the foundry was the highest I've ever seen."

"I suspect it's a smallish river in a remote location but from what he produced he'd struck it rich. A commercially viable stream in an accessible location will attract big interest *far* exceeding the compass of a hobbyist. I told him that when I gave him the ingots. The river could only contain material washed from gold or quartz deposits in the vicinity so the concentration of his stuff implied that gold – and lots of it – lay nearby. I told him to get the rights to that sorted before anything else or he might lose out."

"Was there anything about Mr Peters that was unusual?" asked Bruno.

Harry paused while thinking through his answer, "He was precise," came the reply. "I had to weigh everything. Twice"

"'It is not for me it's for my partners', he'd say. I assume he meant Bartlett. He knew that panning for gold is not really for hobbyists. I've never heard of anyone striking it rich panning. Geologically it is possible, but if you did, how would you handle it?"

"Really, I knew he didn't own the land or the rights to pan at the riverbank. If he'd owned it, he'd have took my advice on methods of extraction. And that's *not* old fashioned panning for gold. There are modern methods using proper equipment that could increase his efficiency many times over."

"I'm always getting approaches from dishonest people with stolen property who want it melted down. A bit like money laundering. I turn them all away. Now Peters, I liked. I didn't think he was intending to be dishonest, and I'm confident he was in the process of legitimising his activities. He was no fool."

Bruno paid for breakfast and the three of them strolled back to the foundry. Felt had told them everything he could. From the way he spoke about Peters, he was clearly upset, and although he'd held it together, he now needed to go somewhere private and react to the awful news alone, as some people are wont to do.

As they said goodbye, Bruno felt that they were making real progress now. Harry had definitely given them some decent information.

***

Twenty-five years in the police force had taught Bruno to constantly re-examine any conclusions from his investigation. So he and Tom re-read Sam's journal beginning on the fourteenth of January. Since his first Island visit, many dates in the diary were blank and contained no Island reports, although his credit card statements revealed that he *had* purchased foot-passenger ferry return tickets to the Island on eleven unrecorded occasions. Without a car and his equipment it would have been impossible to treasure hunt.

So what was he doing on the Island on those dates?

The rail company confirmed that he had used all eleven of the return tickets for the outbound journey on the dates they were purchased, with the return always two or three days later. But Bruno couldn't connect the journeys with any diarised Island activity.

On foot meant that he had to be met at Fishbourne Ferry terminal by someone... or have taken a taxi to some*where.*

Peters' records had given Bruno a number of contacts to work on, but, mostly they were related with business. As yet no one had appeared with a clear motive for killing him. So was his murder connected to the gold mining venture, or something else? Something personal maybe?

The flat's contents portrayed him as rather dull, self-centred, miserly and untrusting, without friends, enemies or girlfriends and with no interests apart from treasure hunting. He was neither a gambler, drinker nor womaniser. It was almost as if no real person had ever set foot in the apartment.

***

Mid-afternoon, in good weather, after their morning meeting with Felt, Tom and Bruno returned to the Island and decided to walk the route of the quartz outcrop.

Following Tom's e-mail to Bartlett requesting a map showing the outcrop, to ensure they went in the right direction, the academic insisted on meeting them at the car park in the Military Road at 3:00 pm, from where he could guide them correctly. It was an offer an unfit 53-year-old copper could not refuse.

Walking with Bartlett was easier than for two inexperienced men to search the Downs alone, and it gave them another chance to discuss Peters with him.

"He never really *understood* the importance of his discovery," said Bartlett. "He would have become world famous for making the biggest gold strike since the 49ers of the Klondike in America."

"Are you *sure* this find is that large?" said Bruno.

"I am," said Bartlett, "and I'm also sure that one day it *will* be mined. To be honest I don't think Sam could accept the magnitude of what he had found and was afraid of progressing with it. I think fear conditioned his approach to everything; he was used to working alone, which means he wasn't used to sharing."

"He looked as if he was getting there, though." Tom interjected. "He had Potter grafting on the river, Harry Felt in the foundry, he was working on selling the ingots, and he had the right man sorting out the legals. Then he had you to add professional credibility to everything. That's not bad from nothing, is it?"

The professor shrugged his shoulders, seemingly to dismiss Tom's point and said, "Apart from the ingots in the bank, nothing was buttoned up. But hopefully *I* can do some of it now."

"*How* will you do it?" asked Bruno.

"I shall continue with Noway," came the reply.

They had by now covered more than a mile over uneven grass surfaces. The weather was good, but on their own, even with a map, Bruno and Tom agreed that they wouldn't have found the quartz.

"In geology you must know *what you are looking for,*" said Bartlett in a conspiratorial tone.

***

When Professor Noel Bartlett finally pointed out the moss-covered quartz to the two detectives, it did not feel like the discovery of the century to them. However, geology wasn't their area of expertise and so they let the professor speak.

"Normally a quartz vein is thin and travels inconsistently over long distances at different heights below ground," he said. "But here it is simply two metres below the surface and solid for at least two metres in thickness. It is two hundred metres wide and stretches for at least one mile. It can be mined opencast. It is *literally* a gold mine."

Having found what they set out for, felt the remoteness of it in the middle of a windswept undulating grass moor, and decided there was nothing more to learn at the location itself, Bruno decided it was time to return to the car. Tom was struggling to understand why they'd come to see the quartz in the first place. The visit had essentially told them nothing apart from confirming Bartlett's desire to seemingly recreate good ol' gold rush fever on the Island.

During the return to the car, Bartlett talked about the uniqueness of this stretch of South Wight, of how it is the only place that one can evidence the formation of the English landscape across the south of the country. Every movement, each strata is visible and verifiable. As they walked, to the west they came upon St Catherine's Oratory, after a detour of four or five hundred metres that Bartlett made them take. It had a strange forbidding tower, built of solid stone, tall and alone, visible for miles. Built as a place of worship in the fourteenth century to celebrate mass for souls lost at sea and abandoned for centuries, it is a place of Island legends, from which there are magnificent views in all directions.

***

After a well-deserved drink at the Chale Inn, they parted and, as there was still several hours of daylight left, Tom and Bruno drove to Niton to explore the source of the East Yar river, where it first becomes visible above ground.

"Are we any the wiser after our trip to the quartz seam?" asked Tom.

"Yes," replied Bruno. "We now know it's *very* windy up there on the Downs. Wasn't it very good of Bartlett to come at such short notice?"

"Why do you think he did?" asked Tom.

"Because we'd never have found it with the map alone," Bruno replied. "And he likely didn't want to see us wasting time looking for something we might not have found."

Bruno paused for a moment, as if playing their entire walk back as a fast-forward video clip in his mind.

"You know, he behaved as if he *owned* the quartz seam, didn't he?" Bruno said thoughtfully. "And by taking us to it, *we saw nothing else*, except the Oratory on our way back – for which he also acted as our guide"

"*Was* there anything else to see?" asked Tom.

"The top of the ridge where the quartz surfaced is obviously a high point on the Downs. You can see for miles from there. To the east there's a hill that is steep and prominent. Ahead, at a distance of about a mile-and-a-half is a farm with plenty of buildings. We need to find out about that because I *think* it's significant. And hiding somewhere in a hollow is Phyllida Glassman's farm."

Tom was impressed with his senior's impressive perception, and felt the need to offer something of worth himself.

"Bartlett was very confident in all his talk. Compared to how he comes across in the diary, it's as if he has a renewed vigour. He seems to think he can handle things moving forward; could he have not pressed his case for being involved a little firmer while Peters was still alive? Or do you think he was *waiting* for him to fall on his face?"

"You are rather suspicious of him, aren't you?" Bruno said.

"He didn't utter *one single* complimentary thing about Peters, his partner and friend, not even after my deliberately positive analysis of what he had achieved."

"Yes, I see where you're coming from, I really do," said Bruno. "But he gains nothing *financially* from Peters' death unless Peters had made a will leaving his share to Bartlett... which I can't believe for one moment is the case. I think he's just angry that Sam got himself killed. To a mind obsessed with a single subject like Bartlett's, a death is just a spanner in the works. The way *I* look at it, if anything, Peters' death is a blow to his endeavours."

***

The towpath alongside the river was a fairly popular walkers' trail, and the distance from source to mouth of the East Yar was nineteen miles – or a two-day hike for the average hobbyist walker. Godshill, with its quaint 'Olde Worlde' charm at almost the midway point, was a convenient stopover.

"Peters is killed early evening, *maybe* late afternoon on a fine warm mid-summer Saturday and his body dumped on a footpath frequented daily by hundreds of walkers. It's almost impossible to think that this man's heavy body could be lifted under the Beacon Alley bridge by one person, without *somebody* noticing *something*," said Bruno as they approached the towpath that led to the bridge where the body had been discovered.

"So are we looking for two people?" said Tom.

"It would narrow the field, but to whom?" said Bruno.

If a walker had seen anything unusual on or around the bridge on the evening of his death it would be a good chance that they would remember. Locating that person required the details of the murder to be advertised on a notice at Police HQ, and entered into the Island newspaper, *The County Press*. Bruno's personal experience of advertising for information was that it had *never* brought anything of value.

***

The six-mile walk from Niton to Godshill took them two hours over level walking trails. Engrossed in the beauty of the river and the surrounding countryside, Bruno tried to place the significance of the river walk in Peters' murder, and concluded that it had none.

On the way they had walked past several quiet parts of the towpath where a man could sit, unnoticed, fishing – or pretending to fish, when actually using a pan to collect the particles that were transformed by Harry into gold ingots. Although they kept an eye out, they did not see Potter, who probably restricted his panning to the times when the fewest walkers were on the towpath.

Thirty minutes before sunset, they arrived at the clearing before the bridge which spanned Beacon Alley, where Bruno had first seen Peters' corpse. They stopped ten metres from the river bank over which Sam's body had been dragged by the killer.

"Can we get a warrant to search the place, on the basis of its location?" said Tom, pointing towards the black house, silent and dark, set back from the bridge but with a clear view of the towpath and the surrounding activity. An observant resident sitting quietly in the garden on a warm summer evening, would have seen something unusual.

"We need something else," said Bruno.

"We *could* make something up to get inside, preferably without the owner knowing. Can't a couple of uniformed guys pretend to see burglars in the garden and break in? They do that on TV..."

"It's an idea," said Bruno, dismissively, but decided an investigation of the dark house or a meeting with the residents *was* certainly called for. It looked unoccupied but not necessarily abandoned. The grass had been cut and the view of the bridge from the upstairs was clear and unobstructed.

"If the murderer had been connected to this house would they really have dumped the body under the bridge?" said Tom.

"Who knows, probably not though," said Bruno.

Putting his head round the door of the Godshill Police Station, Bruno was pleased to see Andy Welsh sitting there. A beer and a pasty later and he was giving them a lift back to their car at Niton.

Chapter 15

When Bruno asked Noway for help to understand the ownership of some of the South Wight properties, he was forthcoming and seemed prepared to tell him anything he believed could be relevant to Sam Peters' murder, beginning with the history of the St Catherine's Down estate where the quartz seam lay.

He explained that St Catherine's Down was not owned by the Island local authority as many Island people believe due to the public footpaths and rights of way across it. Amongst the owners were a Derek Bentley in the centre of the Down, a small farm owned by Phyllida Glassman over the hill to the east and the largest farm belonging to the Klinker family to the west, which had belonged to them for well over a hundred years, but for which the sale was currently proceeding – handled, of course, by Noway. The present family head, Geoff Klinker, inherited the estate on his father Tom's death, five years ago. Geoff had left the Island for medical school in London in the mid-nineteen-eighties, and had never returned to the Island permanently.

Geoff Klinker was an orthopaedic surgeon based in London; he was a leading cardiologist, dividing his time between a Harley Street practice and the NHS at Guy's Hospital. He had never had any desire or intention of returning to live on the Island, even in retirement, nor had he any interest in owning property for its own sake or as an investment. In his father's will, a life tenancy was conveyed only on Clive Hall, the family home, to Geoff's mother, Madeline. On her death the house reverted to Geoff himself. Tom Klinker had in fact been Madeline's second husband. Her *first* son – from her previous husband – was one Arnold Harris, an unmarried man who lived with Madeline at Clive Hall, the very same Arnold Harris who held a position as the chief environmental officer for the Island at Newport Council. Having been brought up and lived almost his whole life there – from the age of one – he had always coveted the house and estate, according to Noway.

To Bruno, this revelation certainly would explain Harris's attitude towards Sam. He had dared to put in a request to crawl all over the Downs looking for treasure, which, in Harris's mind, belonged to the Klinker family, and thus vicariously to him.

Tom had been an excellent step-father to Arnold from the day he married his mother, and the two enjoyed a very happy forty-year marriage together. Geoff and Arnold were treated both the same, one never went without something the other had. There were no problems whilst they were growing up. They both attended Ryde School, the Island's fee-paying public school, attended by boys from around the world. When Geoff left home to study medicine in London, Arnold stayed living in the family home with his mother and step-father for twenty years. But Tom Klinker had wanted to continue the family tradition of keeping the estate in the male line. So he had left the estate and property thereon solely to his son Geoff. After he died, Madeline tried to persuade Geoff to include Arnold in the tenancy so that he could continue to live at Clive Hall when she was gone, but Geoff was simply not interested and did not want to continue his association with the Island after her death. After all, he had hardly visited in thirty years, he felt no connection like true locals do."

Arnold had offered Geoff a pittance for the house – being all that he could raise – which had, of course, been refused. He begged his rich step-brother to grant him a mortgage that he could afford from his local authority salary; Geoff was just not interested.

"Arnold Harris never had a chance of buying the Klinker house." stated Noway. "He had no collateral and the worth was and is far greater than anything he could possibly ever hope to borrow. To be honest, Arnold was bitter and could not accept that some wealthy person was going to buy something that he believed should be *his* inheritance, at least in part."

"Will that be an Island person?" asked Bruno.

"Yes and no," said Noway.

Bruno gave him a quizzical look.

"It is already under offer from a person who owns other Island property: Derek Bentley, who owns the adjoining farm. He doesn't actually make any money from his existing estate; it's a tax shelter of some sort. However, a gold strike on St Catherine's Down might change everything for him."

"What is Klinker's estate worth at today's prices?" asked Bruno.

"Its four thousand acres, and farming land on the Island sells for a premium over the mainland. However, the Downs has shallow soil – it's wind swept, meaning erosion over time has mostly blown away any decent top soil. It's OK for sheep and cattle grazing though, so it should fetch seven or eight thousand pounds an acre. The total sum for the complete estate would come to thirty million pounds, with the house, paddocks and outbuildings."

Bruno recalled that Hamdens had suggested the potential value of the gold deposits on the Downs could easily run into many tens of millions, if not more, a thought he vocalised to Noway. "Will it affect the price?" he added.

"Geoff won't haggle over it to be honest, he doesn't care about the possibility of that sort of thing on his land – he's already getting a premium price he considers perfectly satisfactory."

"And you know this...?" Tom pushed.

Noway admitted that he was acting for Geoff Klinker. "Please regard that as confidential, gentlemen." he added.

"So tell me about the landowners that have river frontage," prompted Bruno.

"There are seven farms between the East Yar source in Niton and half-way to the sea, or three miles north-east of Godshill where the alluvium deposits show only infinitesimal amounts of metal; they are not worth panning. All replied positively to my request for permission to search with a handheld metal detector and to take samples from the riverbanks."

"Did you provide any personal details to the landowners about Sam as being the prospector?"

"Sam *and* Bartlett, as joint applicants. As with the local authority, Bartlett's credentials as professor of geology at Southampton adds credibility to their activity."

"So basically a group of Islanders who are closely connected knew all about what they were doing?"

"Yes, I should imagine," said Noway. "But I assure you, they are farmers who keep animals and plough fields, whose horizons do not encompass collective or individual treachery such as murder. It is not the first time they've been approached by treasure hunters, it's actually quite a regular hobby on the Island."

"Didn't the Romans have a significant presence on the Island?" asked Tom. "A hoard of Roman coins could be found on farmland by a treasure hunters at any time, couldn't it?"

"It has happened," agreed Noway, "but not often. Like a winning lottery ticket, the odds of finding a hoard of Roman coins carries about the same chance, but you have to buy a ticket. Sam was a free one. The landowners are mostly Island families whose ownerships stretch back into at least the nineteenth century," said Noway. "Nothing is farmed directly by the landowners, instead they grant short leases to farmers which keep pace with inflation. The tenants who farm the land qualify for grants from the European Agriculture board."

Bruno was glad that Tom was taking notes. He might have a good memory, but there was plenty of interesting information here that he didn't want to forget.

"What else can you tell me about Arnold Harris?" Bruno asked.

Knowing the Klinker family well, having represented them for various reasons, Noway was able to flesh out some detail for the Inspector.

"Since Arnold left school he has worked in local government. It's a secure job and he has risen up the management grades, which gives him status, locally at least. It has enabled him to stay at home on the Island and continue to be looked after by his mother. He now heads up environmental services for the whole Island," Noway explained.

"Madeline had worked tirelessly caring for Arnold until her eighties, when *she* required daily care from him. This took most of his spare time and energy. They lived in Clive Hall for five years after the death of his step-father. On his mother's death he received a notice to vacate from Geoff's London solicitor. Anticipating the inevitability of the day when he would become homeless, fifteen years ago his mother had persuaded him to buy an old house in Beacon Alley which he rented to a couple who ran a summer bed & breakfast business there. Their tenancy had been undemanding of him, accepting the gradual decline in its appearance externally and its lack of central heating and modern plumbing in return for a low rent until reputation meant they could no longer attract guests and thus moved out."

***

Noway had been helpful to the detectives trying to get to grips with an intriguing network of people.

Since Bruno had confirmed that the Potters were the same couple who had been interviewed in connection with the murder of the Godshill butcher, he had been reluctant to see them – hoping the investigation would either lead him *firmly* towards them with evidence or take him in a different direction. With that unsolved case he had failed to obtain evidence to charge *anyone* with murder, and their presence proved to be a red herring. They were simply family, and likely caused him to ignore the signs which might have led to discovering the identity of the murderer. The idea of visiting the Potters to discuss another murder, that of Sam Peters, did not fill him with joy. He anticipated a degree of hostility with roots that lay in his investigation of the case years ago, where Bruno had pursued them aggressively – although in his eyes not unfairly – because he believed they were involved.

To take his mind off the job for a few hours he called Janet with an invitation to supper that evening in a quiet pub between Shanklin and Sandown. Bruno *liked* to think of her as his permanent girlfriend... which he had no right to do, because he never gave her any indication that was what he *wanted* her to be.

She had recovered from the pain of her divorce and was open to pastures new, but not necessarily with a Police detective who lacked a certain level of creative thinking that would surely help him in his job, and that she looked for in a man. Bruno had long since recognised his own limitations and that was one reason why he chose to see her whenever he needed reassurance, or, perhaps, felt he was making too slow a rate of progress. In this case he still had a number of potential suspects to be interviewed, namely the Potters, Derek Bentley, Phyllida Glassman and Arnold Harris. Hamdens were involved only in a business sense, but should be worth seeing for their man's views on Bartlett and Peters.

When Bruno voiced his reluctance to visit the Potters to Janet, she suggested that he was frightened of them.

"No, I just want to be sure," he replied.

"Of what?"

Bruno could not answer that.

"Am I right in think there was no evidence against them in the old Godshill butcher case, and that events have since confirmed their innocence?"

"No *hard* evidence, and their innocence is *not* confirmed," Bruno stated pointedly.

"You don't like them, do you?"

Again, Bruno did not answer.

"I think you sometimes allow your personal feelings to get in the way of your detective work," Janet said. "The murderer *must* have been a person with either a grudge or something to gain... or both. Don't prejudge the Potters. Dick is clearly at the centre of your investigation. Go and see him ASAP and get his angle on what happened to your victim. Surely he, if anyone, could provide a vital clue? I know you'll be thinking back to that butcher's killing, but what's to stop you thinking about it, anyway? Didn't his awful wife end up taking everything and then selling up and moving away?"

"Yes," replied Bruno. "She was called Steph. She's Sonia Potter's sister."

"Who took over the butcher's shop?" asked Janet.

"A fishmonger from Cowes," said Bruno.

"Was he connected to their family in any way?"

"Not that I know of. It was months later, after his wife obtained probate, that the shop was sold."

"Would the Potters *really* kill someone though? Especially Sonia's brother-in-law. From what I've heard about them, if they had done it, wouldn't they have taken the cash from the till? Look, instead of continuing to think that they're killers who got away with murder, speak to them tomorrow with a fresh, clear mind. It might even help you look at two cases in a different light.

Chapter 16

With Janet's comments of the previous evening still ringing in his ears, Bruno met Tom Craven off the early morning hovercraft and drove him to the Potters B&B in Godshill.

Janet was right, the Potters could surely not have committed the butcher's murder, and there *was* no evidence against them, however Bruno liked to phrase it. All that was certain was that he didn't like them – and if that was a crime, the Island's jail would have been full a long time ago. He decided that permission or not, he'd later re-examine the files on the Godshill butcher's murder.

Bruno raised his hand, hesitated ever so slightly, then knocked loudly on the door.

Recognising Bruno instantly from the front window, Sonia called to Dick from the hall,

"Dick! It's that copper from... from you-know-when, Detective Peach. Actually there's two of them."

"What do they want?" replied Dick, who did not receive an answer.

After a few seconds he came to the hallway and, overcoming an instinctive reluctance to engage with the police, opened the front door.

"Good morning, *sirs*, what can I do for you?"

To Bruno, Dick Potter had not changed.

"I'm Detective Constable Craven and this is Detective Inspector Peach," said Tom, having agreed in advance with Bruno that he'd do the introductions. "We'd like to talk about Sam Peters, with whom we believe you had some connection," said Tom.

"Ah, I read about him being dead; it was in the paper. It mentioned you by name, Inspector, don't know if you saw that?"

"Can we come in please, *sir*?" Tom said quickly, worried that for all his experience, Bruno might just start things off on the wrong foot.

Dick looked at Sonia who had remained at his side like a statue. She didn't speak but stepped backwards and allowed the two visitors to pass into a low-ceilinged room, furnished with a gas fire from the sixties, somehow still working. On the ledges were groups of Capo di Monte sculptures.

"Who told you I had some connection with him?" said Potter, choosing to get his questioning in first.

Tom wondered if it would make any difference before answering, "Professor Bartlett of Southampton University."

"You're right, *and* I know Bartlett. He used to stay here when we was working the river," said Potter.

"And what work do you *do* on the river?" enquired Tom.

"Panning for gold and silver," replied Dick. His first thought was to say 'fishing', but some deep inner voice told him that a murder investigation was not the time to tell pointless lies.

"Was it successful?"

"Very," he said.

"You know that for a fact?"

"The three of us were partners, but now it's just two," said Dick. "Sam Peters did the prospecting and decided on the locations, all scientifically based. I did the panning, the real hard work. I'm still working on two of the locations at the moment. I've collected a big stock of metal particles that need processing. That's something that Sam organised; he collected ten bags weighing ten kilos a piece from me every time he visited the Island."

"Did he pay you?"

"Always," came Dick's affirmation, keen to show that – from his point at least – everything was above board. He took out a copy of the smelter's analysis and what looked like a small stack of payslips from a coffee table drawer.

"I was fairly paid for the graft, and it was a good deal for all of us."

"Who do you think killed him," fired Bruno.

"It wasn't me, if that's why you are here. You've tried that before, but I don't suppose you remember?"

"Only too well, actually," said Bruno, a little quieter than his question. "I apologise if I gave you that impression back then, but routine police work is about obtaining answers to difficult questions, and there was a connection between you and the victim. I was only doing my job, regardless of what *you* think I thought."

"Well there is an even closer connection between me and Sam Peters, but I didn't kill him. And here's why: without him I've got nothing, just bloody heavy sacks of metal out there," he pointed towards the back of the house.

"Can I see them?" Bruno asked, as kindly as he could muster.

"I suppose."

Outside the back door beside a neatly stacked pile of logs was a large pile of thick black plastic bags, each containing a measured quantity of the metal particles that Potter had gathered from panning for gold in the pools of the East Yar river.

"Each bag weighs ten kilograms; any more and they split," he said. "Now he's dead, I'll have to deal with the smelter. Bartlett won't do that, but he's going to take me for my first visit."

"Do you *know* the smelter?"

"Harry Felt, his name and address is on the money slips. It wouldn't be right if I turned up alone would it? It'd look as if I'm money grabbing. I tell you, Sam's death really is a great loss to me."

"How much did you make from the venture?" Tom asked.

"Not enough to bother the taxman," Dick answered, tapping his nose, "but the potential's there. You can see how many bags I've got."

Contrary to Dick's professional accounting analysis, Sam's diary records had confirmed that he'd already earned a good few thousand pounds from their arrangement so far.

Bruno, thinking hard but trying not to show it, had started to get a real feeling that it was unlikely the Potters had any direct connection with Sam's murder. He was pulling in a much better income that his lacklustre B&B's performance, and with his ongoing expectations that the flow of money would continue, it seemed unlikely that he'd do anything to purposefully put a spanner in the works. As was the case with Bartlett, surely a *live* Sam Peters would be an easier and more certain way forward for them.

"Tell me how all this started then," said Bruno.

"He turned up here back in February for a couple of nights B&B, in stinking weather if I remember right. I think he'd been out all that day doing the graft I'm doing now. Then he came more regular. The first few visits were every one or two weeks, and he came alone. After that he brought Bartlett down from the University. It was soon after that they explained what Sam had been doing and made me an offer. We became partners and I started panning for gold."

"Can I see your visitor's book?"

"As long as you're not from the Revenue, sure," Dick said, with a smile.

Sonia, who had remained as silent as if she had been absent, left the room and returned with the visitor's book. A quick scan revealed the occasions since February when Peters had stayed, latterly with Bartlett.

"Thanks. So what happened after you'd made a deal?"

Dick explained that he'd followed Sam's instructions to the letter in the locations he had mapped out for him to pan for the gold.

"He was bang on was Sam, very precise. I improved my methods through joining an amateur mining club on the internet. Lots of people do this in the UK, but I'd bet no one is as successful as me," he said. "Though I shouldn't be telling you this; it's in my contract that everything we knew remained between us."

"Just with Sam?" Bruno asked?

"No, with the two of them, we all signed together," replied Dick. It states that I 'cannot disclose any of my activities to anyone' and that includes *you*, Inspector," he added with amused confidence.

"Is there anything you can tell me about them that could help? Anything suspicious you thought they were up to?", Bruno said, wondering whether Potter had any idea about the quartz seam. "Do you know who might have wanted to kill Sam? Is it possible to think of a reason why anyone would murder him, or for him to be in circumstances where it could happen?" Bruno asked.

"Suspicious, no, secretive yes. It's obvious why we shouldn't tell anyone what we were up to, or hordes of treasure hunters would descend on the Island from all over. So we were 'specially careful not to let anyone see us. If a stranger appeared, I'd pick up my fishing rod and start adjusting the reel until they'd passed by, but no one ever stopped and the walkers are usually talking to each other and don't notice me. Islanders wouldn't like what we were doing, if they knew the details, I bet though. Now whether that would be enough for anyone to murder my business partner, well you'd know better than me, Inspector. But I tell you this. Mainlanders couldn't give a toss. It's an *Islander* that killed him, that's what *I* think Inspector, since you ask."

"What makes you so sure it is an Islander?" asked Bruno.

"Because it has to be something to do with the Island, right? No person would follow Sam over from the mainland to kill him here, they'd do it *there*, wouldn't they? And no one would commit a murder over two men skimming mud out of a stream. It's a person from the Island, and it's *not* to do with panning the river. But, a stranger wouldn't know enough about our business to put him under that Beacon Alley bridge. So *I* think it's someone who knows *what* we're doing, but *not* someone who wants a share or they'd have already asked for it."

Having listened to Potter's theory on the identity of the killer, Bruno and Tom thanked Dick and his wife, and took the opportunity to depart.

Nothing from the meeting suggested Potter was involved with Peters' murder, though – as policemen whether old or young – both Bruno and Tom kept an open mind.

"He *does* have a fair bit to gain with Peters out of the way," said Tom once they were out of earshot.

"*Does* he?" asked Bruno. "There's a finite amount of gold that can be extracted from the river, and who knows how near they are to that already? And surely if all the approvals came in, Potter's small-scale panning would be redundant."

***

Later that evening Bruno talked an attentive Janet through his interview with the Potters, and her take was different to Bruno and Tom's.

"Sam's murder is a gift from heaven for the Potters," she said. "He's mining valuable metals, he's built up a stock which only he knows about and it all belongs to him. From his point of view, he can carry on gathering and gathering. The few thousand he's already made was half of the proceeds, but now it's *all* his. A few thousand to the Potters is a fortune, to them they have literally struck gold. And *they* think it will go on forever. He's only stuck for the time being, until he works out how to sell it for himself. He showed you the smelters invoices so don't believe him when he says he's got nowhere else to go. He could easily find a different smelter. Bartlett must know that, but he doesn't care what Potter does – he's only interested in the big prize. So your Dick will be panning harder than ever now it's *all* for him. Peters' demise is his big chance. He and Sonia benefit far more substantially than you think," she said, "especially now he is the sole participant in the process."

Despite this assessment of the situation from the Potters' point of view, Janet restated her belief that she did not think the Potters were involved in Sam's murder.

***

That afternoon, Bruno and Tom drove back towards the bridge at Beacon Alley. Bruno wanted to think about what happened there, probably in darkness a little over eight days ago, and to try to understand why the body should be hidden under it. Potter's words about it being someone who knew what they were up to echoed in his head; perhaps he was right? If the murderer *had* been spotted on a mid-summer evening humping a heavy body down to the tow path he'd have been bang to rights. The effort involved – especially for one person – was huge, and in view of the discovery only hours later utterly futile, if the murderer's reason for the location was to conceal the body for as long as possible. The risk of being spotted was high, and surely there were other less risky places to hide a corpse?

A sense of dread enveloped the DI as he got nearer to the bridge. The green verge alongside the river was overgrown and it flowed briskly over the undulating river bed creating pools from which Sam Peters and Dick had collected sediment. A short distance before the bridge the trees became taller and the bushes denser and closer to the river banks preventing the sun from shining into the water which ran faster and reached a depth of ten feet directly below the bridge, whilst only twelve feet in width. From the west, the northern bank opened out to a clearing on the left of the towpath. Fifty metres back from the river stood the unloved black house on two floors which Noway had informed him belonged to Arnold Harris. From the clearing between trees, bushes and undergrowth he could see the house was built on ground risen up by around six feet – an artificial mound, high enough to avoid flooding unless the river levels rose significantly, and ensuring the house a full, uninterrupted view of the river and the farmland either side of it. The towpath ran alongside the bottom of the house's sizeable garden, which was not fenced off. Instead there was a natural dip which had become a shallow pond, where bull rushes and pond vegetation grew, up to a dense border of laurel bushes. Any attempt to cross it on foot would mean sinking at least to ankle depth and possibly all the way up to a knee in murky, muddy water.

Taking this opportunity for a closer look at the house, Bruno had parked in a clearing off the road alongside the driveway which had a half-rotten white-painted wooden sign across the top bar of a propped-open rickety farm gate, bearing the name 'Beacon Farm', written in now-faded black paint. The dry stone walls at the entrance were moss covered and clearly in need of repair in many places. Roof slates had slipped and several loose tiles rested in the gutters; one down-pipe had slipped at the joint of the guttering and swayed in the wind away from the eaves. The house looked very much uninhabited.

The closer they got along the weedy, worn gravel drive to the front door, the more tired, gloomy, in need of maintenance, and generally run down the place looked. It had a heavy iron horseshoe knocker that Bruno banged gently at first before trying again somewhat louder. During a brief sideways glance, Bruno saw between half-drawn curtains a middle aged man – whose features he could not determine – watching him, standing in a shadow at the rear of the front room.

After a third and much more deliberate bang on the door, the man had withdrawn out of sight but did not answer the door. There was no car on the drive, so Bruno and Tom assumed the occupier travelled either on foot or by the bus which stopped at the entrance to Beacon Alley only three hundred metres away on the main Newport to Godshill road. With no response, they decided to go away and ask the office to contact the occupier. Despite a reluctance to answer the door, they might be able to shed some light on activities on and around the bridge the night of the murder.

The view of the river from the house and drive was restricted either side of the bridge, but the bridge itself was visible. If anyone had been in the garden on the evening of Sam's murder they could have seen the killer approach the bridge alone or accompanied. If that person had seen *anything* it might help with the murder.

Bruno considered the light conditions, and decided that in dusk it would be tricky, but in full darkness nigh-on impossible to dump a body beneath the eerie and totally unlit bridge.

Further along the towpath, the river widened then narrowed, twisted and turned, producing the perfect conditions from which to take out mud and slush to pan for the valuable metal particles.

Bruno approached the bridge and discovered that only with difficulty could he scramble down the steep bank across long grass, dock leaf and stinging nettles, and approach its brick walls. A tree, one metre back from the riverbank hung over the water, obscuring both the bank and part of the river from anyone looking down from the road as he had done. Three metres back, he could see the flat riverbank where they had found Sam's body. It was surprisingly inaccessible.

The placing of the body, as it had been found, might have been accomplished by *two* people working together. Glancing back from the bank to the towpath one more time, Bruno could easily picture the corpse being dragged the ten metres over the flatter ground to the underside of the bridge.

***

With any unsolved crime, a detective can convince himself that clues still exist at the crime scene that have not yet been seen, and it is these that hold the key to solving the crime. This was why Bruno had begun to retrace his steps to where Peters had lain on the riverbank.

After Peters body had been removed from where it had been found under the bridge, Bruno recalled that he had travelled over to Southsea to inform the next of kin and to arrange official identification of the body. Bruno felt now that his survey of the crime scene at the time had been less than thorough, and decided, with Tom's help, to conduct another search.

Bruno had now concluded that the killer had dragged the corpse by its shoulders until it was completely under the bridge, then pushing it firmly against the side arch of the bridge. To return he'd had to have crawled over the corpse. In the course of doing so, it was very possible the killer may have scraped the low roof of the bridge with some of his clothing or even an exposed part of his body, such as his hands. This would mean there could be clothing fibres, skin, or even congealed blood left there, any of which would prove invaluable evidence.

After a search of the approach to the bridge, Bruno allowed Tom – younger and fitter – to crawl to the position where Peters was found. There, on his back, he lay atop damp grass, staring at the underside of the bridge. It was covered in a layer of moss, the kind that grows in dank, wet places with next to no sunlight; a deep, earthy brown with fibres that stuck to the brickwork. Lying in this position for several minutes, and allowing his eyes to adjust to the light – or more accurately the lack of – he detected tell-tale marks on the arched brickwork where the ceiling moss had been disturbed. Using his Swiss pocket knife, DC Craven scraped off a small chunk of each of the disturbed areas into a plastic evidence bag, which any good detective always carries in his pocket. Tom noted – quite audibly – that crawling across the dew and mud had soaked his shirt, vest and shorts through to the skin, exactly as the effort of placing Peters' body there must have done to the killer.

Lying uncomfortably and staring at the curved ceiling underneath the bridge was a disturbing experience for Tom, a memory that he never could quite let go for some reason.

It took a while to finish a further examination of the other parts of the bridge and the towpath closest to it, but no other missed miracles presented themselves, so Bruno arranged for uniform to give Tom a lift back to the Ryde ferry, driving himself home for a shower before meeting up with Janet for Friday evening supper.

Janet agreed that their revisiting of the bridge and the scraping of the underside of the arch was excellent detective work, and suggested that the scrapings might even reveal the DNA of a suspect.

Revisiting thoughts about the Potters, Bruno expressed his thoughts that although Peters knew the exact value that Dick Potter was producing daily, did Potter *himself* know? From everything Bruno had told her, she suspected he did, and was happy with the split, as he had told the detectives at his B&B.

They then discussed what it would mean for the investigation if it *was* a two person murder. That fact alone did not eliminate anyone, and even bitter loner Arnold Harris might have a hidden accomplice.

One thing Bruno knew for sure was that amongst Sam's small circle of connections, *somebody* had been driven to commit the ultimate crime and take his life. So far it looked as if money was the leading motive, and although from the list of current suspects it seemed implausible that two would have worked together, it was not impossible.

Thinking again about the location and its relevance, Janet suggested if perhaps it was an act of deception, to be as far away from and unconnected to the place the murder had actually taken place. The link to the panning activity either a clever decoy or a lucky coincidence. Perhaps it was simply the most suitable place two people could dump a body in a relatively clandestine way?

***

Tom Craven was not one to let the grass grow under his feet. He had returned to the forensics lab with his wall and ceiling scrapings from beneath the arch of the bridge. There, he persuaded the lab technician to work on them as a top priority.

Chapter 17

Harry the smelter was an important link in the chain. He transformed the sacks of unrefined mud and metallic particles into the valuable precious metal that could be sold for cash. But Bruno had no reason to consider him a suspect. That he may well have adjusted the gold content in the smelting to make a little more for himself was really neither here nor there. But now the dust had settled and Potter still saw him as important in the continuing activity, there could have been something additional he'd since remembered – or had kept back – since the first time Bruno and Tom visited him, so they called on him a second time. They were lucky to find him in on a Saturday morning.

Even the most cautious people sometimes reveal snippets of information that can provide the missing piece in the jigsaw. The number of persons who knew of Sam's activities was increasing, diluting Bruno's search for the killer. Dick Potter endorsed Bruno's current belief that the killer was an Island person with a financial interest; this would therefore include Noway the solicitor, Arnold Harris, Professor Bartlett and – if Sam's will had been finalised as drafted – Phyllida Glassman.

Even now, Harry was astonished at the quantity and quality of pure gold achieved from the metal particles. The alluvium was taken from the river bed, having been washed down to the river by rain flowing over the quartz rock which contained a high concentration of gold.

"That's what this discovery is all about Inspector – quartz. It's where the big bucks are. As a geologist Bartlett will have worked that out, and he'll know where it is for sure," Harry said.

"What happened to the precious metal after giving it back to Mr Peters?" asked Bruno.

"I can't tell you what they got for those ingots because the spot price changes daily. I wouldn't even know *if* he sold them at all."

"So what are the latest developments?" Tom prompted.

"Yesterday morning Bartlett called and asked to bring Potter, the one grafting on the panning. But Potter came alone in the afternoon, saying something had come up and the professor couldn't make it. He said that Sam was dead – *dead* mind, not *murdered* – and that I'd be dealing with him now."

Harry continued freely, Bruno and Tom now saying nothing.

"He'd pulled up in a battered old Peugeot 206 loaded to the gunnels with plastic bags containing metal shards. There were no less than thirty black plastic bags, and he'd put them all in the boot. You should have seen the strain on the rear suspension, it was dangerous! At least spread the load a bit, those bags came to almost six hundredweight.

Harry led them to a corner of the foundry where there were a number of black plastic bags – Tom quickly counting off exactly thirty – each containing ten kilos of the collected particles that Bruno had seen on his visit to Potters' B&B the morning before.

"I said I'd continue producing the gold ingots for him in my soak-up time, and I made a point of telling him that the police had been here to discuss Sam's murder, and that I'd have to mention his visit. Had you not popped in like this, I'd have called you. I want everything I'm doing to be open and above board. Potter told me, smiling, that you'd already seen this stuff," he said, pointing to the plastic bags.

"He knows I'm stuck with it," Harry went on. "And his proposition to me was honest. Without someone to work with who was in-the-know about this business he was wasting his time, he said. '*If you do the smelting and selling, I'll do the prospecting and panning. It's about the same amount of work, I'm guessing. You can't do what I am doing, and I can't do what your doing so we'll split fifty fifty*' – those were his words. If the quality of what he digs up, Inspector, is as good as what Sam delivered, it's worth a *fortune*."

Bruno Smiled at Harry, but still didn't interrupt his flow.

"I told him I'd need to have a signed piece of paper from an authoritative source saying that he was legally entitled to the raw metal. I asked him if he thought he had permission to mine the shards, and he said that was all sown up by Bartlett. He didn't know the specifics, but he swore he'd asked him. I explained that in my opinion, Bartlett would be entitled to a share and so would the people who owned the locations from where he conducted his panning activities. He agreed, had no objections. So that's something we'll be getting onto, Inspector, when we know what it all comes to. Whatever has been agreed between the relevant parties by Sam we will honour, then Potter and I will share what's left."

"He seemed pretty confident of getting what he needed. He left me with the bags of metal over there to get started with, and said he'd already cleared the deal with Bartlett before coming here. With nothing else to discuss, we shook hands and he left."

"For me it's a good deal for the work involved. Plus, as I could obtain the Assay office stamp – although it might take a little time – it would bring clear legitimacy to the project." said Harry. "It's also good for Potter. He's easy to do business with, there's something in it for both of us, and if *you* think he murdered Sam, think again. I can't see him as a murderer. He's just taking advantage of the situation he's now in."

Speaking the first words that he had for some time, Bruno thanked Harry for being so open with them and wished him luck in the venture for the future.

Thinking about what Felt had said, Bruno decided that Potter's behaviour was no more or less than he would have expected. He was an opportunist, presented with the most exciting opportunity that would ever fall into his lap. This was the sort of thing he would have dreamed of in his years of loft- and house-clearance, and stealing old ladies' possessions.

***

Bruno called in to the Potters' on his way past that afternoon to ask Dick for an update on his activities, something he did not object to doing. Potter openly told him he had decided to take direct control of his Klondike-style river panning activity and deal directly with Harry the smelter. He was in business.

"What did you expect me to do after all my hard work?" was Potter's answer to Bruno's question of why he visited him alone. "I've got nothing to hide. Harry was happy to do business with me and he gets a pay increase; he's going to handle the sale of the gold to the dealers in London. And Bartlett still gets the share that he was happy with."

"Have you actually confirmed all of this with Bartlett?"

"Not so far," said Dick. "He'll come calling though."

A smile – kind, but a little conceited – spread across Dick's face.

"I know why you're back here, Inspector."

"Tell me," said Bruno.

"Because you're not getting anywhere finding Sam's killer... otherwise you wouldn't be back here talking to me, would you now, Inspector?"

Of all the people to open up to, Dick Potter was the last that Bruno would have chosen, but in the hope of him saying something of use, he saw no harm in allowing the conversation to continue along its current course.

"You knew him well, so there may be something you can tell us. It might seem trivial to you, but lead to something important for us," he said. "It could be anything. If the panning business that you set up together is connected to his death, you might lead me to his killer; you may know this person and not connect them yourself. Comments from people you have spoken to, quite innocently, might open up a new avenue of enquiry for us... so please tell me if you or your wife have talked to *anyone* about what you have been doing with Sam Peters, particularly if it was immediately prior to his death."

"I've been very cagey, Inspector. You don't need to remind *me* that careless talk costs lives."

"What about your wife?"

"She wouldn't talk to anyone about our business. The only person she talks to is her sister Steph, who lives in Bournemouth. My Sonia knows what these bags contain and she'd prefer it if they weren't stacked up by our backdoor. She knows Sam's been murdered."

"Has anyone ever seen you at work?"

"One or two, maybe a few more than that" Potter replied.

"Where would that have been?"

"Probably the place where I've taken the best metal particles, in North Roud, where the river bends a couple of hundred metres past Berrycroft farm. It's a good half a mile from the bridge where Sam was murdered."

"Nobody knows for sure where Sam was killed, only where his body was found" said Bruno.

"You can't fish the East Yar, but not everybody knows that, so where there is a dredgable pool I set up a rod so it looks like that's what I'm doing. When it's all clear, I get into the river and shovel out the mud. It's messy, cold and wet, and you have to concentrate. After about an hour of that I retire to my tent to warm up, and grab a rest with a mug of hot tea; I've got a primus stove that I pump up. *That's* when you don't notice if anyone's looking at you, but I always leave a rod up with a float on the end. It would be a nice private spot except there's a hump in the road as it swerves round a left hand bend which gives people a clear view of where I'm working. But I can't not pan there, it's easily accessible and it's where the richest deposits are. I'll show it to you if you like?"

"Just mark it on my OS map, please," said Bruno.

"No, honestly, I'll take you," said Potter, who gathered up his jacket and car keys.

It was a diversion, but as it got him out of Sonia's earshot, something he wanted, Bruno accepted.

***

They left Godshill on the Whitwell road, Dick driving, Bruno in the passenger seat, and Tom sitting in the back. He struggled a little to hear what the two in the front were saying due to some rather loud bumps and squeaks coming from the suspension.

Dick took a right-hand turn about a mile south of Godshill and headed towards Roud. Apart from farms, there was nothing *in* Roud itself, but, as he had said, from the bend they were now approaching, the driver of a car passing in the same direction they were travelling would have a clear view of his favourite East Yar mining position.

"No one has ever approached me," he told Bruno. "But there's no way of working that pool without being seen. The land on the west bank belongs to one of the farmers who gave Sam permission to use his metal detector on his land; it's called Pineapple Farm. After here, the next decent pool on this stretch of river is a couple of hundred metres short of the Beacon Alley bridge."

"I'd imagine you *could* have been watched from a number of different vantage points along the river?" said Bruno.

"Through binoculars maybe; I suppose in that case I could be seen from quite a distance," said Potter. "But I'm sure people who pass by just think I'm fishing or camping. Isn't that what you would think if you saw me on the river bank, Inspector?"

As he turned the car around to head back, Dick spoke about how he had improved on Bruno's methods with simple shaking and a spooning device that he used to pick up sediment. He'd researched the panning techniques of the men who had been in on all of the world's gold rushes in the mid and late nineteenth century.

Even with his fresh, 'clean slate' view of Dick Potter, Bruno was a little surprised that his former murder suspect admitted that panning for gold had given him a purpose in life, a kind of satisfaction that he'd never previously felt. He expressed sincere sadness at the murder of Sam, and seemed to genuinely want to contribute *something* that would lead Bruno to the killer, although he didn't quite know what this might be.

Dick's new employment had even led him to research gold mining activity elsewhere in the UK, although unlike the East Yar the streams and rivers were mostly too fast-flowing over granite to create pools with alluvium deposits that might contain gold and silver particles.

As they pulled up outside the B&B, Dick turned to Bruno with a serious look, and stated, "Inspector, Sam's killer is an Islander and he is watching you. Be careful."

The warning sounded almost surreal coming from Potter, but Bruno nodded his understanding before gently reminding him that until the permission of the landowners was regularised and they received their share, he was still effectively stealing.

***

Over supper, Janet and Bruno once again discussed how there was nothing that connected the Potters with Sam Peters' murder, just as there had not been with the butcher's murder.

However, Janet did tell Bruno that after some time thinking about everything about which the two of them had spoken, Stanley Musgrove's widow Stephanie interested her considerably, particularly the fact that she had been married to Andrew Pumpkin, the solicitor from Cowes who had also met a premature death in rather dubious circumstances.

Chapter 18

Delving into Steph's background had been a fairly easy task for a school headmistress. Not only were the teachers themselves amongst some of the biggest gossips around, but she only had to stand at the school gate at home-time to hear the latest scandal. The mums who came to pick up their beloved children were only too happy to dish the dirt when the subject of the butcher's widow just happened to come up.

After obtaining probate, which had taken around three months, Steph had disposed of the butchery business and moved away without telling anyone where she was going. The proceeds from the sale of both the business and the large house she and her unfortunate husband had occupied meant that she was well off, in fact richer than she ever dreamed she would be.

The gossip network spans far and wide though. It was soon discovered that Steph had initially rented a small property in Southampton, but soon felt the area was a little too working class for her newly-acquired wealth; *she* had moved up in the world. She therefore chose to move to an affluent area of Bournemouth to mix with the well-heeled.

The death of Stanley, the respected local butcher, had been the end-point of Steph's third marriage.

As a twenty-one year old, Steph had married a longshoreman named Rod Fletcher who owned a deck-chair license for a stretch of beach in Shanklin, a business that had been in his family for over a century. That marriage had floundered because of their joint promiscuity, *he* with women who fancied a suntanned muscleman who spent his life on a beach. They would give him their hotel room numbers and he'd visit at an appropriate time to do their bidding, receiving a fat tip for his performance. Many of the women who enjoyed booking this additional service returned every year, with husbands who they'd send off on coach trips or fishing expeditions while they spent an hour in bed with 'the Rod'.

The self-styled ladies' man had performed this service every summer since he was a teenager, and it was therefore a surprise to everyone when he married Steph. While he posed in the sun, she worked as a chambermaid across the resort, providing her own special favours to hotel owners and guests throughout the morning in vacant suites. But once the holiday season ended, there was nothing to do – and infidelity as a lifestyle was insufficient to continue a marriage, particularly now that the initial excitement had waned. In less than one year they went their separate ways and eventually divorced.

After Rod Fletcher, Steph took a secretarial course and learned to type, a move which gave her contact with the professional classes. Whilst working in the Cowes Medical Centre, she met Andrew Pumpkin, who would go on to become her second husband.

Pumpkin was sixty-four and close to retirement when they married. He had *some* money but not what most people would consider a fortune. His first wife and children had taken the house and a big chunk of his wealth after she'd found out about an affair he'd had with an office girl. But he had enough to live in some style, with a generous income from private pension plans. He owned a duplex with a sea-view in Cowes, where in the yachting season he propped up the bar as a member of the Royal Cowes Yacht Club and mixed with the sailing celebrities who'd attend from all over the world, including, sometimes, even royalty.

Andrew's status and lifestyle suited the twenty-eight year old Steph. As a prominent – though young – Island solicitor's wife, she climbed the social ladder and managed to escape from the working class environment in which she had been brought up, even losing many of the tell-tale habits that showed she was not born into money.

Despite this, she did not throw off her tarty manner completely, and amongst her new husband's friends she always seem to convey the impression that she was available whenever an opportunity arose. She discovered quickly – and to her enjoyment – that the legal profession on the Island was both a tight-knit and intensely promiscuous community.

Andrew Pumpkin had quite openly married her for sex, and, as a near-pensioner – to be looked after by somebody with energy who could cook and clean. It was one of his greater misjudgements. He soon found out that not only was she a lousy cook and didn't care about cleaning, but was also completely uninterested in sex with 'an old geezer', as she referred to him. He was therefore completely neglected in the marriage.

Steph, simply, was an exploite*r*, not the exploit*ed* and so the relationship with Andrew Pumpkin became exactly what everybody had expected it to become; he with no more control over her than the father of a rebellious teenage daughter, which was exactly how she behaved. They squabbled about everything, but mostly money, over which he had total control. His personal wealth had been reduced considerably by ex-wife number one, and he wasn't going to let that happen again.

Steph had given up her administrative work to enjoy her new life, as Pumpkin's income from pensions and investments was sufficient enough for her to do so. He had bought her a new car and they holidayed abroad as and when, but for Steph that wasn't enough. She wanted *all* of his money.

In Cowes, everybody knows everybody else's business. Many of Pumpkin's female clients had a genuine affection for him and were disturbed that he had married a person of Steph's age and true social standing. Furthermore they did not like the idea of Steph being able to read Pumpkin's personal client records, which by their very nature contained details of their marital problems – solicitors and doctors being the two professions to whom neglected partners tell all.

As a result of this unsurprising animosity, Pumpkin's own inclusion into the Island's social scene was drastically reduced. As he became less invited, so Steph was denied the pleasures of a good-time girl. Without being particularly subtle about her thoughts, she began to wonder how she might exit the marriage and get hold of her husband's cash at the same time.

Internally, Steph felt that she was trapped in a marriage that had promised to provide everything she had been looking for, but it had become claustrophobic beyond bearing, and she could no longer be herself. She was married to an old man living in a dead-and-alive hole with boring yachties.

Steph spent much of her spare time each day searching for sex partners, then when Pumpkin's day was over, found some enjoyment listening to him report on the private details of his clients' divorce actions. One day, during a lunchtime pub crawl, she met Chris West, a fish merchant, who listened to her tale and was prepared to help her extricate herself from Pumpkin.

***

"Steph's relationship with Chris West developed in the usual way and was only of mild interest – even to the gossips – until what happened to old Mr Pumpkin," said Janet, as she tucked into fish and chips, sitting opposite Bruno Peach in their usual table at Bentley's Fish Restaurant.

"Pumpkin's luxury duplex apartment in Cowes had a roof garden with 360 degree views. During Cowes week you could watch the yacht racing in the Solent, then turn around and view for miles across the Island itself, with its beautiful surrounding countryside. The eighteen tiled steps to the roof garden were fully external, because Pumpkin, who had built it himself, did not want a staircase in the centre of the lounge."

Janet went on to explain that Steph's relationship with West was, as always, common knowledge in the town. One afternoon she came home after a heavy, sex-filled lunchtime drinking session with West. Pumpkin was waiting for her on the roof garden, and as soon as she appeared, the two had a wild argument. He shouted at her that he had had enough, and went to climb down to go back in the house. But somehow he slipped on the top step and tumbled down the seventeen others onto to the tiled floor below. His neck was broken and he died instantly. On the steps and the handrail of the stairway were found traces of a high-viscosity motor oil which the police, after Steph told them how Pumpkin had been spending much of his time maintaining his classic 1966 MGB sports car, believed had left him unable to hold his balance properly when he went to descend the steps. They thought it was likely he had picked it up whilst working on the car earlier. When they examined the trainers Pumpkin was wearing when he fell, the soles were full of this oil – so that was case closed as far as the police were concerned.

"But would your ears prick up if I told you that the type of oil they found on the step, rail and trainers was not used for servicing a 1966 MGB?" Janet asked.

Bruno's fork stopped in mid-air, staying there until a blob of HP sauce dripped off and seemed to re-activate his capability of speech.

"Are you *sure*? Who told you that?" he asked.

"Yes, and no one. Due to a public outcry at the time, the coroner's report was made available, and they still had a copy at the local library. I just seem to have studied it more closely than anyone else did."

"Go on..."

"Well, the analysis of the oil in the report stated that it was a formula known as SP104L. I called Gilbert Wright, the father of one of the schoolchildren, who happens to run the Island's classic car club and asked him a few questions about motor oils. As it turns out, SP104L would be a bad choice for anyone working on a 1966 MGB. In fact, SP104L has a very specific use. It is rather a specialist oil, extremely slippery, and is only used in a particular situation – lubricating a kind of two-stroke engine that is required to run for a significant amount of time – like a lawnmower engine, but a bit more advanced. Definitely not the same as any of the oils required for the MG."

"Maybe it was the only oil at the garage when Pumpkin went there?"

"Maybe... but Gilbert knows a whole lot about oil. The only vehicle he could think of on the Island that would use it would be a refrigerated Mercedes van, for which the two-stroke engine drives the cooling unit."

Janet purposefully left a pause here.

"A refrigerated van like the one Chris West delivered his fish in."

Bruno finally put his fork down and began to smile.

"In my opinion," Janet said, "that's something worth looking into, surely? It all feels linked somehow, like there are parallels here – either with Sam's death or that of Stanley Musgrove. I think that if you investigate Pumpkin's death, it may well help you see something you're missing in the other two."

"It will be harder to investigate Pumpkin's death now, because it was never classed as a murder investigation," said Bruno.

"But this is new evidence, so mightn't it be easier?" asked Janet. "One of the school mothers used to pull pints in the Cowes pub that Steph and Chris West frequented. She told me about West; his company – Chris West (Fish and Meat Wholesaler) Ltd – delivered fresh fish and meat to hotels and restaurants all over the Island. He worked hard, made good money, and was ambitious. He had an excellent reputation and was well-liked with a young wife and two baby daughters. He was seen by most as physically attractive and was, of course, a target for Steph the moment she set eyes on him. He did not succumb to her charms at first, though. It was some time before circumstances gave her an opportunity to seduce him. After an extended pub lunch, she headed over to his shop to buy fresh fish as he was closing. Wouldn't you know, that conversation led to him giving her a lift home. With Pumpkin's evening appointments finishing at eight pm, she had a couple of hours to get to know him. That's how it began."

This degree of thoroughness Bruno admired in Janet.

The detectives involved at the time did not treat the Pumpkin death as a crime; to all intents and purposes it looked to them like an elderly gentleman fell down some steps and died. Almost an everyday occurrence. It had every appearance of an accident, so they were not searching for a killer.

"If the steps were oily and he wasn't expecting it, she could have stood behind him and pushed – that's all it would have taken," said Janet. "He would have been habitually careful on those steps if working on his car meant slippery trainers – but that wasn't the case. The slipperiness from the oil was totally unexpected."

"Janet," Bruno asked, "are you suggesting Chris West was part of the plan to murder Pumpkin?"

"Not strictly, Steph may have used him somehow", Janet replied.

"She could have asked him to get her a can of engine oil without saying why," Bruno contributed, his neurons really firing now.

"Quite," agreed Janet. "She carried on living in the apartment, seeing Chris at every opportunity, until she sold it and moved away. Three years later she married Stanley, the butcher. After he was murdered and she obtained probate on Stanley's estate, she sold the butchers shop—"

Another pause...

"—to Chris West Ltd (Fish and Meat Wholesalers)."

Bruno felt that Janet had discovered some truly interesting facts concerning Steph and Chris West, but even though they needed looking into, it wasn't *conclusive* proof of their involvement in the murders of Andrew Pumpkin or Stanley Musgrove.

"Does what I've told you make West a suspect though?" asked Janet.

"Possibly, perhaps as an accessory to Pumpkin's murder, but even if the scenario played out as we both suspect it did, he could still have innocently supplied her with the oil," Bruno stated.

"Yes," Janet agreed, "Did he slip like the coroner concluded? No, he must have been pushed! And surely she'd oiled the steps to make them dangerous? You could re-open the case now. *And* the Godshill butcher's case now there's the information about the sale!"

"I approve of your enthusiasm," Bruno said to Janet, rather affectionately for once, "but I'm pretty sure I'd be told to wait until we have found Sam Peters' killer," Bruno replied.

Despite the words he spoke, the fact that Chris West, Steph's lover, had acquired the butcher's premises firmly planted the possibility in Bruno's mind, that perhaps, at last, the Godshill butcher's killer might be brought to justice. A land registry search would reveal the consideration paid by West for the shop and his financial records would hopefully show if any money had changed hands between Chris West Ltd and Steph herself.

Conversation returned to the more recent murder, and Janet persuaded Bruno that it was worth returning to Harris and his mysterious house, situated only a few yards from where Peters' body was found.

"Make sure he answers this time, but don't talk about the house, get him talking about if there were any *other* applications for planning approval to mine gold on the Island... and if so, from whom were they?"

Janet was now clearly enjoying playing detective. "Give Harris the impression that *he's* the one to trust," she said, "and he might tell you something intended to lead you *away* from himself, if he's involved, and that could be just as useful as something true. You're *nearly* there, I can feel it."

Bruno had his doubts, however. For all the connections they'd made, nothing was falling into place particularly well. There could well be a reason for killing Peters they hadn't even considered yet, and by person or persons not even on Bruno's list.

"You're not like those fictional detectives, who find a string of clues that gradually lead you to the killer, *you* have to work at it," she said.

"They succeed because they're fictional," said Bruno. "I, on the other hand am a copper with an average brain and a few O-levels who served his time on the beat and was promoted because of the time I've been on the force, not because I'm *officer* smart. I'm a normal, lower-middle-class average copper. Why is it that all those fictional detectives are toffs?" Bruno asked, only half-comically. "And that Poirot is the biggest toff of them all!"

He took a deep breath, then continued, a little calmer now, but still on a similar train of thought.

"Did you know that Arthur Conan Doyle lived within walking distance of Sam Peters' apartment in Southsea?" he asked Janet.

"Well then, perhaps Sherlock Holmes will pay you a visit and help out," Janet replied with a smile.

"Watson might," said Bruno.

"Did *you* know that Agatha Christie wrote her books starting from the end and worked her way back to the beginning?" Janet asked.

"No," said Bruno, sipping another glass of Chablis, "Tell me about it."

He only half paid attention to the story she was telling; the other half of him was thinking what a lovely woman Janet was, and how enjoyable the rest of the evening would be now they'd moved on from talking about the case.

Chapter 19

The following Monday morning at 10:00 am, Bruno, accompanied by Tom Craven, met Arnold Harris. He appeared to be in his early fifties, around medium height, and had a grey complexion that matched the colour of his hair. He did not smile naturally and his demeanour supported Sam Peters' description of him: arrogant, self-important, and disrespectful of other people's time. Sam's diary had noted that Harris had kept him waiting thirty minutes once for an appointment – at least he was punctual with Bruno.

As soon as the man approached reception from the back office, Bruno recognised him as the man he had seen hiding in the semi-darkness at the rear of the ground floor of the house opposite the bridge at Beacon Alley.

From his manner, Bruno suspected that Harris remembered the detectives' call to his house when he'd deliberately stepped into that dark corner. Did he now regret not answering the door after so many knocks? How much relevance was there between that reluctance and this incident? Given that Bruno was investigating a murder which had either taken place – or at the very least had been *discovered* – literally on his doorstep, how stupid was it of Harris *not* to have responded to what could surely only have been routine enquiry?! Perhaps he was certain he had not been seen by Bruno, and had been content to watch him eventually go away.

Under any normal circumstances, surely most people would have realised Bruno would only have wanted to know if, from the house, the owner had seen anyone acting suspiciously on the evening of the murder? A simple yes or no would have probably satisfied an initial enquiry, and the location of the property alone didn't imply that its occupants were involved with the nearby murder.

As he did not want it to unsettle his intended interviewee, Bruno did his best to conceal his recognition of Harris.

"Mr Harris?"

A nod and a quiet "Yes?"

"I am DI Bruno Peach, the detective in charge of the investigation into the murder of Sam Peters; this is my colleague DC Tom Craven. I understand that you had some contact with Mr Peters regarding his geological explorations. I'd like for you to tell me about those discussions as we believe that Mr Peters' murder could be connected."

"I can't tell you anything," Harris said, immediately nervous and defensive. "We had two meetings about the permissions he would need to search for treasure on local farmland. I gave him the forms to fill in, and advised him that he'd have more chance of a successful application if he could show an interest other than plundering the Island of its rightful treasures... which is what I tell *every* treasure hunter that comes to the Island, thank you. These people *find* a lot, you know, but they only *declare* the really valuable items – things that are obviously treasure trove which they clearly couldn't sell without revealing chapter and verse the exact details of their discovery."

Harris licked his lips and continued, "He brought in a Professor from Southampton University, so the local authority eventually gave permission over our land – meaning we had two of them prowling around. *I* voted against it, but the others felt it was OK. The rules *clearly* state that the authority would take a share of any discoveries, but neither of them came back with anything, did they? Terrible, isn't it Inspector? You let these people roam all over your land, doing whatever they want to do, yet they never come back, do they? Stealing really, isn't it? Anything else?" Harris finished, seemingly pleased to have got all of that off his chest.

"Is there anything you can tell us about Peters or his associate, Professor Bartlett?"

"Nothing more than that they got their permissions in the end and off they went."

"Were they happy when you told them that?"

"I believe so."

"I understand that you recommended Mr Peters to speak to a solicitor, a Mr Noway?" Bruno asked, for the first time revealing he knew a little more than Harris probably suspected of his dealings with the two men.

"I did," he said cautiously. "He asked about going onto private farmland, so I advised him to speak with an Island land lawyer. Noway is a specialist in that area."

"Understood. So... what did you *think* of Peters?"

Harris considered his answer carefully and replied, "I must say I just don't get them. Treasure hunters, that is. Searching in weather so bad that no honest or sane person would dare to. That's how they get away with finding stuff they don't declare, it's the only reason you'd be out there."

"Has anyone else – apart from Peters and Bartlett – made an application for geological exploration on the Island?

After a slight pause, Harris responded, "Yes. A man called Derek Bentley."

"Is that so?"

"Yes. An application was made on his behalf by a London-based company called Hamdens."

"Do you know the reason for his application?"

"Well, Hamdens are a mining company, so I'd say that's your answer."

Bruno filed this fact under 'very interesting'.

"Do you have a personal view about mining on the Island, Mr Harris?"

"I do not believe it would be a good idea."

"Why not? Surely money would start gushing in, especially to your department?"

"There would be prosperity for the mine owners and even the miners, but they'd need specialist skills and would no doubt be brought over from the mainland. A venture like that would be unlikely to provide any long-term benefits to anyone local, yet there's plenty of unemployed men capable of learning," he said, some truths apparent in his analysis. "And when the mining finishes, what would be left behind? A vast area of unsightly craters and wasteland, any chance of topsoil or grass cover gone forever."

"A fair view, I suppose." Bruno replied. This alternative application was rather interesting, but there were more pressing questions he needed to ask.

"Do you know where Peters was killed?" asked Bruno, his copper's nose twitching now he was getting close to the issue of prime interest to him.

"No," said Harris. "I know where his body was found, but he could have been killed somewhere else, couldn't he? Anyway, it was under the bridge in Beacon Alley."

"Indeed. And if I'm right, you own the black house nearby."

"I do, although for the last ten years I've let it out to a couple, the Youngs – Hilary and Peter. They moved out at the beginning of summer.

They ran it as an overnight youth hostel for walkers; they advertised in hiker magazines. Did alright for the first few years but now the house is so worn out no one wanted to stay anymore. As soon as their tenancy was up this time, they left."

"Can I look inside the house?" said Bruno.

"Why?" asked Harris, unable to sound anything but defensive.

I'd like to know what can be seen from the house that you can't see from the road or river bank thought Peach, although he said, "It would help with the murder enquiry", knowing that this was a good enough answer for most people not to want to deny such a request.

"It's pretty much just as the Youngs left it," Harris said. "They've been gone a while – before the body was found, in fact – but I haven't got round to doing anything with it."

"So it was empty the day before the body was discovered?"

"It's been empty for two months, although I try to call over every so often to check it out. I worry it might get vandalised, or worse occupied by squatters."

"Why don't you live in it?"

"I am a single bachelor, Inspector, and to be honest I'd fear for my safety living there; the location gives me the creeps. Plus, it needs a woman's touch... and none of the women *I* know would touch it. I live in a nice apartment in Newport down by the Medina. My mother had wanted me to move into the black house before she died, but until recently I had a stable income from a good tenant; at the end of her life, mother was bed ridden so I couldn't live anywhere other than with her, anyway." Harris sighed, with genuine sadness there. "I'll show you the house at six this evening, after I finish here, if you like?"

Harris had been as helpful as he could and promised to bring with him contact details for Derek Bentley.

***

At 6:00 pm prompt, Harris drove up to the house and parked next to where Bruno had, on a gravelled piece of land large enough for both cars, in which a notice on a post displayed a 'Private Parking' sign that was ignored by everyone who fancied stopping to take a look at the picturesque bridge and river.

Harris and the detective greeted one another, and after the former had unlocked the farm gate leading to the front door of the property, walked the fifty metres or so to it and entered.

Inside it was cold and gloomy, furnished with the kind of tables, chairs and cupboards you'd have expected to find in a bed and breakfast hotel forty years ago. The kitchen had a hot plate for warming table crockery and keeping cooked food hot, the surface of which was large enough for a dozen plates. There was an old CRT TV in one corner of the lounge and a ragged, quarter-size billiard table in the centre. Prints of Scottish hill-scenes hung on the walls and a gas fire was set in a grate with a wooden fireplace surround on which was perched two wooden candle sticks. Doors opened onto the part of the garden that faced the boggy marsh area alongside the river.

The upstairs was equally uninviting. The five well-sized bedrooms were appointed with post-war utility furniture, some – incredibly – still with utility mark stickers affixed. In each room, it appeared that the wallpaper was from roughly the same period. There was no central heating, although three of the bedrooms had gas fires and two had open grates with fenders for coal burning. There was just the one bathroom and a second separate toilet. All three of the bedrooms at the front of the house had at least one window from which the bridge could be seen. If a body was being dragged along the bank on the eastern side, it would have been visible from these rooms. However, at the side over the lounge was the bathroom and unless the window was fully opened, the frosty glaze prevented anything from being seen.

Having dealt with the inside of the house, and having found no cooking pots containing severed heads, nor clothes fashioned from human flesh, Bruno decided to take a stroll around the gardens, ever accompanied by a politely attentive and not particularly nervous Harris.

Bruno's pleasant perambulation in the summer sun again revealed absolutely nothing that could be connected with a murder, and after a little small-talk about the weather, Bruno thanked Harris, returned to his car and left.

As he drove, Bruno thought about Harris, his upbringing, his lifestyle and that gloomy, forbidding house. On balance, his gut feeling was that Arnold Harris could be demoted down to the bottom of his list of suspects. He was a dull and precise man with a superiority complex, but he just didn't *feel* like a killer.

Chapter 20

Despite the huge commitment to work that a good headmistress must always show, even during the school holidays, Janet had managed to find time to continue her own research into the death of Andrew Pumpkin.

What had nagged at her the most was the fact that the same few people were involved in one way or another in at least two of the three killings. These were Steph – widow of Andrew Pumpkin and Stanley Musgrove, the 'Godshill Butcher', Chris West, Steph's 'bit on the side' at the time of Pumpkin's death, and the man who bought (and at what knock-down price?) Musgrove's butcher's shop, and the Potters, with Sonia being Steph's sister, Dick recently having joined Sam Peters' circle of contacts, and both of them quick to the scene of Stanley's Death after Steph's call. Was there something sinister going on, or were they just a particularly unlucky group of people?

At her evening 'meal-meeting' with Bruno, having covered the usual pleasantries, Janet spoke of her concerns.

"Is Dick Potter a suspect in Peters' killing?" she asked.

"Yes, he's still a potential suspect," said Bruno.

"What about the indirect contacts we've talked about – Noway, Bartlett, Harris and the chap from Hamdens?"

"No, none of them are still on my list."

"They *should* be until you can completely eliminate them," she said. "Look, I know you're focused on Peters' murder, but can't you spare a day to look back at Pumpkin's death? Let's go to Cowes tomorrow and look at his apartment." She said, a driving energy in her voice. "I've said it before, if the murders are related, you might just find something out that helps you make progress in your current case."

"You ask if I can spare a day; what about you?" Bruno asked, but kindly. "Haven't you school work to prepare?"

"It's the holidays so I can afford to take one day out for my own interests. Listen, you've been working non-stop, I've been thinking hard of ways to help you... let's keep up that momentum but just switch tracks for a day. You must be getting pretty tired, especially when you're not making much progress... and a change is as good as a rest, isn't it?"

Chapter 21

The following morning Bruno and Janet drove to The Esplanade in Cowes, to visit the duplex property previously owned by Andrew Pumpkin, from which after climbing the external steps to the roof garden one could see the Royal Cowes Yacht club and a great deal more.

Having parked a few doors down, the two approached the apartment and – both being observant types, Bruno by profession and Janet naturally so – mentally compared what they saw to the information Bruno had shown Janet earlier from the police file on the case. Although not strictly protocol, he'd borrowed the physical file itself, calling in a favour from the current archive officer. Printing the documents off would have been much easier, but would have also flagged up the action on the system. With a current important assignment underway, and the fact he was acting on a hunch which wasn't even his, he thought it best not to have to get involved in any police politics and explain to the higher-ups why he was now looking at a closed case of accidental death.

The most obvious difference from the photos and description in the file was that the present owners had enclosed the staircase, which had in Andrew Pumpkin's time been fully exposed. In addition to that, various minor improvements had been made to the exterior of the property as you would very much expect when considering its current worth.

Shortly after Bruno knocked on the door, it was opened by a woman who, from her well-to-do appearance – he guessed was the current owner.

"Hello. I'm Detective Inspector Bruno Peach," the detective said, showing his card clearly, "and this is—"

Bruno was used to inserting a police rank at this point, but with a civilian in tow – not really the done thing – he simply skipped any kind of descriptor. Thankfully, he thought, he didn't pause long enough for any noticeable doubt to sound in the age-old police introduction.

"—Janet Gibson."

"Yes?" asked the woman, inquisitively.

"It's nothing to worry about," continued Janet and went on to explain about Pumpkin's *accident*; despite her own thoughts, she used the word in consideration of the fact that most people didn't want to live in a house where a murder had occurred.

When she had finished, Bruno took back over.

"I'm currently investigating a murder that occurred near Niton, and knowing a little more about the accident could potentially help solve the case," he said. Not a word they had spoken was untrue, although the police ethics team might have had something to say about it.

However, the woman was perfectly happy to help; she introduced herself as Mrs Helen Lever and confirmed that she was indeed the current owner. She invited her two visitors into her beautifully arranged property, led them up to the first floor and through to the rear, stopping at the staircase that led to the roof garden.

"When the accident happened, these steps weren't carpeted," said Bruno, more to Janet than the owner, although it was the latter who responded.

"Yes, it was one of the first things we had done," she said. "They're tiled underneath and even on a nice day can get really cold. Not very nice if you're not wearing shoes! Would you like some coffee?"

"Please," Janet and Bruno said in unison.

"Of course. Well if it's OK I'll leave you to go on up and I'll follow shortly. It's unlocked at the top, just turn the latch on the door and it'll open."

"Thank you," replied Janet.

It was a beautiful warm sunny early morning and the view from the roof was spectacular. There were chairs, sunshades and a gas barbecue under a canopy. The stair carpet finished at the top of the stairs with a metal strip.

Whilst Helen was making the coffee, Bruno and Janet took great care to inspect the staircase, which felt even steeper in real life that the photo of it in the file conveyed. Descending, one would definitely need to grip the handrail for stability; it was set into the main wall of the house and was obviously the original installed by Pumpkin, matching as it did the one in the photograph.

At the top of the staircase, Bruno noted that the tread was non-standard, and the top of the step was too high by almost an inch."

Pointing to it he said, "Careful, that's obviously dangerous to anyone of *our* age, let alone a pensioner!"

"Mmm," agreed Janet, "a light shove in the back would send you tumbling, especially if you were wearing slippery shoes..."

Helen soon brought up coffee and cream, and the three chatted pleasantly in the morning sun. The mood sobered a little when she told them that her husband had passed away the previous year before Cowes week, and that this autumn she would move away; but Janet skilfully brought the conversation back round to more pleasant details. Soon, Bruno explained that they'd better be on their way and the three all said their goodbyes.

* * *

Janet suggested that their next task should be to discover the whereabouts of Chris West, the Cowes fisherman. Six months after Pumpkin's death – and just one week after Steph had sold the duplex for £165,000 – he bought a pub in Freshwater called *The Crab,* situated right next to the passenger ferry terminal to Lymington. Land Registry records showed that the cost of the pub was £90,000; this matched the £30,000 West had raised from the sale of the lease on his fish business in Cowes with a £60,000 contribution from Steph Pumpkin. Steph's share had been organised by Pumpkin's old law firm who'd undertaken the probate work for his estate. The records detailed Steph's share clearly, and Bruno wondered what kind of arrangement this had been. Did she receive an income from the business, or was it a property investment? Steph had also purchased a two-bed seafront apartment in Freshwater for £90,000.

"So they didn't move in together?" Bruno asked.

"My understanding is that West was already married with a wife and two kids, and anyway Steph aspired to better things," replied Janet. "After all, she'd been married to a solicitor and had acquired a small fortune. Remember, three years later she meets and marries the comfortably-off and widowed Stanley Musgrove."

"So the big question is *where is Chris West now*?" stated Bruno.

"I'm looking into that, don't you worry!" said Janet, playfully. "Bruno, I know all this might just be coincidences and half-connections, but let's keep it all in mind until something shines through and shows us the way. I'm confident it will. I honestly think that the answer to your Godshill Butcher's murder case is in these little details *somewhere*. And I want to find his killer for you!"

Bruno did not question her assertion; he knew that she could see a great deal that he himself could not. He was good at his job, and had caught more than his fair share of serious criminals, but even *he* admitted he always did so by good old slow, steady, solid footwork. Not for him the giant leaps of Sherlockian imagination. Bruno solved his crimes through hard work and doing things by the book. And that's why he turned to Janet whenever the book didn't have all the answers. In many ways, Bruno felt he learned more how to be a better detective from Janet than from anywhere else.

With Bruno's approach, it was often true that gut feeling made up for any deficiencies in his creative thinking. But a good detective wants more than just gut feeling, and when it came to Janet, she was a true artist in this area. Having known nothing about Andrew Pumpkin just a few days ago, his life to Bruno had been a blank canvas. Now, Janet was painting it with detail, and Bruno was starting to feel the same connection that Janet could.

Chapter 22

Today was the day that Bruno had to give a progress report to Superintendent Barlow. As expected, the Super was unimpressed.

Bruno was now into the second week of the Sam Peters' murder case and all he had was a handful of possible suspects, and wasn't even sure he had them in the right order.

Despite the fact that he'd been working flat-out, Bruno was concerned that it sounded like he'd done almost nothing, so he decided to flesh out his progress report by mentioning the Pumpkin death and the Godshill Butcher case.

Barlow had listened to Bruno's recollections of these two historical deaths with a measure of irritation. In his eyes, any potential connection between Sam Peters' murder and the earlier cases was not strong enough to counter his suspicion that Bruno was lost and desperate. Let sleeping dogs lie. The Godshill butcher was murdered by a person or persons unknown, and the Cowes doctor's death was a coroner certified accident.

Bruno had expected Barlow's response to be one of irritability and had not been surprised. He was, however, slightly wrong-footed by the fact that after hearing his summary, Barlow asked Bruno for specific details on a number of key elements of the case. This led to the two of them spending a solid amount of time discussing the various strands – those which were factual at least – and Bruno was somewhat happier to think that the Super at least understood why the case was proving a tricky one on which to make progress.

"Noway," Barlow said. "It sounds to me like he is where you're most likely going to find your breakthrough. Do you consider him a suspect?"

"I haven't written anyone off yet, Bruno lied.

Johnny Barlow, or JB as he was sometimes called (although not usually in his presence) was a career policeman from Southampton. Aged just thirty-two, he had joined the police from University on an accelerated promotion scale; being the top copper on the Island was his first step to becoming Chief Constable on the Hampshire force. Most of the staff under him – many of which were a fair bit older – admitted that he brought intelligence and a kind of computer-brain analysis toward solving crimes, but also felt that he lacked hands on experience. Barlow genuinely liked Bruno and saw him as a hard working detective, albeit one without star quality. Similarly Bruno liked and respected JB.

"Bruno," Barlow said, "I think if you sat down with all of this and went through it from the start with a completely fresh brain, you'd come to same conclusion that I have this morning: you need to put some real pressure on Noway to find out what he's still hiding – because I'm sure that there's something. And you know that the two main motives for a crime like this are money and women. You've been looking into the money angle, but what about the other? It might lead nowhere, but you're missing a trick if you don't get to the bottom of Peters' relationship with Phyllida Glassman."

***

That afternoon Bruno, with a clearly renewed vigour, picked up Tom, and the two turned up at Noway's office unannounced. Bruno exuded an aura of command that had somewhat faded over the last couple of weeks, but that was always an important facet of a successful detective's persona. Tom suspected he'd either figured something important out or had received the tongue-lashing of a lifetime, but was too smart to ask if he was right in case it was the latter.

"I'd like to know your own interests on the Island – all of them." Bruno asked Noway. Not a request, more of a polite demand. "I want to know who you mix with, what you do in your spare time, and anything else you can tell me that will convince me that I should take you off my narrowing suspect list." With these last few words, Bruno tapped his top pocket.

Noway, clearly somewhat surprised, told them that he was a member of Ryde Golf Club, a nine hole course on the hillside at the back of Ryde. He owned a half-share in a 25-foot sailing boat with a local builder which was moored at Wooton Creek. He lived with Marilyn, his partner, in a six-bed house with sea frontage in Bembridge. In her mid-forties, she was an artist who worked from her home studio modelling sculptures and painting seascapes which she sold year-round from a small lock-up shop in Bembridge High Street. Marilyn was well known around Bembridge (for the *right* reasons, he assured them), pretty, petite and absorbed with pretty much any artistic project that took place on the Island. Besides working in the shop, she organised local art exhibitions, the art club, Island fêtes, and twice-yearly art sales from her beautiful garden. Noway, who had a quiet, listening-type personality, was always on hand to help her with her activities and they occupied a prominent place in local Island society. It was these activities that took up much of his time.

Finally, and with some pride, Noway explained to the detectives that he was President of Shanklin cricket club, where he not only got his sporting fix, but also met the kind of businessmen who proved useful contacts.

"OK, that's a start," said Bruno. "Now, I'm trying to build up a picture of *everyone* connected with Sam Peters' venture on the Island. Who can you tell me about?"

"It was a small circle," said Noway. "You can ignore the landowners if you want my opinion. Wisely, Peters involved the Island's geology expert, Professor Noel Bartlett, from Southampton University, and then there is the man Potter, who has been working the riverbanks. He has an agreement which guarantees him a share of whatever gains the partnership produces, which, with Peters gone, should be larger."

"OK..." Bruno said, in a leading manner.

"Personally, I'd say hiring Potter was a mistake for a hobbyist, but then I suppose Peters didn't want to do the hard work. Or maybe he had his eyes on the bigger prize. Regardless, if he was planning a commercial venture then he *could* and *should* have worked with the landowners, who in law are entitled to a substantial share of anything found on their land. All of it, in fact, if they had chosen to deny him access. Greed can be any person's bedfellow."

Bruno could tell Noway was beginning to open up, and did the best thing possible to keep the flow going – he remained silent.

"The three of them had an agreement which they all signed. Bartlett was actually the third to sign it. From what *I* know, he was *not* interested in panning metal shards from the bottom of the East Yar river. The money might have been nice, but professionally, that means nothing to him. I imagine he'd have been perfectly happy not to be involved with any of that, leaving Potter to enjoy any proceeds. Bartlett discovered where the quartz lies and *that* is the big prize in all senses. It will enhance his reputation as a geologist and explorer, *and* will pay him big bucks, which he has no reason to share with Potter."

Noway's tone became a little conspiratorial suddenly.

"The *big* winner in this venture is likely to be Bartlett, Inspector. Take a closer look at *him*," suggested Noway, almost as if they were asking him for advice rather than questioning a suspect.

Tom brought the conversation back to Noway's contacts, and despite the solicitor's suggestion to ignore the landowners, pressed him on the issue.

Eventually, Noway admitted that he'd completed work for Derek Bentley, the actual owner of the land where the quartz deposits lay.

"After being contacted by Peters and Bartlett, Hamdens applied to the council for permission to survey the land for mining purposes. However, the reply that they received from our council friend Mr Harris was that the land they were enquiring about was not actually council-owned, but belonged to Mr Bentley. They have since written to him, expressing an interest in surface mining a certain quartz vein that has been identified on his land."

"And your involvement is..?" asked Bruno.

"I'm handling Mr Bentley's official response – or at least will be at the relevant point in time."

"How well do you know Bentley?" asked Bruno.

"Not very well," said Noway. "Our dealings are formal rather than personal. I am expecting him to send me a copy of the contract when he receives it from Hamdens; I know he hasn't been sent it yet."

"Are Hamdens really confident enough in Bartlett's analysis to send Bentley a contract purely based on what he says?"

"I have no concerns about Hamdens; they have the right personnel to evaluate any evidence provided to them."

"So you're telling me that Bentley knows what is going on, except he *doesn't* know about the panning for gold in the East Yar?"

"That's because he lives in London. He has a mansion apartment in Paddington, where he stays during the week with his a girlfriend. At the weekend he generally comes over to the Island to spend time on his farm. He keeps Alpacas there as a hobby, in addition to developing a vineyard."

"Interesting man," said Bruno, his tone perfectly placed so Noway would be encouraged to continue.

"He has a big passion for cricket. During the winter season, wherever in the world England are playing test matches be that the West Indies, South Africa, Australia, Sri Lanka... *that's* where he will be."

"What business is he in?" asked Tom.

"Pensions insurance. He is an actuary by profession. His company administers pension funds on behalf of blue chip internationals – it's a very successful business. His farmland purchases are made to offset certain tax burdens, so he says."

He buys farmland to escape tax, so he says."

"Sounds like *you* think there's another reason?" Bruno suggested.

"Not really. When you make a lot of money you indulge your fantasies. I am his Island solicitor, and so I conduct some of his business over here, but he'll employ a London firm for anything that's not on the Island. Before deciding on whether to enter into a contract with Hamdens, he'd have considered the tax implications, and any effect that gold mining might have on his Island investments, you can be sure of that. He'd also want to be invisible as far as legality allows him, leaving *them* to handle the publicity of any environmental issues. If an agreement was imminent, one would think Hamdens would be ahead of the game, making some kind of press announcement at the very least... but there hasn't been a peep on that front. I just don't think the idea would interest him. He's not on the Island to *make* money."

"Go on," Bruno said encouragingly, feeling he was getting closer to *something*.

"His two main interests are to create a rare breed through carefully planned husbandry, and to use the *terroir* on his land to create a spectacular wine to challenge even the best France has to offer – although he hasn't had the time to start that project yet. Still, he's young enough that there's still plenty of time to get round to it."

"So, apart from owning the farm and the land on the Downs, has he any *other* connection with the Island? I'd be fascinated to know what brought him here," said Bruno.

"Nothing in particular that *I* know of," replied Noway, somewhat dismissively.

After a brief pause to see if Noway would expand on this – which he didn't – Bruno returned to his previous train of thought. "Can we talk about the other landowners the Peters trio instructed you to contact?" he asked, with a firm enough tone to strongly hint that 'no' was not an answer he'd accept this time.

A flash of a submissive smile, and Noway picked up a folder that he had obviously prepared for this line of questioning.

"All of them," Bruno stressed, ensuring Noway knew that any omissions would *not* go down well at all.

"Let me talk you through the names and explain a little of their backgrounds," Noway said, and did so quickly and professionally, offering just enough of a commentary to keep his interrogators happy. Nothing the solicitor said made any of them stand out; all were Island families going back three or four generations, with two whose local ancestry dated into the late nineteenth century.

"And *all* of them replied almost immediately to your letter requesting access for the purpose of treasure hunting?" Bruno asked.

"Yes, one hundred per cent response rate. That shouldn't surprise you though Inspector; they have been asked the same question before, probably numerous times – certainly once by me. Hobbyists with specialist equipment are forever asking for these kind of permissions, most searching for Roman relics. The landowners know that if the treasure hunters ask permission, they're the type that will stick to the rules – meaning they'll get their fair share of anything found. It's the ones who don't ask permission they're wary of. Dishonest treasure hunters are no more than thieves, and anyone stupid enough to try and sell a valuable hoard without the required provenance would be quickly discovered, swapping their find for a jail sentence no doubt.

From his knowledge of local history, Bruno recollected that two thousand years ago, the Romans were all over the Island – it was a thriving Imperial colony. He'd visited the Roman Villa at Brading, which demonstrates to visitors just how important the Island was to the Romans. Brading was a busy port back then; ships would sail in bringing supplies to the Island's farms, and taking away produce to the garrison towns along the mainland south coast. But that was then. Since they built the dam at Bembridge, Brading was now actually inland.

Snapping back to the present conversation, Bruno realised he was getting plenty of answers now, and despite his excitement about the progress he was making, managed to keep his questioning calm, lest Noway close up on him for whatever reason.

"What do you know about Arnold Harris?"

"As I mentioned to you before, I know he still harbours a desire to buy his half-brother's estate, but he's got no chance. The estate itself doesn't generate an income anywhere near enough to support the kind of borrowing he'd need – there's not a lot one can do with such a windswept, uneven, exposed marshy area. It's also nowhere near the quartz outcrop, so that can't offer him any hope either.

"Would Harris *know* about the Quartz?" asked Tom.

"Surely," replied Noway. "In his local authority capacity, it would have been down to him to reply to Hamdens. As part of their own planning they'd have needed to write to the council to enquire about permissions regarding mining on the Downs."

A raised eyebrow from Bruno hinted to Noway that he considered this an interesting revelation for his murder enquiry.

"Oh, no, inspector. Arnold is not a fan of treasure hunters, but I don't believe the fact that Peters and his colleagues were looking into the quartz seam themselves would have been of the slightest bit of interest to him."

Bruno nodded, and decided to approach the last subject on his mental list.

"Can you tell me anything about Phyllida Glassman?"

"Mrs Glassman has been my client since her husband died. I will handle the disposal of Roud Farm when she obtains probate."

"You know of her relationship with Sam Peters?"

"Yes, insofar as Mr Peters asked me to write a new will in which *she* was his sole beneficiary. We did not discuss her, nor his relationship with her; I just did as I was asked."

"Do you have his will?"

"Yes, it is in his file."

"I'd like to see it, please."

"Ah," Noway replied. "I'm afraid that my secretary has gone home for today and she keeps the key on her own keyring as she uses it so often. I *do* have one myself at home, but goodness knows where. I will send you a copy in the morning. If you need anything else, please do tell me."

Handshakes all round were followed by polite 'goodbyes', and the detectives left Noway to his work.

***

Bruno and Tom agreed that although he was obviously an interesting character for a number of reasons, there was nothing specific about Bentley, the landowner, to connect him with Peters' murder. However, Professor Bartlett, whom both had previously considered open and honest in their meetings with him, now seemed to warrant further investigation.

Bruno took out the copy of the CV Bartlett had given to Sam Peters from the police file. His geological work seemed to commence in his mid-twenties when he spent six years working for a Texan company called *Geological Oil and Gas,* with Bartlett responsible for mapping and exploring the sea bed, mostly in the North and South Atlantic Ocean,. Here he had worked on small ships in relatively shallow coastal waters for months on end, using sonic equipment to bounce radio waves off the ocean bed and using his geological knowledge to identify where oil and gas most likely lay beneath the sea bed. These maps were then used at the next stage by the company's divers to drill exploratory bore holes to confirm whether the sites did in fact contain suitable reserves.

Geological Oil and Gas had three exploration vessels, with two always at sea allowing maintenance to be carried out on the third. These three ships were named after the three ships Christopher Columbus took on his famous voyage – the *Nino,* the *Pinto* and the *Santa Maria.*

The six years Bartlett had spent at GOG was split four months at sea then two months shore leave. The pay was excellent, almost certainly more than a newly-qualified geologist could make anywhere else. This, supplemented by bonuses for hitting targets for correctly-identified sites, enabled him to save enough money to buy a house in a nice part of the New Forest, before marrying and starting at Southampton University as a Geology lecturer.

Sam Peters had clearly done his background work; a report obtained from Geological Oil & Gas had been filed with the CV itself and related to an incident that took place at the company during Bartlett's time there.

The *Santa Maria* had been returning from a three-month voyage searching the sea bed in the Gulf of Mexico. A substantial oil deposit had been discovered. Its precise depth and location had been recorded by the captain in the ship's log. But at some point along the return journey, the folder containing the vital charts and reports about the deposit belonging to the chief geologist, Alan Kemp, had seemingly gone missing. The loss was in fact only discovered soon after the ship returned to her home port of Portsmouth, Chesapeake Bay, USA, when Kemp's dead body was discovered floating in the sea nearby in an apparent suicide. The folder's loss was noted when investigators made an inventory of paperwork from his cabin, and the captain had spotted the lack of such an important folder on the list. When the investigation into the death was complete however, the police could find no proof that the documents' disappearance was directly linked to Kemp's death.

Without the charts from the folders, the company would have faced serious financial trouble – there was always heavy pressure to make the most from each voyage, so to have spent so long identifying one large deposit and then not being able to return to its now-forgotten location would have been disastrous.

But one month later, Bartlett, who had been present on the Santa Maria during Kemp's last voyage, re-created the journey they had made, and – miraculously to some – pinpointed the exact position of the oil deposit. He explained that it was no miracle; he had accurately recorded sun positions on the day of the discovery and used that, along with other notes, to calculate to within less than one minute of accuracy, the location of the 'lost' oil find. Bartlett was rewarded handsomely for his work and over time the awfulness of the entire episode faded from everyone's memory... but not the company files.

The officially-accepted explanation of the whole incident was, to some, open to doubt. Although there was no *direct* proof of anything untoward as such, the strange loss of the investigation chart, the suicide of the chief geologist who lost it, and the remarkable rediscovery of the location by his assistant against normally accepted navigational process, was certainly enough to create suspicion.

News concerning the *Santa Maria*'s voyage and loss of a crew member did not go down well with the longer-standing members of the oil-search industry – a wary, close-knit community that often surpassed company rivalries. Although Bartlett was exonerated, the fact that vital exploration data had gone missing, yet he had re-created it, receiving a large reward resulted in muted but widely repeated conversations expressing suspicion at Kemp's officially-not-linked death.

Of course, there were two ways the majority of people viewed Kemp's death. The first was that he had himself lost the file; perhaps he'd been making additional notes and in a freak accident the folder had been blown clear of the ship from wherever he was working. He had thus taken his own life knowing that he'd likely soon be sacked for his error. Opponents of this theory pointed out how unlikely such a scenario was, especially for an experienced seagoing professional such as Kemp... although in response others said if he was *that* professional he'd have had backup copies of everything.

The second explanation was that a member of the wider crew had stolen the folder in the hope of selling it to a competitor for a fortune. From this particular viewpoint, many thought it possible that the person who stole the map might have killed Kemp, throwing him overboard after being found in his study taking the file.

***

Interestingly, the *Santa Maria* incident did not seem to have disturbed Sam Peters, because although he had kept a copy of it with the CV, he made absolutely no reference to it anywhere in his diary.

Bruno, having read the entire report now, thought hard about it. Kemp's death was certainly suspicious (not *another* one, an inner voice of his commented), but before setting out on the re-creation voyage, Bartlett would have had to have convinced the senior management at GOG that not only did he have evidence of his sun measurements, but also that they had a very strong chance of helping to find the deposit again; there was no way that another four-month trip would be funded if he hadn't presented pretty compelling evidence, and pulling out the missing file would certainly have resulted in a different outcome!

He was also still pretty convinced that Bartlett was not responsible for Sam's murder. The main reason for this was simply exclusion by location – according to all information he had obtained, Bartlett was not on the Island on the day of the murder, nor was he aware of Sam's whereabouts at the time.

As he dropped Tom off to make his way back across to the mainland, Bruno experience an unusual dichotomy of feelings – his gut feeling told him that the conversation with Noway had filled out his knowledge greatly, so much so to the extent that he felt he was at least facing in the right direction. But at the same time, he still had not one meaningful clue, not a single piece of real evidence that led him to any one killer in particular.

***

That evening, Janet, who seemed to be devoting all her spare time and energy to her amateur sleuthing, told Bruno that she had some important information about the older cases that they had discussed.

"You remember Chris West, the Cowes fishmonger?" she asked, more to ensure that she had Bruno's attention that there being any danger he'd forgotten.

Bruno nodded.

"Well, I found out what happened to him after buying the pub."

"Go on," Bruno prompted.

"Well, remember that the pub was bought with the funds from the sale of West's old fishmonger business along with some of Steph's money from the sale of her dead husband's Cowes property?" she continued. "Things didn't go too well there. It wasn't long before his heavy drinking got in the way of his ability to manage the business successfully, and he began to build up serious debts. In the end, the pub gets sold to cover those debts, and Chris West disappears for a while."

"Interesting, but it doesn't really surprise me given what you've told me of his character," Bruno commented.

"True. But when he next turns up, that's the key. Despite the fact that a few months before he'd got no money, the records show that he purchased the Butcher's business – from Steph – and at market value nonetheless. That business was never offered through an agent, it appears it was a done deal."

"So we've got a very suspicious purchase there, haven't we?" Bruno agreed.

"Yes, but *think* about it. There's a clear link between the two deaths now. We've said that we both *feel* that's the case, but can't put our fingers on exactly what it is. Well, the link is that on both occasions it is Chris West and Stephanie who share the spoils. Neither time does Steph take everything she has and use it purely for her own means; both times the fortune that befalls her from the *mis*fortune of the death of a husband is *shared between the two of them.*"

For some reason, to Bruno, this didn't feel like quite as big a revelation as perhaps it did to Janet. Admittedly though, he was having difficulty absorbing anything not related to the Peters case since his meeting with JB, which although had been more positive that he'd thought it would be, had ended with a firm expectation that the case would be tied up pretty soon.

Despite his slight lack of excitement, Bruno respected and trusted Janet, and it was her who convinced him to leave a breakdown of their new discoveries about the Pumpkin and Musgrove cases on the Super's desk for him to consider at his own pace.

The hope was that JB might reach a conclusion that the previous cases need to be looked at once again, but was more likely to accept this if he could be seen to be making the decision himself rather than convinced by a subordinate.

Politics, thought Bruno. Janet certainly knew how to play the game.

After they finished their meal and had said their 'goodnights', Bruno's thoughts wandered back to the Sam Peters case, specifically what lay in store for tomorrow. Earlier, he'd called Nick Hayes, the Managing

Director of Hamdens and suggested they meet on the Island. His plan was to get Hayes talking about the quartz seam – hopefully with a personalised tour. He and Tom would attempt to steer the conversation towards the financial side of the equation, and try and work out what would be in it, for who, and when.

He also decided that in the afternoon, seeing as he'd just *happen* to be in the area, he and Tom would see if Phyllida Glassman was at her farm.

Chapter 23

Wednesday 30ᵗʰ July

The next morning was bright and clear and upon their arrival at their destination on the edge of St. Catherine's Down, Nick Hayes stood and looked at the site, explaining how it would function as a fully-operational gold mine. He talked in expressive language that did a good job of describing to Bruno and Tom – neither of whom had ever seen a gold mine of any size, opencast or deep-mined – exactly how it would look. He spoke of the scale, of the infrastructure, of how many engineers would be needed to opencast mine the quartz rock; he described how the material would be transported by road via the ferry to the foundry on the south coast near Southampton. In describing the new road they planned between the site and the ferry port he told the detectives how it would need a solid ten-inch deep layered and strengthened surface to support the weight of the vehicles to ensure the longevity of its construction. He and his company had clearly prepared plenty of detail.

"So tell me, inspector," Hayes said when his oft-repeated pitch had come to a natural break and he had handed Bruno and Tom sketches of his vision. "What can I do for the Island police with regards to our plans?"

"Of the two people who brought you this scheme, one is dead – and for reasons that are not yet clear." said Bruno, looking closely for any reaction. "What I need from you is—" he thought about the next few words carefully, "—anything interesting you can tell me about them."

"Anything *interesting*?" Hayes enquired with a slightly puzzled look, exactly the reaction Bruno had wanted. Getting an interviewee to accurately remember details of an incident that had just happened was hard enough, let alone a matter of weeks or months. He found it helped to kickstart the process by starting with a question that made them think hard and picture the scene in their minds... and Bruno could tell this was exactly what Hayes was now trying to do.

"They were both secretive – understandably I suppose – but Bartlett significantly more so." Hayes said. "He controlled the presentation and it was obvious that he spent his life searching for something of meaning. His interest was in being the *finder* of the quartz, which is fine from an academic point of view, although for financial recompense he'd have to prove he was the *first*."

"Surely that's not in any doubt?" asked Tom.

"You shouldn't be so sure. Who's to say Derek Bentley, the landowner, didn't find out about the quartz seam when he bought the estate?"

"That is a possibility," mused Bruno to Tom, "after all, Noway told us that Bentley has his alpacas and dream of a vineyard; he could have surveyed to see what his chances of wine-making were."

"True," agreed Tom, although not convinced.

"You're obviously aware of Mr Bentley's hobbies," Bruno said to Hayes, noting he had nodded along when he'd mentioned the alpacas and the wine. "so despite your grand vision, do you really hold out any hope of developing the site into an open cast mine?"

"No, not really. If I were a betting man I'd say ten to one against."

Bruno looked at Hayes as if he was clearly mad.

"Oh don't be so shocked, inspector!" he laughed. "I'd also bet on Mr Bentley eventually boring of his Island pursuits, especially when he realises that no matter how good his wine, the buying cartels won't really care because it *isn't French*! Like Bartlett it's the *status* that's important for him, not the money. I would expect Bentley to move on in seven or eight years' time, which is fine, as we have already paid him a tidy sum for ten-year option to mine. When Bentley sells, the price the next owner will pay would surely include an element of the profit from mining; they'd have no choice but to let us start!"

Although fascinated by the thought of buying a property with a gold mine as an optional extra, Bruno felt that Hayes had exhausted his information about Peters and Bartlett, and decided to leave in time for he and Tom to eat before their afternoon began.

***

"So if Sam and his academic friend weren't the first to discover the quartz, there'd be no money in it for them; that's what Hayes was saying, right?" Tom asked Bruno in the car.

"That's about the size of it."

"So maybe Bartlett found out about it somehow, got annoyed with

Sam for wasting his time, and killed him in anger." Tom proposed.

"Certainly a possibility," Bruno agreed, "except everyone seems to believe Bartlett's true interest was purely academic and not financial. Money was not important enough to him to kill over; that's the impression I have, at least."

"OK," continued Tom, "then what about Potter? Maybe he thought he'd get a share and did it for those same reasons?"

"Except Potter never knew about the quartz," Bruno countered, "and wouldn't you agree he seems excited enough about the money from the panning, which to him is a fortune? I can't see that he'd jeopardise that when he was never involved in that side of the business at any point."

"I suppose you're right," Tom conceded.

"It's all upside down," Bruno said, frustration suddenly clear in his voice. "I can understand why Sam might have got upset and gone and attacked someone *else* if his plans had been scuppered like that, but who and why would anyone attack him? It must be related to the gold, mustn't it? Or is the bridge just another coincidence? I feel like we're going round in circles, and all that's happening is they're getting bigger and bigger all the time!

***

During their stop for lunch, Bruno received a call from Noway with some updates. Obviously, Bruno felt, his firm approach in their last meeting had worked, and Noway now seemed to be helping rather than being obstructive.

The first bit of news was that Derek Bentley had instructed Noway that despite pressure from Hamdens, he had not signed their contract to mine the quartz deposit on the St Catherine's Down section of his estate, and furthermore had no intention of doing so – to both Bruno and Noway this was unsurprising, considering their prior discussions.

The second part of the conversation lasted a little longer, and began when Noway revealed that Phyllida Glassman had visited his office and asked him to act for her in the sale of her farm through a mainland estate agent. Whereas Noway had revealed little about Mrs Glassman in their recent meeting ('*you didn't ask*' the given reason), with a little prodding from Bruno, he provided some background information about her.

Phyllida was in her forties and had been married to Brian Glassman for some twenty-five years, until he had died of Parkinson's-related complications several months ago. For several years he had been wheelchair-bound, making life for the couple both physically and mentally difficult. Visits to the farm by travelling nursing staff had been erratic and mostly unwanted by the husband, but his care was so demanding that by the time he died, she was close to ill health herself.

She had told Noway that she was devastated at hearing of the death of Sam Peters – with whom she confirmed she had enjoyed an intimate relationship since he had begun to regularly visit the Island. It was this relationship that had delayed her sale of the farm soon after her husband had died, but now it was over in the most tragic of ways, she had decided the time was now right to sell.

She had met Sam in February, while she was walking her dog near to her farm; he had been roaming the Downs looking for treasure and rock specimens. It had been a particularly cold and stormy afternoon, so she'd invited him back for refreshments so he could get warm, and there she had told him of her plans to sell the farm. A few weeks later, Sam himself became interested in buying the farm and over a number of visits, their relationship developed into an intimate affair. She therefore changed her decision to sell and move away, however she held a lingering doubt in her mind that Sam's desire to buy the farm – rather than his interest in her – was his reason for continuing the relationship.

Regardless of her concerns, they were both single adults and therefore she felt no reason not to continue the relationship to see where it went. They spent much of their time outside, walking various routes over St Catherine's Down, with Sam genuinely interested in the secrets and stories she told him about the adjoining land, the old Island families, what they did with their farms, and the various skeletons in their closets. "—and *no*, inspector," Noway said, "she didn't tell me what they were."

Talking about the purchase of the farm one day, apparently Sam had shown her a bank statement to prove that – with a little extra borrowing from the bank – he had enough collateral to make the purchase safely. But he had then suggested that instead of purchasing the farm with a mortgage, perhaps they might become joint owners.

Noway explained that Phyllida had told him how although this might sound an ideal solution for their situation, she didn't like the idea of taking his money for the joint ownership – to her it just didn't seem *ethical*.

"The second – and probably principle reason for her visit," Noway continued, "was to show me a copy of Sam Peters' will and to register her interest. If you stop by my office, I will provide you with the file copy I promised which is properly sealed. You will see that it makes her the sole beneficiary of his estate, apart for some minor bequests."

"I'll stop by this afternoon, thank you. I'm actually about to visit Mrs Glassman, as coincidences go."

"Ah, I'm afraid you'll have to cross the English Channel if you want to see her, Inspector," Noway said, unable to see the movement of Bruno's eyebrow that Tom noticed, which somehow managed to convey the words "just my luck".

"However, she returns from Paris in a few days' time, and as I was sure you'd want to speak to her sooner rather than later, she says she'll make herself available for you immediately on her return this Thursday morning."

Bruno thanked Noway for the call. With no other plans for the afternoon, he decided to make his way to the solicitor's office straight away, drop Tom off, and have a much-needed afternoon off.

Chapter 24

Wednesday 30th July

That evening Bruno met Janet once again for their meal together. This time, the conversation began with her views about education on the Island. A visiting education standards chief had highlighted performance-related issues across a number of schools on the Island, and blamed them on high drug use, soaring unemployment and the local government's methods of allocating their budget, highlighting in particular the state of many of the local education authority's buildings, which were in need of modernisation.

But Janet did not agree with his views. In her job she met Island residents from all areas, all classes and all wealths. She knew that although the Island was in many respects similar to anywhere else in the country, but it was the subtle differences at a local level which needed to be considered, and a one-size-fits all approach dictated by London was not the answer – almost all public services could be improved with proper political representation by the local MP in Parliament.

Amongst the young twenty-something mums, there were as many married as unmarried. The sick and the elderly were in care homes starved of funds. The single mothers were housed by the local authorities and claimed the full range of benefits. Widows or widowers lived alone on the Island; many were those advanced in years who had come to retire as part of a couple leaving their families behind and were now reaching the point where they could not cope alone. The costs of their support network was much higher than in the average British town or city, but this was still borne by the Island local authorities. Although this provided many Islanders with employment, it was very much in the low-paid categories – care workers, cleaners and suchlike. Many of these workers would still need to claim benefits, and so the council's budget tended to go on people... it left little for improvements to the infrastructure of the Island.

As the conversation moved on, Janet mentioned a daytime course in Bournemouth she'd been attending through the holidays. This was news to Bruno; definitely the first time it had been mentioned. This perplexed him slightly until Janet said the words:

"...and whilst I was there, I took the opportunity to look into Steph's current whereabouts..."

Bruno doubted that the day time course had actually happened and suspected Janet just didn't want to admit that she had been there especially for this purpose.

The house at which Steph lived at was a two million-pound house on a private estate, a few miles west of the city centre; it was definitely the kind of house that would only have been affordable by someone with considerable wealth.

Bruno knew that one of Janet's skills was engaging people from all walks of life in conversation, but even he was surprised at the amount of information she had found out.

It seemed that Steph's secretarial experience had helped her land a job as a receptionist in a garage selling Range Rover cars, a position in which she could flaunt her sexuality to wealthy purchasers – it certainly seemed like her ideal role.

Despite having moved away from the Island, everyone local still knew that she was a widow looking for a husband... and she certainly dressed to fill their expectations. To her young male and female work colleagues she was frankly a bit of a joke, but to them she was friendly and nice so they tolerated what they saw as her eccentricities.

It wasn't long before Brendan Helland, the 63 year-old owner and managing director of the dealership, had become her main target.

Cars were Brendan's life. As a young man he had raced Formula Fords all over Britain and for three years in the seventies, had actually been the classification's world champion driver. He had made a fortune in the motor trade, eventually buying an ailing Range Rover dealership in Bournemouth for a song and building it into the biggest and best set up in the South of England. His wife of some thirty years had died the previous year, so for Steph he was a natural target.

It had not taken her long to get her claws into him, and using the intangible skill she had which saw smart men fall for her again and again, she succeeded.

Within six months, and against the advice of all who knew him well, Steph became the new Mrs Helland.

Brendan wasn't able to or interested in fulfilling Steph's voracious sexual appetite. He was hardworking, and liked to be at the centre of his business. His twelve-hour days left her all the time she wanted to do the things she enjoyed, most of which involved spending copious amounts of money.

Soon after the marriage she had become very demanding financially, and a classic 'bride from hell'. Even those who had tolerated her before now saw her for the woman she was, and Steph was by a long shot the most hated person in the Helland dealership. Although being wrapped up in his business often meant he was shielded from some of the worst behaviours Steph displayed, when it dawned on Brendan what a mistake he had made, he simply blocked her out of his life. This left her free to pursue her activities with the less affluent lowlife in whose company she generally felt more comfortable.

All of this had happened within little more than a year.

Brendan Helland was the biggest coup of Steph's life so far, and he was by a country mile the richest of her four husbands. In a way, she had what she wanted: money to spend and someone who no longer cared about the company she kept.

Then her past returned to haunt her.

Chris West had failed to create a decent business of the Godshill butcher and fishmonger's business. Eventually his constant womanising had caused his marriage to finally end, and was forced to sell the business to pay his wife the amount the court had ruled. West's wife had taken the two children away and they were now living in local authority housing accommodation in Ryde.

After months of drifting and time spent sleeping rough, West turned up on Steph's doorstep in Bournemouth. With time and money, Steph had begun to spend time at the local gym, attracting whichever horny young man took her fancy. The natural looks she had been gifted with were further enhanced by the exercise she did, and few could resist when Steph had selected them.

On the other hand, Christ West, now a penniless alcoholic, was far from the ideal physical specimen he had once been.

West coming back into her life was undoubtedly one of Steph's worst nightmares.

After telling Bruno this story – to which he had little to say other than the occasional "hah!" or "mm-hmm" – Janet told how she had visited Helland's dealership on the pretence of buying a Range Rover.

She described to him the building, a modern showroom where potential customers can sit in comfort, read a newspaper and drink a coffee while waiting for a 'new customer account manager' to become free.

Janet had sat a few feet away from an attractive and chatty receptionist who she could see was called Helen; she certainly seemed to be a friendly, happy young girl who took to the job well.

Janet was aware that the receptionist in any business like this is usually the one with all the gossip. After all, who puts the calls through? And who *might* just keep a line open and muted if circumstances allowed?! Certainly this Helen had seemed a perfect match to Janet's mental template.

Janet had decided to mention the new Mrs Helland to see what kind of reaction it garnered.

Helen had grimaced.

"Hah!, she had said, as the only apt response to Helen's face, the expression that had said a thousand words.

"So how well do you know her?" Janet had asked.

"Very well," was Helen's emphatic response. "She used to do my job before I got it, actually she trained me. She sometimes drops in, but no one likes her because she married our boss, and they all say it *had* to be for the money. Those two are as different as chalk and cheese. If you'd have known his first wife... they say she was charming, quiet, you know, a *real* lady. Steph is the opposite; she's loud and bawdy, just a different class from Brendan. And, she likes men, if you get what I'm saying. You know, I'm lucky to still be here, I fell out with her a fortnight ago."

For Janet, Helen was a gift, almost too good to be true.

"Oh, I'm sorry to hear that," she had responded. "What happened?"

"Some bloke called, his name was East I think... or was it West... I can't quite remember now. Anyway, he phoned here and asked to speak to her," the receptionist had explained. "He said he was very close to Steph and needed to speak to her urgently. He sounded desperate so I gave him Steph's home number. The next morning she storms in here dressed in her gym gear and drags me into the car park! She was just wild, in a rage, like. I thought she was going to punch me!"

"Good Lord." was the best Janet could muster. "What happened then?"

"She said 'You—'" Helen quietly mouthed the word 'fucking bitch', aware of that fact that there were other customers in the dealership, "—and said how dare I give her private number to anyone!"

"Tch. The thanks you get," Janet said in a motherly way.

"Yeah. Well I did say sorry, and explained that he had made it sound like he was a relative or something, so I thought it would be OK. But she just kept shouting at me! She threatened to fire me – which I knew should couldn't do there and then, but those words are still hanging over my head. My advice is don't talk to her, but if you have to, watch out."

Of course, Janet had planned the conversation from the start. She'd waited until a busy time to visit the dealership, and then walked up and down outside until she thought the maximum number of people would be in there at any one time.

She told Bruno she'd made her apologies that it was taking too long to see a salesman and that she'd be back another time.

"That's some good investigating, Janet," Bruno said to her, genuinely.

"Ah, there's more," she said with a smile on her face. Bruno made a 'rolling eyes' motion, but his own smile indicated that he was only joking.

Since learning that West had unexpectedly turned up in Bournemouth, Janet had also been over to Godshill to ask the locals there as much as they knew about West and his family.

When Chris West bought the pub with the money Steph had given or loaned him, he'd become a drinker, and when it failed under his management, that was his last foray into *that* business. After he acquired the butcher's shop in Godshill, his drinking continued; all the addition of the fish counter did was to give him a convenient reason to 'got out and buy fish', which generally just ended up in a drinking session. By this time he was certainly an alcoholic, lying to himself and others as to his dependence. Eventually he ran the food business into the ground, went bankrupt and his wife left him.

After drifting around the Island, begging from people he knew in his old haunts until he was utterly down and out and desperate, he somehow had learned of Steph's whereabouts – probably on the same grapevine that Janet's contacts had their ear to – and had gone looking for her.

"And is he *still* around?" said Bruno.

"Yes, and I find that rather interesting," Janet replied. "If their relationship had been *only* about sex, I think it would have finished after Pumpkin's death in Cowes. Casual sexual relationships run their course after about eighteen months, it's a psychological certainty" she said, Bruno knowing better than to question her, especially when the subject of relationships came up.

"When Steph left Cowes, I think – at the time – West breathed a sigh of relief. I believe that they had something between them that bound them together inextricably: Pumpkin's death. And you know, I think that the fact that they had gotten away with it meant they felt comfortable planning and executing their murder of Stanley Musgrove, the butcher of Godshill."

The problem was, Bruno thought, it certainly made perfect sense, and Janet was almost certainly not far from some truth – if not *the* truth – in the cases. But throwing around unsubstantiated accusations, loosely based on some facts admittedly, but also hearsay and conjecture, was fine as long as it wasn't your job to build a case that was *beyond reasonable doubt* to pass to the CPS.

"Can't you see, Bruno, that West must have—"

Bruno raised a finger.

"—OK, *probably* fell into his drinking because of the psychological trauma of being involved with a murder? It's enough to break the strongest of people. And now he's turned up again on Steph's door, and he's absolutely desperate, with nothing at all to lose."

"OK, I appreciate it is a possible—"

Janet raised a finger in a perfect pastiche of her dining partner's previous action.

"—fair enough, *likely* scenario." Bruno continued So what happens now?

"Well, I think he's looking for her to buy his silence."

Bruno nodded. He'd been thinking along those lines since Janet had said he'd turned up at Steph's door. Of course, if he'd said that at the time, Janet would probably have marched him down the station to tell JB there and then."

"And I think she'll buy him off," continued Janet. "But consider this. Even with a rich husband, the price he asks might be too high – after all, what price your freedom?"

"And then?" Asked Bruno, already knowing where Janet was about to go.

"And then they have to do the whole thing again."

"Kill husband number four, you're saying?"

"Yes. Can't you see there's a real danger it could happen? Can we not build a case for bringing them in for questioning based on that possibility?"

Bruno smiled to himself at her use of the pronoun *we*.

"Not in a million years," he said. "I can't open up the case without new *evidence*. And as far as *that* goes, we don't have any.

"But you agree that West's arrival is a danger to Mr Helland, right? With Pumpkin *and* the butcher, everything points to Steph leading the way, with them both dividing the spoils... and they've got away with it so far. An evil Siren Steph might be, but she's cunning. Now though, it'll be West who's calling the shots – and he's a broken man with nothing except the hold he has over Steph," Janet almost pleaded.

"What can I do though, Janet?" Bruno replied, his exasperation at his lack of progress more than the conversation with Janet affecting his tone. "This is real life, not some TV programme. Pumpkin's case is *closed*, in fact it's not even murder according to our records. To stick my nose *that* far back in time, I'd have to get the Super's permission and even you know he wouldn't touch it; he's not one for opening up old wounds."

"Even though everything adds up?" asked Janet. "Her investment in the pub, her selling the freehold of the Godshill High Street butchers shop to West at a giveaway price... and yet look how obsessed she is with money; she's certainly not a person who parts with anything easily!"

The truth was, Bruno's workload on the Sam Peters' murder was taking up almost all of this time, and even with that he was not making progress. If he switched focus elsewhere, even for a day, he might end up with another unsolved murder to his credit. He somehow managed to convey his entire thought process to Janet with just a sigh.

Janet took her foot off the gas slightly, but still drove the conversation in her chosen direction. "Did you ever speak to West's wife?" Janet asked.

"No," admitted Bruno.

"Well *she* must have had some knowledge of Chris West's activities at the time of the two deaths. If anything, he'll have told her a particular lie about the circumstances surrounding each of the occasions. And even if that doesn't produce anything fruitful, perhaps she could tell us about West, what kind of man he is. Anything that might give us the advantage."

Janet had obviously invested so much into her own investigation that it was hard for her to accept that things wouldn't move any further.

"Right," said Bruno, kindly. "Listen. West doesn't have a police record, despite his time on the streets. He'll want to keep it that way. He might have nothing, but he doesn't seem to have given up; he wouldn't have visited Steph otherwise, surely?"

Janet nodded, conceding this logical point.

"Now he's obviously very vulnerable, and he might be approaching the stage where he's ready to spill the beans on his involvement, if he had any. But if he's still at the stage of tapping Steph up, then he's not going to want to jeopardise his chances of a payout by being seen speaking to us, do you agree?"

Again, Janet nodded.

"So I've taken on board what you've said, let's keep an eye on the situation."

Chapter 25

Phyllida Glassman, who had promised to return from her visit to her sister in Paris, was Bruno's first meeting on Thursday morning.

Noway had painted a perfect portrait of her. Although she was forty-seven, she did not look her age. She came across as well-educated, confident and sophisticated – as unlike the traditional view of a farmer's wife as a woman could be. She was demonstrably saddened by Sam Peters' death.

Phyllida Glassman was an animated talker who moved like lightning from one subject to another, using metaphor and anecdote to illuminate the myriad of activities which comprised her life on the farm. She insisted on showing Bruno almost every part of her dilapidated farming enterprise, and explaining its history.

During her husband's illness she had naturally taken over the running of the farm. She'd made some decisions that had proven wrong; Bruno laughed as she explained how she'd spent fifteen thousand pounds on a milking machine despite owning no cows at the time.

"The plan was to rent it out to other small farms," she explained.

As she showed Bruno round, he couldn't help but notice the untidiness of the various buildings; it made them feel sad, unloved. In one, grubby piles of shorn wool from sheep lay everywhere.

"Sorry for the mess. I had some sheep to shear and I haven't had time to clear up," she said, dismissing the mess with a wave of her hand.

Bruno smiled, wondering where the sheep had been taken to now, as didn't recall seeing them on their farm tour. He also wondered if Phyllida took care of the shearing herself. Shearing was a skilled craft, and even when experienced shearers were brought in, shorn animals could bleed heavily from cuts caused by going just a little too quickly or clipping ever-so-slightly too close for a particular animal. The sheep from which these offcuts came had clearly suffered from such treatment,

Bruno noted, with blood covering not just the shearings but a puddle having stained the floor itself. He considered how horrible a job it must be to have to clean such a mess on a regular basis.

In another building Phyllida explained to Bruno that, as like many farms, hers was licensed as a pet crematorium, with an oven for cremating animals a necessity due to the safety regulations these days.

"It's big enough to take a small donkey," she said, and took pleasure in demonstrating to Bruno how to use the oven, even down to the method used for draining the fat from the drip tray. Bruno wasn't sure whether or not this was a test of some sort, and wondered if he'd passed.

The office next to the oven was littered with circular cardboard boxes the size of Pringle containers, about 25 cm high with labels stuck to them, indicating the name of the deceased pet.

"Still waiting to be collected, these are," she said.

Some of the dates on the containers were several months old. Bruno gave her a quizzical look.

"Animal lovers who paid for their beloved to be ceremoniously cremated sometimes lose interest immediately afterwards, probably focused on the new pet they have bought to assuage their grief," she said. "They pay in advance though, and so if they never come back it doesn't really matter to me. I keep them for a while out of respect, then have a clear out."

As the tour continued, Bruno felt as if she was showing it to him as if he were a prospective buyer. She was thorough in every detail, even listing the names of people to contact for every activity one might need help for on the farm.

What struck Bruno on reflection later was that in spite of her meticulous attention to small details, it seemed it was only to the small things. A viable business plan – without which no farm could survive for long – was clearly non-existent. Perhaps she was one of those micro-management people, great at small, detailed tasks, but unable to see the bigger picture that was staring them in the face.

As the tour concluded and they return to the farmhouse, Phyllida concluded by reporting on her Eurostar trip and the health of her sister. On making it back to the kitchen, she made herself and Bruno some coffee, which they took into the adjoining conservatory.

"Now what is it you *really* want to ask me, Inspector?" she said, her bright blue eyes looking straight at him, and for the first time since he had arrived, ceasing her non-stop talking.

"I'd like you to tell me everything you know about Sam Peters."

With a near-silent sigh, Phyllida began to talk again, this time a little more slowly, a tad more wistful.

"Do you know where St Catherine's Oratory is?" Bruno simply said nothing and let her continue. "It's the area between this farm, which runs from the Blackgang Road north across Niton Down, then on to St Catherine's hill as far as Downcourt in the north. On one wet, cold February afternoon, I was walking the trail past the old oratory with my dog when I met Sam for the first time. Protruding from his back pack was a collapsible metal detector. One sees a lot of treasure hunters on the Island looking for Roman artefacts and remains. Did you know it has long been accepted that a major Roman settlement was situated in the vicinity of the Down. Sam was looking for feeders to the East Yar river source. The heavens were about to open, and it would have certainly been dangerous for him to have continued tramping the Downs. We were near to this house though, so I brought him in, warmed him up and gave him some tea. As it turned out, we had a pleasant afternoon inside in the warm when all the while outside there was a dreadful storm, with lots of rain. It felt... cosy, somehow. When the downpour eased at about half six that evening, I drove him to the car park on Military Road so he could catch his ferry back to Portsmouth. That's how we met."

"How well did you know him?"

"Rather well, inspector. We were very close, although I should say that I've only known him since February. Things moved quickly, but..." Phyllida paused slightly, "I think I wanted to marry him.

Bruno nodded in a 'further condolences' kind of way.

"Mind you, I was never sure if he wanted to marry me," she continued. He wanted to buy the farm from me, did you know that?"

Phyllida smiled in recollection and continued before hearing an answer.

"He always behaved so nicely. We walked, we talked; he explained what he would do to modernise the farmhouse. He wanted to extend the tree planting, create a shoot and learn to ride a horse. He was perfect for this time in my life, which has been so wretched for years."

"Why do you think he wasn't as keen on marriage as you?" asked Bruno.

"Perhaps he simply got cold feet. He was your classic case of a confirmed bachelor – very private, not used to sharing. Maybe the responsibility or the obligations of a wife frightened him. Maybe. I'll never know for sure now though, will I?"

Bruno introduced the subject of Sam's death as tactfully as he could, and queried Phyllida regarding her own views from a number of different angles. He asked her who Sam might have upset enough to make them turn into a killer – or perhaps kill again.

"I do *not* believe it was possible that Sam could have provoked someone to murder him," she said rather firmly. "He ran his own business, but as far as I know he didn't have a complex social life; there weren't lots of close friends or colleagues or even a boss for that matter. No, Sam wouldn't have done anything to anyone else; they would have picked on *him*.

Since hearing of his murder, I have not been able to speak to anyone about my feelings, Inspector, and for me that is very difficult. I am heartbroken and mystified. That is why, on this occasion at least I went away to see my sister," she said.

She became silent and stood at the open conservatory door with her back toward Bruno and stared out across the fields, oblivious to his presence. He did not speak until she recovered her composure and returned to her seat.

"I did speak to him once about getting married," she said after taking her seat, "and he said he needed to conclude some business he'd become involved with on the Island with Noel Bartlett, the Professor of Geology at Southampton University"

"Do you know what business that was?"

"Yes. It was mining for gold on the Island."

"Do you think that was a real possibility?" Bruno asked, testing the water to see what Phyllida knew.

"Sam certainly thought it was. He reckoned there was enough gold here to cause a Californian-style gold rush. He said that if word of a strike got out, that would affect Roud Farm and ultimately could harm our relationship. He never mentioned to anybody what he was doing and those who came into contact with him probably thought he was just hunting for a hoard of Roman coins. He spent a lot of time on the land to the west of St Catherine's ridge near to where we first met. One day he told me that they – him and Bartlett – had discovered a quartz outcrop which confirmed what he had discovered from the river bed, that the rain water that drained from the high St Catherine's Down to the East Yar river beyond, contained gold particles washed from a rich seam of quartz all of which lay on Derek Bentley's land."

"Did Sam meet Derek Bentley?"

"Yes, he did."

"Do you know what they discussed? I assumed he'd always thought the land on which he'd found the quartz seam was council owned, never finding out that it belonged to Bentley, so why the visit?"

"Somewhat of a coincidence," she said. "He went to Mattins, Bentley's farmhouse half a mile from Chale where he stays when he's on the Island. Sam said it was to get Bentley's permission to search for Roman treasure across his land. Of course Bentley said no. He said he was not interested in replicating what the Oglander family had done near Brading, where there is a Roman Villa well preserved and open to the public."

Phyllida went on to explain that Sam had asked him if he was aware that a rich gold quartz seam might exist on his land. Bentley had said there were many things about his land that he knew about and for the time being he was satisfied and happy with everything he was doing and didn't have time for anything else.

"That was it, I believe," she said before continuing with a different topic:

"Last November, before I met Sam and all this gold stuff surfaced, a Dutch company called Windhoek came to see me and Derek Bentley about the ridge which forms a narrow section of land on top of the hill that divides this farm from Derek's. The summit of the hill is our boundary and is about five hundred metres long. They wanted to put a wind generator on top of the hill. Their plan was to apply to the local authority for approval to erect a single turbine, which they saw no reason not to succeed. With the principal established they would then apply for permission for another four, making five in total. The ridge is a perfect site for wind-based energy; it's high, unobstructed and a Force six rising blows in from the sea most of the year. Windhoek say it's literally the ideal site. They presented a plan that would have given me £40,000 or so per annum, with payments to rise in line with the electricity supply price. That kind of money could have supported the running of my farming activities.

I was happy to go ahead until Derek presented me with a map of the ridge on which his boundary line differed from our deeds. The records we have always held draw the boundary precisely along the ridge, which would have given me and Derek an equal share of the income."

"Although two of the turbines would have been fully on my land, the other three would have encroached onto his, as there is a regulatory space around each generator. Situating the first generator on my land meant that I was responsible for the first application. Although Windhoek did all the work, and thankfully paid all the up-front costs, the planning application was all in my name. I instructed Noway Solicitors to act for me with the application, but it all fell apart when Bentley insisted that he wanted a greater share of the money or he wouldn't give any permission for anything that encroached on his land. Unless Windhoek ended up with at least four generators on the top of the hill, they said it wouldn't be profitable for them, and so that was the end of that.

"Derek is a businessman from London, inspector. He's not in love with the Island, he doesn't feel like he *belongs* here. He's here for the money; what's more, because he visits rarely, nobody can put a face to his name," she added. "They've all *heard* of Derek Bentley but nobody knows who he is."

"Like Gatsby," said Bruno, referring to the fictional recluse.

"You could say that," she replied. "But Gatsby lived in a luxury mansion; Derek comes and goes."

"Was his refusal to let Sam hunt for treasure on his land connected with you?"

"I don't think so, all that wind generator business came up last November before our relationship started."

"Unless he spies on me, there's no reason Derek would have known about that," she said.

"Have you met Bartlett?" Bruno asked Phyllida.

"Yes, once," she said. "It was late March, a Saturday afternoon. Sam had been working with Bartlett on the Downs. They were tired but both had wanted to continue on Sunday so they stayed over. I cooked them supper and we had quite a pleasant evening. Next morning I gave them some digging tools and off they went, searching for their quartz."

"Can you remember any conversations that might have been held during Bartlett's stay?" Bruno asked. "Did anything come up that you think could help us find out more about Sam's death?"

"There's nothing that stands out, although I should say that I don't think Sam really *liked* Bartlett. In fact, I think he was afraid of him."

"Afraid?"

"Yes, I think Bartlett made him feel vulnerable."

"Really? To what?"

"Bartlett seemed to have a way of making you feel that knowledge was power. I noticed it in the conversations we had that evening; it's part of his very character. I suppose all academics do that, don't they?"

"I haven't socialised with enough to know," Bruno admitted. "Did he ever mention a Dick or Richard Potter?"

"Yes, he is another one of their treasure-seeking group. Sam used to see him before he came over to stay with me."

"Did Bartlett ever meet Bentley?" Bruno asked, changing tack as thoughts came to him.

"I'm sorry, I'd have no idea about that," was Phyllida's slightly disappointing reply.

"Hmm. Is there *anything* else you can tell me... about *anything*?" Bruno tried not to sound desperate. "About Sam, about Bartlett, about Bentley?"

"Can I trust your confidentiality?" Phyllida asked Bruno.

"My *personal* trust is assured," Bruno replied, adding in his mind *but anything you say that's relevant to my professional capacity is a different matter.*

"Well, there *is* something that... well, should it have become public knowledge then it might have scuppered the wind farm idea; the same could very much be said for the gold mining. But Derek and I know about it. Six years ago, an archaeologist called Harry Stone found evidence that a major Roman community lived on the Downs beneath the ridge sheltered by the hill that divides our farms. He suggested we invite him and his team to excavate across the Downs. He predicted that apart from the ridge at the top, the settlement lies on the south west side of the ridge, on Bentley's farm land. Beyond the ridge, the Downs are sheltered from the east winds in winter because they lie in a dip like valley. It faces south west and is very sunny. It's near Bentley's new vineyard project. In Roman times it would have been farmed extensively."

"Did you tell Sam about this?"

"Yes, hence his visit to Bentley to obtain his treasure-seeking permission. Although of important archaeological interest, it is of no financial benefit to a farmer to have a Roman Villa discovered on his land. With the potential from wind farm, solar panels and this latest discovery of a quartz seam, if it were public knowledge that proof of the existence of a Roman settlement had been found, any approval of almost any form would be denied no matter how 'cautious' they promised to be."

So it is important to you – and I presume Mr Bentley also – to keep Harry Stone's discovery quiet?" Bruno asked.

"Yes, very much so" Phyllida replied, earnestly. "Although if I'm being honest, the wind farm plan could have been shot down simply due to the certain objections from locals who would point out that St Catherine's Down is a beauty spot. The turbines would be seen for miles, and according to many would ruin the view forever."

"Maybe they're right," Bruno replied, remembering the stunning but desolate beauty of the Down. "So what are your views on Sam's gold mine plans?"

"The prospect of turning a chunk of the Island into an open cast mining desert is utterly unthinkable," Phyllida stated, without the slightest hesitation.

"Why do you think that?" asked Bruno.

"Have you ever seen an open cast mine, Inspector?"

"No," admitted Bruno; neither did he say that he'd seen the drawings and listened to the description from Hayes from Hamdens, and hadn't thought they came across as too bad.

"There is one in South Wales near Merthyr Tydfil. It's mining coal. On what was once beautiful countryside are earth movers, as far as the eye can see, ripping up the earth, extracting the coal seam, just a few feet below the surface. Imagine that outside my front door."

"Did Sam understand these things?"

"Of course, but he didn't want the threat of finding a Roman settlement to stop the gold mining either and Bentley didn't want him anywhere near his land."

"And what are Mr Bentley's views about the mine?" Bruno asked.

"You'd have to ask him," replied Phyllida.

"As it goes, that's what I plan to do," Bruno countered, surprised at such a short answer from someone so open throughout the entire conversation.

"I doubt he'll see you though. He'll generally only meet visitors by appointment, and if he doesn't fancy granting an appointment..."

"In my experience," Bruno replied, a little put out, "People will usually see a police officer. And at the first time of asking if they know what's good for them."

"He has nothing to do with Sam's murder, Inspector."

"I think that is for us to determine, Mrs Glassman."

"I suppose," was her reply.

After the kind of "Hmph!" that only a policeman can do well – it must be a skill learned from years of repeating it during official interviews – Bruno thought carefully if there was anything else he should ask his host.

"Have you ever visited Sam's apartment in Southsea?" Bruno enquired.

"Yes, it was lovely; it was very near to the sea. We always walked along the pebble beach, I shall miss that very much. When I sell up I'll move back to the mainland; that's where I came from years ago. My cousin lives in Purley in Surrey and that's where I grew up."

"How long do you think it'll take you to sell?" Bruno asked.

"I'm not sure... although I know Derek would buy me out tomorrow if I asked him," Phyllida said.

"So why *don't* you ask him?"

"I want *him* to ask *me*," was her reply. "To ask him myself might suggest I'm desperate, and I'm determined to get the best price I can."

"Well, good luck with the sale, Mrs Glassman, and thank you for your time." Bruno said, deciding that this was a natural conclusion for their conversation.

As the two walked towards the car, Bruno noticed what a strikingly beautiful woman the elusive Mrs Glassman was.

***

Despite the suggestion that he had nothing to do with the case, Bruno intended to see Derek Bentley as soon as possible. Phyllida Glassman had portrayed him as an adversary, but as a trained copper Bruno was able to see many arguments and disputes from both sides of the story. He also understood Bentley's reticence to allow treasure hunters on his land. He'd asked Phyllida for a number or other contact details, but she insisted she didn't have any, explaining that most of their conversations of recent years had been through their solicitors.

Bruno shared the main points of the conversation with Janet, although left out the final thought he'd had just before leaving.

Janet's view was that Phyllida's answers were probably accurate. Her relationship with Sam was consistent with his general behaviour; he was secretive and had an agenda, which he wasn't prepared to allow anyone to be party to.

"What did she say specifically about Sam?" she asked Bruno.

"She said that she was in love with him, that he was a breath of fresh air. They were certainly in a kind of relationship that *she* saw as close."

"Was he an attractive man?"

Bruno couldn't answer that question, it was a woman's question, one that a man – especially one like Bruno – found impossible to judge. He attempted to explain as much in his reply, asking Janet in return what a well-spoken and "to some people I'm sure, very attractive" woman see in a lonely building surveyor from Portsmouth?

"You said he was rich?" Janet asked.

"To some people's definition of the term, I suppose so," Bruno agreed.

"So he's moneyed, not *unattractive* and available. That's often more than enough," she surmised. "Was *she* in on the gold deal in any way?"

"No, her farm is some distance from the quartz," said Bruno.

"It seems to me," Janet concluded, "that you've got all these people – from Arnold Harris at the council to Noway the solicitor, and at the front line Hamdens, Bartlett and Sam – all running around dreaming of riches, when really the only one who'd ever profit is Derek Bentley himself? If the quartz seam is entirely on his farm, then he's the only one who'd be getting anything worthwhile. I agree with you wholeheartedly for once. Go and see him immediately."

Chapter 26

Friday 1st August

Bruno decided that the best way of getting to meet Bentley was to rely on pure pot luck and show up at his place of residence at a reasonable time at the weekend... so that is exactly what he did. When the front door opened, he presented his card to the lady standing there, who he presumed – rightly – was one of the large house's staff, and the authority a warrant card commanded worked. After a call to the master of the house from her mobile phone, it was agreed that Bentley would meet Bruno the following afternoon at three pm on arriving from London.

***

Saturday 2nd August

Bruno turned up near to Mattins Farm early enough to see Derek Bentley arrive by helicopter. Bentley was accompanied by a lady who, on the basis that he was in his fifties, looked about half his age. The helicopter landed neatly on a preferred spot on the lawn and took off almost the moment the two passengers had cleared the rotator blades. They were met by the staff lady Bruno had spoken to the previous day, along with a man, who grabbed their hand luggage and led them inside.

Watching this from his car, Bruno decided that he wouldn't approach the house quite this early, giving Bentley time to ease into his country house. A relaxed interviewee was a good interviewee, and Bruno wanted to find out what Bentley knew about Sam Peters. As always he hope was that there would be *something* which could help him find Sam's killer, but he was not feeling particularly optimistic.

Bruno timed things so that by the time he'd parked his car where it looked like it wouldn't cause a fuss, and walked to the door to press the doorbell, it was one minute to three. The same lady as before greeted him and led him through into a grand lounge arranged like a film set in an Agatha Christie mystery.

Bentley – a young, clean and energetic fifty-year-old – strode with purpose into the room and shook Bruno's hand. "You're lucky to catch me on a weekend when I am available, Inspector. My farm manager is away today, so I've brought my daughter for a first visit to show her what I do secretly at weekends. This is a place I *escape* to, and the last thing I ever want here is any kind of interruption."

After tea and pleasant but forgettable small-talk, Bruno explained that he was interviewing everyone who had a connection to Sam on the Island. His first question, as always, was where Bentley had been on the evening of the murder. Having been provided with details of an address on the mainland which could be easily confirmed, Bruno mentally crossed Bentley off the suspects list, but realised this was probably his one chance to get as much information as possible from the man.

"As you met him, you might have discovered – that is, he might have mentioned – something about his personal or work life that will help me find his killer," stated Bruno.

"I don't think I can help you much with that," Bentley replied. "I only saw him the once. He wanted to explore the Downs that led up to Mattins, which is the productive part of my estate. He said he was looking for a Roman settlement and wanted permission to use his metal detector on the land. There are Roman remains all over the Island."

Bentley paused for a moment before continuing.

"Maybe that was true, maybe it wasn't. Personally, I did not believe that was his sole reason, so I had him checked out. I found that he had discovered the gold-producing quartz seam that is on my land. A few basic enquiries and it turned out he'd already alerted Hamdens the mining company that it existed, who've since propositioned me with a fully-detailed plan to turn my retreat into an opencast mine."

"Which you have declined?"

"It's not something I'd welcome, Inspector. It would simply ruin what I am trying to do here. The Island has several small vineyards producing inferior wines. They are inferior because the grape they use suits neither the climate nor the terroir on which the vines are planted. Over ten acres here, I have planted a dozen of the world's finest grapes. Some will fail and the wine will be undrinkable, but one or two will succeed; when I know which, I will plant fifty whole acres and produce Chateau Mattin, a medal-winning wine."

Bruno noted the confidence with which Bentley spoke.

"Once I have won the right kind of accreditations, I shall market the wine throughout Europe – and who knows where else – but at present I'm still very much at the early experimental stage. We also have Alpacas, I'm sure you've been told. One herd we've got; you can't see them easily, but they occupy some fields on the lower slopes of the middle hills. I employ a viticulturist, Mike Pelham, who manages the farm. He is university educated, has served an apprenticeship in wine-making and he is part of a number of plans I will eventually get round to here. What I've told you is not secret, but of course many nosey Islanders think I am engaged in some kind of secret activities, which, sadly in a way, I am not."

"And those plans don't involve gold mining?" Bruno asked.

"A number of people, including Nick Hayes of Hamdens, have been trying to persuade me to mine the quartz seam they now have knowledge of, located on St Catherine's Down, but as I've said, it would ruin my current and future projects." Bentley replied firmly.

"When Sam Peters asked me if he and his partner could roam the farm looking for treasure, I said *no*. Not as emphatically as I should have done because Mick reported seeing them on a few occasions walking the Downs taking measurements, or that's what it looked like at any rate. I told him to leave them alone, because whatever they were looking for I already know is there. And even if they discovered something else, it would eventually get back to me; whatever they could find belongs to me anyway."

Bentley paused and looked Bruno straight in the eye.

"Inspector, do you think I would invest a fortune on the Island and *not* know what every acre contains?"

Bruno did not answer the question, but felt he should try and gain an element of control; *he* liked to be the one to lead the conversation.

"Mr Bentley, do you have *any* idea who would murder Sam Peters, and for what reason?"

"I didn't know him, I've explained this. I only met him the once, and it seems we mix in entirely different worlds so the answer is *no*," said Bentley. "Have you spoken to Bartlett, his partner? He seems to be all over everything. *He* came to talk to me about the geological importance of my land and how it came into being, tens of thousands of years ago. He spoke about the strata and about the quartz deposit. Things I already know. His real interest was in something that he said he knew about and would not divulge, unless I signed a confidentiality agreement, which of course I did not. There is a rude word for our Professor Bartlett which I won't repeat to you Inspector. He said that he knew Peters had asked me for permission to explore my land, to which I had said no".

Bentley paused to think for a moment and Bruno let him continue.

"Inspector, I think Bartlett was suggesting that Peters hadn't explained everything to me, and that he should, but I didn't give him the opportunity to have the conversation he had wanted to have with me. That might have angered him."

Bruno did nothing and said nothing, hoping for Bentley to continue, which eventually he did.

"This Island is very insular, Inspector. After seven years, I am still an outsider. But some can see what I've brought to the Island, and I've not *taken* anything from it, I haven't exploited the Island's resources. I've *invested* here, and I will eventually make whatever I do a prosperous business for the whole Island's benefit."

"An honourable approach," Bruno said, thinking *if you're telling the truth.* "Sir, do you know Phyllida Glassman?" he asked instead.

"Yes, she is my neighbour. Is she part of your investigation, Inspector?"

"She's on my list of people to talk with," replied Bruno.

"I think she was having a relationship with Sam Peters, wasn't she?"

"I can't comment on that," the obvious copper's reply.

"She is very attractive, a widow, and she is quite lonely. And from what I know, she's the sort who uses her beauty and charm on men she *wants* something from. She is not my type, but Sam Peters had something she wanted and I'd go so far as to say vice-versa. What was it he had? I think he was comfortably off from what I extrapolated from my conversation with Bartlett, and maybe he provided her with an opportunity to escape from that farm. At the very least it stopped her for a while from pestering me to buy her farm, which I have no absolutely no interest in."

"That's quite interesting, Mr Bentley," Bruno said, making a mental note of as much of the conversation as possible. "Why does she pester you so much?"

"I wonder if you know just how broke she is? The bank are taking action to force her out, but she won't go. It's... unpleasant."

"She seems to struggle to keep up with work on her farm," Bruno said, a defence of sorts but more to keep the conversation flowing.

"She has stopped pestering me to buy her out, but with the death of Mr Peters, I expect another approach anytime soon. Have you spoken to the man who does for her?" enquired Bentley."

"She has help?" Bruno asked, rather taken aback.

"Certainly; Steadman is his name. He lives in a cottage near the farm. The Steadmans are an old Island family who actually used to own her farm – until Steadman's father's second wife spent everything they had. In the end the poor man had to sell everything, except the small cottage he now lives in. The Glassmans bought the farm, but they never did anything good with it. Phyllida's in the same boat now; it's all too common – idle spendthrifts resting on the financial laurels of the past. Money doesn't last forever."

"No one I've spoken to has even mentioned this Steadman," said Bruno, still wondering how his name had never previously surfaced.

"Really? John Steadman? He takes unemployment benefit, but also does odd jobs for cash. I'll admit to you now Inspector that he's done a bit of labouring for Mike; of course you'll appreciate that the requirement to report any additional income is his, not Mike's or mine."

"Of course," agreed Bruno, who saw that Bentley was doing his best to show how straight-along-the-line he was... *but was it all for show?*

"So what's this Steadman like?"

"Well, if you ask me – which you have done – he has a sinister countenance, which makes one feel rather uncomfortable. I am sure he'll know everything there is to know about Phyllida Glassman... and more than likely all about Sam Peters too."

Bruno made a note in his book to call John Steadman; this was too important to leave to memory alone.

"Mrs Glassman mentioned a wind farm plan..." Bruno said, wondering how differently Bentley would tell the story.

"Indeed. Last Autumn, Phyllida introduced me to a Dutch company called Windhoek who wanted to destroy the beautiful landscape with a row of giant wind turbines. They'd never have got permission in my opinion, but *they* were convinced they would. I listened to their pitch but I simply wasn't interested. I told Phyllida so, and that I would oppose their application, but she kept on. Windhoek produced a bunch of calculations showing the cost of setting a turbine up, and the return on investment. I didn't believe the numbers, they were far too optimistic; neither did I have any confidence in their prediction of the payback on capital – seven years, if the supply price reached the reserve. It was far too optimistic a forecast. I told Phyllida that I was opposed to wind generators in principle anyway, yet she still tried to persuade me to help her do the deal, by re-partitioning an area at the top of my farm so she could go ahead. I could have let her have the land, for a price of course, but I just don't believe in that method of generating electric power at the current time. It's far less environmentally friendly than the companies pushing them would have you know. Were you aware of that, Inspector?"

"It's not something I've ever had the time to consider," admitted Bruno, whose environmental commitment just about stretched to separating his rubbish into the various bins the council provided.

"It's been tried on a mass scale in California and it failed spectacularly. The generators wear out before they've paid for themselves and what's worse is that they leave a whole host of toxic materials that are very difficult and costly to dispose of. Inspector Peach, the truth is that over the years, various consortiums have presented all kind of plans to put my land 'to use'. None of them will go ahead because I simply won't allow it. Not everything is about the money, although I make that where I can. Do you know what I do?" Bentley asked. "I'm sure you do, you'd have checked me out before coming here like a good policeman."

"Actually, no, I didn't do that, sir," Bruno said, a little off-put. "If Mrs Glassman hadn't told me that Sam Peters had visited you, I would probably have never made contact. I don't believe that knowing your background is of any importance to the case – although I can't deny I'm now interested to find out."

"Well, regardless I am happy to assist however I can now you have called. For your information my Island business is called the *Brown Sugar Investment Company*. It's 'Brown Sugar' because we used to import it to the Island, but not any longer. Now we are an investment company. If there is a serious investment opportunity on the Island, Brown Sugar will be interested as long as it is profitable, and designed to benefit – or would result in helping in some way – the people of the Island."

Bruno nodded and stood up to signify that the interview was drawing to a close, feeling that he'd just about managed to be the leader of the conversation. *Small triumphs*, he thought.

"If I knew of anything that could help you find the murderer of Sam Peters, I *would* tell you, Inspector. In my opinion, although he came from Portsmouth – a fact he told me when discussing treasure hunting – but I suspect he was murdered for something he was involved in *here*, on the Island... and by an Islander," added Bentley.

As the two walked back towards the entrance hall, Bruno decided to ask for a tour. Throughout the conversation with Bentley, he had slowly begun to feel he could trust the man more than he'd supposed initially.

But if there was something fishy going on at the farm, it would be a certainty for an excuse to be found for such a tour to take place another time.

"Of course I can show you, it would be a pleasure," beamed Bentley. "Let me call my daughter, Emma, she's dying to see around too!"

A pleasant pretty young student – the young woman who had arrived with Bentley in the helicopter, was introduced to Bruno. For some reason he now felt a little guilty he had assumed that she was the older man's latest squeeze.

The tour was a little shorter than Bruno had thought it might be, with the highlight consisting of what could be best described as a village of greenhouses. Each one was full of vines in pots or in long beds; some were large, some small, all were planted in a range of soils and substrates. Some of the vines had only minor differences, whereas others were clearly from wildly different varieties. The number of combinations, Bruno thought, must be extraordinary.

"As I mentioned, Inspector, we are cultivating vine specimens from the main wine-growing areas of the world: France, Hungary, Spain, Australia, California... Mike is aiming to produce the best wine in the country from amongst this lot. It *will* take some time, but I have no doubt that we shall end up with something both special and unique."

As the tour came to an end, the three of them returned to the main entrance of the house. Emma politely said 'goodbye' and ran back in. Bruno put out his hand to shake Bentley's, and thanked him for his hospitality. As he did so, the man rested a hand on Bruno's shoulder and spoke in what seemed to the detective like an honest tone.

"Mr Peach, I suggest you look into Phyllida Glassman's activities. You won't get much truth out of *her*, but look to her close acquaintances; even a women like her can make... *unusual* choices when it comes to rather dodgy characters."

"Like John Steadman?" Bruno asked.

"Absolutely," replied Bentley, clear that the barb had been aimed at the individual.

Chapter 27

Bruno had been thinking about everything he'd learned to date and was throwing various thoughts and combinations together in his mind.

Derek Bentley had told him that the gold mining idea was dead in the water, and Noway had confirmed the contract from Hamdens regarding the mining of the quartz had been returned unsigned. The reason he'd given to Bruno for his refusal was that he wanted to focus on rearing alpacas and developing his vineyard; he had told of his belief that a gold mine in the centre of his estate would ruin these other ventures and would also be unpopular on the Island.

But Bruno couldn't help thinking that this altruistic approach wasn't the whole story.

The unmined quartz no doubt added considerable value to Bentley's property, possibly even more so than the proposed gold yield at current prices. It could happily lay underground just as it had done for millennia until he changed his mind or until a new owner bought the farm. But whichever way Bruno looked at Bentley, even though he doubted the man's explanation for his position on the mine, there was nothing that linked him to Sam as a potential suspect, and so he was removed from the detectives list.

Bentley had, however, progressed Bruno's investigation, even if only slightly, by introducing the existence of John Steadman, a factor not previously taken into account. Whether this would lead anywhere or not was still to be seen, but it was progress nonetheless.

Bentley had suggested there was something of a relationship between Phyllida and Steadman, and furthermore had expressed what came across as a sincere dislike of her. Despite what he had said, Bruno in fact thought that she seemed exactly what he imagined Bentley's cup of tea would be.

In addition to the information about Phyllida Glassman, Bentley had also indicated a mild indifference towards Sam, but a certain dislike for Bartlett.

The true effect of Bentley's decision to refuse permission was essentially that nothing had changed for most of the people Bruno considered to be part of this Island circle. To Hamdens all it meant was that the minerals moved over from the 'immediate' profit column to the 'future' one; the gold wasn't going anywhere, and their option meant that the next owner would surely agree to their plan, as Bentley would include it in his price, should he sell.

It seemed that the one person it made a difference to – who was still alive – was Bartlett, who would now not get the chance to gain recognition for his amazing discovery, especially as he wasn't even the first person to have made it.

That put Bartlett at the top of the list of people Bruno needed to move things forward with. There was also this Steadman character; he'd definitely be worth speaking with. Then, mainly due to the discrepancies between her version of various points and Bentley's, surely Phyllida Glassman had to be up there as well.

Bruno thought hard. At some time during Sam's attempt to buy Phyllida's farm (*why had she not sold if she was in that much trouble?*), he had obviously disclosed his true wealth to her. More so, he had written a will leaving his entire estate to her, which included his cash, property, and the flat in Southsea. Bruno understood the idea of love at first sight, but knowing that Sam's bank balance was near to half a million pounds and the apartment worth almost the same – there had to be suspicion over the fact that he had signed all of it over to someone he'd really only known for a few weeks.

Bruno realised that he'd previously discounted financial gain as a motive, but having learned that the apartment was in fact mortgage free, there was now a significant amount of money at stake – especially as there was someone with financial troubles in the picture. This meant Phyllida Glassman needed a complete re-think, especially with the changing of the recipient of the will into her name.

Then there was that delay between asking Noway for the will and him producing it. Did Bruno believe the story about the secretary and the key? Was there a connection between the solicitor and Phyllida that needed looking into? The question he required an answer to was whether there was a personal, as well as a professional relationship between them.

Bruno had, of course, checked that neither Noway nor Glassman had police records or any recorded misdemeanours with the civil authorities. Often reports would contain details of a partner, but nothing of that sort would help here. It would be difficult to approach such a subject, and may result – if neither were involved in the murder – in two potentially good providers of leads closing him down after being offended.

Noway. He should speak to Noway. The circumstances that induced a cautious, quiet, personal man such as Sam Peters to bequeath his entire net worth to a lady he hardly knew, with no more than a relative pittance going to his sister and her family were quite puzzling, but perhaps the solicitor picked up on something. Other questions surfaced in Bruno's mind, and he picked up his phone.

***

"I wondered when you'd next be calling," Noway said on hearing Bruno's voice. "What can I help you with today, Inspector?"

"I want to know everything about the will, Mr Noway, confidentiality be damned!"

Bruno heard Noway sigh.

"Mr Peach, let me explain. As you know, my duty is to whatever client is – or clients are – in front of me at that particular time. Let us consider a couple, seemingly very much in love, who visit me to discuss the writing of a will."

"I'm considering it Noway, now tell me what happened."

"Well, I advised the two of them on the physical aspect of writing the will, and – for my usual fee – helped them to draft a document that would pass legal muster. But I was not asked to be a witness for it, and the copy of the document I assisted with is not signed."

"So at this stage not even you know what the true status of Sam's will is?"

"Correct, Inspector."

"And you didn't tell me this before because..?"

"Conf—"

"Of course, confidentiality," Bruno interrupted, determined not to let Noway use the excuse. "When Sam asked you to help write the will, did you think it was strange that he should leave everything to her so early in their relationship?"

"I did, and when we met again, I repeated my caution, but he seemed keen to do it. He said that if they were going to marry and he was going to invest in the farm, then that would have been the position anyway. In fact, at the beginning he wanted to buy the farm outright, but the liabilities were too great, even for Mr Peters' liquid funds."

"Really, I'd have thought the amount he had available would be a sensible amount for the property."

"Negative equity, Inspector, negative equity. The bane of the housing market. Phyllida Glassman's husband lived as a 'gentleman farmer.' Whenever he needed cash – which he frequently did – he'd take out a further mortgage, a loan secured on the house. The valuation he'd provide them with would be far in excess of the true realisable amount of the farm."

"I can't believe he'd get away with doing that!" Bruno replied, rather surprised.

Noway smiled. "Yes, you'd think that financial companies would have been more cautious with their lending, particularly checking up on valuations... but this was before the recent financial crash, and money flowed freely. A little too freely in the Glassman's case. But Mr Peters was in that business, wasn't he? So the minute he looked at the actual figures, he'd have cottoned on straight away. He'd certainly have realised he had to back out the minute he learned of the true debt attached to the property. But this kind of thing happens all the time in the market, Inspector. I'm surprised you've spent so much time on the Island when I'd have thought the most likely culprit would be somebody amongst his commercial clients that had it in for him over some dodgy property deal that he scuppered, perhaps."

Bruno admitted – internally – that this was still a possibility, although he and Tom had been fairly sure that there was no indication of anything of the sort in Sam's diary; if there'd been an angry client, surely he'd have made at least *one* note? Of course, he didn't say any of this to Noway; it didn't do for a detective to reveal anything about what leads or information he may or may not have.

"What will happen to the farm now then?" asked Bruno, having realised what Bentley had been talking about with regards to Phyllida Glassman's financial situation.

"It will be sold when the mortgagor obtains a possession order, which he can when probate on her husband's estate is granted. It is a lengthy process, mainly because of the number of creditors' claims – although it isn't exactly speedy even in the simplest of circumstances. Until then she'll stay living in the property I would imagine. I suspect that Mr

Bentley will snaffle the property up eventually."

"Wouldn't he buy from her to avoid the risk of losing it?"

"No, he's a smart man with money, Inspector. It's a buyer's market at the moment. When the bank fails to sell the farm at the price which they'll ask for – that being an amount that pays off all the debts – their next most sensible move will be to go to auction. Then Bentley will pick it up at a sensible price; everyone knows he can outbid them so few will try."

"And what happens to Mrs Glassman if the amount Mr Bentley pays is less than her current liabilities?"

"The bank could still pursue her for the money, even if she ends up paying it off at a pound a week from whatever work she finds. Other times they write it off. It's an unknown factor as things stand...

Their conversation came to an end at this point, when Noway's secretary knocked, popped her head round the door, and advised Noway that his next client had arrived. Bruno thanked Noway who – yet again – had proven helpful, even if he had only revealed information the detective wished he had done before. The solicitor promised to keep in touch with any developments.

**

Bruno's thoughts shifted back to Phyllida Glassman, the one person who had known Sam Peters intimately during the four months leading up to his murder. Other than to admit they were lovers she had disclosed very little else more. She admitted that she had visited his home in Southsea and they had strolled the shingle beach, but after a phone call or two Bruno had learned that he'd not taken her to see his sister and his three young nieces, who by all accounts were an important part of his life. Bruno was searching for something of substance in their relationship, to support a closeness which would persuade a sane, professional man to leave her all his worldly goods. The lack of this was seriously disturbing him. He needed answers.

**

After a second unanswered phone call to Phyllida Glassman, Bruno decided to drive over to her farm early that evening on his return to the Island. In their previous meeting, she had projected an image of a genteel lady who was vulnerable, able to cope, but in need of support, and whose present circumstances were not of her own making. If it was true she was fully aware of the financial situation she was in, and yet she was determined to remain in-situ until evicted, she was entirely different than the character she had portrayed.

Bruno wondered if she was not taking any phone calls in order to avoid the multitude that no doubt would be coming from the various financial institutions. Regardless, he hoped that his surprise visit would catch her unawares and get at least *some* truths out of a conversation with her regarding Sam Peters.

The approach to Roud Farm was along a narrow lane that opened out into a concrete quadrangle about fifty metres square. There was a tractor in the yard and several pieces of equipment that could be hooked up to it for various reasons, whether that was lifting hay bales, or transporting heavy loads to various parts of the farm. None of the equipment looked to be in current use.

Bruno stopped his car in front of the tractor and walked around to the main entrance of the farm house. It looked deserted, as if there was no one at home so he prowled along each side of the building looking for signs of life, but without finding any. The lady of the house was not present, and unopened letters indicated an irregular visitor.

Walking back through the courtyard, Bruno noted that on two sides of the courtyard were large farm buildings, each one a six-metre high typical agricultural work building made from steel, with large sliding doors for access. Trying his luck, Bruno found that one wasn't locked and he was able to slide a door back far enough to step inside.

Inside the creaky metal construction was a collection of farm equipment and tools strewn about haphazardly at one end, and at the other a small red car, a Volkswagen UP. There were personal possessions inside that looked recently used – gloves and a tube of hand cream. It was not locked, and for some reason Bruno decided to get in. The position he found himself was a little cramped, and he adjusted the seat and rear view mirror to suit, before placing his hands on the wheel.

He sat in the car – obviously Phyllida's – wondering where she had gone to. He thought it unlikely that she'd have returned to visit her sister in Paris so soon after her previous trip. Perhaps she had friends on the Island who offered her some support at what for anyone in her present circumstances would be extremely distressing events?

After getting back out of the car some time later, Bruno walked back to the courtyard and stared at the buildings. What suddenly struck him was the sheer loneliness of the place. Even on a summer afternoon like this, the wind coming in from the ridge whistled around the abandoned and empty shacks, barns and other buildings nearby. Other farms would still be full of hustle and bustle at this kind of time, staff hard at work on the animals or produce; here however, the whole thing felt... dead.

How had Phyllida Glassman managed to survive this atmosphere of abandonment? What was her reason for staying? She didn't grow up on the farm, and she must have known she was fighting a losing battle with the banks.

It made sense what she'd seen in Sam, though. The relationship with him must have been a welcome distraction from the decay and the isolation. But then to stop tending the farm altogether as it appeared? Had she invested too much into her relationship with him at a cost of absolutely everything else around her?

Another thought came to Bruno as he considered their relationship. If, as Phyllida had proclaimed on Bruno's previous meeting with her, they really were in love, then for two mature adults, the distance between Southsea and Roud Farm was certainly no obstacle to an intimate relationship; surely considering their situations the two could have lived together either here or in Southsea without it having too much of an effect on each's daily responsibilities? And yet they had behaved as if they had lived in different countries, with irregular weekends together, and no contact in between.

As a detective, Bruno had learned to read a great deal from people's property. Here, on Phyllida's farm, it was easy enough even without his experience. There was an air of untended abandonment in the gardens and flowerbeds around the house; the grass was long, un-mown. It was clear that Phyllida only ever stayed here for a couple of days at a time – three at the most. It was somewhere she obviously just dropped in to pick up the post; there was no way it was her home, somewhere a person could live permanently – there would be tell-tale signs; tiny little things that said the place was *alive*.

After a half an hour, Bruno left. He hadn't enjoyed the loneliness one bit, but on top of that he began to get an uncomfortable feeling that somebody was lurking around the farm out of sight, watching his every move.

Chapter 28

Derek Bentley's comments about Professor Bartlett, Phyllida Glassman and the others persisted in Bruno's mind as he drove towards Newport. Heading south, he took a left at Chale along the Military Road that took him into Ventnor. There was a small luxury that the detective allowed himself when he needed to sit and think – a Mingella ice cream purchased from the Ventnor beach café. Thankfully, a space to park appeared along the beach promenade not more than three spaces from the one directly outside the kiosk.

Bruno fed the meter £2 and exchanged £2.50 of his coinage for a single vanilla cone at the ice cream counter. Not the best value, but worth it. Savouring the first bite, he strolled off in the direction of the Spyglass Inn at the western end of the promenade.

In the nineteen-fifties and sixties, Ventnor had been a highly popular holiday town for the lower-middle class families from southern England. The town had dinner, bed and breakfast guest houses with sea views facing the beach along the entire promenade. There was a mixture of families with toddlers on the beach and grandparents sleeping in the deckchairs, owned and managed by longshoreman families, whose names appeared in early Victorian photographs of the town on sunny summer Sunday afternoons.

In those last few years of the nineteenth century, the promenade had always been crowded with ladies in fine dresses and gentlemen wearing their best Sunday suits – always with a hat; the go-to accessory for the ladies of the day a parasol, and what fashion there was dictating that the young boys would all wear sailor suits. There would scarcely be an open space on the beach, which was crowded with bathing huts pushed thirty metres or so into the sea, from which ladies wearing swimwear that covered almost every single centimetre of flesh from head to toe would emerge to paddle about with as much dignity as such exercise allowed.

In the fifties, Ventnor had its own laundry and brewery, with the hundreds if not thousands of holidaymakers arriving by steam train.

Nowadays there was no train, no laundry, no brewery, not even a cinema let alone what Bruno would have called a 'proper picture house'; one had to search hard for a traditional B&B, with self-catering apartments having taken over as the norm for the millennial generation of visitors to the Island.

Bruno loved the cinema. He never missed a major film release, nowadays travelling into Newport to see it at the charmless multiplex, but in previous years he half-remembered visiting the Regent in Shanklin and the various 'bug hutches' to be found across the Island. His ice cream made him think of *The English Patient* and *The Talented Mr Ripley*, great films made by Anthony Mingella, who'd died young – just fifty-four. The name was no coincidence; the director's mother still owned the ice cream parlour, and the young Tony had worked there as a schoolboy. In Bruno's opinion – with which he felt confident the real cinema buffs would agree – Mingella had had so much more to offer, leaving this life before fulfilling his incredible talent. He had also cared passionately about Portsmouth FC, the club whose stadium was just across the Solent in an area of the city called Fratton; so much so in fact that he'd tried to save them from bankruptcy when they faced serious financial difficulty in the nineteen-nineties. Bruno remembered another fact; that Portsmouth were the team that had held the FA Cup for the longest: seven years in total. Of course, this was because they'd won it in 1939 before the Second World War had broken out, only relinquishing the title of 'current FA Cup holders' when the competition resumed in the 46–47 season.

As he took further small bites from the ice cream, Bruno's thoughts turned to the complex and frustrating puzzle of Sam Peters' murder.

Bentley had spoken about both Phyllida Glassman and Noel Bartlett in unflattering tones and he certainly came across as the type of person who *would* have known about the gold seam on his land since day one. He did not seem to enjoy the intrusion into his privacy the 'discovery' of the quartz had caused, neither did he have any time for people running around in circles trying to organise something that because of his unique veto ability was simply not going to happen any time soon at least.

Despite the alibi, Bruno wondered about Bentley, and just how angry he might have been with Sam's intrusion into his private world, whether that be extracting the gold particles from the river beds, or his crawling across land he had no right to search.

Bruno also felt slightly guilty about what he felt may have come across as an uninterested dismissal of his friend Janet's rather professional and impressive detective-like research into the 'Steph Helland murders' as she had now somewhat tongue-in-cheek coined Pumpkin and Musgrove's deaths... although Bruno knew despite the humorous approach that Janet really did feel that way.

He reconsidered the Andrew Pumpkin case, and on reflection felt that Janet had presented a re-analysis of available evidence which would potentially justify the re-opening of the case. The specialist motor oil supplied by the fishmonger detected on the upper steps of the staircase had certainly caused the solicitor to slip on and tumble down eighteen concrete steps to his death. But would the CPS be able to convince a jury that this was a case of deliberate murder? And if Steph had actually *pushed* him, how in blazes could such an act be proven? Nobody witnessed the slip, so no push could be determined. What they did have was that the type of oil used could only have been provided by Chris West. The fact that a significant amount of money was given by Steph to West after the death – to buy the waterside pub he ended up running into the ground – was certainly suspicious, but enough to bring a murder charge or even convince the super that it would need an investigation? It wasn't quite there yet; there was some tiny factor missing, he thought.

Then look at Steph. Two husbands meeting violent deaths after rather short marriages, and the resulting beneficiaries Steph and her bit-on-the-side Chris West.

The thing that had been causing Janet serious discomfort was that Steph's *present* circumstances mirrored those at the time of the previous two deaths, and should she – or Bruno – fail to prevent another murder then she knew she would struggle to cope with how that would make her feel.

Bruno *had* to put the facts to his station commander and get that permission to re-investigate with full authority Janet's pet case, and the one of the Godshill butcher that had haunted him since the day it happened.

***

Once the Ventnor sea air had cleared Bruno's mind, he returned to his list of principle suspects for the Sam Peters case. Bentley had suggested Phyllida Glassman was always up to something that *he* considered 'no good' most of the time. If it wasn't the wind turbine saga, it was Roman villas, not to mention getting involved with Sam and his gold mining scheme.

Bruno was keen to interview her again, and would be doing so right now if it wasn't for the fact that she'd disappeared – and for how long, come to think of it? The more times he had replayed the conversation with Bentley in his head, and the more he'd thought about that visit to the strange, almost morbid desolation of Roud Farm, the more he'd been convinced that there was some kind of murky depth hiding behind her calm, reserved front.

Bruno thought back to what Phyllida Glassman *had* revealed about her relationship with Sam.

In the weeks leading up to his death, Sam had stopped staying with Potter and had stayed with her. She had learned a great deal about him – well, certainly his situation. Recollecting the various things Glassman had said during his conversation with her, Bruno surmised that she'd established he was an unattached and somewhat wealthy bachelor, in fact at some point discovering exactly *how* wealthy. She had enjoyed visiting Sam's apartment in Southsea— *no, Bruno, think carefully about what is certain and what is not* —she had *said* she enjoyed visiting Sam's apartment in Southsea... but this had not been mentioned anywhere within Sam's diary, on any other computer document, or in any notepad or paperwork he had left behind.

And if she had visited, how much time had she spent there? Bruno recalled that the flat certainly hadn't looked like it had had even the slightest female touch, yet surely if she'd stayed over more than once or twice there'd be *some* sign? Was Phyllida Glassman's professed love for Sam simply a means to an end? Or, even worse, was there something more sinister here?

She had claimed the person who took up most of Sam's time was Noel Bartlett, the geologist from Southampton University. According to her, Bartlett had always wanted to know when Sam was coming to the Island, what was he doing, who he was seeing and what it was about. She also said that Sam never told Bartlett that he was staying with her; apparently he let no one into his private life.

She thought that was probably to do with his childhood, that sort of behaviour usually begins with something that happened then, she had said. Bruno replayed this part of their conversation in his head.

"It didn't really come to light much, except in his dealings with Professor Bartlett – Sam's secretiveness, that is. Perhaps if he'd been more open, whoever killed him might not have had reason to. I don't know. But as our relationship developed, he lost interest in treasure hunting on the Island. I think I may have convinced him that gold mining in the middle of a beauty spot was wrong, and that to cause such a monstrous thing would play on his conscience. Bartlett, on the other hand, thought the opposite. The way *he* saw it, this was his moment, his chance for fame, for recognition. His obsession is exploiting the natural riches of the earth – with no real care for who would gain! Every day that passed Sam felt worse about it though. He said that 'experts' would come to the Island, certain in their knowledge that a single quartz seam couldn't exist in isolation. He talked of seeing a vision of the Island being ripped up from top to bottom, but couldn't do anything to stop it; he'd opened Pandora's box, it was too late."

Bruno thought hard about this. Had Sam really had a change of heart? How did that tally with his activities, with the people that he spoke with? At which point had he turned? Most importantly, if he was now against gold mining, there were a whole host of possible new motives. As a priority, Bruno needed to find out what Sam had been doing on the Island between the time he arrived that day, and the point at which he was murdered.

And he needed to get hold of Phyllida Glassman urgently.

***

Bruno was now driving to Godshill to find Dick Potter.

Thinking about his conversation with Phyllida, he also recalled that she'd said that she wasn't aware Sam had been on the Island between the Wednesday the sixteenth and Saturday the nineteenth of July. It had seemed a little strange at the time, but now he thought about it even more so. If they were as close as she suggested – and that's close enough to give her everything in his will – why would he have visited the Island without telling her? Furthermore, where had he stayed if not with her?

Thus he had decided to speak to the one person who might be able to answer that question.

Bruno knocked on the door of the depressing B&B, and for some reason jumped when a voice suddenly spoke to him from the open hall window.

"You're lucky Inspector, I was just going fishing today! We had no punters last night, so *she's* still in bed, taking a day off. Now what can I do for you?"

***

Over coffee, Bruno asked Dick Potter to recall every incident in his relationship with Sam during the two or three weeks before his death.

"Did his demeanour change; was he preoccupied; did you feel he lacked interest in what you were doing?"

Potter was keen to be helpful, and put on somewhat of a show of silently thinking before answering, then speaking slowly and thoughtfully. Of course, this in fact made it harder for Bruno to decide whether or not the truth was making a particularly strong appearance today.

"I did think at one time, near the end, that he was more interested in the quartz than in the gold panning, even though I was going at a great pace. He seemed to have lost interest even in the money. I got the feeling that there was something else he was doing on the Island, otherwise – if he really didn't care about things, why still come over from the mainland?"

"Have you got a record of which nights he stayed with you?"

"I remember, Inspector... because he stopped staying here, except for when Bartlett came with him. Wondered if we'd upset him or something. We reckon he must have stayed somewhere over towards Freshwater, because there were times he turned up to see me early enough that he couldn't have come over from Portsmouth that morning."

"Perhaps it was a *slightly* more modern guest house?" Bruno said, doing his best not to sound offensive, or smile too much.

"Hmm," Potter replied, noncommittally.

"It's important I find out where he stayed; after all, if he became acquainted with the owner of another guest house, I'd have to consider them as a potential suspect," Bruno said, wondering if the hidden message that Potter was still potentially under suspicion would force the truth out.

"*I* think he might have had a fancy-woman," Potter said, cocking his head to one side.

Bruno raised an eyebrow.

"I don't think Sam would have been killed by a new lover," Potter assured Bruno. "I mean, he was a bit boring, wasn't he? Type of woman he'd go for would be the same – not interesting enough to be a killer, right?"

It was now Bruno's turn to say "Hmm," after which he continued along a different line.

"How's Professor Bartlett?"

"Honestly haven't seen him since Sam's death. What he's doing gives him what he wants, which isn't a share of this" he said, pointing with an arm towards the coal shed at the rear of the bungalow, where he kept and sorted the metal shards from his gold panning on the East Yar. "He wants the quartz mine, and he hasn't been here to see me, basically because I'm the treasure hunting partner. Apart from Harry, nobody knows that, Inspector, and that's how I like it. Bartlett doesn't actually want to be *seen* as a treasure hunter or a panner like me, turning over stones. He's Mr Big Shot, a wise guy, he wants *recognition* for his discovery... which I suppose he'll get *now*, won't he?"

Bruno looked at Potter quizzically. The way he'd said this last sentence seemed to leave an unspoken undertone hanging in the air.

"You suppose he'll get *now*?"

"Well, really, Sam found the quartz, didn't he? He discovered it when he saw rock chippings fall from the cliff during a storm. He retraced it from the cliff fall back from the cliff until he exposed it on the Downs. Now *Bartlett* is claiming to have discovered it, and as Sam's dead, there's no one to say he didn't. Now that's not my business Inspector, I couldn't give a monkey's. For me, the river deposits that have been washed out of the quartz, *they* are heaven sent. I've never been so lucky in my life. I'm not stupid, Inspector. I know it's going to run out eventually, or the owners of the river banks are going to find out what I'm doing, and then I'll have to stop stealing their gold... but by then I'll have flushed out what's worth anything, and what's left will be such hard work they're welcome to it!"

"So you're saying Bartlett's my man, then?" Bruno asked, feeling a little queasy at the fact that Potter seemed to have taken control of the whole conversation.

"Now I'm not saying he's a murderer, Inspector, at least not without something more concrete than you've got at the moment. Last time we met, I said I thought it's an Island person, I *still* think that, but I am not a detective. But if it isn't Bartlett, I'd say the killer is somebody *close* to your list of suspects. Maybe it's someone you haven't even run in to yet, but I'm sure you will if you keep at it, Inspector."

***

Potter's final words hung around in Bruno's head for a long time after their conversation had ended.

Considering his recent discovery that Phyllida had a handyman do odd jobs around the farm according to Bentley, he found Potter's words strangely relevant. But was that just another coincidence? Or did he actually know something? But how would Potter know who was even *on* his suspect list?

Bruno started to wonder if it wasn't the time to spread the net as wide as possible. What if it wasn't an Islander but someone on the mainland? A mainland killer would surely have needed to come to the Island by car, and so he requested his desk officer at Newport Police station ask the ferry operators for the records of all car, van and motorcycle registration numbers that had passed through one of the three ferry terminals within a couple of days either side of the murder. It was a standard 'wideband' technique, but in many cases such a search had proven highly useful, so in this case, he thought, it might just lead somewhere. Similarly, he asked Tom to handle the request from the Portsmouth side, knowing that depending on the service, the registrations might only be taken on boarding and not departure from the ferry.

Bruno's next thought turned to Arnold Harris. From what he himself had told Bruno, there was motive there alright – Sam coming over to the Island as a treasure hunter, plundering the local area of its precious hidden secrets. And there was no doubt that Harris was boiling inside with resentment; people like him could certainly turn into killers. But if Harris were to take a cudgel to someone, there were surely people on his list higher up than Sam, one of a thousand treasure hunter's he'd probably processed applications for, and although clearly didn't like him, he didn't know Sam Peters from Adam. No, if Harris flipped, his first target would be whoever he felt had 'done him' out of his rightful inheritance, and whatever Sam's crimes in his eyes, that would not be one of them. No, Harris was someone to discount at this juncture.

Chapter 29

Janet had been busy since Bruno had last seen her. She had spent the day planning a search for Chris West, who was surely in the areas having discovered the whereabouts of his former mistress, Steph, from the receptionist at Helland's car dealership.

Janet's view was that if she was correct about the two past deaths, West would be looking at Steph's new wealth with an eager eye, and with nothing to lose would possibly look to blackmail her.

What would Steph do, though? Keep the peace, avoid hostility and pay him off with some cash? And if it had to be cash, how much? Surely there's a limit to what she could spend without her disinterested husband asking questions that she wouldn't want to answer.

It was Janet's opinion that the two of them had collaborated in two murders and split the spoils. Maybe the temptation to repeat what had succeeded twice before might actually be attractive to Steph. Maybe Helland's wealth was such that she saw it as the ultimate goal, enabling her to escape all links to her previous life for good.

But similarly, Steph might simply want rid of West; he could be an unpredictable danger, an unknown quantity, a bomb ready to go off, the timer hidden from view. Maybe she'd look to 'deal' with West? But he was physically strong and wary of her; desperate he may be, but Janet felt he was unlikely to allow himself to be manipulated into a dangerous situation.

Could it descend into the two of them plotting and planning to such an extent that their own lives were at stake from each other?

The more Janet thought about it, the more convinced she became that Steph could never pay West off. He was too unstable and too far gone on his road to alcoholism and self-destruction. With an understanding of psychology and her appreciation of the human condition, Janet was sure that West would blame Steph for steering him along his current path, that it was him who was suffering for the sins that she had committed. No amount of money would be enough to restore his self-respect, so Janet's concern was that West was in serious danger of taking Steph down with him somehow or somewhere. Clearly both their lives were in danger.

Every summer, around this time, Janet took her own aging parents on a short holiday break so that they could spend time as a family unit, and enjoy themselves; these were often the few days that the headteacher *truly* got away from her school.

This year, Janet had chosen to take them for a four-night stay at the Royal Bath hotel in the centre of Bournemouth, a stone's throw from the pier, the beach and centre of town. She knew they'd be happy to entertain themselves during the day, which – by pure chance, of course – would enable her to continue her investigation into the troubled twosome of Steph Helland and Chris West.

***

On the first day of the holiday, Janet set off on her quest starting at Helland's motor showroom. She was pleased to see Helen was still employed as the showroom receptionist; her previous visit as a 'potential customer' had resulted in an interesting exchange of information – although most of it had been one way.

Helen recognised Janet the moment she walked in, and after the 'hellos' and coffee, but before she was whisked away by a salesman, the two engaged in a purposeful chat.

Janet expressed her surprise that Helen was still happily in her job considering Steph's previous threat to her.

"She hasn't turned up here since," said Helen. "The damage was done when I gave him her number. You know, a few days afterwards, a detective from Bournemouth CID called me, Detective Morrison I think. I was so worried, I thought she'd reported me to them and *I* was in trouble, but actually he was interested in the man – West, that was definitely who it was, *West*. Well this detective didn't tell me much, but asked what I'd said to him, and what he'd said to me. All he told me about why he was asking was that something had happened to this West, but he wouldn't tell me what it was. It all seemed a bit over the top to me, you know, storm in a teacup kind of thing."

"And you say she hasn't been back in?"

"No, but I bet she's just biding her time. When I make the tiniest mistake, she'll hear about it somehow and then do anything she can to get rid of me then. But I'm careful, and I don't think she'd sack me without a good reason – she knows I'd go to an employment tribunal, and I doubt Mr Helland would want the publicity."

Unfortunately, Janet's time was up as a beaming salesman strode over with the latest brochure.

Janet suddenly remembered an appointment that had previously slipped her mind, but assured the salesman that she'd be back to talk through the options sometime soon.

Chapter 30

Much though Bruno trusted Janet, he felt that it wouldn't be wise for her to be speaking to Detective Morrison at Bournemouth CID without him there to gloss over any questions that might arise regarding the slight steps made outside normal police protocols and procedures he'd personally afforded her.

At Janet's insistence that it really *was* important – "*What* has happened to West?" she must have asked at least six times – Bruno arranged to come over from the Island on Thursday evening, and speak with Morrison with Janet in tow on the Friday. He arranged an off-the record meeting with his mainland counterpart, which usually meant food and drinks would be on him. It certainly wouldn't help his progress on the Peters' case, but he knew Janet, and that meant he knew there was no getting out of this one.

***

Friday 8th August

Bruno, Janet and Detective Morrison from Bournemouth CID met in a small coffee shop around the corner from the local HQ. Bruno introduced Janet as his 'specialist civilian advisor', which had the unintended consequence of Morrison complaining about how his budget didn't come close to affording such extravagances. Bruno thought about letting on that Janet's work was on a voluntary basis, but decided to hold onto the truth for *just* a little longer.

Morrison came across as the kind of copper who preferred to avoid some of the red tape that had found its way into policing over the last decade or so. Cut corners, yes, but cut those corners *by the book*. Such a trait meant that he and Bruno naturally got on quite well.

After Bruno filled his new friend in on as much of the story as he needed to, he listened eagerly as Morrison told his tale.

"It was a break in, that wasn't a break in," he said. "We had a call from Mrs Helland—"

"That's Stephanie Helland, yes?" Janet interjected.

"Correct," Morrison replied before continuing. "She said that someone was attempting to enter her house through the conservatory at the rear. When we arrived, this Mr West was sitting alone in the conservatory itself, happily drinking from a whisky bottle! My colleague went upstairs to look for Mrs Helland, who it turned out had been too frightened to go and investigate... generally the right choice, I'd say."

"Indeed," Bruno replied. "So what was the story then?"

"Well," Morrison said excitedly, "*He* seemed taken aback that we had turned up, and claimed he'd been invited in. He was smiling and sipping at his glass as if he was meant to be there. I thought it was all a bit funny, took his name and details down and starting checking him out, but then my shift partner brings the lady of the house downstairs and as soon as she saw him she apologised and said it had all been a mistake – that she'd simply forgotten he was meant to be visiting that evening."

"Sounds a bit unlikely to me," Bruno stated.

"Well that's what we thought. I asked if there was anyone else in the house, and she said no, her husband was away on Business in Birmingham. Between me and my partner we must have asked if she was definitely OK three of four times, but she was very insistent... in fact she seemed pretty keen to get *us* out of there, not him!

Well, we left, but it didn't stop me checking him out. He doesn't have a criminal record, which is unusual because he's supposedly sleeping rough or living in a squat. Mind you, if he carries on with that kind of behaviour, he'll have a record soon enough. But it turns out, from what I was told, Mrs Helland *does* know him – although quite how well I never found out.

"Mr Morrison," Janet began, "what did *you* make of Mrs Helland?"

"Hmm. She seemed very embarrassed when she saw him; she regretted calling us, simply told us to go. It was all a bit odd. When I spoke to my shift-mate, we agreed he had to be a ghost from the past, you know? Like a brother she'd fallen out with, or an old lover."

"And was that it?" asked Bruno.

"Not entirely," Morrison replied. The following day I called her, as routine, and enquired if everything was OK. She said that it was and that there had been a simple misunderstanding between her and this West about their meeting, but there was no problem with it. She then asked if I would not raise the matter with her husband, who would worry unnecessarily about her when he was away."

"I thought that might have been in there somewhere," Janet chuckled, but without any real humour.

"So where is West now?" asked Bruno.

"Frankly, he could be anywhere, although I'd bet he's still in Bournemouth. If we run into him for any reason, I'll let you know. How's that?"

As a quid-pro-quo, Bruno gave Morrison a little more background information on West's activities on the Island, without mentioning murder suspicions. The two accepted their respective information gained was a fair trade.

They also agreed to share any future actions involving West. Morrison further reminded Bruno of current policy.

"Don't forget that if anything happens to him in the near future, Mrs Helland will be one of the people contacted by the community liaison team." he said, before the ritual shaking of hands and the 'goodbyes'

***

"It's impossible to know what went on", Janet said, "but I'd imagine she feels that her current status is under threat."

"True. I think that just shows how ruthless an operator this West can be. In my opinion, something will happen between the pair of them, and we need to be around to find out about it."

Bruno was no expert on the mind of a serial killer, but if you could recover from the emotional trauma involved in your first kill, and succeed with a second, he reckoned a third would hold no fear or thought of being caught. It was clear that Janet's thoughts fell somewhat along the same lines.

"To escape from the situation she's now in, she has to kill West or her new husband," was Janet's dramatic conclusion. "West's demise will solve her problems, *if* she can get away with it," she said.

As she finished saying these words, it dawned on the pair that they were genuinely considering the possibility of Steph being not just an opportunist, but a fully-fledged serial killer."

Janet's train of thought got there first.

"West is not going to be considering the possibility that *he* might be a target, is he?" she said.

"No, that's just what I was thinking."

"Should we warn him?"

"First we'd need to find him."

"You're right. we don't know where he is."

"No," said Bruno. "And to be honest, we're still only really guessing that the two of them committed those two murders together. And we still have no actual proof as is required by the laws of our country! That's the one piece of the puzzle that we need."

"And I believe," Janet replied, "that West will give that to us, given a little time."

"Time I don't have, Janet. I need to report back to JB otherwise I'll be in big trouble."

"*One* more day?" she begged.

"*One* more day," he agreed.

Chapter 31

Saturday 9ᵗʰ August

At midday, Bruno received a text from Detective Matt Morrison of Bournemouth CID, informing him that Chris West had been arrested after a drunken disturbance at a bed & breakfast in Bournemouth the previous evening.

West had returned to the six-bedroom guest house with two drunken 'friends', whom the owner would not allow in the building. Unsurprisingly considering the amount of alcohol consumed, a fight had broken out, the police had been called, and the three drunken men had been arrested on charges of being drunk and disorderly and of violent behaviour.

Bruno called Morrison back at Bournemouth Police Station where the arrests had been processed, and found out some interesting information. It had been Steph Helland who had paid the bill for West to stay in the B&B. The owner had refused to allow West to enter the building to pick up his belongings, so suggested she would therefore have to do so.

The three men were bound over to keep the peace and given a conditional discharge.

"I should imagine they'll all return to sleeping rough now the fun's over," added Morrison.

Janet decided to visit the B&B and see what information she could find out from the owner.

***

The Bournemouth Bed & Breakfast Guest House at Alma Road had exactly six letting rooms and, by the owner's admission, was small enough for three drunken men to cause chaos.

"And turn this place into a doss house in five minutes if I'd have let them in," said Jim Watt, the owner.

"I allowed West to keep a room because Mrs Helland paid for his whole month's bed and breakfast up front. But he's not coming back now, so if she wants a refund she can come and pick up his things."

"Do you know where Mr West might be now?" said Janet.

"Sleeping rough on the beach if it's still warm enough outside, or maybe you could try the YMCA in Suffolk Road. Best thing would be to ask her though, I'd imagine she'd know. I reckon they must be related – can't think why else she'd pay for a room for him."

***

Janet had been thinking about it for a while, but decided now was the time: she wanted to speak to Stephanie Helland, if only to see if she did know of Chris West's whereabouts.

Bruno agreed that the best way for Janet to proceed was a 'cold call' at the Hellands' home and scribbled the address he'd learned from Morrison out onto a piece of notepaper.

"I'll say I'm from the court probation service, as her booking the room for him would have been noted either on his arrest or release," said Janet.

Bruno put his fingers in his ears, jokingly, suggesting that he'd rather not be told the finer details of Janet's plan if it meant bending the rules (or outright lying, his deeper conscience added, a little embarrassed).

"Look, I know you can handle yourself Janet, but... be *careful*," Bruno said, the kindness clear in his voice. "You've been fantastic so far, and I appreciate everything you've done, but Stephanie Helland is dangerous. That I think we both agree on."

***

It was a three-mile drive to the Hellands' property in Sandbanks on the Poole side of Bournemouth, home to football managers and the nouveau-riche of the city. For Steph, Janet knew, living there was a giant step up, and had brought her into contact with people of a class she had only dreamed about before.

After locating her house and seeing a white Mercedes SUV parked on the drive, Janet dropped Bruno at a café around half a mile away to await her return. He had wanted to sit outside in the car but Janet had dissuaded him, reassuring him that she had a mobile to hand.

At the agreed time, there was no sign of Janet. She'd told him to sit tight if this was the case.

Twenty minutes later and Bruno was getting worried. Where was she?

Forty minutes now and Bruno was quite concerned. He decided that when the hour was up he'd go looking for her, agreement or not!

His watch signified the hour and Bruno got up to leave—

—just as Janet walked in through the door.

***

"She bought the court story hook, line and sinker," Janet said, beaming. "She was alone, the house was beautifully laid out, modern, well-furnished and clean. She took it that I was providing a support role for drug and alcohol abusers. I told her that paying for accommodation for a homeless man was such a kind thing to do, and asked if she'd considered volunteer work in the sector."

"Have I ever told you that you're a genius?" Bruno asked her. He had realised straight away that assuming (or at least *pretending* to assume) that Steph had no prior relationship with West would ease any fears she might have, and would likely get something out of her.

Janet described to Bruno how Steph had seemed a little distressed about her name being linked with Chris West's – she'd asked a number of questions about the procedure, and how private the information was, which Janet had winged the answers to... thankfully, it seemed, to Steph's satisfaction.

"I don't know Chris West," Steph had said. "He broke into our conservatory a couple of weeks ago. He was just a wandering drunk who was after liquor. I felt sorry for him, but was also frightened he might come back, so I rang a B&B from the phone book and checked him in for four weeks. He was sober enough when he left here for them to give him a room. I drove him there to get him off the estate as quickly as possible, without anyone else around here being troubled."

Janet said she'd then asked Steph if she'd been in contact with West before.

"No," she had said. "I'd never set eyes on him until that night, I know nothing more about him so I can't help you with his whereabouts."

"Of course, that was contrary to what she had told the two police who had been called out on the night of the burglary; then she had claimed it had been a misunderstanding and that she did know him," Janet added. "But I didn't' say that."

"What did you say?" Bruno asked.

"I said I supposed he might turn up again considering how kind she had been to him."

"Next time I will rely on the police to deal with him." had been Steph's response.

Janet said that she had then asked Steph once again about potentially volunteering to assist the city's needy."

"I can't," Steph had said. "I am busy helping my husband's business. If you give me your card, I'll send you some money through."

"I said I would send her some literature and reminded her that Jim Watt at the B&B had West's belongings and a refund for the nights paid and not taken. I noticed that my reminder irritated her, as I was highlighting her indiscretion in how she had handled the West encounter at her home, and she seemed to want to move on."

"The significance of her denial of knowing West could be enough to get him talking, if it's put to him correctly," said Bruno.

"What if she knows where he is?" asked Janet.

"I think he's on the streets, so she won't know *exactly* where he is. But he is an uncontrollable threat to everything she has, and if what you say is correct, he won't go away. We must be cautious; There are many ways an alcoholic can meet an untimely death, they are accident prone in every part of normal life," said Bruno.

"If she finds out where he is, I don't give him much chance, all things considered," said Janet. "I honestly think that we should find him to stop anything bad happening to him."

She was right. As a matter of urgency Chris West had to be protected.

***

Saturday 9th August

After a visit to the YMCA and Salvation Army hostels in Bournemouth town centre proved negative, Bruno and Janet strolled through the Winter Gardens and the neighbouring bars, but saw nobody resembling the mug shot of Chris West that Inspector Morrison had sent over to Bruno's phone.

"Let's ask the guys on the beat to help us find him," said Bruno, who called Morrison's mobile number and asked if he'd help. He duly got the message out to the coppers on the streets and told Bruno he'd be in touch as soon as he was spotted.

Bruno was suddenly reminded of his wider duties when he received a message from Tom Craven saying that they had located Sam Peters' Golf GTi in an NCP car park at Portsmouth Harbour. It had been there since 10:10 pm on Saturday the nineteenth of July, and had now been transported to Hampshire Police's car pound.

Reluctantly leaving the warm summer seaside, not to mention her parents on the final evening of their holiday together, Janet drove Bruno to see Sam's car, the pound being located adjacent to Portsmouth Police HQ. The car had 'WARNING' stickers in a number of prominent areas, indicating that it had been left sealed, awaiting the forensic team to examine.

Bruno was optimistic that the forensic report would include finger prints, and maybe even traces of blood in the car if Peters' body had been lifted in and out of it. He also knew that in an emotional state after having committed a murder, many perpetrators would forget to take important evidence away with them, and couldn't help hoping that would be the case here. Bruno could hear a voice inside his head, urging him to break the seals and have a poke around in the car... although prudence directed him to follow the rules which prohibited him doing so until it was officially released by forensics.

Thankfully, Bruno's presence at the pound persuaded forensics to get a move on, and within two hours they had finished their examination and released the car to Bruno just as Tom arrived.

Tom watched as Bruno silently looked around the car, bending down here and there, taking a look at this and that, then eventually just getting into the car and sitting in the driver's seat.

Bruno suddenly had a shot of déjà vu. He knew he'd been thinking of how he had sat in Phyllida Glassman's Volkswagen on the farm, but couldn't place that strange, annoying pang that he felt.

Shaking his head as he climbed out of the Golf, Bruno paused for a moment. He then thought about what he'd just done.

Most people, when getting into a different car to normal, adopt the routine drilled into them all those years ago when they were learning to drive. Check and adjust the rear view mirror, adjust the driving seat, then check and adjust the wing mirrors before finally checking the handbrake and gearstick are at a suitable distance.

This is exactly what Bruno had done when he had sat in the Golf, and carefully thinking back to the adjustments made, realised that the last person to drive it couldn't have been Sam Peters himself – he was taller than Bruno and would certainly not have been able to control the car from such a cramped position. Therefore, the last person to drive it was surely connected with – if not directly responsible for – his murder.

Bruno wondered out loud to Tom if any CCTV footage would be found of the car being driven, and if so, what secrets it might show. Tom smiled and led him inside the HQ to his computer.

The Portsmouth to Fishbourne views of the car, on the outbound journey on Wednesday the sixteenth of July, showed Sam Peters, a six-foot tall man, in the driving seat of the Golf. More interestingly though, on the car's return journey, in the early evening of Saturday the nineteenth of July under a grey, rain-threatened sky, the film showed the rear view of the Golf driving on to the 8:30 pm ferry at Fishbourne in a line of traffic. Sight of the VW was lost once aboard the ferry and no on-board camera identified the driver. On the return to vehicle instruction, called on the ships speaker system, a person was seen to emerge from the lowest level door, walk a dozen paces to the Golf and climb into the driver's seat. That person was of *medium* height, wearing bulky clothing, a hooded jacket and walking boots, and interestingly determined not to be recognised.

The car left the ferry in convoy, before breaking off, presumably to make the mile- long journey to the NCP car park across the road from Portsmouth Harbour train station. Tom studied the video images of all passengers returning to the Island later on that same Saturday evening, the nineteenth of July, to see if the strangely dressed driver of Sam Peters Golf was amongst them, should they have made an immediate return to the Island.

There was no sign of a similarly dressed passenger returning to the Island on that route up to the last departure at 11:35 pm that evening. Later Tom examined the Hovercraft departures and the possibility that they travelled to Southampton to travel on the Red Funnel line to Cowes, with similar results.

Was it a mistake for the driver to have driven the car to a registered place to park it or would it have been better to have abandoned it on the Island? If the killer *was* from the mainland, surely he would not have driven the car back to Portsmouth, unless it was someone trying to *pretend* that the murderer was from the mainland.

It turned out that the return portion of the car ferry ticket purchased by Peters for his outward journey from Portsmouth, was discovered in the car.

***

Neither Bruno, Tom nor Janet were deluded by the killers returning Sam's car to Portsmouth, and they all agreed that such an act suggested the killer was an Islander, narrowing Bruno's 'priority list' to five people: Bartlett, Potter, Harris, Noway and Glassman.

Bruno talked through his reasoning for the exclusion of the first four people on this list, now leaving Phyllida Glassman as his prime suspect – and even more worryingly, she was not returning his calls.

To be honest, if he had wanted, Bruno could have made a *case* for suspecting Bartlett, but it would be mostly based on psychological factors, profiling and predicting human nature rather than any actual evidence; and generally that theory would ignore the most important analytical point of all: Bruno's gut feeling. Bartlett certainly wasn't everyone's 'cup of tea', but he did not come across to Bruno as someone who was capable of murder.

Tom pointed out the fly in the ointment here – the report about the disappearance of the files from the Santa Maria, along with the suspicious death of the First Mate. Yet Bruno was convinced that Bartlett's knowledge of his subject would have allowed him to re-plot the course.

Tom did however convince Bruno to have a quick look for Bartlett and see how he reacted to the latest news.

***

Finding Bartlett was surprisingly easy; he was at the University preparing for the new term set to begin in a month's time.

Bruno decided to share elements of progress with him. He began by telling him that Peters' car had been driven back to Portsmouth from the Island after the murder, but the driver could not be identified by cameras and that the car was still under examination by police forensics. Bartlett's reaction was neither disturbed nor anxious – in fact he seemed genuinely interested, so Bruno felt safe telling him a little more.

"When time has passed with any Police investigation, the crime goes out of focus. People begin to mis-remember details, or to question their own memories... so it's most important that we make progress as soon as possible," Bruno explained.

"I understand," said Bartlett.

"Professor," Bruno began firmly, "I need to know if you can give me *any* further information or if there's something else you have lately remembered that perhaps slipped your mind in a previous discussion?"

"Inspector, if I had any knowledge that could help you I would have already told you. What sort of thing do you mean?"

"In your relationship with Peters, do you think he was afraid of you?"

Bartlett did not comment straight away, but made a face to suggest that he thought this was a strange question, certainly not one he was expecting.

"Not to my knowledge, no, Inspector."

"How do you explain the instances of him keeping secrets from you, of not telling you everything that was going on?"

"Oh, I don't believe he trusted me, but from what I gathered Sam Peters trusted nobody. This paranoia didn't get in the way of what we were doing. In my opinion, he had a complex. In particular, I believe he could not stand criticism of anything he did. That's why he worked alone – so any mistakes he might make were known to him alone. I'm sorry Inspector, but you're barking up the wrong tree I fear. Sam's relationship with me was no different to his relationship with anyone else."

"What about Phyllida Glassman? You met her, I believe?"

"I did, yes. I spent a night at Roud Farm with her and Sam."

"What was she like, in your opinion?"

"She was a threat to him, the way I saw it."

"Oh? How so?"

"Ah, excuse me inspector, perhaps not my best choice of words. She was a threat to his way of life I should say. I wish he'd spoken to me about her; I feel I could have helped Sam. I don't believe they suited each other, and she was a distraction from his way of life. I couldn't quite see what she saw in him."

"Perhaps there was simply no one else on her radar?"

"I suppose that's true – and admittedly that surprised me. She was charming, interesting, good looking and had a wealthy air about her... although incidentally I don't believe she actually had any money."

"Was she a threat to you and your plans?"

"I suppose she was, at least to the project I was working with Sam on. She wanted to keep him to herself – women always do. But I wasn't having any of it. I had my objective and I was getting on with it," Bartlett added somewhat pompously.

"I understand you were hoping to take a year off to manage the mining operation. Is that right?" Bruno asked, deciding to see if Bartlett's responses would tie up with the facts he'd already gained from other sources such as Noway and Bentley – presuming *they* were true.

"That was my initial proposition to Hamdens," Bartlett admitted, "but I never held out any real hope of them putting me in charge." Bruno was convinced this statement was simply to help himself restore his damaged pride; why submit the suggestion if it was pointless?

"In the end we agreed that I would write a book about the entire mining project from a geological, business and environmental point of view. I shall become the expert on the Island's gold mining opportunities. And in time something will happen with the quartz deposits on Bentley's land. Inspector, in my job as a University Professor, I can take a sabbatical for a year if I want to do research or write a book, unpaid of course. The University do in fact *expect* me to publish, in order to raise the profile of the faculty, which I do every so often. It also enables me to keep up to date in my profession."

"Do you keep in touch with Dick Potter?"

"He has everything under control, and we have an arrangement over money which includes Harry the smelter. If I make anything from that I'll be lucky. But I don't mind, I was never in it to share the profits from the panning."

Bartlett paused, took a break, and continued.

"Inspector, your questions indicate to me that you are focusing purely on Sam's involvement in this gold mining business. Are you sure you're focusing on the right area of Sam's life to detail? Forgive my offering of an opinion, but have you looked at some of the property deals Sam was involved in? There are many dodgy people in property. Some of their deals rely solely on surveyors' reports. It can make a difference of millions one way or another in what you pay, or what you get for something; Sam had some large clients, where everything he worked on was big money stuff. There were insurance claims which ran into hundreds of thousands, every single one of which relied solely on Sam's survey opinions, which – no matter how hard one tries – are always opinions. With the projects on which Sam worked, there were bound to be situations and disagreements, sharks working fiddles. The property business makes the gold business look small fry," he concluded.

Normally Bruno would have felt somewhat angry about a 'civilian' such as this doesn't-live-in-the-real-world academic offering opinions about how to do his job better... but for whatever reason, Bartlett's observations created a feeling of anxiety within Bruno: *had* he missed the point from the beginning? *Had* he concentrated on the wrong thing? Were the Island and Sam's activities thereon irrelevant and the killer connected to his day-to-day business? Bartlett had reminded him of his track record of failing as a murder investigator (which was how Bruno saw the result of the Stanley Musgrove 'Godshill Butcher' case).

It was true, Bruno had ignored Sam's list of surveying business clients for the most part, concentrating on his Island activities purely because of where he had been found. Was this a serious oversight?

"Take a look at his big deal clients, Inspector," Bartlett was saying. "You don't know what kind of people he's been doing business with."

No, Bruno decided. He was *not* wrong. Everything pointed towards the gold mining activities. Opening up Sam's business files would be a blind alley, a waste of time... and would not produce a single clue. To begin a line of investigation into Sam's business contacts would be like searching for a needle in a haystack, fraught with blind alleys that even a specialist financial fraud investigator would struggle to unwind. Even JB had agreed with his analysis of the case. To completely change tack now would be professional suicide.

After all, Bartlett was still a suspect, even if he was mostly discounted. His suggestion to look elsewhere could be genuine concern, but it could also be a ploy to get him to alter the course of his investigation *away* from his present suspects, of which Bartlett *knew* he was one.

***

Bruno returned to the Island on a Red Funnel ferry as a foot passenger and took a taxi home from Cowes, all the time switching between doubt and assuredness that because of the significance of Beacon Alley he was concentrating on the Island.

Tom had long since returned home to rest, and Janet was somewhere between Bournemouth and her home, collecting her parents at the end of their holiday.

Bruno lay in bed going over and over the case in his mind. He was tired both physically and mentally, but the sleep he desperately needed was a long time coming.

Chapter 32

Sunday 10th August

Bruno was woken at 7:00 am by Janet who was already en-route back to the Island with her parents. She agreed to come over as soon as she had delivered them home.

After explaining what Bartlett had said to him, Bruno confessed to Janet his concern that he'd been heading down the wrong path since the start of the case.

"Listen," Janet replied, "let's both talk through where you're at, and see if there's anything – even the tiniest little detail – that has been missed. After that, if you really are at a dead end, then you can start on the business files tomorrow. It might not be the most appealing prospect, but it's not as if you have any other choice."

I could quit, Bruno thought, not sure himself whether he was serious or not.

"Forensics have finalised their examination of the car and are preparing the report, which I'll be given tomorrow," he said, "so I suppose today's free if you don't object to giving me some help."

***

Bruno had only just finished showering and dressing when another call came through.

It was Morrison.

And it was about Chris West.

According to witnesses he'd been hit by a car that had sped away from a public car park. He'd been taken to Bournemouth General Hospital and was currently in the ICU.

Bruno thanked Morrison and called Janet.

"Fancy a visit to Bournemouth? It's been ages since we last visited!"

***

On arrival at the hospital, Bruno and Janet received an update as to West's situation.

"He has a broken knee cap, broken pelvis, broken ribs, cracked sternum and some minor internal organ damage." the doctor explained to them. "It seems that he was falling over drunk and lurched into an oncoming car. He's being kept under at the moment, but he's stable. You might be waiting a while to talk to him, but there's no rush – he's going to be here for some time yet, and he won't be walking for weeks."

Bruno nodded his thanks to the doctor who smiled, and went off to fix the next poor soul who arrived on a stretcher. He and Janet quietly opened the door to the single room in which West was lying, and entered. Each found a seat to occupy and waited.

Despite what they knew about Chris West, it was impossible for them not to feel sorry for him, lying in this hospital bed, unable to move, under the influence of pain killers but suffering terribly from the withdrawal symptoms that had begun to kick in.

It wasn't until six pm that evening that West stirred, at which point Bruno – having discussed strategy with Janet – got up and left the room.

***

Sunday 10th August, 6:00 pm

Despite the painkillers, the injuries Chris West had sustained in the hit-and-run eclipsed much of the pain of being sober. His trembling body added to the discomfort he felt, and in his mind he wondered just how close to death he might be. The only positive thought he had was that he was alive – and that wasn't much consolation.

But the things this kind woman was saying were helping him. A police officer was she? Maybe one of those community support types. Certainly not like most of the police who treated him like he was a bit of turd on their shoe. She'd said she was with a detective, so must be some kind of assistant or liaison officer, right? Was this detective in the room? No, couldn't see him, they'd probably be sitting together. What she'd just said made sense. What was it again? That's right, he couldn't ever feel worse than this. No matter what happened, he'd never again feel as bad as he did now. Strangely comforting, that thought. She assured him he'd completely recover; didn't sound like she was lying, why would she? Kind words. Light at the end of the tunnel. Funny, he felt that there was, but hadn't seen that light for a long time. She's going though, going to leave. But she says she'll visit again tomorrow. Said not to worry. Think about the accident, if anything came back. What *had* happened? Need some sleep though.

***

Janet smiled at Bruno as she closed the door softly behind her.

"It's hard to tell, but I think he took to me," she said. "I'm sure there was the hint of a smile when I said I'd be back tomorrow afternoon."

"You did great. Well done." Bruno replied, thinking to himself just how much he was relying on Janet's help at the current time.

Chapter 33

Monday 11th August

After a satisfying breakfast, Bruno and Janet walked along the beach in the morning sun, and talked about West and his accident. Was it *really* an accident or was their suspicion that he had been in danger from Steph Helland now a reality? The two spoke of the need to treat West as gently as possible, but at the same time push for information. Bruno felt that his investigation had slowed down considerably and needed to pick up the pace somehow.

***

That afternoon, Janet was at Chris' bedside prompt at 3:00 pm with Bruno sat at the end of the ward, ensuring their visit complied as much as possible with police guidelines. Although Janet was an unofficial helper, in their last meeting JB had encouraged Bruno to make use of *all* the resources available to him, which he had taken to refer to Janet specifically. He was therefore confident that should some meddlesome hospital worker speak of *procedure* and *privacy*, the Super would have his back.

Unsurprisingly, Chris West was heavily dosed up with painkillers, but seemed to recall Janet's visit the previous day. He lay there beaten up, unable to move, de-toxing (surprisingly well, Janet thought, compassionately) and, in all honesty, desperately in need of help. Although West still thought of this woman talking to him as 'police', he warmed to her and felt she was someone he could talk to and trust – at least to a certain extent.

Taking her time, and asking the most pertinent questions when he was lucid, Janet managed to obtain West's recollection of the incident, which was in fact quite clear. He had been drinking inside a pub opposite the car park, then at some point had bought a six-pack of Stella Artois from an off-license – much cheaper than the pub – and had drank his

216

way through those while sitting on the wall between the car park and the main road.

The car park, which was near to the pier and Winter Gardens, was almost completely empty when he and a fellow acquaintance had decided to return to the Salvation Army hostel in which they were staying. He had just begun to walk along the narrow car park exit road – only wide enough for a single vehicle – when he heard a car approaching at speed from behind him. He looked around and saw it coming towards him, but – in his inebriated state – was unable to get fully clear of the car. In front of him, jutting into the road, was a large plastic black, white and orange cone.

"That cone saved my life," West told Janet. "If I hadn't been moving to avoid falling over the cone, the car would have hit me full on. The driver hadn't seen it though, and when they hit it I reckon it took enough of the blow to save me. Still hurt more than anything though. Caught me on my right side and knocked me down. I heard a loud crack, must have been some bone or other. Then I was sick. I was glad the bloke I was with stuck around until the ambulance came, cos I passed out. People might've thought I was just drunk if he wasn't there to help."

"Was it deliberate, or an accident do you think?" Janet asked softly.

"It wasn't even dark, and anyway he had his headlights on. Bright they were, I remember seeing them behind me. He must have seen me. He hit me, then the curb, then drove off. Bloody hit and run. That's a criminal offence, that is."

"You say 'he'?"

"He, she, they, who knows? It all happened too fast to see who was driving."

"Can you remember what car it was?"

"Great big white one. Chelsea tractor thing. SUV they call them now, right? Dunno the model though. They all look the same, don't they."

"Chris, I promise you we'll find who was driving."

"Don't matter though, does it? They'll say I was drunk, and I'll get the blame, won't I?"

"Being drunk is no reason to blame you for a crime someone else committed," Janet said firmly. "And it's not like the driver would know you were drunk anyway. We'll find them, and they'll be arrested for a hit and run offence."

West was surprised that this woman, Janet she'd said her name was, really did seem to want to help him. It had been a long time since anyone had shown him kindness. Still, she was wrong about the hit-and-run, he thought. When you're drunk, everything's your fault.

"Thanks," he said, trying his best to make it sound like he believed her.

Janet smiled and continued to talk to him about anything but the accident; of course she wanted to solve her case, but regardless of what West might have done, and where his life had led him now, she believed that people deserved compassion, especially when they were lying in a hospital bed with god knows how many broken bones.

***

It was a good two hours before Janet finally emerged from West's room on ward six, acknowledging Bruno's raised hand with a wave of her own.

Janet considered herself a good judge of character, and the more she spoke to people, the more she believed she learned about them. Having spent the time with Chris West, she was certain she had a good feel for the kind of person he was. Although neither she nor West had spoken about the deaths of Pumpkin or Musgrove, he'd told her a fair amount of his life story, including the odd mention of Steph.

She was absolutely convinced that West had been an accomplice to Steph in the two murders, but wasn't sure whether he was aware of the intention to kill in either incident. But she was convinced he was in no way the instigator; he was a simple man, easily led. In the hands of someone as cunning and evil as she believed Steph was, he wouldn't stand a chance; she'd be able to manipulate him into doing anything... including helping commit murder.

Janet told Bruno everything Chris West had told her, also expressing her thoughts about his personality; something Bruno knew better than to question.

"Regarding the hit and run, it was dusk, he was drunk and there are no witnesses other than the fellow hostel inmate who was even drunker," said Bruno. "I know you want to help him, but I'm not convinced we'll get anywhere with that one."

"That's no kind of attitude to take," Janet admonished. "We should have a look at the scene of the incident to see what we can find."

"Is that an order?" Bruno asked.

"It is indeed," Janet replied. "And you might not be confident about finding the culprit, but do you think it's a coincidence that when I visited Steph Helland's home there was a white SUV on the drive?"

Bruno chuckled and jingled his car keys.

***

At the car park exit there were half a dozen cones in two stacks of three alongside the pay-and-display machine. They were well worn with black rubber tyre marks over their white painted bases. Above the heavy 5 cm-thick base – designed to keep the cone static in the wind – was a band of around 8 cm painted black, then three further fluorescent circles: two 28 cm-thick red bands surrounding a 14 cm white one. On the upper sections of each cone were scratches and dents, most of which were clearly from older collisions. However, one of the cones clearly had a fresh band of white paint impressed into the top two fluorescent areas.

"Evidence," said Bruno as he picked the cone up. Janet opened the boot of the car and he placed it inside.

As they drove over to the Hellands' residence, Janet explained to Bruno that any damage to the car would be on the nearside bumper, according to Chris West's description of the incident.

"I think the best plan is to carry out this mission in secret," Bruno said to Janet. "I'll grab the cone from the boot, take it with me to the SUV, and if there's any damage I'll take photos on my phone to show it matches the marks on the cone itself. Got that?"

"Sounds like a good plan to me," Janet replied, smiling.

"Although," Bruno continued, "You are taking a leap of faith here."

"I'd prefer to think of it as an educated guess."

Janet parked as close to the drive as she could without a clear line of sight from the windows of the Hellands' property. Bruno grabbed the cone from the boot and, moving as fast as a crouched man of his age could, made his way to the car, hoping his presence wouldn't be advertised by the instant brightness of a motion-controlled security light.

Luck was on his side, and he made it to the SUV without alerting the occupants of the house.

There was indeed an indentation and several black and red scratch marks around the nearside front wheel arch. There was a clear match with the white paint marks on the cone, and thus there was no doubt whatsoever that this was the car that had hit the cone.

Bruno took a number of photographs on his mobile showing the cone and the damage from different angles, then hurried back to Janet's car.

As they drove away, Bruno dialled Matt Morrison's number and told him what they'd found. He agreed to pay a visit to Steph Helland in an official capacity as a member of the local CID.

"She must have known there'd be damage on the car," Janet said as Bruno hung up. "You'd have thought she'd have hidden it the garage workshop and got straight onto a workshop, wouldn't you?"

"Hmm," was Bruno's reply. "I suspect she panicked after knocking West over, thinking she'd killed him – and I don't believe that was the intent. She'd have wanted to warn him, not get more blood on her hands. Even if she'd killed before, that thought grabs hold of you and takes over your brain. I'd bet she's focused so hard on getting over that feeling that she's forgotten all about the damage."

***

Whereas Morrison was looking to deal with Steph Helland, Janet's priority was to see West again.

It wasn't hard for her to sympathise with him. A few years ago he'd had status, a loving family, friends and money. In his fish business he had demonstrated the ability to succeed, but as often happens in life a single but vital character flaw had destroyed that stability, gradually dragging him down until he arrived here – physically and mentally broken, a man at rock-bottom, the lowest one can reach.

Janet hoped he was at the start of a journey to recovery, in spite of what he may have to endure because of his involvement with Steph. West was only forty; young enough that even if he was sent down for his part in the deaths, he could eventually enjoy life again.

Janet opened the door to West's room, and at the sight of her, his spirits rose visually. He expressed sincere thanks at her coming to see him again; his enthusiasm and gratefulness registered encouragingly with Janet, and helped her start the conversation that would lead to areas she was interested in. But although such information might be useful, it was not her main reason for visiting – that was her natural compassion.

"Do you come from Bournemouth?" she asked, a smile on her face still from his reaction at seeing her.

"I'm from the Isle of Wight, actually."

"You must have a connection with this town?"

"I know a woman who lives here called Stephanie, that's all."

"Has she visited you? And would she help you when you're discharged?"

"No, no way," he snorted. "She won't help me. On the contrary, she wants me well away from here. Since I knew her she's moved up in the world, and look at me. I wasn't always like this, you know. Me and her were lovers for years – even when she was married. But when her husband died, she left the Island. If I'd had more sense I'd have followed her."

"What happened with this Steph? It's OK, you can tell me the story," she said softly.

"It wasn't what happened *then* as what happened *before*." West began.

Janet gave him a look that said 'go on' better than any words could, and he continued.

"Our relationship began years and years ago, when we both lived in Cowes. She married the local solicitor, Andrew Pumpkin, a good old boy. He was a widower who'd practised in Cowes all his life. She was fun to be with, and he was flattered by the attention from this pretty young woman. But to her he was a means to an end. That Steph is a lady without morals. Every man is a target, and quite a few are susceptible... me included, although it took me years to realise it. She cast a spell over me, and I was trapped. I couldn't escape and everything went to pot, even the business that I'd built up since I was a young man. Then Andrew slipped and fell down the stairs that led from the roof top. He slipped on the top step and broke his back as he tumbled down. By the time he hit the bottom he was dead."

"Oh that's *awful*," Janet cooed. "It *was* an accident, wasn't it?"

"Hah. She was alone with him. She said it was, but no one saw it. I had my doubts later... not at the time mind, so I didn't say so to her. I remembered that she'd said to me a number of times that she hated her husband, 'and all his lah-de-dah friends' was her words. *They* certainly hated her, she's common as muck, not a solicitor's wife. To be fair, that's why *we* got on so well. I might have had my own business, but I've always been and always will be working class, just like Steph."

Janet gave him another kind smile.

"She was generous with money – well, with *his* money – if you gave her what she wanted, which was sex. And before poor Andrew Pumpkin died, that's all it had been really, a bit of a fling, a bit of fun. OK, I shouldn't have done it, but since the day I met her it was like she targeted me somehow; I never stood a chance. But when he fell, well, it turned into a nightmare. There she was, with money that hadn't been hers and in a place where everyone hated her – and not a soul believed it was an accident. She turned to me, even though I tried to say no. She didn't care that I was married, she never left me alone. I was her pawn, she could make me do *anything*, I didn't dare cross her, not after seeing her temper.

Soon, the whole town were talking about us, and it ended up ruining my business. My wife tried her best to keep us away from each other, but under Steph's spell no one has a chance."

Chris was now on a roll and seemed to want to tell Janet his side of the story. The words flowed out of him.

"After everything was sorted out, and she'd got all her dead husband's money, she gave me sixty grand to buy a pub on the harbour in Cowes. Having lost my business, how could I say no?! She used to come to the pub when we were shut, or I'd go to her place if the wife and kids were about. Then she married her next husband, Stanley. He was a butcher in Godshill; wasn't as old as Andrew Pumpkin though. Anyway, his wife had recently died. Now as a solicitor's wife in Cowes, Steph had learned how to behave better and so didn't always come across as the common or garden tart that she actually was. I actually think that at first, poor bloody Stanley thought *he* was going up in the world marrying *her*! He soon learned otherwise though, because within a year she was being talked about in Godshill."

Janet could hear Chris's throat had begun to dry, and poured him a drink of water which he sipped at, thankfully before continuing.

"A couple of years passed, and occasionally we still saw each other from time to time. Then one evening, a few days before Christmas, she phoned me from the butchers shop, totally hysterical. She begged me to come to the shop right there and then, which I did. Oh God, it was horrific. Her husband was lying face down on the floor; he'd been hit on the back of the head with a great big meat cleaver, and was clearly dead. There was blood *all over* the marble floor. I was in a state of shock I think, but she seemed pretty calm. When I asked her what happened she didn't answer. Instead, she just said 'I want you to take me home now, I'll call the police from home, I don't want to disturb anything here now.' I could tell that she was fully in control, and by the time I was inside her house, even though I was still shaking a bit, she seemed to have put it out of her mind completely. She gave me a whisky while she showered, and when she came back down she said that I should take her back to the butchers shop. Her car remained parked at the shop, while I'd taken her home."

"What had happened to Stanley?" Janet asked.

"Even back then my first thought was that it was her that had killed him," West replied.

There was a moment of silence before he spoke again.

"Look, I don't know why, maybe it's the drugs they've got me on here, but telling someone about this is making me feel better, God knows why," he said, just about holding back the tears that he surely wanted to cry.

"When I took her back to the shop, I dropped her a few doors down and scarpered as quickly as I could. Not with any feeling of relief mind. After all, she'd deny any involvement wouldn't she, and where would that leave me, if I'd been spotted near the shop at the time of the murder? I tell you, I sweated blood for days, expecting that knock on my door from the police, but it never came. I don't know *how* she got away with it. If they'd have come for me, I'd have told them everything, but she told me to keep quiet, and it worked. When she realised I could be trusted to keep my mouth shut, she offered me a deal that I couldn't say 'no' to. I know I should have gone to the police straight away and told them what happened, but she twisted it to make it seem like I'd be in trouble no matter what I said. She was always good at convincing me to look at the world from a particular point of view. She would always persuade me to do things I didn't want to – whether that was not going to the police, or something as stupid as having one more drink with her instead of doing my fish round!"

At this point the tears came, but silently.

"*Did* she kill him?" Janet asked softly.

"I'll never know for sure, but I'm convinced she did," he said.

"What was the offer you couldn't refuse?"

"She promised me the freehold of the butchers shop in Godshill, once all the legals were tied up."

"Was it out of generosity or to implicate you further?" asked Janet.

"Hah, you're sharp!" he replied, but there was no humour in his laugh. "It could have been both. Steph never tells you what's on her mind about *anything*. If she's the only one who knows the facts, it gives her control. That's probably why she's got away with these terrible, awful things."

"There's no statute of limitations for murder though, Chris," said Janet, "the police could always re-open the case."

"She's smart, she always thinks of a way out." he replied, dejectedly.

"What if there is conclusive evidence that she tried to kill you in the Royal Bath car park?"

"She wouldn't do that to me."

"Are you *sure*?" asked Janet. "If *she* was the hit and run driver, she could have been trying to silence you considering what you've just told me. Did you ever say anything, or cross her, before finding her in Bournemouth recently?"

West was still shocked at Janet's suggestion that he might be in danger from his old flame, and tried to think of the best way to refute the idea... yet not a single argument came to him.

"If you say you think she killed Stanley, that butcher, then surely she's capable of trying to kill you?" said Janet.

The thought that Stephanie might be out to kill him frightened West; he shook his head and closed his eyes, perhaps hoping to shut himself away from the world. Whatever the reason, he fell asleep.

It was only a brief drift into unconsciousness, and when he awoke some fifteen minutes later it was with a start. But he was pleased to see Janet was still there, a guardian angel looking over him.

"I can come in tomorrow if you'd like me to," she said, "and if you tell me now I can bring in anything you need... soap, toothbrush, something to read?"

"Thank you" was all he said. Janet scribbled her mobile number on a piece of paper that she left on the dresser next to the bed, then waved West goodbye as she left his room to go and meet with Bruno in the hospital canteen. There she barely mentioned him, instead engaging in small talk about the hospital, staff and the building's decor.

But as soon as they made it back to the car and climbed inside, Janet pulled a portable audio recorder out of her pocket and told Bruno to prepare himself. Bruno gave Janet a serious look, and asked,

"You did ask his permission for that, I hope?"

"I did ask, and he said 'yes,'" Janet replied, a little flustered. "He might not have been one hundred per cent clear about it, but..."

"Hmph. I suppose it's still consent. Good enough for our boys, good enough for you," he said firmly, before glancing at her with a smile.

After listening to the entire thing without saying a word, Bruno told Janet that he believed West's story was sufficient to arrest and charge him with being an accessory to murder. However, he agreed that Matt Morrison needed to tell them how things had gone with Steph Helland before they actually rolled the dice.

**

It was late that evening when Bruno received a call from Morrison, and his faith in his mainland counterpart proved well-placed. Rather than go directly to the Helland's residence, Morrison had actually paid a visit to the Salvation Army hostel at which West and his acquaintance had been staying. After a few basic enquiries he'd managed to find a man known as Tiny Jacobs, who confirmed he had been Chris West's drinking buddy at the time of the incident.

Unlike other times, Jacobs hadn't been blind drunk; in fact he had been capable of walking back to the hostel, which – for an alcoholic like him – was about as good as it got. He'd actually seen the car knock his friend Chris sideways, and while he'd been unconscious, Tiny had attracted the attention of a member of the public, who'd called the ambulance on their mobile phone.

Tiny had gotten a clear view of the car, which he described as a white Mercedes (he'd recognised the star logo) driven by a blonde lady. He knew that the registration number began with 'TJ', because he remembered thinking how much of a coincidence it was that they were the letters that made up his name.

"Do you think it was an accident? Perhaps the driver hadn't seen Chris?" Morrison had asked.

"No," was Tiny's reply, "she aimed for him. There's no way she couldn't have seen him, he was standing in the middle of the road, and she was facing dead ahead. She certainly wasn't on a phone or anything."

"What happened after she hit him?"

"Well, I think she hit one of the big car park cones as well, 'cos there was a clunk and a screech, then almost right away she sped off. Poor Chris was lying on the floor in a puddle of sick and piss."

"And what did you do?"

"When I saw how bad he was hurt, I ran and stopped a couple, told them that he'd been hit by a car. The girl went over to help Chris, and the guy called for an ambulance. I waited around until the ambulance turned up – it seemed to take ages, but probably wasn't as long as it felt. Anyway, when they loaded him into that van, I got a horrible feeling come over me, so I went back to the hostel. Since then I've kept seeing it over and over again in my head."

Morrison had thanked Tiny, and explained that he may need to give evidence in court at a later date, so he'd very much appreciate him not suddenly deciding he didn't want to stay in Bournemouth. As it was, Jacobs had said he wanted to help his friend Chris, one of the few people who'd shown him respect of late. He'd even told the detective that his *real* name was Frank Jacobs, although no one outside of the court system ever used it.

Bruno answered a few of Morrison's questions about Janet's discussion with West, then told him to sit tight and wait for developments as he went back to the station and prepared an arrest warrant for Stephanie Helland.

***

Midnight was approaching. Yet despite the late hour, Morrison managed to get approval, and sent two uniformed officers to arrest Stephanie Helland and bring her to Bournemouth Police station. The charge was for failing to stop after a road accident, which, at the current time, Morrison felt was the best strategy.

At a few minutes past one am, the uniforms arrived back at the station with Stephanie Helland in the back seat of their car. Right behind them was a second car, out of which Brendan Helland and a family lawyer stepped.

The following hour or two were very much occupied with dull, police procedure, the filling-in of forms, the signing of documents, and the meeting of lawyer with client.

The interview was over almost as quickly as it had begun, with Stephanie staying silent other than to confirm her details.

Bruno received a call at the crack of dawn from a very tired-sounding Morrison telling him that Steph had been released on £10,000 bail, to appear the following morning at the Southbourne Magistrates Court, where she would be bound over to stand trial in a higher court. The two agreed to discuss how to increase the charge to attempted murder at the next possible opportunity.

Chapter 34

Bruno's inability to interview Phyllida Glassman was hampering his progress in finding Sam Peters' killer. He didn't have the address of her sister in Paris, or anybody whom she knew to ask about her whereabouts. If she was on the Island, who was she with, and why had she decided to go away now? Each question could have a perfectly acceptable answer. But what she would be unaware of was that because of her continued absence she had become a hunted woman. It was apparent to Peter Noway, Dick Potter, Noel Bartlett, Derek Bentley and of course to Bruno himself that she should be able to contribute far more than she had so far. Above all, Bruno needed to know what she had been up to in the three days leading up to Sam's murder on Saturday the nineteenth of July.

Bruno had tried to call her many times on her mobile and left messages on her land-line answerphone both of which she had apparently ignored. Initially he had mentally given her the benefit of the doubt, but now...

Janet's view was, unsurprisingly, a sympathetic one. She set no more store in Phyllida's disappearance than that the lady had endured two awful experiences close together – her husband's death and her lover Sam Peters' murder; after discovering the brutal manner of the latter, surely most people would have been frightened and wanted to vanish off the face of the earth. Thus it was Janet's opinion that she had simply taken a holiday to restore her faith in herself, or perhaps human nature in general.

But then there was Sam's will. She stood to inherit a considerable fortune, and no doubt whenever she returned, the spotlight would shine on her and her activities. If she had nothing to hide, then she had no problem, however, her sudden disappearance from Roud Farm undoubtedly saw suspicions arise in those that were aware of the situation.

In spite of her failure to answer his communications, Bruno returned to Roud Farm in the hope that she had returned in the same, sudden way in which she had left. He also believed the farm was connected with Sam's whereabouts prior to his murder, but after leaving the Portsmouth-to-Fishbourne ferry late on Wednesday the sixteenth of July, especially as the Potters had told Bruno that he'd not stayed with them around that date – or, in fact, for some time.

Phyllida Glassman's insistence that *she* had not seen him at this time either didn't ring true to Bruno given their supposed close relationship. Was it *really* possible someone would sign their will to someone, then not long afterwards come over to the Island and *not* see them?

Bruno did not think so and even Janet agreed on that point; she could see neither why he had come late on Wednesday to the Island if it was not to see Phyllida, nor where he might stay if it were not with her or the Potters.

After completing a walk around the farmhouse and having knocked repeatedly on the front door for some time, Bruno concluded that Phyllida still hadn't return to the farm. Yet something was bothering him and it took a while to figure out what it was.

Although the quadrangle in front of Roud Farm was deserted, it did not seem to have the unkempt appearance he remembered from his previous visit. Someone must have spent some time cleaning it up. The two large metal farm buildings with their floor-to-ceiling sliding doors were shut but still not locked and opened easily. Bruno tried the one closest to him first, and as soon as he felt the door slide easily, he pushed it back and crossed over to the one opposite, opening it up wider before stepping in.

Preoccupied with his thoughts about Phyllida Glassman's whereabouts, Bruno wasn't looking for anything in particular, rather he was partaking in the policeman's version of window shopping.

Living alone on a farm that was not being worked must have been lonely and soul destroying, he thought. There were no animals nor evidence of proper farm activity anywhere, despite the comments she had made. Bruno considered this fact as he wandered through an area which contained unused, now rusty farm implements. Despite the obvious activity outside, the mud-covered, blood-stained fleece cuttings from the sheep she claimed to have sheared herself were still laying untidily across the floor.

Bruno shook his head and turned to leave, but as he turned to face the door through which he'd entered, he got the fright of his life.

There, standing in the entrance was a tall man standing stock still, watching him.

The sun bright in the sky outside contrasting with the darkness of the barn meant that all Bruno could really discern was a silhouette, the watcher's face featureless and dark.

Bruno's heart suddenly seemed to kick back into life after a pause of who knows how long. He couldn't help but admit he was frightened, for some reason transported back to being a schoolboy watching Hitchcock's Psycho, terrified as Norman Bates appeared as the same black silhouette, framed by the upstairs window of his motel.

How long had he been watched for? The unease turned Bruno's world upside down, making him feel like a burglar caught red handed, not a policeman going about his investigative duty.

Bruno squinted and managed to make out colours within the blackness. The man was at least six feet two inches tall, the height exaggerated with a felt trilby hat. His clothes looked utilitarian, like farmer's clothing – a hard-wearing green shirt and brown corduroy trousers, held up by buttoned-down braces. The classic countryside look was perfectly finished by ankle-high, mud-caked, brown leather working boots.

"Can I help you?" spoke the watcher, an Island twang in his voice.

The politeness of the question didn't stop Bruno from jumping a second time, the sudden disturbance of the silence causing his already jittery nervous system to overload once again.

Bruno snapped himself out of his state of terror as quickly as he'd entered it.

"I'm Detective Inspector Bruno Peach from Newport police CID. I'm looking for Mrs Glassman; I was hoping she'd be here today."

"That won't be possible, I'm afraid. She went away yesterday morning. Said she'd be gone for a couple of weeks."

If she was here yesterday, she's definitely ignoring my calls, thought Bruno, who'd left messages on both mobile and landline early the previous morning.

"Any idea how I can contact her?" Bruno asked.

The man didn't answer, as if he'd not even heard the question.

"Has she gone to stay with her sister in Paris?" he tried.

"She left with a gentleman," the man said.

"And can you tell me which gentleman?" Bruno asked, a little exasperated, feeling that the conversation was almost as unworldly as the man's sudden appearance in the doorway.

"I think he's an estate agent. I've seen him here before, but I don't know which one he works for. I'm looking after the dog. That's what I do,

I come over to help with odd jobs. Some farm work needs two people or at least one strong man."

"Ah! You must be..." Bruno desperately racked his brains to think of the 'helping hand' that Derek Bentley had mentioned.

"Steadman. John Steadman," said the man.

"Of course, thank you, Mr Steadman. I'm quite pleased to have bumped into you actually, I've been hoping to have a chat."

"Always happy to help the local constabulary," said Steadman, with the kind of tone that suggested his 'help' was usually given in a room containing chairs, a desk, a tape machine and not much else.

"Do you know if anyone other than this estate agent visits Mrs Glassman regularly?"

"Only Mr Peters, but he's dead," came the oddly matter-of-fact reply.

"And did you know Mr Peters?"

"I met him a couple of times, but I didn't *know* him as such."

"How often did you see him?"

"He used to come a lot, until he was murdered."

"And this estate agent?"

"He came to value the farm, as she's trying to sell up. She can't farm... some women can, but *she* can't, she wasn't born for it, too toffee-nosed," he said, using an expression Bruno hadn't heard in a long time.

"Can you describe this man?"

Steadman just looked at Bruno quizzically.

"Was he thin? Fat? Old? Young?"

"He's young, I think. I saw them drive off together. Yep. Young."

"OK, that's very helpful, thank you." Bruno replied, sarcasm getting the better of him.

Steadman smiled as if he'd been genuinely thanked.

"Were they going somewhere together do you know, or was he just giving her a lift?" Bruno continued.

"Now *that* I'm afraid I don't know, Inspector."

And you've been so knowledgeable up to this point, Bruno thought.

"So you were here when they left?"

"Uh-huh; I was cleaning up, so I just waved them off."

"Do you remember what sort of car it was?"

"A BMW I think, not sure what kind though."

"OK, never mind. Perhaps you know a local estate agency that mainly sells farms? That might help," Bruno said, hopefully.

"Well," Steadman started, offering a ray of hope, but it was quickly extinguished. "There are several on the Island, but he ain't necessarily *from* the Island, is he? I'd buy the farm, if I had any money."

Bruno wondered if Steadman was playing a game with him, or if he was just friendly and a bit simple.

"Used to own it once, you know? Not me personally, the family. My father actually sold it to the Glassmans. It is on a hill you see, difficult to plough. It's too small for sheep either, so it's not very profitable. My Dad should have let me have it, *I'd* have made it pay."

"How?" asked Bruno.

"Hard work."

Of course, thought Bruno, *something no one else would have thought of*.

"Hard work," he repeated. "That's what *real* farming is."

"You still live nearby though, Mr Steadman?"

"Yep. I live in the cottage three hundred yards back down the road, you'd have passed it on your way here."

"OK," said Bruno, "Is there *anything* you can tell me that could help me locate Mrs Glassman? I really do need to speak to her urgently."

"She said she would phone me, so I expect a call, maybe tonight, definitely tomorrow, when she'll have been away for two days."

"Right. If she does call you, *please* could you find out where she is, then let me know? It really is important."

Bruno hoped that the way he'd worded this meant Steadman might not mention him.

"I'll do my best," was Steadman's response.

Bruno, who had gradually (but carefully) stepped closer to Steadman, was now close enough to hand over his card. "You can get me on that number," he said.

"Inspector, have you arrested anyone for the murder of Mr Peters yet?"

"Police investigations are continuing," said Bruno, surprised by this question. Surely the man didn't expect to be told anything?

"But seeing as you ask, did you murder him?"

"Nope."

"And can you remember when exactly you last saw Mr Peters?"

"I only ever saw him when I popped in to see Mrs Glassman, which wasn't that often, but he was often here though," Steadman explained. "I saw his car parked outside and he behaved like he lived here. Familiar, like. You know."

"During the week?" said Bruno.

"More at weekends," he said. "Last time was a few weeks ago, Inspector.

I can't remember *exactly* when that was, It was always only by chance that I saw him. He was alright sir, yes, he was alright."

"How do you mean, *alright*?"

"He was friendly."

"Friendly? What did you talk about?"

"We didn't, he didn't know anything about farming."

Bruno made a mental note to tell his colleagues about *this* one.

"What did you call on Mrs Glassman for?"

"Just to see if she wanted anything from the shops."

"Even though it was the weekend and she had visitors?"

"Yes, Inspector, she never minded me calling in anytime."

"And can you think of any reason why somebody would want to kill him?"

"People kill for all sorts of reasons, don't they?"

Bruno decided that he wasn't going to make much progress like this, and frankly the conversation with John Steadman had exhausted him more than anything else during the investigation.

He was now convinced Phyllida Glassman knew more about Sam Peters' final hours than she had let on, and he wanted— no, *needed* to talk to her again.

"Before I leave, I'd be grateful if you could show me inside the building opposite this one," he asked.

"Sorry it's locked and I don't have a key with me."

Having tried the other building's doors when he had arrived and had found them to be open, Bruno knew Steadman was lying about this. He wondered how much truth he'd actually heard. Rather than amusement, Bruno had in fact decided there was deliberate obfuscation here. He remembered that Derek Bentley had a very dim view of the man.

"OK, I'll come back when she's here instead," he said. "So where's this dog?"

"I keep her down at the cottage," he replied.

"Well... Thanks for your... help, John. You *will* call me when you hear from her, or when she comes back?"

"I'm sure she'll call you when she is back sir," Steadman replied before wandering off towards the far end of the courtyard.

Bruno stepped outside into the sunlight. It was like waking from a strange dream. As he walked back towards his car, he noted that although Steadman appeared to be cleaning, inspecting and generally 'attending to' various areas, he always kept a line of sight to the courtyard, specifically, Bruno assumed, to his car, next to which an old dark brown Volvo estate was parked.

Bruno did not drive away immediately, but picked up his phone, ensuring that Steadman could see him. He mouthed a few silent words as a bluff to make the farmhand think he was phoning the office, or some other such business call.

But Bruno was thinking. Still holding the phone in a 'talking' position, he pulled up his contact list and selected the entry labelled 'Phyllida Glassman'. Oddly, it wasn't his brain telling him to do this, but his copper's nose, a suspicious organ if ever there was one.

After no more than half a ring, the detective got his second shock of the day when what sounded like Phyllida's voice said "Has he gon—" then abruptly hung up.

Bruno did not return his hand set to his coat pocket, and instead continued 'talking' silently to let Steadman, who was now doing nothing on the far side of the yard, think he was still speaking with the office. To his surprise he found it quite easy to do this and think.

That was definitely Phyllida, he thought. So what was that all about? Surely the logical explanation was that she had been expecting a call – hence the quick pick-up – and had carelessly not checked the identity of the caller until it was too late – hence the cut-off. Even though Bruno's phone automatically dialled out as an unknown number, she'd have known it wasn't who she was expecting... the logical conclusion being Steadman. Most likely the 'he' referred to Bruno himself, with the curious odd-job man having alerted her to his presence prior to intercepting him in the metal building.

Something that stood out as interesting – and that perturbed Bruno – was Steadman's refusal to let him look into the second building, which he'd outright lied about. He wondered if there was something specific hiding in there that he hadn't wanted the detective to see, or if it was just a general 'no looking' policy he'd been asked to enact.

Not wishing to give Steadman any sign of his thoughts, Bruno mouthed the word 'bye', and put the phone down on the passenger's seat before driving off, but not before making a note of the Volvo's registration plate.

Around three hundred metres down the narrow lane that led away from Roud Farm, Bruno noted Steadman's cottage, then continued driving for around a quarter of a mile until he reached a crossroad junction.

With the words 'has he gone?' still ringing in his ear, instead of taking a right towards Newport, Bruno turned left up the hill, slowing down at the point where he could look down on the road he'd just come from that went past Steadman's cottage. He parked his car out of sight, and removed from the boot an old dark brown leather case which he carried by its strap. He scanned the bushes and shrubs for a moment before spotting exactly what he was looking for, and went to crouch down behind his chosen vegetation. He was now in a natural depression in the ground, completely hidden from sight from a wide angle, but able to see through a small gap between two leafy shrubs. He unzipped the heavy leather case and pulled out his treasured binoculars, just in time to see Steadman get out of his Volvo which was now parked in front of the cottage.

Bruno wondered what was with Steadman's odd attitude and behaviour at the farm. Considering he had nothing to do with Sam Peters, why the question about his murder? He hadn't seemed genuinely interested, he'd been fishing for information. But why? The only reason that made sense is that he was doing it for Phyllida Glassman. What if he knew of her whereabouts? Perhaps they were hiding something together?

He thought back to one of the first things Steadman had said. It was true that in order to reach Roud Farm you *had* to pass Steadman's cottage. He would no doubt have seen Bruno drive past. How long had he been keeping an eye on him? Hadn't he felt like he was being watched once before?

Bruno thought for a moment and then looked all around him. There was no one within sight, and anyway, he knew Steadman was down at the cottage. It was then that he realised just what a beautiful day it had become. There were the hints of a warm summer breeze that would no doubt continue gently into the evening. The grass on which he was sat was surprisingly comfortable, the birdsong pleasant and relaxing. He couldn't help thinking how nice it would be to be sitting here with Janet, the two of them sharing a glass of Merlot and with no one else around. No waiters, no screaming children, no murder investigations.

Snapping back to reality, the more Bruno thought about the whole setup, the more convinced he became that she could be a lot closer than everyone had assumed... maybe she'd simply been keeping a low profile in Steadman's cottage? This thought grabbed him and wouldn't let go. He *had* to find out before *anything* else. Within seconds he'd thought of a plan and as quickly as a man trying not to be seen could move, he got back into his car and drove away.

***

Janet found Bruno's brief summary of the conversation he'd had with John Steadman rather amusing, but didn't linger on the humorous aspects for too long; they had work to do – and more importantly there was pleasure to be had.

She was the type of woman who always had a full fridge, so it wasn't hard for her to put together a fairly impressive picnic basket, with cheese, meat and a full-bodied, mid-priced, new world red complete with two glasses.

***

As Bruno watched Janet lay plastic plates, the two wine glasses, ham, Camembert, nuts, the Chilean Merlot, a plastic carton of grapes, condiments and a corkscrew onto a white nylon table cloth, she mentioned how even now she was thinking about 'poor Chris West' and the Pumpkin and Musgrove cases.

Well, two out of three ain't bad, thought Bruno.

In fact, when they'd each had a little wine, and begun to tuck into the cheese, conversation veered well away from work. They talked about the geography of the Island and how hilly it was, as it appeared from where they sat on the edge of a clump of trees. There were rolling downs and between the hills far into the distance, fields of yellow and brown. There was an early evening haze, generated by the hot sun setting. It was a half hour before the sunset in the west, over fields, wheat and corn coloured all shades of brown and yellow bounded by hedgerows, bathed in the tranquillity of having existed for eternity.

Eventually, conversation did return to the reason they were there. Janet asked Bruno about Steadman, and the two agreed that he wasn't strictly a farm labourer – certainly not a full-time one. His assistance to Phyllida Glassman could easily be considered that of a good neighbour rather than paid help.

"So how does he earn his living, then?" Janet asked, Bruno realising that it wasn't something he'd thought about but perhaps should have done.

They also talked about the female voice on the phone and those three words. It was a woman, certainly, and chances are it was someone who had been made aware of Bruno's presence at Roud Farm, and who knew what Steadman was doing at that moment.

"But it could have been her sister?" Janet asked, again playing devil's advocate.

Bruno was just framing his answer when he thought he saw movement at the cottage.

Steadman had let a dog out of the cottage's side door, and followed it outside himself. It seemed well trained, sticking close to the man as the two walked up the hill, heading towards their picnic location.

"Let's put this plan into action," said Bruno, picking up the basket and opening the hatch of the car. He reckoned there was plenty of time to pack up before man and dog reached them; Janet was not so sure. But having bundled everything into the car boot. Bruno had time to climb into the spacious rear, lying himself down into the footwell and pulling the picnic blanket to fully cover his body. Janet hopped back into the driver's seat, started the car and began to drive.

As far as Steadman would have known, it was just a passing car, a single female occupant.

Now for the difficult bit.

Janet stopped at the crossroads, and made a point of looking around. She then headed towards Roud Farm, but stopped outside John Steadman's residence from which he'd emerged with the dog some ten to fifteen minutes earlier.

As she climbed out, she seemed to accidentally bump into her wing mirror, which now sat at slightly different angle to the normal driving position.

Approaching the front door, she knocked and waited.

Nothing happened.

Breathing in deeply, and trusting Bruno's instincts, Janet knocked again, calling out a polite "hello?" as she did.

Suddenly, the door swung open and a woman answered. Explaining she was lost, Janet asked for directions to the nearest petrol station. The woman pointed her back the way she'd came, told her to continue along the road until she reached a town, then quickly withdrew back into the cottage.

Janet returned to the car and began to follow the directions.

"I got the angle right, I hope?" She asked.

"Perfect. Couldn't have done it better myself!" Bruno said, pulling the picnic blanket off his head.

"And?"

"Oh that was Phyllida Glassman alright."

Chapter 35

Bruno had reached a stage in his investigation of Sam Peters' murder, where he could not make a mistake, or the evidence he had yet to discover might seep away. Glassman might be gone by the following morning, and that had to be considered. But also, there were pressing issues at Roud Farm. What had Steadman been so keen to hide? Or was there nothing specific, Bruno's imagination simply on overdrive. Phyllida or the farm... *Phyllida or the farm*, thought Bruno.

Bruno could certainly have arrested Phyllida last night, but one of the rules a policeman learns is that preparation is the key; *fools rush in* an axiom that had saved Bruno from mistakes in the past. But he certainly had no intention of standing still. On the drive home, he had called Tom Craven in Portsmouth, whose assistance he had missed lately. Although Janet had accompanied the detective on a number of missions in the past few days, there was something about his young apprentice that seemed to make Bruno more active and decisive – and it was now that those two qualities were going to be needed in significant amounts.

Tom smiled and said "Good morning, sir," as he got into Bruno's car. It was just gone 6:15 am and he'd just hopped off the first Portsmouth-to-Ryde hovercraft of the day.

"It is indeed!" Bruno replied, and during the drive towards Steadman's cottage and the farm filled Tom in on everything that he hadn't had a chance to the previous night.

***

Tom's thoughts were to check the farm quickly first for any signs of activity, then return to the cottage to pick up their two targets; as they had driven up the road to both cottage and farm, they'd noticed Steadman's brown Volvo still in place outside the cottage.

"We can always give chase if we see them leave," he suggested.

At the farm, a quick scout around revealed an identical scene to the one Bruno recalled from yesterday's visit. Parking in the centre of the courtyard, Bruno's first wish was to see what was in the outbuilding from which he'd been prevented seeing yesterday.

"You keep a lookout Tom, and I'll just open this—"

"Problem, sir?" the younger man asked.

"Locked!" Bruno replied, angrily. "And it certainly was not yesterday, whatever that shifty bugger said!"

"I believe you, boss... but—"

"I know, I know. If I force it then any evidence will likely be thrown out unless we get a warrant."

"I'm surprised you haven't come with one," Tom said, hoping his mentor wouldn't see it as a criticism. Thankfully, Bruno explained the situation without taking offence, although there was an obvious bitterness there, perhaps more aimed at the system than anything else in particular.

"I don't think I'd have got one. There's nothing *directly* linking Glassman or Steadman with the murder yet, and these judges have a habit of being far too fair. I'd have asked to search this building, and the wig would have asked why. I'm *suspicious*, I'd be saying, because when I was trespassing on this woman's land, I tried opening a door I shouldn't have touched, then when I was in another building that I had no legal right to be in, someone probably well up on police search laws caught me red-handed and told me something which I only knew was a porky-pie because I'd already broken the rules by opening the door in the first place."

"I think I get the idea," Tom acknowledged.

Bruno tried the other buildings; each one was heavily padlocked, with no keys hidden under plant pots or tractor parts. The farmhouse was equally locked and clearly devoid of human or canine occupants.

"Right, back to the cottage then."

***

Although the walk would have taken no more than a few minutes and would have given the two some 'good exercise' according to Tom, Bruno decided to drive in the unlikely event a chase might occur. It would be just their luck that Steadman and Glassman would be jumping into the car just as they arrived on foot.

The Volvo was still in its parking spot, and Bruno started to get an ominous feeling. As they stepped out of the car, Tom must have noticed the sudden change in his demeanour as he asked, "Problem?"

After three heavy knocks on the door, Bruno replied. "I've got a funny feeling about this. With my visit yesterday, they'd have no doubt been feeling pretty nervous. I know it's early, but I'd have thought Steadman would have appeared at the farm again."

"On look-out all night?"

"Sharing shifts, perhaps. But it's either that, or—" Bruno banged the knocker a good six times as hard as he could.

"They've done a runner," said Tom, now as grave-faced as his boss.

"It seems so. If they were still here, the dog would be as well. And I don't hear barking."

After looking in through every window, the two came to the conclusion that this was definitely the case. Usually a pretty calm man, Tom was surprised to hear Bruno express his feelings in one particularly succinct four-letter word.

As Bruno drove back to the station, he and Tom agreed on how to progress. Firstly, they would list Phyllida Glassman as a missing person. That was the quickest way to ensure that ports, airports and other transit networks would be looking out for her.

After the missing persons report, they would request search warrants for both Roud Farm and Steadman's cottage, requesting to remove anything they found for which there was reasonable suspicion that it was connected somehow to the death of Sam Peters, or their own disappearing act.

It took them most of the day to get all the paperwork completed, especially as JB was a real stickler for documentation. Having let a criminal free early in his career because he had forgotten to put the right date on a particularly important evidence bag it was understandable – but that didn't make it any quicker.

It was coming up to five pm. The last note on Tom's checklist was to speak to Noway, to see if he'd heard anything from Phyllida; Bruno was sure that at some point she'd need to speak to him about the inheritance. A quick phone call to him confirmed that he'd not been able to contact her either, and Tom tore the page out of his notebook, throwing it into the bin.

"Come on, let's get you home," said Bruno.

As they made their way out of the building, he took out his phone and pulled up Phyllida Glassman's mobile number. Pressing the 'call' button he lifted the phone to his ear.

The phone was most definitely now switched off.

Chapter 36

The following morning, Bruno drove Tom Craven out towards Roud Farm to execute the search warrants they had obtained. A regular police car followed them, with three uniformed men on hand – both to assist in the bagging and tagging, but also to rely on if things got ugly. There was also a fourth man, a police engineer, whose fascinating bag of lock-picking tools and sundry items had been carefully placed in the boot of the car.

Their first stop was Steadman's cottage, which was silent and unattended, just as it had been the previous day. The twelve-year-old Volvo estate stood in the same parking area beside the cottage. With the anticipated lack of response to knocking, a cursory look quickly confirmed that still no one was at home.

Before the engineer got to work on the front door to Steadman's cottage, he skilfully employed an often-used Policeman's trick to open the car door, albeit using a more professional tool than the coat-hanger Bruno would have suggested. He slid it behind the top of the driver's window, manoeuvred it around the door handle and opened the car door from the inside.

Both Bruno and Tom could see that the driver and passenger seats were tired, but clean. The rear seats seemed to have been permanently folded forward to provide space for moving things. Bruno had appreciated Tom's instinct and professional approach from the start of the investigation, so was not surprised in the slightest when Tom spoke exactly his thoughts:

"We shouldn't touch *anything* in this car. I should call forensics down from Portsmouth. They can be here in just under two hours. I really think we should get them to go over the whole car and to tell us everything they can about it, particularly the questions of exactly *what* it has been used for."

"Agreed," replied Bruno. "If he was working with Phyllida, then perhaps there's important evidence to be found within."

Tom made the call, and gave Bruno a 'thumbs up' to indicate they'd be on their way. As he did so, the engineer succeeded unlocking the cottage's front door. The cottage was certainly old, there was no doubt about that, however the lock itself was very much a modern addition to the structure.

Inside the cottage Bruno, Tom and two of the uniforms searched for anything that could be potentially connected with a murder... a weapon perhaps, or maybe some soiled clothing; perhaps even something previously belonging to Sam Peters.

In the bathroom, it was clear that Phyllida had been using it for some time. The bathroom contained the type of shampoo, conditioner and bath soaks that only woman of her age would generally use. But there was certainly no implement that could have been used as a weapon. The clothing in the laundry bins amounted to very little – none of which was soiled in a way that suggested foul play.

The kitchen, on the other hand, contained something of interest. There was a drawer packed full of the Tesco supermarket-branded plastic shopping bags of a similar (or the same) size as those that Bruno vividly recalled covering Peters' head and being tied around his neck.

Bruno wondered if there was any kind of serial or batch number on the bags... *anything* that might help... and grabbed a handful so they could be compared with the ones used for the murder.

Just as the two detectives finished their initial look around the cottage, the same team of two specialists who'd examined Sam Peters' car arrived, each shaking hands with their welcoming party professionally before changing travel dress into forensic gear and getting to work.

***

Soon, Bruno, Tom, one uniform and the police engineer made the short trip up to Roud Farm. Choosing to tackle the main house first, the engineer took no more than ten minutes to carefully inspect each lock and open the front door.

The house was kept in a tidy, clean state, as one might expect, and it did *not* indicate that Phyllida Glassman *had* gone on an extended visit, or was *not* returning, and like Steadman's abode there was nothing at first glance that might suggest evidence of Peters' presence on the morning of the nineteenth of July.

Moving upstairs, one bedroom on the first floor was used as an office, cluttered as it was with household paperwork, alongside magazines that went back to the previous year. There were copies of *The County Press*, the local Island weekly newspaper, from early summer; additionally there were two copies of The Times, dated the seventeenth and the eighteenth – the Thursday and Friday before Sam Peters death, Bruno noted. He bagged up the newspapers, as they came under the "something suspicious" category – he knew that Phyllida did not regularly buy a newspaper... so *why* on those two days?

Although the house felt very much empty, the presence of a number of personal items satisfied Bruno's concern that Phyllida was not quite yet at the stage of arranging a complete disappearance – but she could well be close to doing so.

Moving onto the farm buildings, the first contained a collection of tools, bicycles, an old green bus in the process of being restored, empty tins, oil drums, doors, broken farm gates, no entry signs, rubbish, oily rags and a kitchen roll. Everything looked as if it had been there for years.

The second building, the one which Steadman had refused Bruno access to recently, was used as a garage, it seemed. Although it could easily have housed ten cars. Phyllida's small red car was in the same position as when Bruno had sat in it a few days previously.

Ever since Bruno had realised the importance of the similarity of the seat position of her car and that of the driver's seat in Sam Peters', Bruno had become increasingly convinced of Phyllida's involvement somewhere along the line. In addition to the state of the car, Bruno had a suspicion that she was outright lying to him about the weekend beforehand, claiming that she hadn't seen him at all.... although he currently had no way of proving this. Another gut feeling to add the host of others he'd been having.

When Tom's Hampshire Forensics team had finished their examination of the Volvo, they had collected a number of finger prints and blood and animal samples, on which they'd report as soon as possible. Before they departed the farm altogether, Tom got them to scrape up some samples of earth from the floor around Phyllida's car and take hand and finger prints from its interiors. Steadman's deflective interview answers (and somewhat odd behaviour) coupled with his recent concurrent absence linked him to Phyllida's activities.

Just before the forensics team were about to leave, Bruno grabbed one of them. "Follow me," he said. Leading his captive to the building which contained the blood-covered shearings of the sheep that he still had yet to see evidence of, Bruno pointed to the pile.

"Bag up some of that, if you'd be so kind. I don't reckon there's been sheep on this farm for months, and when there's blood involved, *I* want to know where it came from."

"Of course, sir" was the technician's reply as he knelt down.

After picking up samples from throughout the pile, the two of them made their way back outside, where the others were standing in a group.

"Pretty sure that's everything, right Tom?" Bruno asked.

"Right," Tom replied. "Thanks," he added, nodding towards the forensics team.

Changing back into their civvies, the technicians promised Tom and Bruno that they'd aim to have the results within twenty-four hours.

***

As it was, Tom received a phone call from the forensic team as he and Bruno were taking in a spot of lunch.

"We thought you'd want to know asap", said the Forensics team leader, "a sample of some dried matter on a rear internal panel of the Volvo is human blood."

"Human blood? Thank you," Tom said.

And you can tell your boss that his hunch was correct; so was the blood on the sheep shearings that we picked up."

"Uh-huh," said Tom.

As he continued listening to the forensics results – and somewhat to Bruno's frustration – he nodded a few times, said the odd "yes", another "uh-huh" and finally finished with "Thanks, let me know if there's any more developments, we really do appreciate it. Yep. OK, will do. Thanks, bye now."

As he put the phone down, an excited Bruno was the first to speak.

"Interesting about the blood! I wonder if they can run it through the database and—"

"It's Sam Peters' blood," replied Tom.

***

The news that Sam Peters' blood had been found on John Steadman's car was the first piece of evidence that linked any person to Peters at the time of his death. Filled with renewed energy and confidence, Bruno requested the importance of the arrest warrant be increased to maximum, and all units on the Island as well as further afield in Hampshire would be supplied with her photo and detail file in the hope of finding her.

Thinking back to the evening of his picnic with Janet, Bruno now felt that these two 'wanted' had probably left that very night... but obviously not in either of their own cars.

This matching blood sample in Steadman's car was a key clue, confirming his involvement in the killing, and, being of tall, strong farming stock, answered the question of how a man like Sam Peters – not exactly light himself – could have been taken and hidden beneath the bridge where his body was found.

With this news, he decided to visit Noway the solicitor, still happily accompanied by Tom Craven.

***

In the solicitor's classily-furnished office, Bruno told Noway that Phyllida Glassman *and* John Steadman had seemingly vanished, and that he'd issued a warrant for their arrest in connection with Sam Peters' murder. Should she make contact, Noway agreed to tell Bruno immediately, and not to disclose any detail to her of the progress of proving Peters will for probate.

Noway was happy to concede to the probate hush-hush, mostly because he knew it would take weeks.

"Every 'I' will be dotted and every 'T' crossed before it is signed off," Noway said. "That's just how it is in a murder case. I've known it to take two years. in the past."

***

If Janet was right, Phyllida and John hadn't left the Island. They'd have travelled by public transport or taxi, or alternatively were staying somewhere *very* close by.

Bruno now felt the time was right to issue an arrest warrant for Phyllida Glassman and John Steadman. After obtaining the required permissions, he sent out a notice to all Island Police stations along with file photos, descriptions and a little background – enough to make it clear that they were wanted in connection with a recent murder.

If the Island Police couldn't discover their whereabouts, he'd have to try going national – but that was not a step to be taken lightly, considering the pressure it would put straight back on Bruno himself.

Chapter 37

Thursday 14th August

Bruno decided that until Phyllida or John showed up, he could afford to spend some time on trying to prove that Steph Helland had murdered Stanley Musgrove; he'd also look to re-open the investigation into the Andrew Pumpkin 'fall'.

The best way to do this and keep face politically – especially with JB sure to be asking for another progress report soon – was to demonstrate the links not hide them.

So, working with Morrison, Bruno aimed to increase the charge to attempted murder, with the motive being Steph's desire to extinguish one of the only people with knowledge of her full-scale involvement in the two deaths.

Following Detective Morrison's initial interview, Steph Helland had been charged with failing to stop following a serious accident, where the victim had suffered life threatening injuries. She had appeared before Magistrates in the Southbourne Court, where she had entered a plea of not guilty, had been granted bail against a surety of £10,000, and had been sent for trial to a higher court. At this time there was no reason for her husband to think this was anything other than a driving 'mistake', or that she was anything other than the person he *believed* she was when he married her. The case had been set down for trial at the Winchester Assize Court in December, by which time West would have recovered, would have been discharged from hospital and would be able to give evidence.

However, before then, West's statement concerning their activities relating to Musgrove and Pumpkin took precedence. It was Bruno's view that the key witness had to be detained, or he would slip back into his old ways, drift off and disappear. Bruno intended to prevent this by charging West as an accessory to the murder of Stanley Musgrove, and remanding him in custody.

Bruno explained to Morrison, "We can do that in a week or two, as long as he stays in hospital until then, once we have tested the evidence we have against Steph. Then they will both be charged, she with murder and he with assisting her. We can bring the evidence to prosecuting counsel for them to build the Crown's case."

"Whether guilty or not of the actual murder, and we believe not guilty, his behaviour after seeing the murdered Godshill butcher, particularly taking Steph home to clean up before doing anything about the body in the shop, he will not get away with," said Janet. "I think it will depend on the judge and how he presents himself. A good lawyer will save his skin," she added.

Bruno knew that was true. Guilt could stare a courtroom in the face, but a cunning and charismatic lawyer could wriggle even a dangerous criminal free.

***

Having agreed the plan with both Morrison and Tom Craven, Bruno returned to Newport Police HQ to present the Chief with his report on the Chris West accident in Bournemouth and its connection to the Godshill murder, together with West's confession to Janet. The top man demanded a signed statement from West under caution before he would consider charging him and Steph Helland with murder.

Typical, Bruno thought, *that's not going to be easy.*

Everything he had disclosed to his boss was based on a private conversation with Janet which West could deny... and, under the circumstances, probably would – it implicated him in a murder, and he certainly did not trust the police enough to take Bruno's word for it that his arrest was part of a master plan which didn't involve him spending his life in prison! So, without a signed statement under Police caution, the risk of *everything* he had told Janet being retracted was simply too great.

Although late in the afternoon, Bruno picked up Janet, and headed over the channel, saying 'goodbye' to Tom, who made his own way back home when they arrived on the mainland.

***

Bruno believed (and secretly hoped) that a lesser charge could be made against Chris West, particularly as he believed West wasn't even present at the killing, nor did he have prior knowledge of what he was about to witness in the butchers' shop, and no knowledge of what had taken place between Steph and Musgrove when responding to her call for help from the butchers' shop. He would have had no idea that by responding to her call to him, he'd be placing himself at centre stage in a murder enquiry.

Having had a great deal of time in hospital to think about his life, Chris West had undergone an important change or two.

Firstly he had come to accept that the car park hit and run 'accident' was anything but; that it was a serious attempt to kill him which had very nearly succeeded.

Secondly his eyes had been opened to just how far he had fallen since first meeting Steph in Cowes all those years ago. His life since then had been a downward spiral of deceit and lies, to satisfy a sexual ego, over which she had full control, and from which he had not been able to escape.

West understood that after Pumpkin's death, when Steph had invested money in the pub, she not only owned the building, but him as well. He had been at her beck and call for years, summoned for her own sordid pleasures whenever she wanted him. During this time he had descended into alcoholism, lost all his money, self- respect and his family, which he had always cherished dearly. He was now prepared to admit to anyone who might listen that the biggest mistake of his life was thinking his life had been stuck in a rut, and that there had to be 'more'. He hadn't been mature enough to realise he actually had everything he could ever want.

West felt tremendous guilt about Andrew Pumpkin and Stanley Musgrove. With the awful thought that Brendan Helland was on Steph's radar for an 'assisted removal' from life, he had to do what he could to help.

Janet, who had in a more recent visit told Chris West the true nature of her job – that she was a school headmistress helping out her detective friend – had shown West more kindness and understanding than anyone had done for years, and in his vulnerable but lucid state he trusted her without question. So when she introduced Detective Inspector Bruno Peach as a police officer who could also help him to re-establish himself, West was not only not frightened to reveal the details of his long relationship with Steph Helland anymore, but was brave enough to fully appreciate the implications for his own freedom. He was now well aware that he may receive a custodial sentence, but was prepared to accept any punishment that may result. It was time to start telling the truth – to himself and to others.

***

Bruno's manner towards West was a continuation of Janet's. Despite the fact that he did not quite share the level of forgiveness and compassion that Janet seemed to be able to do, he did appreciate here was a man who wanted to change. And such a man deserved respect. He therefore ensured this was clear in the way he spoke to him, making it clear that such respect existed, even in the police.

Bruno assured West that he was not there to *charge* him with a crime, but that under correct police procedures, he had to caution him. He stressed that the force was gathering information as part of an investigation into Stephanie Helland, and as everyone had hoped, he signed the documentation with purpose.

When Bruno knocked on the Chief's door at Newport, he was just putting on his jacket to leave.

"Sir, I'd appreciate you looking through this paperwork," Bruno asked.

"Do you need me to? I take it everything you told me about is in there?"

"Of course, sir."

"Then you have my blessing to re-open any such historical cases as you feel you can solve. But I have one piece of advice.

"I'm all ears, sir."

"Don't re-open a case you can't solve. We've got fascinating historical records to tackle at some point, but as you know, statistics rather than justice seem to be what drives the force in this day and age!"

***

Bruno's next task was to interview Steph Helland, who had been granted bail and was awaiting trial for the hit and run accident. Expecting that mud would fly and there would be cross accusations between her and Chris West, he decided to wait – perhaps a week – until West was sufficiently recovered to appear in court as a witness. This would also allow Bruno the time to re-examine the files on these two murders.

Having come to rely on the input of Tom on the Sam Peters case, Bruno put in the paperwork to request his assistance on 'cases ongoing'

Again, Tom hadn't taken his foot off the pedal, but had continued to try to be productive. To start with, he had re-visited Sarah Bates, the aging lady who managed the Cumberland Terrace residents group, to discuss her statement in which she said she had seen Sam Peters' leave his apartment early on that July Sunday.

Tom had arrived at her apartment at 3:00 pm. She had been in, and was 'only' drinking tea and watching a quiz show on television. She repeated what she had told him previously: that it was Sam Peters she saw leaving early on Sunday the twentieth of July. Tom asked her in the politest way about her age and eyesight; She confided in him that she *was* admittedly seventy-three next April, but still went on fortnight-long cruises where she loved to dance... insisting her eyesight was still good enough to 'pick out the handsome ones'.

Tom produced the photo of the driver of Sam's car on the ferry; the person walking away from the camera.

"Is *this* person Sam Peters?" he asked her.

She studied the photo for quite a long time, first lying flat through her glasses, then she lifted it up and held it at arm's length.

"I was going to say yes at first," she said. "But the person in that photo is definitely too short. Sam would have stood taller against the cars. No, that is definitely *not* him."

Tom had also discussed the question of whether it was definitely Sam's front door she'd heard slam closed. This Sarah proved to him by demonstrating how it was the only other door on the ground floor.

After crossing that off the list, Tom felt it important to address the issue of her insistence that she had seen Sam after hearing his door open and close that morning.

Tom explained that she must have been mistaken, and although she might be sure it was him, there was a chance she could be mistaken... and asked if she accepted this.

After contemplating the question for a minute or so, including pacing from bed to window, Sarah agreed.

"I must have put two and two together having heard his door close. I could easily have been mistaken," she admitted. "in fact I do remember thinking something looked odd, and it's just hit me what it was. I could tell from the gait that this person had shorter legs than our Sam."

***

"Shorter legs, eh?" wondered Bruno.

"I thought you'd like that," replied Tom.

"Indeed."

Although it was getting late, the pair decided they could get a couple more things crossed off their 'to do' list. Opening up the folder containing the various photographs associated with the case, the two re-examined the camera shots of Sam's car being driven on and off the Fishbourne-to-Portsmouth car ferry, late on the evening of the murder. Bruno was hoping one of them would spot a physical characteristic that he could match with Phyllida Glassman's description. He'd also received an update that there were several fingerprints inside the car, all of which could be helpful. This just added to the reasons why he must interview and obtain her prints at the earliest possible opportunity.

Bruno added an additional report page to the file. Tom gave him a quizzical look.

"It's my notes on the drivers' seating position in both cars," Bruno explained.

"Sorry sir, I still don't quite—"

"Come on Tom, don't you see? I sat in both the car that came back over on the ferry that we're looking at now, *and* Phyllida's sporty potential future barn find. They were both set up for a driver of somewhere just under five and a half feet to about five-eight. That is definitely not Sam's size, is it?!"

Bruno's train of thought continued, although he did not vocalise further. He considered that for the murderer to have to returned Peters' car to Portsmouth so soon after the murder suggested that a plan was in place *before* the killing – this was a premeditated crime, not a lover's quarrel. But why move it? Was it to give the impression it had never left Portsmouth, or had it to do with how long he had stayed and where it might have been on the Island? It also suggested the murderer had an accomplice who might have helped to place the body beneath the bridge – with one party covering each aspect.

"I'm going to be honest, sir, and say I don't think we're going to get anything from these photos," Tom admitted.

"I agree, Tom. How about we call it a day there. I'll drive on back home, and tomorrow we'll pick up Steph Helland for an interview. How does that sound?

"Like progress, sir."

Chapter 38

Stephanie Helland was aggressive right from the start of the official interview conducted at Bournemouth Police HQ.

She was accompanied by a lawyer, Charles Clementson, a senior partner from a local law firm, which – as she had still not told her husband anything close to the truth – he had paid for, as well as being in attendance himself. For some reason he couldn't place, Bruno found his presence a little unsettling.

After the introductory speech volume level setting and the stating of the interview time and date, Bruno fired his opening salvo:

"Mrs Helland, can you explain the nature of your relationship with Christopher West?"

"The incident in the car park was an accident," interjected Clementson defiantly.

"Excuse me, *sir*, but prior to discussing those particulars, we would like to understand Mrs Helland's relationship with West *before* the accident," repeated Bruno. "When did you first meet Mr West, Mrs Helland?"

"I'd never set eyes on him until he turned up at my house," she replied, simpering like a misunderstood angel. "I felt sorry for him."

"And although he was a total stranger to you, you booked him into a bed & breakfast hotel, and paid for an entire month's accommodation in advance, just to get him out of your house, is that correct?"

"Yes," was the simple answer.

"It was most magnanimous of you to behave like that towards a potentially dangerous stranger who'd broken into your home," Bruno continued. "I find it very hard to believe, in fact. But let's carry on. Mr West claims that you knew each other well, and that the two of you have engaged in a sexual relationship when the circumstances have suited you over the past several years. Hmm? I seem to recall being told that this started in Cowes when you were married to Andrew Pumpkin?"

"And can you *prove* that?" she spat.

Ignoring the question Bruno continued, "I understand that during your relationship with Mr West, you met in various Cowes-based locations for sex, but principally at the residence you shared with Mr Pumpkin."

"Inspector, I do not see the relevance this has to the accident in the Bournemouth car park, and I respectfully suggest you change your line of questioning," interrupted Clementson.

"On the contrary," Bruno retorted. "If Mr West's claims of an intimate relationship with Mrs Helland going back many years – and the activities that we're told have taken place between them during those years – are true, it would make a huge difference to the 'accident'. In fact, it is our belief that the collision was in fact a deliberate attempt by Mrs Helland to kill Chris West."

The solicitor snorted in the way that only people of a certain financial security can.

"If you have brought me here to listen to the tales of a raving alcoholic, you're wasting my time Inspector, I've never heard such a load of rubbish," said Clementson.

"Yeah," came a further defensive shout from Steph. "You're out of your mind. I loved Andrew Pumpkin, and I've told you, I don't know this West. Mr Clementson," she said as she turned to her lawyer, "I'd like to terminate this interview and leave now," she said to her lawyer.

Her husband had not spoken one word, so it was difficult to know how much of his wife's past life he already knew about.

"Mrs Helland, we are investigating a number of allegations against you by Mr West, all conducted over a considerable period of time," said Bruno. "These are serious accusations and we are offering you the opportunity to clarify your relationship before we continue."

"And what accusations are these?" demanded Clementson.

"We *will* cover them, one at time," said Bruno. "The first is that you and Mr West actually know each other very well, and that you have indulged in sexual activity over many years. Do you deny having a sexual relationship with Chris West during your marriage to Andrew Pumpkin?"

Clementson had a look of panic and shock on his face, but it was nothing compared to Brendan Helland. Clearly, neither had the faintest idea about Steph's sordid past, and the lawyer had been introduced into this police interview situation without being briefed about any of these older revelations.

"I would like to terminate this interview, Mr Clementson," Steph repeated to him. "I do not see that my private life is of any relevance to the offence with which I have been charged, a charge nonetheless which I am innocent of."

"Inspector, I believe that to continue this interview could prejudice my client's position in the upcoming court appearance, so I am advising her not to continue with this *voluntary* appearance," said Clementson.

Bruno saw that Clementson was out of his depth; he was obviously a friend of Brendan Helland from the local well-heeled set, but as a lawyer he was used to processing paperwork, or discussing dealings of a contractual nature... certainly not this kind of criminal proceedings.

"Mr Clementson, I do of course agree that your client has attended this particular meeting by invitation and she has the right to end it now as she is not being interviewed under caution. Are you absolutely sure, Mrs Helland, that you want to end this voluntary interview?"

"Yes!" she almost shouted.

"I understand," agreed Bruno. "In that case then, I am charging you with the attempted murder of Christopher West on the evening of August the third this year. You do not have to say anything. But it may harm your defence if you do not mention when questioned something which you later rely on in court. Anything you do say may be given in evidence. Now, I shall adjourn this interview for one hour to allow Mrs Helland to consult with you, Mr Clementson."

Tom escorted the lawyer and the Hellands to a spare interview room.

Bruno was pleased; it had been a good meeting so far. He had achieved his objective, not only working her up, but also seriously putting her on the defensive. He had set a cunning trap, appearing to accept various things she had said, but now made sure she knew the answers HAD to be the truth, as very few people were able to lie successfully at this stage and get away with it. She had been cornered by a new, sober West, focused on repairing his own life and therefore now both able and determined to bring her down. He regretted his own downwards spiral, especially those times where life had been at its lowest ebb and he had drunk himself into oblivion, fully knowing that he may not wake up from those deep, dark clutches. But even so, that would be his choice, not anyone else's. Who had a right to end his life? No one. And *certainly* not Steph Helland, who Chris West finally saw for what she was.

***

An hour later, Bruno resumed the interview with Steph Helland and her lawyer; the husband was no longer present. Clementson began by asking Bruno to present the evidence charging his client with the more serious charge.

"There is sworn testimony which will be presented in court on Monday at 10:00 am with a view to altering the charge to attempted murder. In the meantime, Mrs Helland is to be held in Police custody pending her appearance, at which bail conditions will also be discussed.

Clementson was utterly lost for words. He had not known anything about Steph's relationship with Chris West, and until he did he could not advise his client. The situation Steph was in right at this moment in time was very much of her own making.

Tom was told by a friend in uniform that about twenty minutes into the break, a silent and clearly distraught Brendan Helland had walked out of the interview room, through the police lobby and outside to the taxi rank. Apparently he had looked like a zombie, and everyone on duty, who had been absolutely silent as he walked past them, felt a sincere sense of pity for such a man who had just found out a small number of the lies his wife had told him.

Chapter 39

Friday 15th August

The speed of the developments of late had given Bruno and those he now considered as his 'task team' – Tom and Janet – plenty of work to do before the next working day's afternoon court session, where sworn evidence would be provided to the court. They had to proceed with the utmost care, or the plan to ultimately charge Steph with additional crimes – the murders of Andrew Pumpkin and Stanley Musgrove – would fail.

The most important evidence was that provided by Chris West himself, yet he remained in Bournemouth Hospital, still in a serious (but improving) condition, unable to attend court. This was not necessarily a problem as well as it was presented correctly.

An internal call to the Bournemouth Police HQ's legal office provided the team with details of the barrister who would represent the Crown on Monday's hearing. A huge amount of responsibility was on his shoulders, as it was he who would be presenting the case to upgrade Steph Helland's charge from the fairly common 'failing to stop at an accident' to the much more sensational one of 'attempted murder'. Tom was told that this William Calter would take a stroll over to their office at four pm for a pre-court conference.

***

William Calter knocked on the door of the room that Morrison had kindly arranged for Bruno, Tom and Janet to use whilst working on the Helland case. Bruno looked at his watch and noticed that it was 4:00 pm precisely. He looked back up at the barrister.

"Hi, you must be... William Calter?" he asked.

"I am indeed – but please, call me Will." the man replied. He was a lot younger than Bruno had expected – he seemed only a few years older than Tom. His clothes could best be described as 'scruffy casual' – or at least whatever the opposite of '*smart* casual' might be. In one hand he was carrying a motorbike helmet, in the other a baseball cap which obviously – judging from his messy hair – he had just removed before knocking.

The detective knew from experience however that age had no bearing on capability, and welcomed their new acquaintance warmly.

"Great to meet you, Will. I'm Bruno, DI Bruno Peach." he said, shaking Will's hand. "This is Tom,"

"DC Tom Craven. Pleasure," said Tom as it was his turn to shake hands.

"And my close friend Janet," Bruno gestured.

"Janet Gibson. Pleased to meet you."

"Likewise, Janet. A civilian then?"

A little embarrassed, Janet asked "I am... but... how did you know that so quickly?"

Will laughed. "You didn't say any letters before your name like these two did!"

It was a pleasant introduction, after which they all sat around the tables pushed together in the middle of the room. Bruno took a deep breath and began by describing the background to the case.

***

It took the two detectives a little more than an hour to convince Will of the need to upgrade this offence, and the bearing it had on the planned murder charges which would hopefully follow in due course.

After the long discussions in the office, Bruno suggested taking Will to the scene of the incident. The barrister agreed, but said he'd take his own transport and meet them there.

When the task team arrived, Will was already standing there next to a powerful motorcycle, still in his biker's leathers.

"Nice Bike," said Tom.

"Thanks," replied Will, "I'll tell you about it some time, but not now. We've got work to do."

In his notebook, Will began to write notes as Bruno and Janet talked him through the exact details of what had happened, as best put together from the information from West himself as well as Tiny Jacobs and others they'd since spoken to such as the ambulance staff. After listening to everything they had to say, Will strolled around the open air car park, took particular interest at the brick bollards that guided the cars driving into and out of the car park, examined the pay-as-you-park machine, and wrote down plenty more information into his notebook.

After asking a number of questions, most of which Bruno had to admit that they didn't know, Will seemed happy that he had everything he needed from them.

"There's a couple of things I'd appreciate you providing for me," he said.

"Of course," agreed Bruno.

"First, I'd appreciate a copy of the Land Registry Certificate of the pub bought by West after Pumpkin's death, and a similar document for the transfer of the Godshill butcher's shop to West. Monday morning not a problem, the hearing isn't set until two pm.

"I'm sure we can provide those for you, Will," said Bruno.

"Fantastic. Right, it's six pm now; do you think Helland's showroom will be open?"

All three had to admit they weren't sure.

"Not to worry, I'm going to pop over there now. I'll meet you in court at one pm, OK?

"Excellent, see you then."

"Ah. One more thing," Will said.

Janet looked at him and asked kindly "What do you need?"

"Which way is Helland's showroom?"

After brief directions he sped off, leaving Bruno, Tom and Janet to go for a drink and discuss their chances, which Bruno felt were about fifty-fifty. His main concern was whether this scruffy young lad would have the confidence and ability in a court setting. He turned to Tom and said, "Don't suppose you fancy presenting the evidence to the judge do you?"

Tom's response was drowned out by the glass he was drinking from deliberately, although Bruno did catch the words 'above my pay grade' in there somewhere.

***

Saturday 16th August

Obtaining the Land Certificate from the Land Registry was straight forward, and Tom did so online on Saturday morning. Bruno visited Roud Farm and Steadman's cottage, where nothing had been disturbed since his last visit, and clearly neither had returned to their homes.

He *had* to find Phyllida Glassman quickly, so he issued a notice to all Island police stations that this was a priority arrest, and that he should be notified immediately on sight of these two fugitives.

***

Sunday 17th August

Thankfully for Bruno, Sunday was very much a day of rest. He chose to meet with Janet for lunch, and they both agreed they would try not to talk too much shop. After eating, they took a stroll along Ventnor beach, soaking up the sun, before relaxing with a read of the Sunday papers.

They both did very well to keep their promise, until the point at which Janet was due to depart, at which Bruno invited her to accompany him to Bournemouth on Monday for the Steph Helland court appearance at two pm.

Janet's reply was that as it was *real* Police business, he should go alone, but he reminded her that, in many ways, this was *her* case so she *must* come. On top of this reason, Bruno knew that her presence would give him real confidence... and that secretly he was sure she wanted to come!

Chapter 40

Monday 18th August

Will Calter was almost unrecognisable from the scruff that had shown up for the conference on Friday afternoon. He was suited (obviously bespoke), clean shaven (with a hint of expensive aftershave) and looked every bit the handsome young professional barrister that Bruno had been hoping for.

After examining the Land Certificate, and the statement from West, he changed the subject away from the trial to small talk before entering the court room fifteen minutes before two.

On the opposite side to where the police team were sitting was a local barrister whom Will indicated he knew, accompanied by Clementson, Steph Helland's solicitor. Her husband was the sole occupant of the public section at the back of the court. Bruno felt sorry for him, but wondered whether the hearing might well be a blessing in disguise.

***

After the "All rise" and the generic court preliminaries, it was time for this hearing to get fully underway.

The hearing started with complex legal points being made by Will, referring to various cases and highlighting certain lines of text to the judge that he believed relevant.

Stephanie Helland was smartly dressed in clothes that had been brought into the remand centre where she had spent the weekend. She had clearly softened her personality under instructions from her legal advisers, and in appearance she could have passed for a respectable middle class Bournemouth lady, in a plain navy blue suit and white blouse, flat hair and little make up.

As time wore on, Will Calter explained that it was important to clarify Stephanie Helland's relationship – both current and past – with Chris West, the victim of the road accident at the Bournemouth car park.

He argued that if we could prove that she knew him prior to the point she was claiming, then precedent stipulated that a charge of attempted murder could be sought, and therefore the judge should allow the more serious charge to replace the existing one.

"Mrs Helland," Will said, "can you tell the court about your relationship with Chris West?"

"I did not have a relationship with him."

"But you know him?"

"Yes."

"When did you meet him?"

"When he came to burgle my home. He broke in and I called the Police. He hadn't stolen anything, so I took pity on him, and sent him to a local bed and breakfast."

"And you paid the one month bill in advance for a complete stranger, Mrs Helland, correct? So then, what happened after that?"

"He was thrown out of the B&B for drunken behaviour, then he came to see me for money."

"Where did he come?"

"To my home, one morning, he just showed up."

"Did you give him any money?"

"No, not at first, but he wouldn't go away, so I gave him £100, and he promised he would not come back. But he had got my telephone number and kept calling me, always drunk."

"Were you frightened when he kept calling?"

"Yes."

"What did he say to you?"

"He always just wanted money."

"Why didn't you tell the Police, Mrs Helland? That would have been a normal reaction to a phone pest. And with the recent stalking laws introduced it is very easy to deal with such situations."

"I don't know."

"Was it because in fact you *know* Chris West *very well indeed*, and you are frightened that he might expose your past to Mr Helland, your current husband?"

"No, it was not," the reply, still relatively calm.

It was now very clear to Bruno that Will's way of working was in complete contrast to the scruffy individual that he'd last seen replacing a baseball cap with a motorbike helmet. Not only was his knowledge of case law excellent, but his skills of persuasion were impressive. Bruno smiled with satisfaction, confident that this man would do as good a job as anyone could, and his fears were totally unfounded.

"Mrs Helland," Will continued after an uncomfortably long silence in which he waited and waited for Stephanie to speak. "I put it to you that you have known Chris West for at least ten years. I believe that because you recognised it was he who was in your conservatory the day when the Police arrived in response to your 999 call, that you sent them away. You were frightened when you set eyes on him that he had come to reveal secrets of your past life. And here's the scenario that played out: you were helpful to him at first until you realised that his petty blackmail would not stop, that he is now an alcoholic, and it would continue to put you at risk until you put a permanent stop to it, one way or another. You tried to kill him in the Bournemouth car park by driving into his body. You knew where he would be at that time of the evening because you knew where he'd be drinking!"

"No! He didn't tell me that!"

"I didn't say he did, Mrs Helland. No, he left a message for you with an employee at the reception desk of your husband's business, which she passed on to you at 5:30 pm by phone at your home. Because of the content of the message, you *knew* that he would be drinking in the pub opposite the car park all evening. Mrs Helland."

"No. It's not true," Said a visibly angry Stephanie.

Now I have here in my possession a certificate issued by the Land Registry regarding the butchers' shop premises in Godshill on the Isle of Wight, which you sold to a – let me just make sure I'm reading this correctly – ah yes, a Mr Chris West some four years ago. Would you confirm that your premises were at number eighteen the High Street, Godshill and that the building was bought from you by Chris West?"

Stephanie did not answer as the document moved from Will Calter to the judge and then to her. All the time she kept looking around at no one in particular, ensuring that she never focused on one person enough for their eyes to meet.

"Do you recall that transaction, Mrs Helland?"

Still she did not answer.

"The parking set-up at the town car parks mean that you are required to enter your registration number prior to making payment, and yours is recorded on the machine as having entered that particular car park at 8:05 pm. You put £2 in the machine, but never left your car, according to the cameras trained on it. You simply sat watching the pub exit until nine o'clock, when Chris West appeared with two friends. He crossed the road and sat on the wall at the exit to the car park drinking from cans. One man left after around fifteen minutes later, and I put it to you that not long after that, you saw an opportunity to rid yourself of Christ West for good as he stood standing in the middle of the car park exit finishing a can of lager.

However, you did not kill him as you had hoped, did you?

**

After the court hearing, Janet paid a visit to Bournemouth hospital to report the details of the hearing to Chris West.

She explained the court proceedings and how the Police barrister had compiled new evidence and presented it to the court; much of the detail was met by her with a muted silence. Janet explained how the barrister had proved to the court their relationship was long-standing and that the accident in the car park was premeditated.

Steph had tried to kill him, to eliminate him from her life and prevent him exposing her past.

Chris West now fully accepted that it was his *duty* to prevent Steph from continuing her murderous life.

He was concerned that he could be found guilty of a number of offences, that he ran a risk of being adjudged to have been involved with her crimes, even though he did not *knowingly* assist her to commit murder.

He knew he'd likely be charged with assisting her on some charge or other, but he trusted the court to be fair.

The importance of West's testimony in the case was paramount, and Bruno wanted to get as much detail as possible.

The butcher's murder was far more sinister and incriminating for Steph Helland than the attempted murder of West, because she had actually succeeded. Actual murder definitely trumps attempted murder, Janet explained, and so to present his statement about this would be instrumental in bringing her to justice.

West agreed, and Tom began to fill out the top boxes on a 'statement sheet'.

**

"On the day she murdered Stanley, she had called me from the butchers' shop at about five o'clock to come and meet her urgently. It took me thirty minutes to travel to Godshill High Street. The shop was closed and in darkness. I knocked with my hand on the shuttered door, which was opened by Steph, who seemed calm and was dressed to leave. 'What's the matter?' I said. As I had been summoned by what seemed to be a life or death call. 'He's dead,' she said, pointing to a pair of legs protruding from alongside the counter at the back of the shop.

'Good god,' I said, terrified. 'Have you called the Police?'

'No,' she said back to me.

'What have you been doing for the past half an hour, call them now!' I said to her.

That Stanley lay in a huge pool of blood, still seeping from his head the blood covered the tiled floor surrounding his body.

'Why haven't you called the police?' I asked her.

'I waited for you,' she told me, then paused.

'What the hell for, why involve me in this?' I countered.

'Because I need help, that's why,' she said. 'You always said you'd help me if I was ever in trouble.'

'In trouble, what do you mean? Did you do this?'

'I want you to take me home, she said.'"

"I was terrified," continued West. "I tried to get her to call the police and ambulance, but she refused, she wanted me to take her home. Stupidly, instead of insisting on doing the right thing, she managed to convince me to do what she wanted. Always the same it was.

"On the journey home she did not speak one word. She stared ahead, eyes wide open. When we got to her house she started to undress until she was completely naked, she picked up everything and put it into a black plastic bag, tied a knot in it and stood it in the kitchen. She took my hand and led me into the bedroom and we made love. After she showered, then dressed in plain clothes, she asked me to drive her back to the shop. I dropped her round the corner, turned around and drove back to Cowes, praying that nobody had seen my car. There was no explanation of what had happened in the shop. When I left her she'd worked it out. She had a plan and a story to tell the police."

"Do you think she killed her husband?" asked Bruno.

"Yes, I'm certain," he said.

"Why?"

"She was tired of the old butcher, and his family hated her. When I saw her about a month later, she never mentioned him to me and I was frightened to ask her."

"Why didn't you tell the police later?" asked Bruno.

"I just blanked that afternoon out of my mind. She had convinced me that I'd be in trouble more than her if I said anything. At that point in my life, I never wanted to see her again. After the murder she went quiet and I didn't hear from her much. I expected any day to hear she had been charged with murder. She knew I had drunk the pub dry, so when I did hear from her it was to offer me the butchers' shop. I was skint, my wife and kids had gone to live with her mother, so I jumped at it, went back to the fish, which I was pretty good at. It did alright.. until I went back on the booze, and then it all slid away from me again. When she signed the shop over to me she said it was because I'd been a good boy about the butcher's murder."

"I said, 'What do you mean?'"

"She said, 'You never told anybody what happened.'"

"I said, 'That's because I don't *know* what happened.'"

"She smiled and said, 'That's the spirit'"

"If I think about it now – which I really don't like to do – I'd say that she hit him on the head with a butchers axe, which killed him outright," said West. But obviously it could have been any of a number of things.

Everything that West had recalled about his relationship with Steph, Tom had written down in statement form, which he read back to the bedridden man, let him read it, and then got him to sign.

***

Bruno was pleased with the statement they had obtained, and left West with promises; Janet likewise. With his signed statement, Bruno was now in a strong position to put the case of the Godshill butcher to bed. Andrew Pumpkin on the other hand was a different prospect.

The facts he had to support a charge were paper invoices of the lubricant obtained by West from his supplier which was later used on the steps of Pumpkin's penthouse, and also, bank statements showing her gift of £60,000 to buy the pub.

The team certainly believed that West was telling the truth, however, one person who had not been mentioned was West's wife. It was likely she could reveal something about the final days of their relationship together that would add to the knowledge they had about West's behaviour during the business ventures in Cowes and Godshill.

The compilation of all the evidence in the Pumpkin and Musgrove murder cases was completed, fully compliant to all procedural requirements, by Bruno alongside a little unofficial help from Janet, and passed to the Criminal Prosecution Office of Will Calter, who would compile the case against Steph Helland.

Sadly for Chris West, it would include charges against him as an accomplice – yet he assured Bruno this was a necessary part of his repentance and recovery.

Chapter 41

Bruno saw Chris West's wife the following afternoon, and he learned a great deal about their relationship., and Bruno was admittedly surprised that she had tolerated West's behaviour for so long.

"He is still my husband, I won't divorce him. Even if I wanted to, in my church it is forbidden... I can't. And anyway, besides, I am ever hopeful he will come back to me," she said. "Regardless of what has happened between us, I still love him."

It certainly seemed that Judy West had not only been a good wife to Chris but also a loving mother to two well-adjusted daughters. She now worked in St Mary's hospital in Newport as a part-time receptionist.

During her marriage she had worked in her husband's fish business, doing the accounts and paperwork and offering the kind of professional approach that helped keep the businesses on the road for a while. She dealt with suppliers whose orders were delivered late, and restaurants who didn't pay up on time. Under her management the fish business increased at a decent rate, until its success went to Chris's head and he developed other interests. Sadly, the principle interest he found was Stephanie Helland... or, more accurately for the time, Steph Pumpkin. She chased him all over the Island whilst he delivered fresh fish to the best hotels and restaurants. She kept him out late and by the time he got home he'd had a skinful of booze.

Judy just could not even remotely fathom what Chris saw in Steph. Almost everyone else in their circle saw clearly the dreadful, greedy, adulterous, amoral person she was, and Steph felt that somehow she would come to a bad end.

"Everything bad that's happened to Chris has been because of Stephanie Pumpkin, or whatever surname she's onto nowadays," Judy said, for the first time allowing a tear to streak down her right cheek.

"She is an evil predator who stole *my husband*" the emphasis she put on the words was significant "because she *could*. I know about the sex. That's why she gave him money for the pub, and when that went bust, the butchers shop. She was always hanging around.

And you know what? My Chris wasn't the only one. She was absolutely anybody's at the yacht club. Talk to old Steve Davis, who owns the Chandlers in Cowes; he's one. She is a poisonous person to know." Judy paused and then asked kindly: "How is Chris?"

Bruno gave her the details of his injuries and she promised to visit him in Bournemouth hospital.

"He'll come home one day," were her hopeful last words.

***

"A visit from Judy would definitely help him," Bruno said to Janet after he returned home. "A tear of sympathy and a hint of forgiveness would give him strength to battle through his physical and mental recovery."

Judy promised Bruno that she'd attend court, and if needed, be cross examined about Chris and Steph's activities on the Island as she understood it, and the time scale their activities had covered. It was just possible that her presence at Steph Helland's trial, pleading on behalf of her husband, could evoke the sympathy of the court. Steph's defence lawyers would , of course, try to shift the blame onto him. She might even come up with some wild story that implicated him as the main killer of Andrew Pumpkin and Stanley Musgrove.

A woman with Steph Helland's guile could present herself to the court as a simple woman controlled by a man in trouble, who had planned and executed the murders, and who in both instances had profited substantially.

Chapter 42

The joint arrest warrant for Phyllida Glassman of Roud Farm and John Steadman of Artisans' Cottage contained a description of the couple and a photograph of Phyllida, enlarged from a framed photo taken from a sideboard at Roud Farm. It showed her head and neck, and stated that they were wanted for questioning in connection with the murder of Mr Samuel Peters, on or about the evening of the nineteenth of July. The details were circulated as a priority e-mail to all Island Police stations. Rather than go fully national Bruno decided on a limited county-wide expansion, so he also wrote to all Southampton and Portsmouth constabularies. The Island Police units confirmed one-by-one they had put the wanted details on Police noticeboards inside Police stations and in some community centres and Post Offices.

Bruno had no idea what response his e-mails would have. He had absolutely no idea as to where the pair were, although Janet was convinced they were still on the Island. The forensics confirming Peters' blood in Steadman's Volvo estate was enough evidence to involve and implicate Steadman at least; further proof of his involvement could come from matching the blood-soaked Tesco shopping bags that covered Peters' head with those found at Steadman's cottage.

Bruno was now sitting in his office, trying to think about any way he could improve his chances of finding them. He was never particularly hopeful for speedy assistance in these cases; police uniforms not directly involved with the case were known to see a wanted suspect but deliberately not arrest them because of the amount of extra paperwork they'd be required to complete.

He was also not convinced about Janet's theory. She said they had to be somewhere within easy walking distance of the cottage, so were sure to be local. But Bruno knew that the main Niton-to-Newport bus route was a ten-minute walk from Roud Farm, and Steadman would have been familiar with it. From Newport they could have travelled *anywhere* in the four days since they were seen together in the environs of Artisans' Cottage.

"August is a busy month for holiday visitors on the Island, there are strangers everywhere," said Janet. "They might have gone walking, staying in a tent. They can stay one or two nights in a B&B anywhere and move on, even hire a campervan."

"They must have a plan," said Bruno.

"Why?" said Janet. "They thought they had got away with it, surely? Or they'd *both* have disappeared a lot earlier. Your position is strengthening with every day that passes, theirs is getting weaker – and they know it! The blood in Steadman's car is a breakthrough. We know they're in it together, and there's surely more to come from Sam Peters' car. Look, I'm sure someone will report them to us. Our best bet is that they see their own mug shots and panic, which will induce something irrational, like trying to leave the Island. Someone will spot them, then we'll catch them. The public read and respond to notices, the station will be deluged with calls."

"Hopefully, if you think so," said Bruno, "although I fear the people who run holiday accommodation in August are often too busy to stand around reading notice boards."

Chapter 43

The following morning, Janet's theory was proven somewhat correct. She had assured Bruno that Glassman and Steadman were close by. "Just a little stroke of luck" she had said.

In Bruno's mind, there was no such thing as luck... and, if there was, it always seemed to favour the accused.

Yet sometime around eleven am, a call from a Newport uniform informed Bruno that Phyllida Glassman had been apprehended by local Police in Newport after a 'catastrophic occurrence' at Carisbrooke Castle at 10:30 am. that same morning. They gave no details by phone, but requested his immediate presence at Newport Police Station.

His first concern on arrival at Newport Police Station was *why no mention of Steadman?* As he arrived he was told that Phyllida had been brought to the station alone.

"So what room is she in?" Bruno asked.

Unfortunately, he was told, she was no longer there. It was rare for DI Peach to blow his top, but those listening to the conversation prepared to run for cover as his face changed shade rapidly.

It was at this moment that Tom burst through the door, surveyed the scene and went to stand loyally at his master's right-hand side.

As he took his place, it was explained to him and Bruno that on arrival at the station, Phyllida Glassman had collapsed in the detention area, and – as per current policy following criticism of a number of deaths in custody – she had been transferred to a secure ward at St Mary's hospital in Newport; it was here where hospital patients from Parkhurst Prison were normally held and treated. *At least she's secure there*, thought Bruno.

Amazingly, Phyllida had rapidly recovered the moment she arrived at the hospital, and expressed her wish to be released from custody there, not relishing a return to Newport Police station.

Of course, her request had been denied. This news seemingly led to another collapse, and she was currently 'being monitored'. Unfortunately, this meant she was 'off limits' for police interviews.

"So where is John Steadman?" implored Bruno.

"Steadman is still down the well," a brave young female in uniform stated.

"The *well*?"

"Yes, the well at Carisbrooke Castle."

"He's down a *well*?"

"According to Ms Glassman, he jumped. It was only the two of them there, apparently".

"*Down a well...*" Bruno thought about this.

Even Tom was struggling to make a comment.

The brave officer continued, "They've closed the Castle and the fire department are there with their tackle to bring him up. As for Ms Glassman, we've been told that when she's better, she'll be brought back here.

"She'd bloody better be," grouched Bruno.

"Why don't we go to the castle, sir?" Tom asked Bruno. "By the time we've finished there, we might be able to talk to Mrs Glassman."

It was as good a suggestion as any; at least they'd have an independent report as to what happened.

The Castle had been closed since the incident and several fire department vehicles with men moving to-and-fro had assembled close to the Castle gates. News of the incident was now common knowledge and visitors were being turned away by uniformed Castle employees who, rather than following official policy and offering no comment, were turning people away with the melodramatic and unofficial statement "Sorry, you can't visit today, because a man jumped down the well."

Shaking their heads, Bruno and Tom flashed their cards, but were told that there were no special favours for service personnel, and they *still* couldn't visit because a man had jumped down a well.

Tom explained that they were actually policemen here to investigate the incident of the man jumping down the well. He asked if anyone could fill him and DI Peach in on the details of what had happened.

"I'm sorry sir, we're not authorised to provide comment," was the reply.

Thankfully at that point, a senior member of staff made their way over, and escorted the two men to an office which had been set up as a kind of crisis-centre.

A man was called over to help bring the two policemen up to date with happenings. A badge indicated that his name was Barry and that he was a historical expert and tour guide.

He explained to them that the incident had happened in the 'Well House' which is open to the public every day between the hours of 10:00 am and 6:00 pm. The well itself dates from medieval times, when the ability to draw water from the subterranean rock guaranteed the Castle's impregnability as a fortress to invaders. The treadmill, dating from 1291, by which spring water is drawn up from a depth of over 160 feet, was hauled by prisoners until the early eighteenth century, when donkeys were introduced.

Nowadays a team of four donkeys rotated in two-hour shifts for the benefit of the tourists. Even today there is always a good forty feet of water at the bottom of the well, from which bucketfuls of ice-cold water fit for drinking are drawn up.

The most famous resident of the Carisbrooke Castle was King Charles I, who was imprisoned there for fourteen months before his execution in London in 1649.

From 1896 until 1944 the Castle was the home of Princess Beatrice, daughter of Queen Victoria, who was the Island's Governor.

"Although I'm always interested in local history," said Bruno, "today my focus is more on the more recent happenings. Perhaps you could enlighten me as to the incident in the well house?"

"Of course, forgive me inspector," he said before continuing, "at about 10:30 am the Castle superintendent reported a woman emerged from the Well House screaming for help, explaining to an attendant that a man had just fallen down the well. The well itself was almost exactly 161 feet deep, so as Island records go, the interesting thing about it is that the—"

"If it's *that* easy to fall down the well, why was it left unattended?" Tom asked.

"Well that's the issue, inspector. At first there was disbelief amongst the uniformed employees within the castle, because they all knew that the well is *caged off* and *locked from the public*."

"So what happened?" Bruno demanded.

"Well, it turns out that the man responsible for the donkeys left the cage open when he released the animals on Saturday evening, and was late bringing a donkey back, so anyone could enter the cage that encased the well shaft."

"Hmm," said Bruno.

"The lady was distraught, in a terrible emotional state. She said that the door of the cage was open, so anyone could indeed enter and approach the edge of the well, which she and her companion did thinking it was a normal part of the tour. Now it also seems that the grill that usually covers the Well opening had been removed for some kind of maintenance. So there's a fair amount of bad luck here.

"Yes, bad luck indeed"

"So this woman, a Mrs Glassman I believe; it seems she did not remember any noise from the fall and the landing of the man or anything really, other than watching him step off the stone ledge of the surrounding wall with his left foot, and disappear from view."

"It seems that safety has been a little lax around here," Bruno stated. "How often does something like this happen?"

"Oh, never sir, *never*. In fact, I'm proud to have been called into work today. This is a totally unique moment in the life of Carisbrooke Castle. No one has *ever* fallen into the well in its nine-hundred year history. The story "Man commits suicide by jumping down well" will go down in history, and I can say that *I was there!*"

"You think he's dead?"

"He has been at the bottom of the well for over two hours now, sir. I should think that would do it."

"I see", said Bruno again.

The historian introduced the policemen to the castle receptionist who had taken Phyllida to a quiet staff area and sat her down with a cup of tea.

After speaking with the receptionist for a minute or two, it became clear that they were too frightened to ask how it happened, worried that her account would reveal evidence of negligence on their behalf, or – perhaps even worse – some kind of foul play. Either way certainly the incident could lead to the closure of one of the leading visitor attractions on the Island. The staff feared their jobs were at stake.

In a recent accident, a man had fallen twelve feet into the Castle moat while taking photographs. Although dry and grass covered, the Castle management had been adjudged liable, for not putting up a notice within viewing distance, and the man had made a claim.

A more serious accident would be a disaster for them, as they would be liable if the access gate to the Well had been left unsecured, and the grill removed by their staff.

A number of uniformed police officers had arrived in a black Maria within ten minutes of the reported suicide jump, having recognised the name Phyllida Glassman as a wanted person.

Speaking to one of the uniformed officers at the castle, Bruno completed the jigsaw when he was told that once Phyllida's emotions had subsided and she had recovered from witnessing the demise of John Steadman in the Well House, she composed herself and attempted to leave the Police Station, but was prevented from doing so. It was then she had immediately collapsed and was transferred to St Mary's for medical attention.

"OK, thank you," said Bruno. "Can you point us in the direction of the Well House?"

***

Bruno and Tom examined the Well House, the cage built to prevent public access to the well, and the low brick parapet that surrounded the well.

Rescue work was currently underway. The fire chief had abandoned the initial attempt to drain the well, as their equipment was not capable of being set up to pump any decent volumes of water from 160 feet down. Considering alternatives, the diameter of the well was noted as large enough to lower a man on a swing chair to survey the well at a great depth and moveable lights were lowered at the side of the well to assist with visibility.

The man currently dangling in mid-air above the well was wearing a harness and was sitting on a swing-like platform attached to a strong rope that could haul him up if the platform got into trouble.

"Going down?" Bruno asked.

"Nah, just come up!" the man replied.

He proceeded to explain to an audience of Bruno, Tom, the site manager and a few others that a diver would be required to bring the body up from the bottom of the well. On Tom's suggestion, a request was sent to the Royal Naval diving school at Whale Island in Portsmouth for a diver with specialist body-retrieval equipment to attend.

It was also necessary to check the firmness of the walls of the well, to ensure it was not capable of caving in. Additionally, the erection of the mechanism over the well head and checking its safety was a lengthy task. in itself. Recovering Steadman's body was no easy job, and it was anticipated that Steadman wouldn't be raised until early evening.

"Didn't they raise the Titanic recently?" Tom asked.

"I'm not sure, you know," replied Bruno.

"Just that considering how much work it is to get just one man up a couple of hundred feet, how hard must it be to raise a ship?"

"I remember seeing them raise the Mary Rose on Blue Peter back in '82", Bruno mused.

"The museum's in Portsmouth, you know," replied Tom. "It's really impressive, you should visit one day."

"I'll try to... *if* we ever reach the end of this case," Bruno laughed.

With almost perfect timing, he received a call to let him know that Phyllida had now been transported back to Newport Police station.

***

Bruno and Tom mutually agreed that they would try their best to steer clear of the events at the Well House until the fire service had recovered the body and the pathologist had provided them with some initial thoughts.

Phyllida was already seated in the interview room when Bruno and Tom entered. Standing behind her was a bulky uniformed PC, to whom the older detective nodded his thanks; he left the room, advising just loud enough that Phyllida could hear him tell Bruno that he'd be standing outside in case he was needed.

"Thank you," stated Bruno. Starting the recording and turning to Phyllida he asked "No lawyer?"

"I'm innocent, Inspector, I don't believe I need one," she replied.

Thinking about her money problems, Bruno said "If you can't *afford* your own, then we can contact the on-duty legal aid cover for you? There's no need to be embarrassed."

"I have plenty of long-term funds, inspector, I don't require charity, thank you" she replied.

Bruno wondered if she was talking about Sam Peters' will.

"As long as you can assure me this is a considered decision?"

"Of course", she replied.

Bruno began with a short summary of the fact that Phyllida had been impossible to get hold of recently, and then explained that she and John Steadman were wanted for questioning about the death of Sam Peters. At first she feigned surprise and demanded to know why she had been lumped with John Steadman in the man hunt.

"Inspector, the man who jumped to his death down the well was John Steadman, the man who lived in Artisans' Cottage a few hundred metres from Roud Farm. I know him because he has done odd jobs for me over many years up until now. After my husband died he became very familiar, in fact overly so, at times forcing himself on my attention. When he discovered I intended to marry Sam, he became jealous and began to spy on us. He seemed to know Sam's every movement. He spied on the farmhouse from various places around Roud Farm, of which he knew every nook and cranny. He was born and grew up on my farm, because previously it had belonged to *his* family... until his father sold it to us. The Steadman family continued to live in Artisans' Cottage; mother, father and John, their only son. They were a strange bunch; they never went out or away. The Steadmans were an old Island family, going back to the early eighteen-hundreds and possibly even before then. On Saturday morning they all went food shopping in the Tesco's in Ryde, followed by lunch at that Busy Bees garden centre restaurant opposite, it was their only enjoyment."

Phyllida Glassman was getting more composed as she spoke. Bruno, however, gave her a look that said 'this story had better be going somewhere'. His patience with her was already thin and the interview had only just started.

"While my husband was alive," she continued, "we got on well as friends, but within a month of his funeral John would turn up, early mornings or late evenings to 'see if I was alright'. He would hang around, sitting in my husband's favourite arm chair, something that I found irritating. Now, I am not going to say he *definitely* killed Sam, Inspector, but if you have suspicions or evidence against *him*, which you might well have, please do not involve *me*."

"If you had nothing to do with Sam's murder, why ignore all my calls?" Bruno asked, frustration getting the better of him.

"I had no idea you wanted to talk about Sam."

"What else could it have been?" Bruno said, exasperated.

Seeing his mentor's frustration and knowing only too well the danger of it increasing, Tom interjected on an alternative tack.

"You are one of the *only* people on the Island who had any knowledge of what Sam Peters was doing here, and he was to marry you, we are told. So something that particularly interests us is why Mr Peters would come over to the Island, stay for a long weekend, and not even inform his immediate fiancée?" he asked.

The question clearly irritated Phyllida. "Sam had a *number* of business activities on the Island. He did surveys for building companies, he was involved with Dick Potter dredging river beds for gold particles, and he was involved with both Bartlett and Bentley in their quartz mining venture. He did not *always* tell me what he was doing or when he was coming to see me. Anyway, Steadman said not to bother calling you." This last sentence seemed an odd addition.

"Why would he say that?" asked Tom.

"He reckoned that I should let you get on with finding Sam's killer first," responded Phyllida.

"Why would you listen to a man who was stalking you, as you say?"

"I didn't say I didn't *like* him, Inspector. You asked him to get me to call you, Inspector. You did not say call *urgently*, you said to call *when I got back*. When you visited the farm again he said perhaps you were planning to pin Sam's murder on me."

"Why would he say that?"

"You tell me, Inspector."

"What was your reaction to his suggestion?"

"It was his observation, not mine. He suggested we go away to a cottage he sometimes rented. He said nobody would know where I was, which would give you time to find the killer. So that is what we did."

Bruno was playing a very careful game. He was perfectly happy with her responses so far, as she was drifting towards a corner, and was now gradually digging a hole for herself with a story that had started out as sounding plausible, but was becoming confused and ill thought out as it expanded. Soon she would have told so many lies it would be too hard to track them all.

"So where is this secret cottage?" asked Tom.

"It's a walk," she said "A long walk from the farm. It's a mile south of Carisbrooke at Gatcombe. We put on our walking boots, we could have got on a bus, but it was a beautiful evening and we wanted a country walk. So we walked the Yar river trail, which starts at the farm and tracks north across the Worsley trail, past the mid Island farms to Gatcombe Dairy cottage in Gatcombe. It's high up, but south of Hill Farm."

"How long did you plan to stay there?"

"A few days, while I got myself together," she said.

"I am surprised that you chose to disappear with a neighbour rather than respond with a phone call to me at the station."

"I didn't disappear, I just didn't consider a phone call to you a big deal and, there was no urgency, according to John."

"You still haven't explained why you've been avoiding having this conversation, Ms Glassman", said Bruno.

"You might find this hard to believe, Inspector, but I hadn't got over Sam's murder, and I didn't want to go through all the pain again, certainly not in front of a typical policeman! I had and have nothing to add to what I'd already told you," she added, in a manner that was moving from the defensive to the aggressive, targeting Bruno.

Bruno knew that attack was the best means of defence and, if he was right and she was involved in killing Peters – and he believed she was – she would no doubt defend her position aggressively.

"You may say you have nothing to add, Mrs Glassman, however I haven't yet asked you all the questions I'd like to. And one of the biggest questions I have is why you've been avoiding me like you've got something to hide?"

"Do you know something Inspector? We needed some food, and so John suggested we walk into Newport along the Whitcombe Road, past Carisbrooke Castle. Just before the entrance to the castle is a car park and a post office. On the notice board outside the post office do you know what I saw? A photograph of me and a notice which read, 'Wanted for questioning in connection with the murder of Sam Peters on 19th July. Please contact Newport Police Station, if you know the whereabouts of this person.' Surely that explains why I've been avoiding you?"

"I'm afraid I don't follow," said Tom, "so you'll have to treat me as if I'm a bit on the slow side. Can you explain what you're trying to say?"

"I'm trying to say that you've both already pinned this murder on me, haven't you?"

"We don't 'pin' a murder on anyone until we're sure we have the right person, Mrs Glassman."

"But you will publicly embarrass me with a notice like that?"

"That is how we work Mrs Glassman. We gather evidence and that leads to further investigation and questioning. If people avoid us, especially in such a serious matter as a man's life that was ended brutally, we have to use tried and trusted methods to find them"

"Was it your idea to use a 'tried and trusted' advert like *that*, Inspector? If it was, you should be demoted, or whatever they do to policemen who make false allegations and ruin people's lives, which is *exactly* what you have done to me. That notice with my photograph worried Steadman to the core and look what has happened to him now! You may try, but you are *not* going to ruin my life."

"Mrs Glassman, I shouldn't need to point out that the notice did not constitute an allegation in any form. You were a missing person, and it was most important for me to interview you in connection with Sam Peters' murder."

"That's tosh, Inspector, and you know it. You implied that I was a bloody killer," she said, clearly becoming more riled. "John and I were so worried about your false accusations that we decided to go into the castle to think carefully until we decided what to do next. We paid our entrance, and hoped the person at the desk had not seen the notice board outside of the Post Office. We walked through the entrance of the castle, hiding our faces, and across the courtyard into the Well House. The cage that surrounds the treadmill was open, as if they were about to bring in one of the donkeys that turn the wheel."

Bruno wished that he could communicate silently with Tom. If he had telepathic skills, he would have said *"Look Tom, note how I haven't even asked about John Steadman's death, but she's about to tell us 'exactly' how it happened. Often you'll find people prepare their stories so well that they want to tell them as soon as possible. They're so keen not to make a mistake that they tell you things without being asked. And who gives a policeman information freely? That's right Tom, no one except a liar!"*

In the real world, the best Bruno managed was a meaningful glance at Tom that said 'pay attention'.

"John went inside the cage," Phyllida continued, "and stood close to the edge looking down the well shaft. I stood back and watched, the depth of the well scared me... but then he just disappeared. He had jumped down the well, without making a sound. I screamed for help and ran out of the Well House, and an attendant arrived, I don't remember what happened after that, all I remember is being brought here."

The dramatic tale of Steadman's death did not change Bruno's view on Sam Peters' murder, of which he was now convinced was a Glassman/Steadman combined effort in some form or another... although he certainly didn't believe it was *purely* Steadman's doing, which is what he suspected Phyllida would soon suggest.

The evidence discovered in his Volvo estate, the blood of the victim Sam Peters, implicated Steadman in the murder. His demise in the Well House changed nothing for Bruno in his search for Sam's killer. Steadman had not played a direct role in his investigation, until now, and now he was dead. That left Phyllida even more exposed. Now she would surely try to wriggle out of the accusation by blaming everything on Steadman, who couldn't answer back now.

Bruno could tell that she was emotionally tired, and was vulnerable to questioning if she was lying. He hated the idea of being too harsh with any interviewee of his who was innocent, although he could count on one hand the number of times he'd got to the stage of pushing a suspect hard and them *not* being responsible for the crime.

Bruno now wanted to know about her personal relationship with Steadman. She had changed so much from the sophisticated lady of the manor persona that she had presented at their first meeting. Now she was a woman hiding away in a neighbour's cottage to avoid interrogation by the Police, and the merest hint that she might have to answer some questions she runs away.

Perhaps it was it a Lady Chatterley experience that Phyllida was engaged in with Steadman? What persuaded her to hide away in a cottage, ten minutes from home, and then de-camp to another cottage, many miles away, in Gatcombe? It surely wasn't just to avoid phone calls from the local police, was it? She was almost certainly running away from what Bruno had to prove in a courtroom. But with Steadman dead, she had probably started planning how everything could be put down to him.

It had only been a few seconds since Phyllida had last spoken, but she clearly felt uncomfortable with silence, as she decided to throw another accusation Bruno's way.

"Because you can't find the killer, you've latched onto me, Inspector, haven't you? Do you realise that by issuing that abominable notice you, you *personally* have caused the death of John Steadman? Police incompetence knows no bounds when you start accusing innocent people of murder," she said indignantly, with a tremor in her voice.

At that moment a police officer beckoned Bruno and Tom Craven out of the interview room, while their friendly uniformed guard came back in to act as a sentry.

"Inspector, there is something I think you need to see before you continue your interview with Mrs Glassman," the Desk Sergeant said to Bruno.

***

After a short discussion, Tom and Bruno drove back to Carisbrooke Castle to view a video recording of the comings and goings of all visitors to the Well House, from opening time at 10:00 am.

"You'd think with the money they make, they'd be able to afford a decent security system that allows them to transfer files digitally to use in an instant, instead of sitting in front of two old, large bloody CRT TVs!" Bruno complained to Tom.

They were taken from the reception area through to another office, where a large man with a bluetooth headset permanently affixed to his ear greeted them.

"Thank you for coming chaps, I'm Rod, head of OpSec here," the security manager boomed. "I think you'll be keen to see our latest submission for *You've Been Framed*, ha ha."

It was common for civilian security folk to assume a buddy-buddy relationship with police officers, due to their belief that they were pretty much 'in the same game'. Bruno did *not* consider this to be true, mainly because of the number of mistakes he saw happen due to their lack of professionalism. He often found that door staff or shop security assistants broke all kinds of rules when faced with a shoplifter or drunk idiot, but would assume their 'mate in the police' would turn a blind eye. He recalled one time he had no choice other than to prosecute the security chief from the local electronics supermarket store when he had broken a teenager's arm restraining him after claiming he'd caught him shoplifting – yet when the poor lad's bag had been searched, it contained nothing more than schoolbooks. All the security chief could say was "well, he looked like the kid on the camera."

"I don't find death amusing in the slightest, sir." said Bruno in his gravest voice.

"Very well. Right, uhh, take a seat just here, gentlemen," Rod replied, indicating two seats, each one in front of a giant old CRT TV.

"Because it's dark in the Well House, most guests don't realise there's a security camera in there. It's lasted us pretty well, but in a couple of years we'll need to replace it."

"Yes," Bruno replied, "amazing how quickly technology moves on, and what was cutting edge last year is average this one."

Somehow Bruno managed to nod towards the TVs and subtly point towards the VHS tape that Rod was loading into the ancient machine at the same time.

Tom had to bite his lip to stop himself from laughing out loud. But as soon as the tape begun to play, it was no longer a necessity.

The screens showed Phyllida Glassman and John Steadman entering the Well House. They were inside, alone, for ten minutes arguing, which could not be audibly understood. Tom made a note to book a lip-reading expert to see if they could suggest what was being said.

The two visitors to the Well House did not observe the artefacts and interesting writings that adorned the walls; instead they continued with their animated conversation which finished when Steadman seemingly decided that he'd had enough of listening to Phyllida and turned his back on her. He moved towards the rear of the room and leant over the low brick wall surrounding the well opening, looking down into the gaping black hole.

As he was leaning over staring into the well head, with his hands resting on the low brick surrounding wall, the camera showed Phyllida stepping back so she stood behind him, then suddenly she moved forward quickly with her arms raised, and clearly summoning every ounce of strength in her upper body, she pushed him in the centre of his upper back. He near somersaulted into the open mouth of the well. As fell, for a split second there was an angle at which Phyllida must have seen the expression of horror on his face as he vanished down the 160 foot-deep well shaft, his limbs no doubt ripped to shreds on the jagged brickwork as he ricocheted from side to side. It was a terrible death, perhaps the only consolation being that he would surely have lost consciousness before hitting the ice-cold water, and sinking forty feet to the bottom of his temporary icy grave.

It was clearly murder. The aggression displayed could not be interpreted as anything else.

Now, whatever story Phyllida told about Steadman's death, the evidence was there to convict her of *his* murder now.

Chapter 44

Thursday 21st August

The video of Steadman's death got no easier to watch with subsequent viewings. The fact that the recording, now copied, backed up and in the hands of the police as a digital video file in mp4 format, was silent made it so much worse. It was almost as if Steadman fell into a void, into another dimension. He was pushed by his former neighbour, and then suddenly he wasn't there any more. It was as tragic a reminder of what death actually meant as one could get. *No wonder people want to believe in an afterlife*, Bruno thought to himself.

Once again, Bruno clicked back to the start of the video, and Lydia, the interpreter who was sat with him, made more notes. Every time the two of them watched the clip, even though there was no more speech after the fall, they somehow felt they had to reach the end, where, after two or three minutes of standing still – obviously thinking what to do – Phyllida turned towards the exit and could be seen to scream, waving her hands as she ran out of the well house.

This time though, as they got to the end, Lydia said to Bruno, "OK, have a look what I've got."

Bruno clicked back to the start of the video again, but this time focused on the page in front of him, occasionally looking up to make sure he was 'in sync' with who was speaking on the screen. This is what he read.

[JS] *"They know about Peters."*

[PG] *"That's impossible, and stop shaking. They just want to ask me, not you, some questions, I should have spoken to that guy Peach when he phoned."*

[JS] *"Why didn't you?"*

[PG] *"Because you said not to bother, he'd wait two weeks, you said, then you thought he'd go away. How have they got onto me? What have they got on me? What do we do now?"*

Bruno noted that these worried questions seemed to be supported by her body language.

[JS] *"I'm frightened, I don't know!"*

[PG] *"Let's give ourselves up. It's only for questioning, so just behave like we've got nothing to hide. There's no connection between you and Peters, you never even properly met him."*

[JS] *"It's riddled with mistakes, I should never have done it for you."*

[PG] *"You did it for yourself, John."*

[JS] *"I did it for us!"*

[PG] *"Look, if we tell them we know nothing and keep to our story it will all blow over."*

[JS] *"It won't, I know it won't, and so do you. I'll get done for murder. You might get off, but not me, I struck him last."*

[PG] *"But they could never know that."*

[JS] *"They'll prove it."*

[PG] *"How?"*

[JS] *"That detective is onto us already, snooping around the farm."*

[PG] *"John, it's me they want to talk to, it's my face on the notice."*

[JS] *"But that's from last week! By now I bet they know it's me. We're in it together."*

The last statement seemed to silence Phyllida for a minute or so, but also anger her. When she spoke next, her body language was animated, but certainly not in a positive way.

[PG] *"Stop talking like that, you're getting me down."*

[JS] *"What shall we do?"*

[PG] *"Go and see the police, ask them what right they've got to accuse us by putting up that notice. We'll be very indignant and threaten to sue them."*

[JS] *"Sue the police? You're out of your mind."*

After this line, the few words that remained were spoken with backs to the camera, so were lost to eternity. But they didn't matter, this was plenty.

"OK, thanks Lydia, you're a genius. Get this transcript typed up on an official form as soon as you can if you don't mind. I'm going to need it *very* soon!"

He hoped that by showing Phyllida the video, she would confess, and they'd avoid a lengthy trial.

***

By the time Bruno returned to Newport police station, four hours had passed. Glassman was tired and angry, having tried in his absence every reason to persuade the station officers to allow her to go home.

Bruno and Tom discussed their options, and in the end decided to carry on the interview the next day. They were both tired, and could not afford to make mistakes. Similarly, a night in the cells might well scare their suspect into confessing, making a mistake, or simply being less skilled at fabricating stories.

So Phyllida glassman was transferred to a night cell, given standard prison-fayre food, and told that she'd be continuing her interview the next day.

Bruno offered Tom a bed for the night in his spare room, and offer that he gladly took up, meaning he could put his head down two hours earlier than if he chose to get the hovercraft back over to the mainland.

On the way back to Bruno's house, they both agreed that Phyllida saw herself as a cut above most people, and exhibited the most selfish of characteristics, with a form of narcissism.

The evidence from the Castle Well House also convinced them both that Phyllida Glassman was guilty of *two* murders, and would not taste freedom outside of a prison cell for a very long time.

Chapter 45

Phyllida's marriage to Mr Glassman would have been a trial for them both, although her persistent absence, spending the equity in the farm, was sufficient for her to hang onto their marriage, knowing full well that the loans and mortgages her husband had to borrow to finance her lifestyle were entirely his responsibility.

Bruno wondered if it was possible that before his demise, Peters had identified the evil traits of the fashionably-dressed fading beauty, he had met on that cold winters day, prowling St Catherine's Down with her dog, and was manoeuvring his exit from her.

Tom's mind was on the video. He knew he'd be visiting the police councillor when the case was over; these days there was plenty of assistance to help you get over the more traumatic experiences of a case. He considered the bleakness he felt watching that video, and realised that overnight, Phyllida Glassman would surely have felt it a thousand times worse. She would surely be unsettled today.

Together, the two men compiled the evidence to charge Glassman with the murder of John Steadman. During this time she was once again offered access to a lawyer to represent her. This time she realised she needed one. She had phoned Noway, but although he could not assist her on a criminal charge, he arranged for a local solicitor to appoint Lewis James, a criminal law barrister in Newport, who accepted the brief and was introduced to her before the interview recommenced, allowing him time to hear her version of the situation she found herself in.

Meanwhile, Bruno and Tom re-examined the Well House video which graphically displayed the evil nature of Phyllida Glassman as a ruthless, clever killer. She was no doubt still unaware that her murder of John Steadman and the incriminating conversation they'd had prior to his death had been filmed on CCTV video.

Yet Bruno did not intend to question her immediately over that incident. First it was the murder of Sam Peters he wished to charge her with.

***

Saturday 23rd August

After a night in an uncomfortable cell, with the threats that hung over her, Phyllida Glassman managed to come across as a remarkably controlled lady; in just thirty minutes she had told her side of the story to her newly appointed lawyer. After the formalities, in which Bruno explained the reason for holding her for questioning and her rights, she provided full personal details, her name, address, age, and profession.

"Mrs Glassman, on Saturday the nineteenth of July, Sam Peters was murdered. You were engaged to marry him, and he visited the Island that weekend. Did you see him in the three days prior to his death?"

"No."

"Did you *know* he had been on the Island since Wednesday the sixteenth of July, three days before he was found murdered?"

"No."

"Did you speak to him on the telephone?"

"Probably," her answer this time.

"Did Mr Peters tell you *why* he had arrived on the Island on the sixteenth of July?"

"I don't recall him saying he was coming to the Island."

"What did you talk about?"

"I don't remember."

"Can we see a log of your calls for that weekend?"

"I don't have one."

"Will you authorise us to obtain one from your phone provider?"

At this Lewis James interrupted, "Inspector, I will advise my client to refuse this request until you officially charge Mrs Glassman with a criminal offence," he said.

Bruno did not push the issue further; it was her *reaction* to the question he wanted, which was exactly as he had anticipated. He didn't really need the log from her phone, as he had already seen the log of calls on Sam Peters' mobile, which showed that he had called Phyllida twice on the Wednesday evening after his ferry had arrived at Fishbourne, but not thereafter. This convinced Bruno that he had met Phyllida on that Wednesday and stayed with her until his death.

Nevertheless, Bruno played along.

"When you discovered he had visited the Island without contacting you, what was your reaction?"

"Inspector, Sam and I were in each other's hearts, not each other's pockets. He had several things going on over here, which I've already told you about. He was searching for treasure."

"But you said he had given that up when we last spoke."

"He was mapping the quartz seam, not looking for gold deposits in rivers or Roman coins buried in fields," she said.

"Do you know where he stayed for those few days?"

"Dick Potter's Bed and Breakfast I expect; they have an ongoing business relationship."

"When I called at Roud Farm last week to see if you had returned, I met John Steadman, your occasional farmhand. He said you had gone away. *Did* you go away?"

"I wasn't at the farm, so I did go away."

"Where to?"

"I was staying with a friend, is it relevant?"

"Yes it is. Can you tell me the name of this friend?"

"Why?" said Lewis James.

Bruno did not say why, and although he was tempted to answer with the classic '*who's asking the questions here*', instead he said "I'll record that your client declined to say where she has been staying since she left her home at Roud Farm on Wednesday the thirtieth of July. OK?"

"Yes," confirmed James.

"Was your relationship with John Steadman an intimate one?"

"He was a friend," Phyllida said after a pause.

"The problem I have, Mrs Glassman, is that it appears that you hid and then ran away with your odd-job man to avoid being questioned about the murder of the man who was shortly to become your husband. Weren't you *desperate* to find out who killed him? And therefore wouldn't you want to *co-operate* with us in finding his killer? Furthermore did you not fear that whoever murdered Sam might come looking for you?"

"What for, Inspector?"

"I thought you might tell *me* that."

Phyllida just smiled her non-answer.

"What did you do before you went to Carisbrooke Castle today?"

"John and I had breakfast together."

"John Steadman told us that you had gone away for two weeks. Why would he say that if you were staying at his cottage just a few hundred metres from the farm?"

"Well I am here *now*, Inspector, and I want to go home. I am *very* tired."

Glassman was starting to show a confidence that had been steadily growing throughout the interview. She suspected from the questions that Bruno was asking that he had nothing solid on her, and with her taking the opportunity to remove Steadman from the picture, she had begun to believe everything had been neatly tied up. He would get the blame for Sam's murder, and she could carry on with her life. She knew that if Bruno had anything on her, he'd have surely started with it, not asked these questions he probably thought were cleverly planned to trick her into giving him the wrong answer.

"When did you discover that Sam Peters had left you everything of value he owned in his will?" Bruno continued.

"It was a couple of months ago."

"That was when you accepted his proposal of marriage?"

"Yes. I was devastated by his death, his possessions did not matter to me. I didn't kill Sam Peters, Inspector." she said.

"You admit though that his fortune *will* come in extremely useful in your present financial predicament?"

Phyllida narrowed her eyes and stared at Bruno. "What predicament?"

"Aren't you soon to be evicted from the farm to clear your late husband's debts?"

No answer.

"Back to the evening of July the nineteenth, please will you be specific regarding your movements?"

"I was at the farm, alone. All night."

All night was an answer Bruno had not expected. Was it her visit to Sam's apartment in Southsea late on the nineteenth that had prompted her to answer his question by covering the night? Bruno could not currently prove that the person who drove Sam's car to Portsmouth on the 8:40 pm Fishbourne-to-Portsmouth ferry and stayed in his apartment overnight was Phyllida. He filed that away under 'interesting'.

"This morning you and John Steadman went to visit Carisbrooke Castle. Did you drive?"

"We walked. That's how I saw your bloody notice – walking past the post office."

Her attitude unsettled Bruno somewhat. She truly seemed to believe she could talk her way out of Sam Peters' murder, and Bruno realised that despite the circumstantial evidence, a jury could easily be persuaded that it was all John Steadman's doing. He therefore decided to focus back on Steadman. Perhaps if she realised the game was up, the truth would come out freely.

"Mrs Glassman, I have reason to believe that the death of John Steadman was *not* an accident, and that you committed a deliberate act which resulted in his death."

"How absurd, Inspector. I watched him approach the well, and when I guessed what he might be doing I tried to save him... but I couldn't stop him. I leaned forward but there was nothing to hold onto. I tried to grab him round the waist but he disappeared before my eyes. Poor John," she said. "I will say this only one time, Inspector. I did not murder John Steadman and as I have already told you umpteen times, neither am I involved in the murder of Sam Peters. OK?"

"OK." Bruno agreed.

"So may I leave please?"

"You can leave this room, Mrs Glassman."

A smile spread across her face, but as Bruno continued speaking her lower jaw dropped until she was sitting there fully open-mouthed.

"Mrs Glassman, it is now 10:30 am on Saturday the twenty-third of August. I am charging you with the murder of John Steadman in the Well House at Carisbrooke Castle yesterday morning at 10:17 am. I maintain that you intentionally caused his death by pushing him down the well in a violent and calculated way. You are *also* charged that on or about the afternoon of July the nineteenth, together with John Steadman you murdered or significantly assisted in the murder of Sam Peters. You are therefore remanded in custody until your appearance in Newport Magistrates court on Monday morning.

Still Phyllida sat open-mouthed.

A baffled Lewis James was speechless, but managed a reply.

"Inspector, can you present your evidence to me?"

"Presuming you are representing Mrs Glassman in court, it will be provided to you in line with standard trial procedure," Bruno replied.

"Is it *really* necessary to remand my client in custody?"

"Yes, Mr James, absolutely. Considering she ran away for several days just because we wanted to question her, do you not agree she is a serious flight risk now she has been charged with two counts of murder? The only way I can be sure that she appears in court on Monday morning is if she remains in custody. You're welcome to appeal my decision to a judge, but you know full well that there isn't a beak in the land who'd go against it."

Finally Phyllida found her voice. "You will never prove anything against me, Inspector," she said.

Despite his own optimism, the confidence with which she spoke these words sowed the tiniest seed of doubt in Bruno's mind. Surely the video was sufficient evidence to prosecute for murder, it couldn't be read any other way, could it? And there was no way she could know about her act being filmed otherwise she'd never have committed it. But what about Sam Peters' murder? A jury wasn't going to believe that just because she murdered one man she had definitely murdered another. And the only real evidence was the blood that the forensics team had found – and that was on Steadman's car. Had he been too hasty? The forensics team had told him they still had plenty of analysis to conduct, but it had been days now, so he guessed there was nothing more from that side.

Desperate not to show his sudden concern, Bruno hastily stated "Interview concluded at eleven thirteen am. Tom, take her to the cells," before standing up, nodding at Lewis James, turning around and leaving the room.

***

Bruno was now particularly worried about his second murder charge. Later that day he was due to present the video evidence of John Steadman's death to the Island Prosecutor, along with the lip-reader's interpretation of what was being said. Although the conversation hinted at the Sam Peters murder, it was all Bruno had. He knew his case was weak, and he knew that the Prosecutor would say so.

He was now hoping that the lack of strength in the Peters charge would not adversely affect the decision about the Steadman one. But what if it did? What if the decision was made not to continue with the charges. If Phyllida Glassman was let go now, Bruno had no doubt in his mind that she would disappear from the face of the earth, never to be seen again. And in some warm paradise, an aging beauty with a mysterious past would turn up, find a local husband and settle down to a quiet life.

No, he couldn't let that happen. Justice must be served.

***

The time came and Bruno was in a panic. He was now absolutely sure that the Prosecutor would turn down the Sam Peters charge. All his work for nothing. All this time chasing clues, speaking to so many people, all for nothing. Sam's death would not be avenged.

"Sir, have you got a moment?" asked a young policeman in uniform. "There's urgent news from forensics! DC Craven said you *had* to see it!"

Bruno stopped in his tracks.

"News?"

The young lad handed Bruno a good, old-fashioned fax which he immediately unfolded and read.

Bruno actually whooped with joy and punched the air.

"Talk about leaving it until the last minute," he smiled. "Thank you. Thank you *so* much!"

Although someone had done their best to wipe it away, a bloodstain containing a partial palm print had been found in Phyllida Glassman's car. There was enough of the print there to test against a match.

For now, the fact that there was a direct link to Glassman herself was enough. Bruno said "Thank you," again, this time to no one in particular.

As long as Phyllida was remanded in custody – which Bruno was now sure she would be – he could obtain her palm print on admittance to the prison remand centre. He guessed that the blood in her car could have been deposited after she helped Steadman lift Peters into his Volvo estate, or after she helped him unload the body at Beacon Alley. Bruno's primary theory was that she *did* help him put Peters' body into Steadman's car for him to take the body to the bridge, then drove Sam Peters' car back to Portsmouth on the 8:40 pm ferry from Fishbourne, staying overnight at his flat. His theory was now beginning to be supported by fact.

Although the conversation between Phyllida and John Steadman in the Well House saw Steadman admit to striking the killer blow to Sam Peters, Bruno felt that under the group responsibility laws that were introduced a few years back, he could still secure a full murder conviction for Glassman for partaking in the act.

When Bruno presented his information to Maurice Coleman, the Prosecutor, he was relieved to be told that his charges would be supported by the crown, and that time in custody would help them clarify a number of important issues. However, Coleman warned him that it was not a black and white case, and he was not certain of prosecuting one charge successfully, let alone two.

***

When the court resumed at two pm, Lewis James requested an adjournment. He argued that he had not had enough time to fully understand his client's version of events, and this was not disputed by Coleman – he knew it would help prepare the case better. Additionally, James highlighted Glassman's emotional state following the incident at the Well House and her subsequent collapse at the police station. This, Bruno didn't agree with... but knew better than to say anything. Small victories like that did not impact on the overall course of the war.

The hearing was set down for 10:00 am on Monday the twenty-fifth of August, and Phyllida Glassman was ordered to remain in custody over the weekend.

***

Bruno, Tom and Maurice Coleman were stood outside the court discussing the case. Bruno reminded the prosecutor of the elements he considered most important; the fact that Phyllida Glassman had evaded police questioning from the very start, the clear video evidence of the murder at the Well, and the blood from both the Volvo and from Phyllida's VW, which had turned out to be on the steering wheel.

Tom chipped in, "and don't forget Sam Peters' will. That's highly suspicious, right? There's no way she'll get away with this."

"Don't be so sure," Bruno cautioned; Coleman nodded his agreement with the statement.

"A good defence lawyer like Lewis James could tear us apart. No doubt he'll say that Steadman was responsible for everything, including the blood in her car."

"Do *you* think he was?" said Tom.

"No, I don't think so," said Bruno. "She is beyond any reasonable doubt *in my mind* guilty of Sam Peters' murder."

Chapter 46

At the hearing on Monday at two pm, Phyllida Glassman was remanded in custody to stand trial for both the murder of Sam Peters on or about the nineteenth of July, and the murder of John Steadman at 10:17 am on Thursday the twenty-first of August.

She pleaded not guilty.

Maurice Coleman was the most experienced prosecutor on the Island. This case, a double murder, would represent the summit of his career, and he was determined to enjoy the publicity that would arise. Thankfully for Bruno and Tom this meant he would work his hardest to obtain a conviction.

The police evidence associating Phyllida Glassman with Sam Peters' murder consisted of the forensics report on the VW, and in particular the palm print which had now been confirmed as hers, her full set having been taken as she was enrolled in the long-term custody suite over the weekend. Noway the solicitor had also provided a statement regarding his suspicion that the adjustment to Sam Peters' will was fraudulent. Additionally, it was decided to highlight Phyllida's denial that she had seen Peters for the three days prior to his death, despite their apparent closeness as evidenced by the change of will.

Steadman, according to those who knew him, had been a controlling person with one obsession: getting Roud Farm back. It was entirely possible that although he was clearly Glassman's lover, his only interest was the farm, and he didn't necessarily feel the way about her that she did about him. The belief was that it may well have been Steadman who talked Phyllida into committing murder, somehow convincing her that it was the only way she could save her farm. As her lover and with his controlling personality, he would surely then see the farm as his own, everything now rightfully back in his family name.

Maurice Coleman had listened to the circumstantial evidence in the detectives' reports on their investigations as well as considering the hard, factual evidence. He himself was certain that Phyllida Glassman had had significant input into Peters' murder. But was it a convincing enough case for the jury to consider it *beyond all reasonable doubt*? In his opinion it was marginal.

The blood impregnated palm print on the base of the steering wheel of Phyllida's car proved that the driver had been in direct contact with Peters' body, and therefore that person must have been involved in some way of transporting the corpse from the murder location to the bridge. As it was Phyllida's hand print, it proved the contact... but not necessarily guilt of the murder itself.

If her motive was Sam Peters' money, perhaps she genuinely *had* persuaded him to make her the sole beneficiary to his estate on the pretext of marriage, him being far from the most experienced man around women. But Steadman, who wasn't just an odd-job farmhand but was her *real* lover, and had been since the death of her husband, stood guard over her like a watchman in the tower.

It was highly likely that when Glassman had invited Peters in to get out of the rain, it was out of genuine kindness. But he must have said something that let her know he was monied and single, and afterwards, when she'd mentioned this to Steadman, the two had concocted a plan. It would have to be a long-term sting, but the payoff was that the two could live together on the farm having paid off all the debt.

It was highly likely that Phyllida grew to like Sam Peters a great deal, perhaps even love him. It was hard to tell, but those who spoke to Phyllida whilst in custody all felt that there was a genuine sadness in her that Sam Peters was dead.

Steadman's body had been recovered from the well, and had undergone an autopsy which matched up with what could be seen from the video. He was dead before he hit the water.

Steadman was gone.

Peters was gone.

Phyllida Glassman was all alone.

Chapter 47

Monday 10th November

The trial of Phyllida Glassman on two murder charges commenced before judge and jury at 10:00 am on the tenth of November, at Winchester Crown Court, defended by Lewis James QC.

It had taken Bruno thirty years as a police officer to try to understand the complex rules of evidence, which Lewis James would methodically exploit during the trial, and which would force him to question both his methods of collecting evidence and the basis on which he approached his job as a police officer.

Bruno's task had always been to protect the public, to report offenders and bring them to the courts. He had never attempted to bring a criminal to justice when he had not been convinced they were guilty, and that was as true of this case as any other.

Yet in a little over two months, Lewis James had prepared a defence of Phyllida Glassman that threatened to tear to shreds the evidence that Bruno, and Tom Craven, had diligently compiled and which ultimately constituted Maurice Coleman's prosecution's case. Maurice too had prepared meticulously the case for the crown, and although he believed everything that Bruno and his clever young assistant had unearthed in the course of their investigations, and was confident of obtaining a conviction, it just felt that *something* was missing. The smoking gun, as they say.

Phyllida did not present herself to the court as she had to the Police when she was charged with the double murder. Her manner on arrest had been aggressive, harsh and spiteful. She had obviously been coached that any such behaviour would go very much against her in court; she therefore wore her best country clothes, and looked the epitome of a gentile country lady. Oddly, she had no supporters come to the trial and sit in the public gallery. There was not a single relation or friend, and the oft-visited sister she had always visited was nowhere to be seen.

Whilst she was in custody at the Parkhurst Remand Centre, Roud Farm had been sealed off by the Police. Whilst the trial was in progress, the banks were not permitted to re-possess the property, and so it lay untouched for months.

Witnesses for the prosecution were DI Bruno Peach, DC Tom Craven and the forensics team. Maurice ignored the evidence from the lady who claimed to have seen someone leave Peters' Southsea home the day after his murder. She'd had no clear view of the departing person, and therefore could not describe them accurately enough. Apart from hearing his apartment door shut, there was no certainty that the person had come from Peters' apartment, and therefore it sadly added nothing to the case.

Maurice began his address to the jury recounting that stormy afternoon in February when Phyllida had rescued Sam Peters from the storm that would have led him into difficulties if he had attempted to return to his car in the Military Road car park nearly two miles away across the treacherous Downs. It was she who had encouraged this chance meeting into a serious relationship once she had discovered that he was a man of substance, with his own small but thriving business. With her 'dear' husband of twenty-five years dead and buried, without life assurance or pension and with creditors banging on her door, she had become desperate.

Phyllida Glassman was attractive and feminine, and to Sam Peters she must have seemed vulnerable. In truth it was *Peters* who was vulnerable, and by late spring she had him so wound around her finger that he was planning all kinds of intimate activities, including him buying Roud farm. By then she had visited his home in Southsea and confirmed his assets – she was cunning and cautious, and would not just take someone at their word. Maurice commented that Peters was 'just what she was looking for', a phrase which raised an objection from Lewis James, and was upheld by the judge, Justice Aurelia Kennedy.

Maurice continued to explain his version of what had happened. Sam Peters had been ready to buy the farm, but his plans had been shelved due to the various loans and mortgages on the farm being far more than the property was actually worth. Despite the probability that the property would end up at auction and make even less, the banks were not prepared to work together to accept a lower offer from Sam Peters. Coleman produced for the court to examine a file of correspondence from building societies, banks and lenders backing up this assertion.

Maurice stated these debts had come about by her spending the capital value in the farm. Financially, she was in a desperate situation, but if Peters would marry her, she could pay off the debts and as his wife still own the farm.

In the course of the negotiations, Peter Noway, the solicitor, had been instructed by Sam Peters, a lonely forty-four-year old bachelor, with a married sister living in Southsea forever telling him to settle down, to write a will, in which he left his entire estate to Phyllida Glassman. This he did because he genuinely was in love with her, and was so far under her control that he was happy to do so.

What Sam Peters did *not* know was that Phyllida's *true* lover, John Steadman, who lived three hundred metres from Roud Farm, had been told about his wealth and his adjustment to the will. Together he and Glassman planned Sam Peters' murder and set a trap, which started with getting him to come to the Island late on a Wednesday evening.

In his cross examination, Maurice Coleman frustratingly failed to rile Phyllida enough to get her to answer his questions in the way he wanted; he therefore was unable to prove her a liar.

Coleman also suggested that Phyllida's complete denial of any knowledge of *Steadman's* involvement in Peters' murder, in view of their relationship, was incomprehensible. If she was to pin the entire murder on him, how could she, his intimate lover, not have known a single thing about the plan? Whichever way you looked at it, she was a willing partner to his murder.

At each step, defence counsel Lewis James was forced onto the back foot as he tried to discredit each piece of Police evidence. *His* argument was that Phyllida had reluctantly accepted that the farm would be sold by the creditors to pay off her debts to the bank and building societies and back in that March she had been preparing to leave the farm, having applied for live-in work. He showed the court offers of employment she had received that gave her a good job, a salary and a home. He maintained that she was not in any way desperate and that Sam Peters' arrival on the scene had simply been a most welcome opportunity to let her behave *normally*. The idea of him buying the farm had excited her in the beginning, but she soon decided that he should not buy the farm, as it would have needed a huge injection of cash to bring it up to date and it was uneconomic as a business.

Under oath she denied that Steadman was her lover. She had stayed at his cottage for a few nights because, since Peters' murder, she had become frightened being alone on the farm. She had stayed in one of the three bedrooms at his house and he had walked her dog for her. Moving to the holiday cottage away from the farm was his suggestion, with which she went along with as it was a change that helped her to relax and avoid the continual and harassing approaches from Detective Inspector Bruno Peach.

James tried to disconnect Phyllida from the killing of Peters. He suggested that Peters could have been killed at Roud Farm in one of the metal farm sheds, without her knowledge of any of the circumstances that might have led to his killing.

He also said that the suggestion that she had helped Steadman somehow transfer the body to the bridge at Beacon Alley had no basis and was absurd. James claimed that the bridge had been selected by Steadman to dump Peters, because it was far enough away from the Roud Farm that it would not be automatically connected, and he probably hoped it would not be discovered for some time.

James questioned Glassman, in particular asking her if Steadman ever drove her car.

"He did have a set of keys and moved it around the farm if he wanted space," she had replied.

James explained how if, on the day of the murder, Steadman had moved the car, then later on in the day Phyllida had driven it back into the garage, her palm print could easily have appeared in drying blood on the steering wheel deposited by Steadman, without her ever having come into contact with the body.

As for the incident in the Well House that led to Steadman's death, Lewis James dealt with it in two stages: the conversation prior to his demise where he'd admitted killing Peters, and the prosecution's claim that she pushed him into the well.

James objected to the *use* of the video and doubted the authenticity of the lip-reading of their conversation. He argued that Steadman's confession to the murder absolved his client completely, and the accusation that she pushed him down the well was illogical, despite what it might look like on the low-resolution, old, grainy videotape.

Steadman was a big man, six feet two inches, sixteen and a half stone of mostly muscle and with a low centre of gravity. James argued that even the biggest push from a small, nine stone woman could not have tipped him over the well parapet. He would surely not even have stumbled.

He claimed that the video showed her with her arms outstretched trying to *grab* his coat, as she had suddenly realised he must be thinking about jumping.

When James finished his defence statement, the judge in her summing up re-stated the facts presented by the prosecution, before the jury retired to consider their verdict. She stated that the facts that formed the prosecution case against Phyllida Glassman were:

- Her reluctance to be interviewed by DI Peach following the murder of Sam Peters and her subsequent disappearance.

- Her statement the she'd had no contact with Peters on Wednesday the sixteenth of July, when both her and his mobile phone showed two calls late that evening between them.

- The suggestion they'd had no contact when he'd come to the Island for three days, despite the defence not providing any proof of where he might have stayed other than at Roud Farm.

- The bloodstain found beneath the sheep shearings still scattered in the metal outbuilding on the farm, where the prosecution suggested the murder had taken place.

- The blood-impregnated palm print in the VW that proved she had driven her car after coming into contact with Peters body.

- The close relationship between Phyllida and Steadman indicated they had conspired together to get their hands on his money.

- The transcript of the conversation between Glassman and Steadman in the Well House that indicated she was both aware of, and a participant to, Sam Peters' murder.

The jury retired at 4:00 pm to consider their verdict.

***

At 5:30 pm the jury returned and advised that they had reached a consensus. When asked to deliver the verdict the foreman stood up.

"On the charge of the murder of Samuel Peters how do you find the defendant, guilty or not guilty?"

"Guilty, your honour."

"On the charge of the murder of John Steadman how do you find the defendant, guilty or not guilty?"

"Guilty your honour."

***

The trial had in all honesty been abnormally short for a double murder trial. For Bruno and Tom Craven it had gone to plan. In a strange twist, they believed that pushing Steadman down the well had sealed her fate as a murderess, and on that basis the jury believed she could have murdered Sam also. Both policeman admitted to each other that had there not been video evidence proving her evil side, she would have probably been acquitted of the murder of Sam Peters.

Bruno was rather elated at the trial's outcome, as he had never been particularly confident she would be convicted. All through the trial he had questioned his own occupation. Why be a policeman and work so hard to bring certain criminals to account when a court can let them walk free with no punishment? He felt a renewed sense of purpose.

He wondered how he'd have felt if the jury had announced the opposite verdict, and he'd seen Phyllida Glassman walk out of court not only with her freedom, but also nearly a million pounds worth of Sam Peters' money, which it was assumed would – after some complicated legal wrangling – go to his sister. He shook off the thought, not wanting to consider how he'd have reacted.

Tom Craven, always looking to learn something new, asked Bruno if there were any lessons in particular he should take away from the case. Bruno thought for a moment and then replied, quoting the statistics of murder.

"Most people think most women are incapable of murder," he said. "But at the start of a case, you should never make any assumptions. Just because statistics tell you that most murderers are male, don't automatically exclude female suspects. At first I couldn't bring myself to believe that Phyllida Glassman could hurt a fly, but the more I thought about her, the more convinced I became that it was just a mask she was wearing. We all wear masks, Tom. The trick is to see what's under them."

Tom nodded and said, "Thank you, sir," before shaking hands and walking away.

Bruno was left standing alone. He felt good today. Since his failure to catch the Godshill butcher all those years ago, a black cloud had followed him around every day. Today it felt like that cloud had been lifted.

The Godshill butcher... of course! Bruno had focused so much on the trial of Phyllida Glassman that he'd forgotten Steph Helland's trial was coming soon!

Chapter 48

Coming to court Monday one week to the day after the conviction of Phyllida Glassman was Steph Helland.

Could she blow away the evidence to convict her of the murder of Stanley Musgrove, and the attempted murder of Chris West? The Hampshire Constabulary had decided to set aside the charge of the murder of Andrew Pumpkin because they felt it clouded their case, thus diminishing the chances of a conviction on the other two charges. They knew that there was always the possibility that it could be resurrected for trial at a later date, if any new evidence supported the case.

Janet attended the trial, sitting in the public gallery every single day. Having contributed so much to the case, she felt she needed to see it to its completion.

Bruno told Janet that it was very much her case; it was her analytical approach and persistence not to let anything go that had resulted in getting this far. She had worked out that Chris West was at serious risk from Steph Helland, and if Janet had not conducted the investigative work that she did, West would currently be just another alcoholic released from hospital, lucky to be alive after stepping out in front of a car... and who knows how long it would be before it happened again?

***

The Steph Helland trial opened on a sunny November morning at Winchester Crown Court. She was charged with the murder of Stanley Musgrove on December the twenty-second four years prior, and the attempted murder of Chris West on the thirty-first of August in a Bournemouth city car park.

Just like Phyllida Glassman, she pleaded not guilty.

The prosecution counsel had been appointed by the Hampshire Constabulary and the Police Officer representing was Bruno's now friend-for-life DI Matt Morrison of Bournemouth CID.

West had recovered sufficiently to attend court, but operations to repair his hips and pelvis were still ongoing, meaning he could only walk with the assistance of a cane. Charged with being an accomplice in the murder of Stanley Musgrove, he had been detained in the Winchester Remand Centre Hospital. He was accused of being an accessory in the murder in that after witnessing the man's dead body on the butchers' shop floor, he should have immediately informed the Police.

In view of the injuries West suffered as a result of the hit-and-run attempt to kill him, Janet hoped that the judge would show compassion towards him.

It was impossible to gauge the attitude of Brendan Helland towards his wife standing trial for the murder of her former husband. It seemed he had escaped his predecessors' fates by good fortune, and now, released from her spell, he could not understand how he had succumbed to the charms of such a woman.

The fact that Steph had been incarcerated in West Dorset's remand centre for three months awaiting trial on charges which she denied had not persuaded Mr Helland that she was innocent. In fact, he already considered her guilty, and had taken steps to erase her completely from his life. Even if the unthinkable were to happen and Steph were acquitted, she would be divorced and never be permitted to return to his inner circle. The court proceedings had exposed her lies about her past and proven she was not the person she had led him to believe she was – more than suitable grounds for a quick divorce to be granted.

He had withdrawn financial support for her legal services, and thus she had to settle for assistance provided by court-appointed personnel.

DI Morrison managed to craft the investigative work of Bruno, Tom Craven and Janet skilfully into an impressively tight and complete case for Prosecuting Counsel Jasper Johnson, who would act for the crown against Steph Helland.

Stephanie's lawyer, Hugh Field, took the only approach that he could – hide as many aspects of the defendant's personality as possible, and present only facts that put doubt on her capability to be a cunning, scheming murderer. It was a strategy that had worked for others, sowing just enough seeds of doubt in the minds of the jury.

It was impossible not to compare Steph's experience at court with that of Phyllida Glassman. Whereas Phyllida had been presented by the defence as an innocent lady who had suffered a misfortune of circumstance, Field presented Stephanie as a stupid, poorly-educated and loud-mouthed tart, quick to speak and slow to think. Someone you wouldn't want at your dinner party, but *not* someone capable of planning a murder.

Steph was dressed plainly in a tidy, inexpensive, woollen two piece, but her choice of skirt length and her general demeanour betrayed her common character to the older, class-aware court personnel. Wearing an adversarial countenance, Steph did not look kindly about the courtroom and couldn't help herself from staring at the judge and jury aggressively. She had been a caged animal for three months, and it showed.

The trial opened by hearing the hit-and-run charges against her, the attempted murder of Chris West, who was present as both a witness and defendant, for now seated in an adjoining room in the court. After giving his evidence, he would return to prison to await the trial of the second offence, where he was jointly charged with her for the killing of Stanley Musgrove.

The defending counsel successfully petitioned for the two charges to be heard sequentially rather than consecutively, arguing that because they happened years apart there was no direct connection between them.

The fact that Chris West was involved in both cases in different capacities did not persuade the judge otherwise.

***

On the charge of the attempted murder of Chris West, Stephanie Helland was acquitted, found guilty of the lesser charges of dangerous driving and failing to stop after an accident.

Bruno was surprised.

In fact, he was alarmed. This was not how it was supposed to go.

On the charge of dangerous driving and failure to stop, the jury accepted the defence's suggestion that it was purely an accident, the dusk light playing a part in the verdict on the basis that West was drunk and swaying all over the place directly in front of her car. For this she was told she would receive an eighteen-month custodial sentence.

***

Next came the charge of murder.

This was a trial for a crime that took place years ago, and was intricately woven into the lives of two questionable individuals. Steph Helland appeared to be the instigator and ringleader, who profited from her ability to find weak men to join her in activities of low moral worth.

The murder of the Godshill butcher was the most famous unsolved case on the Island, and if Steph were to be convicted of it, she would go down as one of the Island's most evil women of the twenty-first century.

Although the demise of Andrew Pumpkin was not relevant to the case, the prosecuting counsel opened with a description of how Stephanie and Chris West's relationship started – namely that she was engaged in a sexual relationship with West whilst she was still married to Andrew Pumpkin, a local Cowes solicitor, who had fallen to his death in an accident at home in Stephanie's presence. It was a clever move, as even though the defence objected to the statement, the fact that another of Stephanie's husbands had died when they had not been long married would surely be picked up by the members of the jury.

Following the death of Pumpkin, the prosecution continued, there was the gift of a large sum of money to Chris West to buy the lease on a pub. Tens of thousands of pounds was a huge sum of money to give to a married lover by a woman who had recently acquired her wealth by the death of an elderly husband of just two years – the point was highlighted in an attempt to show scheming on Steph's side.

The prosecuting counsel continued to paint a picture of a destructive relationship between Steph and West, indicating that she was in control of him, he very much at her beck and call.

Jasper Johnson described the years whilst West's pub business failed and he descended into alcoholism, sadly the fate of many publicans. He pointed out that during this time he continued to be summoned for sex by Stephanie, and as she had paid for the pub he could not say 'no'.

"One December afternoon you received a call from Mrs Helland, can you tell me about that?" Johnson asked Chris West when he was in the witness box.

"It was two days before Christmas Eve, I was in the pub in Cowes and she called. She sounded desperate and said she needed me to come to the business her husband ran in Godshill, the butchers shop, immediately. I drove the thirty-minute journey to Godshill to find her alone in the shop with her husband lying dead, in a pool of blood, on the tiled floor beside the chopping block."

"What did you do then, Mr West?"

"I was horrified. Terrified," he replied.

"But what did you *do*?"

"I asked if she'd called an ambulance, she said 'no, he's dead'. I said 'what about the Police,' she said 'no, take me home Chris'. So that's what I did."

"Then what?"

"When we got to her home, she took all her clothes off and showered, she made me do it too, then we, you know, made love like we always did." West was genuinely embarrassed, but to some onlookers, his sheepish grin made him look a little too cocky.

"And then what?"

"I had to take her back to the butchers. She said 'just drop me off, I'll call the Police from the shop. You should scarper before they show up', she told me, which is what I did."

"After that what did you do?"

"How do you mean?" said West.

"Did you call her to find out what happened?"

"No, I was too scared."

West's evidence in the trial was consistent with the tale he had told Janet in the hospital. Janet *knew* it was the truth.

However, despite his recent alcoholism, West was not a regular in court, and was not used to being questioned. Steph's defence lawyer got him to admit that he hadn't witnessed the murder, and then presented her version of the events which was completely different.

She claimed that she had a prearranged rendezvous at her home in Godshill with Chris West at 2:00 pm.

"He was late," she said. "We'd agreed to meet at my home at 2:00 pm, so I could get to the shop at 4:00 pm, with a car load of Christmas presents that Stan always gave to his best customers in the lead-up to Christmas. I had spent all morning wrapping them up. Chris had arranged to come to the house when I knew Stan had to be working alone in the shop. As it happened, he didn't show until 3:00 pm; he was half-pissed and still wanted to go to bed. I let him, thinking it wouldn't matter if I was a little late taking the presents to the shop. But the shop wasn't busy, so at 3:45 pm Stan put the door to the shop on the latch and drove back home in the van to give me a hand loading the presents into my car. He let himself in, came upstairs and caught me and Chris at it. He was a tough man, Stan, and he grabbed Chris by the throat, nearly throttling him. He beat him up, and said to Chris 'I know you, and I'll see you, your wife and family later', and stormed out. He said he was going back to the shop. That was it as far as I was concerned, I knew it was over for Stan and me."

Steph was growing in confidence as she continued.

"Chris left and after a short while I drove down to the shop with the Christmas presents, dropping something off to a friend's en-route. But

Chris didn't leave Godshill, he went to the shop and got there before me. When I got there, I could hear Chris from outside, he was shouting at Stan, who was slicing some meat with a small knife, 'You keep away from me or I'll kill you', he said. 'And you keep away from my family', I heard Chris say."

Hugh Field was nodding, encouraging Steph to go on.

"I was frightened because Chris was drunk, I reckon he had a bottle of vodka in his car. It was dark outside the shop so I stood out of sight in the shadows, hoping he would just go away. But I could see what was happening through the windows. He leaned forward and put his face inches from Stan and was threatening him. Stan straightened up holding his knife and caught Chris on his forearm, cut him badly, it was at least six inches long. I'm sure it was an accident, and I thought Chris would have realised it was as well. But while Stan was bending over to get a bandage from the first aid box, Chris picked up a chopper and hit him on the back of his head. It smashed his skull, and he slid forward onto the tiled floor. It shocked me rigid."

"What happened then Mrs Helland?"

"As soon as I broke free from my terror, I rushed into the shop and up to Stan who was lying on the floor. Chris rushed into the toilet with blood streaming from his arm, grabbed a towel and ran off. He was bleeding badly."

"What did you do next?"

"I went home."

"You left your husband, dying, on the stone floor?"

"He wasn't dying, he was dead. I checked his pulse. I didn't know what to do, so I had to get out of the shop and think it out. When I got home I tidied the house and changed the sheets – I was in a complete state of confusion. At about 7:30 pm I went back to the shop and phoned the police. They asked me what happened and I told them, he hadn't come home, so I had come to find him. I said that's all I knew. I didn't tell them anything about the afternoon or Chris West."

"Why not?"

"I was frightened. I thought my best chance was to say nothing. If I'd told the truth he'd have come for me... or the police might have even accused me of being a part of it. He sure wouldn't have said it was him alone. So I made it look as if I'd found Stan dead at 7:30 and had called the Police straight away."

"What happened after that?"

"There was the Police investigation. I think they thought I did it, but they couldn't prove it, obviously. Chris kept contacting me to see what had happened. I told him what I'd told them and nobody suspected him, he got away with it. When it all blew over, I gave him the shop in Godshill, but he wrecked that, like he did the pub."

"Why did you give him the shop?"

"Because I hoped it would keep him happy, and keep him in Godshill, so I could move on, away from him, no longer scared. But when he came after me in Bournemouth, well, I just didn't know what to do."

"So you tried to kill him in the car park?"

"No, I didn't. I know it looks like I did, but I did not. You see I really did love him, once, but he was intent on ruining my life."

It was a different Chris West who returned to the witness box for cross examination.

When Chris West returned to the witness box, it was obvious he was angry about the story Steph had told.

"It's my word against hers, and I don't lie." he said.

"Would you show the court your left forearm," said Hugh Field.

"What's that got to do with anything? She knows I got a lot of cuts from slicing fish and that's one of them."

"Please show the court the cut I am referring to on your left forearm, the cut that Stanley Musgrove gave you, when you were threatening him in a drunken rage, after he caught you red handed in bed with his wife."

Reluctantly West rolled up his left sleeve and presented his damaged forearm to the jury.

"It wasn't Stan that did it though!" protested West.

"Thank you, Mr West, you may return to your seat."

Hugh Field then called Chris's wife, Judy West to the witness box.

"Mrs West, on the evening of the December the twenty-second, your husband returned home with a serious injury to his arm, is that correct?"

"Yes, it is," she said. "He had a very bad cut along his left forearm. It was bleeding heavily and wrapped in a blood-soaked towel."

"And how did he tell you he obtained this injury?"

"He said he did it changing a car tyre. I took him to A&E at St Mary's hospital in Newport and they stitched it up."

"And what happened then, Mrs West?"

"I took him home and put him to bed."

During the time Hugh Field had been preparing Steph Helland's defence to the charge of murder, he had visited Judy West and she had given him the towel that Chris West had wrapped around his bleeding arm.

He explained to the court that the towel was one of a matching set used in the butcher's shop lavatory, which Steph Helland had bought from a local shop.

"Mrs West would you look at this towel, and confirm it is the towel you washed after your husband returned home that evening?"

"Yes it is," she said.

"Thank you Mrs West, that will be all."

"Your honour, here is a copy of the hospital A&E report of 9:00 pm on that twenty-second of December. The cause of the accident as reported to the hospital was that Mr West was slicing fish, but he no longer had a fish business, and his pub did not sell food. So I ask the court, why was a different reason given to the hospital compared to the one Mr West told his wife, and why would he be slicing fish with such a large knife?"

The counsel for the defence had turned the case on its head.

***

Tuesday 18th November

Bruno didn't sleep a wink. The next morning it was raining heavily. His car had a flat tyre. His coffee tasted foul. It all felt ominous.

The verdicts handed down were as follows:

Stephanie Helland was guilty of obstructing the police, making false statements relating to the killing of her husband Stanley Musgrove, and concealing evidence. She received an eighteen-month suspended sentence.

Christopher West was found guilty of murder of Stanley Musgrove and was sent down for eighteen years without parole.

Everyone else was satisfied with the outcome of this trial. They believed Steph Helland, but not Chris West.

Bruno felt physically sick. He was not satisfied. He needed to think and then to talk. But first there were formalities to deal with.

Epilogue

It was a fond farewell to Tom Craven at the end of the trial of Steph Helland. He had contributed a great deal, and Bruno knew he would be going on to have a highly successful Police career. Bruno was proud of his young apprentice, who told him that he'd learned a great deal from him during the case.

Bruno and Janet had had time to think. Between them they realised that it was without any doubt that Chris West had murdered Stanley Musgrove. Although Janet had believed West, if she had not built up enough trust in him to get him to sign an official statement of his version of events, the trial would never have happened. It was West's own lies to Janet that had been ripped apart in court; it was his own lies to someone who trusted him that saw him found guilty of murder. Bruno managed to persuade Janet that this was why a policeman never trusts anybody. And at the end of the day, the person who murdered the Godshill butcher was now in prison for his crime.

It was this last point that banished Bruno's black cloud forever. The two trials had helped him regain his self-belief.

**

To celebrate in style, Bruno took Janet to the Royal Hotel in Ventnor for a five star dinner, where they discussed the characters involved in the two murders. In several ways the outcome of this trial had changed the landscape of many lives. Although the murder of Sam Peters had finished his treasure hunting, Dick Potter had continued panning the East Yar river in secret, and would carry on until its yield did not justify the time spent at it. Harry Felt, Potter's smelter, was happy, the extra income paying for some of the luxuries he'd always wanted. Bruno was happy to let them carry on, his sympathies much more with them than the wealthy landowners.

Bartlett would carry on trying to get somebody to mine the Island quartz deposit and, in any event, would write up the finding as the geological expert on the Island he believed he was. Bentley was the type of man who shied away from any publicity whatsoever, so there was no one who was going to dispute Bartlett's claim.

Sam's sister Wendy and her family eventually inherited his hard-earned money, but not one day would pass that she didn't shed a tear for the brother whom she worried she had neglected and had allowed to fall into the clutches of an evil woman.

Steph Helland was divorced by Brendan, but was comforted by a cheque for a six figure sum and a luxury apartment overlooking Poole harbour. It wasn't long before she sold it and moved to Brighton after bumping into a potential suitor at a luxury hotel who spent half the year there when he wasn't in the Caribbean.

Janet said she wondered about the others. "What's Harris going to do with that spooky house?"

"He has to do it up and sell or let it, or sell it as it is," said Bruno. "If I were him, I'd find a woman to replace his mother and go and live in it. It's in a stunning location."

***

Bruno and Janet's relationship had developed during the course of this investigation. He was no longer feeling like a failed detective, afraid to express and share his views on people. He had shared every aspect of his investigation with Janet and she had responded helpfully, bringing her clever mind to his formal Police work. On his own Bruno thought he could have floundered. Janet had enjoyed helping his investigation, and *she* didn't see him as a failed detective at all. She saw Bruno in a positive light and admired the way he had steered the investigation to a successful outcome, and how he had helped Tom Craven in his first case of murder.

Janet was ambivalent about the verdicts; she was pleased that justice was done with the conviction of Phyllida Glassman, although she thought Steph Helland's punishment was far too lenient. Was she a corrupting influence on the men she associated with, or did her loose morality spark a fire that exists in many kinds of man?

Her experience in seeing Chris West kill her husband, and then her continued support of him, did not sit well with Janet. And although leopards don't change their spots, perhaps the experience might have changed Steph for the better.

Janet loved Police work more than she ever dreamed she would. Tom confided to her how much he enjoyed his career as a Police officer, with one exception – trying to find missing persons. He said this was because most of the time missing people didn't want to be found.

***

That night, lying in bed, Bruno thought again about the sentences, but only for a moment. A thought struck him. A Police officer cannot be judge and jury, and more than any others, they know that sometimes the guilty go free. However, that is not as troubling as when the innocent are convicted. *That* haunts and keeps a Police officer awake at night.

He rolled over onto his side, and slept soundly.

THE END